KING OF DEAD THINGS

KING
OF DEAD
THINGS

NEVIN HOLNESS

 New York London Toronto Sydney New Delhi

atheneum

An imprint of Simon & Schuster Children's Publishing Division
1230 Avenue of the Americas, New York, New York 10020
Text © 2024 by Nevin Holness
Jacket illustration © 2024 by Taj Francis
Jacket design by Sonia Chaghatzbanian © 2024 by Simon & Schuster, LLC
Simon & Schuster: Celebrating 100 Years of Publishing in 2024
For information about special discounts for bulk purchases, please contact Simon & Schuster Special Sales at 1-866-506-1949 or business@simonandschuster.com.
The Simon & Schuster Speakers Bureau can bring authors to your live event. For more information or to book an event, contact the Simon & Schuster Speakers Bureau at 1-866-248-3049 or visit our website at www.simonspeakers.com.
Interior design by Irene Metaxatos
The text for this book was set in Minion Pro.
Manufactured in the United States of America
First Edition
10 9 8 7 6 5 4 3 2 1
Library of Congress Cataloging-in-Publication Data
Names: Holness, Nevin, author.
Title: King of dead things / Nevin Holness.
Description: First edition. | New York : Atheneum Books for Young Readers, 2024. | Audience: Ages 14 and up. | Summary: Eli, who possesses unique magical abilities, and Malcolm, desperate to escape his past and save his mother, join forces to retrieve a dangerous magical artifact in the mystical underbelly of London.
Identifiers: LCCN 2023013929 | ISBN 9781665946919 (hardcover) | ISBN 9781665946933 (ebook)
Subjects: CYAC: Fantasy. | Magic—Fiction. | Ability—Fiction. | Friendship—Fiction. | Black people—Fiction. | LCGFT: Fantasy fiction. | Novels.
Classification: LCC PZ7.1.H6467 Ki 2024 | DDC [Fic]—dc23
LC record available at https://lccn.loc.gov/2023013929

Nana and Grandad,
thank you for always
telling the best stories
at Sunday dinner

—N. H.

KING OF DEAD THINGS

NOW

CHAPTER ONE

ELI

The soul slipped from the boy as easily as removing a sheet from a bed.

It felt a little like that, Eli thought as he took it in his hand; thin, weightless, like releasing a kite in the wind. He got a sense of the life as it passed through him. He had read before in one of Max's old books that the magic in each soul had its own individuality; this one felt like motor grease on fingers and grass stains on knees, the smell of petrol, the hum of an engine. He was a mechanic, Eli realized belatedly. He had spent a lifetime working with his hands.

In theory, it was simple. The boy's soul was battered and broken; Eli was just stitching the fragments back together one at a time, like patchwork. It was a complicated magic, healing; one wrong stitch and it wouldn't stick. Plus, it took from him as much as he gave. Afterward, Eli would feel worn out, nauseous, and it usually took a few days for his own magic to return.

He didn't have the luxury of going a few days without magic, not when he had bills to pay, so it had become habit for him to take a piece for himself in the form of payment—a single thread of magic, small enough not to be missed. Most people were oblivious to magic, even when it was right under their noses, and the ones who weren't existed the same way as Eli, in hushed voices and behind closed doors. It was easy for Eli to go unnoticed. The only real risk of failure lay in human error, but Eli had practiced incessantly, ghosting the movements over and over with his fingers, like surgeons' sutures into oranges.

There was an art to it. The first time he'd tried taking magic that wasn't his, it had wrapped around his palms like razor wire, tight enough that he'd needed stitches. Since then, Eli had bled magic from a soul enough times that he knew the rhythm of it. He knew what kinds of magic to stay away from and what kinds he could upsell, which would get stuck beneath his fingernails and which would crumble and turn to ash if he held on too tightly. He had strict rules. He only took magic that had been corrupted or warped into something wicked. Magic that had soured and rotted from wrongdoing. Magic like *this*, that smelled like . . . death.

It didn't take long before he was finished. The soul slotted back together with a click that reminded Eli of clockwork. When he stepped back, the boy let out a deep exhale. He wore a thin golden chain around his neck, a pendant of a snake wrapped around a dagger. Eli watched it rise and fall against his chest until he was sure that he was okay. The magic was weak with fatigue and confused, probably, at having been tampered with, but it had listened to him.

"You're getting good at that," said a voice behind him, and Eli turned to see that he had an audience.

Sunny leant against the doorframe, a cigarette between her lips despite the very clear, capitalized sign on the wall behind her indicating that it was prohibited to smoke. At some point during the short twenty minutes since Eli had last seen her, she had gotten into a fight, because she now sported a bloody nose, a swollen eye, and a crooked grin.

"Who'd you piss off this time?" Eli asked, entirely unsurprised.

Sunny smiled. There was blood on her chin. "Why do you assume it was me doing the pissing off?"

"I've spent more than fifteen seconds in your vicinity," Eli answered, and Sunny gave an unladylike snort.

They were standing in the back alley of some Camden pub, one of those nameless ones that seemed as old as it did new. The asphalt gleamed in sleek pinks and purples from last night's rain. Across the street, a tattooed guy was fruitlessly flogging his mixtape. A few drunk people hovered outside the kebab place, and if Eli craned his neck, he could just about make out the last of the tourists leaving the Lock with dusk. It should have been unnerving, probably, that it was only the cover of the night that kept them shrouded from onlookers, but Eli had always liked busy places. There was something in the comfort of not being alone.

"That's not our guy," Sunny said, peering down at the unconscious boy.

"Nope," Eli said, and it most certainly wasn't. Eli pushed his glasses further up his nose to get a better look. Their contact was supposed to be a gray-haired seer man. Instead, they'd found a boy around the same age as them. When they'd first found him, he'd been moments away from death. He might have been mistaken for sleeping if it hadn't been for the small, bleeding puncture at the base of his stomach, slowly oozing magic. Now, his chest rose and fell in even breaths. He would be fine when he woke up. Something would be missing, maybe. A memory. A friend's face. A favorite song. Eli tried to avoid thinking about it too hard. He had saved a life, after all.

"Shit," Sunny said. "Pam's gonna be vex."

"When isn't she?" Eli said, and Sunny snorted in agreement. "At least we've got something else for her."

The sliver of magic Eli had taken from the boy was no bigger than a ten-pence coin, probably only slightly larger than his thumbnail, but weighed heavy in the palm of his hand. Most magic Eli had encountered was tinted with color, a reflection of the soul it had come from. Eli's own magic, for instance, had the habit of staining his fingers moss-green. This magic, however, was completely clear and white. It cut through the darkness of the alleyway like moonlight, bright enough to leave spots behind Eli's eyelids. Eli wondered what it might feel like to use that sort of magic but quickly cast the thought aside. Thinking like that only led to trouble.

The boy most likely wouldn't notice the magic was gone, but for Eli magic meant survival: from just this fragment, he would be able to cover at least a month's rent, maybe a couple of weeks of credit on his Oyster card, and at least a momentary reprieve from the sinking sand of financial instability that he was constantly up to his neck in.

"We should probably get out of here, then," said Sunny, yawning. "There are some drunk guys inside who are going to be realizing any second now that they no longer have their wallets."

Eli rolled his eyes, but it wasn't like he could comment. He was just as much a thief as she was.

Eli had always thought of London as two halves. There was the tedium of everyday London that most people existed in, full of commuters, coffee shops, and tourist traps. Then there was the secret side of the city, full of winding, serpentine streets and back-alley bargains. This was a London you only knew if it ran in your blood.

Pam's West Indian Takeaway was one of those places. Far enough off Camden High Street that it was easy to miss, it was nestled between a vegan sandwich shop–cum–tattoo parlor and a record store that, as far as Eli could tell, only sold obscure Serbian jazz on vinyl.

In truth, this was the side of London that he loved. Not the sleek gray industrialism of Zone One, full of overpaid suits and twenty-something upstart gentrifiers. For Eli, this was home. Corner shops next to kebab shops next to unisex barbers. Nail shops next to chicken shops next to funeral homes. It was the outer crust. He liked that everyone here knew what it was to be on the outside.

Pam's, in particular, was a place of in-betweens. The magic of the restaurant, like a lot of places in London, lay in the fact that it existed just outside linear time. Eli didn't understand the technicalities of it, honestly. Sunny had attempted to explain it once, but since she had the unfortunate habit of lying compulsively for the fun of it, Eli wasn't sure how far he could believe her.

Still, he'd figured out the basics. Pam's was a sanctuary. If you knew the right spells and which doors to use them on, you could even enter at any time of the day, stay for as long as you liked.

For Eli, it was home. The top two floors had been converted into flats, and Eli and Sunny each rented a room from Pam for half the market price, under the condition that they spend their free time downstairs washing dishes and folding pastries. It was, objectively, a bit of a fixer-upper—there was water damage in almost every room, the smell of food permeated the walls, and it was somehow both freezing in the winters yet suffocatingly hot in the summer—but Eli had grown fond of it. It was a place that was theirs.

Max, the final piece of their trio, was behind the counter flipping through a comic book when they entered.

"Hey," she said at their arrival, "what kind of West Indian time do you call this? I was just about to close up." She took in Sunny's bruised and bloody face, then turned to Eli with a resigned yet wholly unsurprised sigh. "Do I even want to know?"

Max, like Pam, was a girl of in-betweens. She was close to Sunny and Eli in age, but nobody this side of London knew more about magic. The daughter of an imam and a retired activist, Max was a healer some days, a thief the others, but a cashier on most.

"Probably not," Sunny said, closing the door behind her and flipping the OPEN FOR BUSINESS sign hanging out front to SOON COME. "Anyway, you worry too much. Probably only, like, forty percent of the blood is mine."

Eli tried not to roll his eyes. Sunny's judgment about whether something was worth worrying over seemed to exist on a scale from one to a-human-being's-death-has-transpired.

"Besides," Sunny continued, flinging herself onto her usual stool by the counter. "You won't be mad when you see what we've got."

He wasn't sure how it had happened, but in the short time they had known one another, this act of exchanging gifts after every job had become something of a tradition among the three of them. Of course, the big things they found, things with actual worth, Max would pass on to Pam. Magic that was owed. Debts that were overdue. It was how he and Sunny stayed afloat. Well—that, and a hellish amount of monotony; weekend retail work in between shifts at Pam's, part-time waiting tables, freelance call center temping. Eli was just nearing the end of his teen years, yet he'd had more jobs in the first two decades of his life than most people had in whole lifetimes.

Their smaller finds, the peculiar magical tidbits that didn't have any worth outside of their strangeness factor, those Max kept for herself. She wasn't a collector, necessarily, but she liked deconstructing things, stripping them down and seeing what they were made of.

It was the same reason that Max had first decided to help Eli with his own business. *Okay*, Max had said after she'd heard his story. *Well, you're definitely a mystery.* And that was all it had taken.

A boy who plucked the magic from a soul like petals, who had no memory of who he was before three years ago? She had peeked once at the hollowness inside him, the crack right through his center, and decided instantly that it was something of interest to her.

In return, it had become a fun little game for Eli and Sunny while they were on their adventures: Who could bring Max back the weirdest find? Scales from a water spirit, hair of a lagahoo, cursed knives, phoenix ashes; somewhere along the road, the two of them had inadvertently become a pair of proprietary house cats, filling their jaws with feathered gifts.

It was Max who had dropped Pam's request in their group chat a week prior, between links to personality quizzes and twelve-minute-long YouTube videos dissecting pop star feuds. *Pam looking for ancient fang,* she'd texted, *says it nyams magic. Allegedly stolen by Anansi himself from Osebo, leopard god. Last heard whispers that it's with some seer man looking to sell to the highest bidder. Pam says if you find, DO NOT TOUCH (obvs). (It eats magic.)*

pass, Sunny had replied, *sounds like some old-time bush fable.* But then a week later she'd come back with the lead on a Camden pub and a simple follow-up question:

how much?

"Pam's not going to like this," Max said, after suffering through their lengthy explanation of how they'd searched for the seer man and instead stumbled on the boy in the alleyway, a hole pierced through his gut, half dead, and no sign of the fang.

Sunny and Eli exchanged a look. Pam sent them on a lot of errands. Some of the things they were sent to retrieve were hefty enough to keep their stomachs full for whole months. Other times it was just the matter of passing on a message. Pam never gave any indication of the significance of her requests, and Eli and Sunny never asked. This felt different.

"What's so special about this fang?" Sunny asked. It came out, as did most of Sunny's words, dripping with derision, but Max's response was sincere.

"At the moment it's just rumors. You know people like to run their mouths. But you should have seen the way Pam spoke about it. She told me she *needed* it. She seemed, I don't know. Spooked."

Truthfully, he hadn't even known Pam was capable of fear. One time a group of guys had tried to break into their cash register and Pam had dispensed with them using only the blunt end of a broom. Another time, a kitchen fire had started out back and the whole building had been flooded with thick, blinding smoke. Pam had casually waded through the flames, wafting the smoke from her face like it was a fruit fly. She hadn't left until everyone was safe, and only then did she leisurely amble outside, a handbag nestled in the crook of one arm and a wad of cash in the other, looking less like she was escaping a burning building and more like she was on her way to the bank.

Max gnawed at her lip, and Eli could tell that she was debating how much to reveal. "Mrs. Taylor came in the other week. She told me her son—you know the tall one, plays the clarinet?—well, he was missing."

"Eddie," Sunny said, and Eli cast her a sideways glance. She somehow always knew everyone, which always took him by surprise since his own social circle was pretty much limited to the two people in this room. "What? He comes in here sometimes. He's nice."

Max nodded. "They found him two days ago; he'd had the magic ripped out of his soul. Clawed straight out of his chest. The same thing happened the week before, some guy on Green Lanes. They pried apart his rib cage, picked it clean out of his heart."

Neither Eli nor Sunny uttered a word, both quietly horrified.

"There's been a couple of other missing cases. Word is that

someone's clawing souls out of hearts and feeding off people's magic. It's all anyone can talk about when they come in here."

"You think Pam wants the fang for protection," Eli said.

"Your guess is as good as mine," Max said. "All I know is that it seemed very important to her to find it."

Eli winced. "Well, maybe this will help." He dug into his pocket and pulled out the little satchel that contained the slice of magic he'd taken. He threw it to Max, who caught it one-handed and then pushed her glasses up from the end of her nose and whistled. The magic rattled like copper pennies at the bottom of a purse. A pair of tweezers materialized in Max's hand within seconds, and she used them to reach into the satchel and pluck hold of it. Behind her glasses, her eyes were magnified to the size of saucers. "Where'd you get this?"

"The boy in the alleyway," Eli said. "We didn't want to come back empty-handed."

They watched as Max flipped the magic over again and again, fascinated. She put it to her ear like a seashell, gave it a little shake as it rattled, then sniffed it. "Whoever this came from, he's powerful. This is serious magic."

"Yeah?" Eli asked carefully. "I know it's not the magic-eating fang of a leopard god, but I figured it would sell. How much you thinking?"

Max looked up then, the humor sobering from her expression. "Eli, I'm not taking this."

"What? For real?" Sunny asked. She'd been stretched languidly along the counter, braids trailing on the marble, playing a one-man game of foosball with the salt and pepper shakers, but at the mention of money, her head popped up.

"You need to get rid of it," Max said. "The fang was one thing, but this . . ."

Officially, Pam's dealings were wholly aboveboard. The takeaway was a sanctuary, but it would stop being so if angry mobs were to turn up at the door, demanding retribution for what was taken from them. Unofficially, however, Pam's willingness toward the nefarious tended to work on a sliding scale. It was a balancing act; she didn't accept anything that was more trouble than it was worth. Exhibit A: the supposed fang of a leopard god that could eat through magic. Exhibit B: the slice of stolen magic of some no-name boy they'd found in an alleyway.

Eli wasn't even entirely sure what Pam did with their findings, if she sold them or kept them on display somewhere. Sunny had theorized once that Pam simply ate them, nyamed up the magic for herself, and coughed up the bones, which might've seemed plausible except for the fact that Pam rarely used magic. Eli had only ever seen Pam use it once the entire time he'd known her, and it had been to cheat at a game of rummy. He wasn't even sure she *could* use magic anymore.

"Eli," Max said. "This magic smells like death. A lot of people are looking for this fang. If duppy magic is involved, you should do yourself a favor and stay out of it."

Eli fell quiet, feeling sullen and chastised, and Max leant forward to flick him in the head.

"Did you send off your application?" she asked, softer now.

It was a seemingly innocuous question, and yet it succeeded in swiftly causing Eli's mouth to snap shut. Despite the many and increasingly passive-aggressive texts Max had sent him reminding him of the looming deadline, he hadn't, in fact, sent off his Sixth Form College application. He'd spent weeks agonizing over which course he'd even want to pursue before settling on a foundational history course. He'd been drawn to the idea of learning about what came before him. Though he kept insisting to Max that he simply

12

hadn't gotten round to it yet, the truth was he'd been avoiding it.

He just kept thinking about what would happen if he woke up tomorrow and remembered who he was. What if he'd already been partway through his A Levels and had simply forgotten? What if there was something, some secret talent, that he was exceptional at, that he hadn't realized yet? The act of applying for a college course seemed like a betrayal to who he was or might have been. It would be the nail in the coffin of finding his former self.

Max, who had never scored anything lower than an A+ and who treated preparing for further education like it was training for an Olympic sport, did not seem to grasp that.

"No," Eli admitted, "I haven't sent off my college application yet."

Max sighed. "Did you even start it?"

"Not . . . exactly," Eli said, though that wasn't quite true. He had opened the application a few nights ago, but one of the very first questions had requested a vague description of where he saw himself in five years and Eli had just—he'd panicked. He didn't know where he saw himself in five years. He didn't even know where he saw himself in five *days*. Whenever he thought about his future, he'd get this tight, nagging feeling in his chest that would follow him around and keep him up at night. He couldn't explain that to Max, whose bedroom walls had been covered in glittery mood boards carefully strategizing her future since she was ten years old.

"I say bun the whole education sector," Sunny said. "Get a degree? Why? 'Cause some old white men decided I'd need it to have value in society? Pass."

Max shook her head but didn't bother protesting. This was an old argument between the two of them, and one that they would never see eye to eye on.

"You trust me, don't you?" Max said. She dropped the magic

back in the satchel, pulled the string tightly shut, and placed it firmly back in Eli's hand.

"You know I do," Eli said. His friendship with Sunny and Max was about the only thing he did trust these days.

"Then hear what I'm saying. You can't hide behind magic forever, and that magic stinks of death. Get rid of it, and quickly. The last thing any of us wants is duppy problems on our doorstep."

"Fuck," Sunny said.

The two of them stood across the road from Pam's waiting for the bus. The night wasn't over for them yet. They both still had a few more errands to run for Pam before the end of the night, and they'd lined up a temp job tomorrow waiting tables at some black-tie, members-only event in Central where they'd been told they were going to be needed until at least midnight. Eli's bones were already aching at the thought of it. He briefly contemplated flaking and going straight to bed, but without the money they'd anticipated for the fang, they were already behind for the month. What they really needed was a way to sell the stolen magic somehow. It was one of their rules: whatever they found, they sold. They never kept any of it—magic, especially. Keeping anything meant a trail. Plus, it was a dangerous thing to keep magic that wasn't yours for too long. It had a way of changing you.

"It's not that bad," Eli said.

"Really?" Sunny pulled a face. Instead of giving them the paycheck they'd anticipated, Max had handed them a beef patty, and now there were pieces of pastry stuck to Sunny's fingers and braids. "How is it not that bad?"

Eli shrugged. "Legs will probably take it."

Legs was Sunny's slick-talking roadman friend; he bought all their seedier finds, the stuff a little too high-risk for Pam to take, but he also tended to shamelessly lowball them at any given opportunity.

"Yeah," Sunny grumbled, "but at what cost?"

Eli knew she was thinking about the last time Legs finessed them. "Our dignity, probably," Eli answered. Sunny went to laugh but ended up wincing as it stretched the swollen skin over her cheek and busted lip.

"You know I can fix that if you want," he offered, purposefully light. Sunny hadn't been exaggerating when she'd said Eli had been getting good at the whole healing thing. He'd gotten cuts and bruises mostly down and could even fix a broken bone if he really concentrated, though if he didn't, they tended to stitch their way into his own skin instead.

"I'm fine," Sunny said with a glare. "Worry about yourself."

"I'm pretty sure you do that enough for the both of us."

Whatever cutting remark Sunny was about to make was lost when her phone began to ring. She looked down at the screen and cussed under her breath. "I've got to take this," she said, though not without flipping him the middle finger first. "Yell if the bus gets here?"

Eli watched her, phone balanced between her ear and shoulder, back hunched against the wind, gesturing theatrically, the way she only ever really did when she was angry. Not for the first time, Eli wondered who she could be talking to. This wasn't the type of thing they discussed. Their conversations in general would probably seem largely vacuous to an outsider; they could spend hours ranting over something as nonsensical as the rankings of a Quality Street selection, or who would win in a fight between the Avengers and the X-Men, but the subject of family, by some weird, mutual unspoken agreement, had become something to be avoided early on. In some ways, he thought it was a kindness on Sunny's behalf, some covertly altruistic attempt to not put salt in the wound, since they both knew that Eli's personal life started with Sunny and ended with Max. Secretly, Eli suspected there was more to it.

Sunny had always been private. She rarely mentioned her family, if ever, and whenever Eli would ask her about it, she would talk in vague, uncertain terms. He knew the basics: she didn't get along with her mum, she had a brother she didn't talk to, she'd been born and bred by the River Lea, and even though she was probably a year or two younger than Eli, she had left home young. He knew that she couldn't use magic anymore, that a spell had turned sour and blackened the tips of her fingers, but the details of it were a mystery. He'd asked her one Christmas if she had any plans to go home, and she'd stared at him as if he'd proposed they take a leap off Tower Bridge and then said, like he was stupid, *I am home, idiot.*

Although Eli thought about it a lot, the truth was that it didn't bother him if Sunny was a little reserved. He chalked it up to another trait in a long list of baffling Sunny-isms, like her perpetually foul mouth and mercurial temperament. Whatever the reason for keeping her secrets, Eli figured, Sunny probably had a good one.

He was still very much dissecting the thought in his mind when a flaky piece of pastry hit him square in the middle of the forehead. "Ow!" Eli said. "What was that for?"

Apparently, Sunny had finished her phone call, because she was now standing in front of him, eyebrows raised. "Eavesdropping, yeah?"

"No," Eli lied, and Sunny gave him a deadpan look. "Okay, maybe a little. Everything good?"

Another piece of pastry hit him in the jaw, and Eli flung it back. "What, you want me to write you a sonnet?" Sunny snorted. "I'm good. You know how it is."

Eli did, was the thing.

Above them, the sky was black and starless, empty in the way that it only ever was in the city and stark compared to all the business beneath it. On nights like this, it was easy to convince himself that things weren't so bad. He had made it through the day. There was no reason that he wouldn't be able to make it through the next one.

He didn't register the silence that had snuck up around them.

This kind of quiet didn't happen where Eli came from. He was used to falling asleep to the background noise of passing police sirens and barking dogs or the distant bass lines of a neighbor's party. No matter where in London he went, there was never truly silence. It was another magic of the place, possibly even Eli's favorite kind.

This, though. This wasn't a tranquil kind of quiet. This was almost funereal.

"Do you feel that?" Eli asked.

"Feel what?" Magic didn't affect Sunny the way it used to. She once described it the same way someone might describe losing their sense of taste. If she ate, she would still be full, but there would be something missing. It was the same thing with magic; she saw it, she understood it, but it didn't cause an itch in her fingers or raise the hair on her arms. She couldn't hold it in her hand and sculpt it into something material.

"I don't know," Eli said. There was an odd tang in the air. It smelled a little like the sky after heavy rainfall. "Something's off."

"Okay," Sunny said, suddenly low, cautious. "That's not ominously vague at all."

Standing like they were, in the middle of the street, it struck Eli that they were completely out and in the open. He looked down at his phone, wondering why the bus hadn't arrived yet when it was scheduled to have come five minutes ago, but the battery had conveniently opted to die.

"I don't like this," Eli mumbled.

"You don't like anything," Sunny replied, which was correct, yes, but this was different.

There was a faint electrical hum, and in the distance, Eli saw a streetlight start to flicker. For a second, that was all there was. The soft buzz of a blinking light bulb, like the flapping wings of a hover-fly. Abruptly, it burst, a satisfying little crunch of a noise that seemed amplified amid the nothingness. Glass clattered to the pavement.

Sunny opened her mouth to speak—probably some kind of sarcastic comment about the local council—but they were silenced when it happened again. Another streetlight shattered. Then came the next one. And the next. It was almost musical. One by one, in perfect succession, each streetlamp cracked into darkness, until there was no light in the entire road except for the single bulb that hovered above their heads.

Eli willed for it to stay on with all the magic in his veins.

"Okay," Sunny said, breaking the silence. "What the hell was that?"

"We should go," Eli said.

Before either of them could move, however, something across the street caught Eli's eye. Thick tendrils of smoke curled out of the shadows and toward the shop. It traveled with the darkness, a shapeless black ghost. Eli knew dark magic when he saw it, and this was walking the streets as plain as day. He wondered fleetingly what it could possibly be doing here—and at Pam's, of all places, which had been a sanctuary and neutral ground for decades before Eli had even been born—when something dawned on him.

"Max is still in there."

The lights were off, but Max would still be inside, locking up the register and doing one last sweep of the kitchen floor. Across the street, the shadow hardened into something solid. A man—or at least, that's how most people would see him. People like Eli, Sunny, and Max, those who inherited the magic in their blood, they saw something else. It wore a person's skin the way a coat hanger wore a mac. It stopped a few yards away, straightened its tie as if it were preparing itself for a meeting, and then strolled straight toward the shop.

There was something familiar about this. Something just on the edge of Eli's memory that he couldn't quite reach. Distantly, he became aware of panic brimming at the back of his throat, but then fear was funny that way. For Eli, it had become a near constant in his life these days. He would wake up anxious, and the feeling would only fester. Now, he could feel it reaching boiling point. He knew he wasn't imagining the way that each hair on his body had suddenly become erect, or how the air around them seemed to drop several degrees. He imagined Max inside, obliviously sweeping the shop floor, mouthing along to whatever bashment mixtape filtered through her earphones. Eli couldn't leave her there alone. He wouldn't.

"Eli," Sunny repeated, and Eli blinked, realizing that she'd spoken and was waiting for him to reply. "I'm gonna go get her. Stay here, keep watch."

"What?" Eli's reflex was always to argue, even when his gut was telling him to do the opposite. "No, you stay here."

"Look," she said calmly. "It's okay if you're scared—"

"I'm not," Eli snapped, and Sunny raised an eyebrow. She wasn't being accusatory, was the thing. It was a simple observation. Of course Eli was scared. He was constantly scared. He felt himself bristle with frustration, partly at his own cowardice, partly at how Sunny could see straight through to it. He could tell from that quirk of her eyebrow that she was thinking about all the times she'd found him, huddled and trembling at the kitchen table in the middle of the night, skin sticky with sweat from thrashing through nightmares.

The concept of being genuinely frightened by something was probably unfamiliar to Sunny. There was nothing that stumbled into her pathway that she couldn't demolish with pure strength of will.

Eli glanced back toward the diner, determination settling in his gut. Max was inside, grossly outmatched and entirely unaware. The light above their heads had started to rattle, but Sunny's gaze didn't leave his. He could be like Sunny, Eli thought. Just this once.

"Let's go," he said, and he turned back toward the shop to make his way across the empty street before she could protest.

There was a trick to entering Pam's undetected. Max had taught Eli and Sunny right at the beginning of their friendship. They'd been drunk at the time, and Max had forgotten her keys after spending an entire bus journey waxing lyrical about a supposed crater of left-over macaroni cheese that she'd been longing for. After realizing that their midnight snack plans had been foiled, Eli had been more than happy to call it a night, but Max refused to admit defeat. She'd ushered them to the back of the building, giggling and stumbling the entire way.

"Wanna see a life hack?" she'd said, and Eli had shushed her because it had been nearing four a.m. and her voice always got a decibel too loud after a few drinks.

"You sure you want to break into your own workplace?" Eli had asked, because at that time he hadn't known Max long and the diner was yet to become his home. It had seemed excessive to risk incarceration over a dish of pasta.

Max had just patted his face, her own full of sympathy for the poor macaroni-less boy with no memories. "Don't worry," she'd said, "you'll understand once you try."

There was a window at the back that didn't close all the way, no matter how hard you pulled. It had been spelled to keep out intruders after a couple of break-ins started happening locally, but the secret was intent. If you meant ill, the window stayed locked. If not, it was simply a matter of wriggling your way in.

Now, Eli's intent was clear.

The window opened with an almost expectant sigh. Not without great difficulty, Eli scrambled through, shakily landing on the balls of his feet.

The first thing that hit him was the smell, pungent enough that he had to cover his mouth with the back of his sleeve. It was the unmistakable stench of rot and decay. Of death.

"Now, I'll ask you again," a voice said. It was distinctly male, the voice of somebody who had never been told no before. Eli glanced at Sunny, who had soundlessly dropped in through the window behind him. They exchanged a nod, and then the two of them followed the sounds through the kitchen, crouching behind the counter to keep out of sight. "Tell me where it is."

"I told you, I don't know what you're talking about," Max said.

"Now, now, Max. We both know that's not true. I can smell death on you."

Eli crept around the corner, ignoring the unpleasant stickiness of the kitchen tiles, and peeked through the beaded curtains onto the main shop floor. Around the corner, he could just about see Max pinned against a wall, a hand to her neck and her feet inches from the ground.

Sunny cursed under her breath.

The man holding Max was wiry with graying skin, as tall as he was thin. There was a spiderlike quality to him, something in the way he moved, all legs and joints, bends and knobbles like an aging tree branch. Underneath his coat was a black suit, like he was dressed for a funeral, and when he turned his face, Eli caught a glimpse of eyes that were milk-white.

21

"That's enough of the games," the man said amiably. "If I must, I'll kill you, little witch."

"Even if I did know," Max spat, "do you think I would tell you? I know what you are."

Eli took a second to be momentarily impressed by Max's fearlessness; her scuffed Converse kicked fruitlessly, but the man didn't even flinch.

"You know what the ancient Egyptians used to believe about the afterlife?" The man continued as if she hadn't spoken. It wasn't the voice of evil, really. He sounded more like an overzealous history teacher. "The ancient Egyptians believed that when you die, the black-headed jackal Anubis, protector of the dead, leads you across the threshold from the world of the living to the underworld. There, he reaches inside you—"

Eli tensed as Max began to whimper.

"—takes out your heart, and places it on a scale. If your soul is lighter than a feather, then you ascend to the heavens and live out your eternal life in bliss. But if your heart is heavier, well . . ."

Max's body was obscured from his line of sight, so Eli couldn't see what caused her shout, but this time he felt it all the way to his bones. If they didn't get to her, he was sure she'd end up like the others she'd warned him about. Like Eddie, who'd been found with his chest clawed out. Her magic torn out of her and a hole through her heart.

Think, Eli thought frantically. *Think, think, think.*

"Tell me, little witch," the man whispered. "If I cut out your heart, will it be lighter than a feather?"

Eli took a deep breath, his heart pounding. He moved as if to stand up, but before he got the chance, Sunny's hand clamped over his mouth.

"Old Street," Sunny whispered, and Eli understood immediately.

Old Street: the time he and Sunny had been chased up and down Shoreditch High Street by a gang of dreadhead soucouyants, like they were protagonists in some old-time Charlie Chaplin film. They'd made the mistake of stumbling into the wrong ends after sunset, when the soucouyants were at their hungriest for blood; the only reason they'd gotten away was because, by some weird twist of fate, a moped had cut off a bus on the road they'd been crossing and the two drivers had pulled into the middle of the road to scream red-faced at each other, allowing Sunny and Eli the perfect opportunity to slip away. It was something the two of them still laughed about to this day, the rush of absolute glee as they bumped the barriers at the station and slipped to safety, the burn marks from the soucouyants' flames they'd narrowly missed, how close they were to being caught, how surely they would have been if not for that tiniest sliver of luck. *Something was looking out for us that day*, Sunny would say. *Nah*, Eli had told her repeatedly. *We were looking out for ourselves.*

In short, Eli knew what Sunny meant now. She meant that they needed a distraction. She meant for them to run.

Eli looked back toward the dining area, conscious of every moment that Max was in there, alone and in pain. Sunny didn't have magic; it would be easier for her to go undetected.

"When I give the sign," Eli whispered, "grab Max."

Sunny frowned at him, clearly hesitant, but then she nodded and disappeared around the other side of the counter.

Eli leant back against the wall and pulled from his pocket the small velveteen pouch that held the piece of magic he'd stolen from the boy in the alleyway. Even through the material, Eli could feel it pulsating, aimlessly floundering like a goldfish dropped into a glass of water.

It would have to listen to him. Magic was funny that way. It had to be coaxed into doing what you wanted, otherwise it would just waft stubbornly, like oil in water. Really, it came down to a mutual understanding, somewhere deep in your core.

Eli focused on the memory of it as he'd plucked it from the boy's chest; the sensation of grazed elbows, scuffed trainers, and bloody noses that he'd felt the first time he'd touched it. It had felt lonely, and Eli understood. When he opened his eyes, it was there, hovering in front of him. No satchel; just the tiny white glowing fragment of magic, drifting at eyeline.

Eli didn't hesitate. The magic hit his palm and sizzled, and Eli let out an involuntary hiss at the contact. Its light streamed through his fingers, hot enough that he almost let go, that he was sure he would have a scar. Eli didn't drop it, though, and the base of it thrummed against his palm, steady like a heartbeat. Eli was entranced; he raised his hand and saw all the tiny veins and capillaries lining his skin, the red of the muscles under the flesh.

He took a deep breath and stood up.

"Hey!" he called out. He'd never noticed before, but Pam's place had an echo to it when you shouted loud enough.

"Ah," said the white-eyed thing. Its head whipped around fast enough to give a normal person whiplash. He peered at Eli with translucent eyes, then sniffed, once, like a bloodhound. Eli's mouth soured with fear. "Well, this certainly makes things more interesting."

It took a step toward Eli, and Eli saw its face twist into something else entirely. Something hungry.

"She doesn't have what you want," Eli said. Another step. Eli almost stumbled backward, but he forced himself not to move. He kept his fist clenched tight by his side, the magic pounding against his palm, like he was brandishing a flare.

The creature had stepped away from Max, but its magic kept her pinned against the wall, half-heartedly clawing at the invisible grip seizing her neck. The creature barely seemed to notice. It cocked its head ever so slightly, interested. "And what have you got there?"

"Let her g-go," Eli said, stuttering a little around the words, "and it's yours."

"Eli," Max choked. "Get out of here. Don't be stupid." Her face was red; she looked, perhaps for the first time that Eli had ever seen, genuinely frightened. It was enough to glue Eli's feet to the ground.

The thing waved a hand without so much as looking, and Max's head slammed—*crack*—into the wall. She should have slumped to the floor like a rag doll, but instead, she stayed suspended, clawing at the invisible grip around her neck. The creature raised an eyebrow in appraisal.

"I wonder . . ." It hummed and took another step. "How much does your soul weigh?"

Max's breaths were fraught as she struggled. They needed to hurry. From the corner of his eye, he saw Sunny rise. She gave him a small nod.

"Well," Eli said, mostly to himself, "I guess there's only one way to find out."

Before he could think too much about it, he opened his palm and slammed the magic, hard, into his chest.

There was a yell of protest—perhaps even his own—but it was too late.

Something cracked, and then the magic filled him, sweet and fizzy, like a carbonated drink. At first, that was all he felt; giddy and light-headed, with a chest-deep warmth that spread all the way through to his bones. Then the heat started to deepen and deepen, until it felt as if his veins were on fire.

Everything faded to blackness; then, all at once: perfect clarity.

He'd had the same sensation before, when, after months of stumbling into doorframes and repeatedly missing his stop on the tube, Sunny had finally dragged him to the optometrist to fix his shortsightedness. He remembered looking at the trees for the first time through his new glasses and being surprised that he could make out the individual leaves, watching Max talk animatedly about something or other and realizing that she had a scatter of freckles across her nose that he'd never noticed before.

The thing about magic was that it usually hurt. It didn't hurt now; with every stitch of the magic into him, it was as if he had turned the dial on a microscope and made everything sharper. Colors were brighter. Even smells were stronger. The scent of freshly fried salt fish fritters from the kitchen clung to the inside of his nose. He could even taste the ozone outside from the afternoon's rain on the tip of his tongue.

And then there was the magic. He could feel it all.

When he opened his eyes, Max, Sunny, and the man were staring at him with mirrored expressions of horror. Eli felt strangely distant from it all.

He reached out a hand and let his new magic cut through the air like scissors through muslin. The white-eyed thing let out a scream like nothing Eli had ever heard.

Then everything went dark.

CHAPTER TWO

ELI

The first time Eli remembered using magic was on Sunny.

It had only been a few weeks into what he had internally nick-named *Post-Memory*. A lot of those early days were foggy and dreamlike. When he thought back to them now, he could only recall various sensations: his stomach hollow with hunger for days on end, his fingers cold to the bone. During that time, he walked through the city like an apparition. He'd remember things only to immediately forget them, and what he did remember, he wasn't entirely sure he could trust. He'd had very few possessions: his name, which he somehow knew at his core; money, a few wads of it rolled together in a rubber band and stuffed in his coat pocket, not enough to survive on long-term but enough that he wouldn't die of starvation; he'd had a backpack full of clean clothes that fit him, a toothbrush, and a wide-tooth comb. While this wasn't a lot, it made one thing clear: wherever he'd left, he'd done so intentionally.

He'd spent a lot of those early days just wandering around, hoping to stumble into familiarity. He'd walked into a police station a few times, but every time he did, he was treated with such immediate hostility and suspicion that he'd turned around and retreated, feeling shamed and embarrassed. If he had a home, he didn't remember it, though that in no way lessened the aching, gnawing homesickness that suffocated him.

It had been on a particularly bad day that he'd met Sunny.

He remembered standing at the edge of an underpass, and there at the far end, right in the line of its mouth, a girl lay on the ground. It took Eli a moment to register her for what she was. It was very dark and her body was strangely contorted. Plus, Eli had never seen a dying person before.

Her breath was ragged, she was covered in blood, and half of her face was masked by a curtain of braids. They were vicious, heavy things, Sunny's braids. Later, Eli would learn of the six hours of laborious handiwork that went into them, and he would think of that every time he saw her wearing them. Even that first day, curled up on the ground and bleeding, Sunny wore them the way a snake wore its rattle.

He remembered his feet taking him towards her without thinking.

"Try not to move," he might've said. Or maybe, "I'm going to get help." He couldn't recall his exact words, but he knew he'd been babbling reassurances, mostly nonsensical, and that his hands had trembled the entire time. Sunny had just stared at him, wary and unmoving, like she was being cornered by a wild animal, so Eli had paused, put his hands up. "It's okay," he'd assured her. "I'm not going to hurt you."

Something in Sunny seemed to have resolved at that, and she relaxed slightly. She smiled briefly, and there was blood on her teeth. "Right," Sunny said. "As if you could."

That was the first thing Eli remembered noticing about her: she was *funny*.

28

"No," Eli said. "I mean yeah, obviously. Sorry. Tell me what to do."

"First, stop asking questions," Sunny said. Eli almost protested, but Sunny shot him a look that immediately silenced him. "My hands, I can't— Could you— My phone. It's in my pocket."

"Oh." When Eli got closer, he saw why she couldn't use her hands. They were covered in vicious-looking cuts and bruises that seemed to go right to the bone. Her fingers were burnt black right up to her knuckles, almost as if they were frostbitten. It looked painful, but Eli kept his face neutral. "Sure, I got it. This one?"

"Yeah."

Careful not to rustle her any more than necessary, Eli dug around in her coat pocket and pulled out a small white card embossed with the words PAM'S WEST INDIAN TAKEAWAY, and underneath, a phone number.

Eli wavered, suddenly unsure. "Are you sure you don't want me to call an ambulance, or—"

"No. No ambulance." She closed her eyes and breathed heavily. "Call. Tell them it's Sunny."

"Sunny?" Eli frowned, and then the realization dawned on him. *Oh.* This sour-faced, bleeding girl was Sunny. The absurdity of it was almost enough to make him laugh. The truth was, he'd found Sunny a little bit terrifying that first day, and frankly every day since. "I'm Eli, by the way." It was more of a self-revelation than anything. The list of things that Eli knew about himself was short enough to count on one hand. But this—his name—this was his, and it was all he had to offer.

Sunny just gazed at him, eyes glassy and confused. "Okay?" she drawled. "So?" And that was the second thing Eli learned about Sunny: she was able to make a single syllable drip with sardonicism, even on the brink of death.

"Just try and stay awake, yeah?" Eli asked. "I'll make the call."

"Mm. 'Kay." Sunny's eyes were already drifting shut, so Eli reached over and took one of her bruised and bloodied hands. Eli had never seen anyone die, but he had a sudden flash of visiting an old lady—his grandmother, maybe—as a child. She had been close to the end, at the time. He remembered hugging her and feeling nothing but bones, taking her hand and feeling ice. It was funny that he could look back and remember this, but not her name or who she was to him. Sunny's hands felt the same that day, and it took everything in him not to flinch.

"Please don't die," Eli whispered.

It worked. He felt the first pinpricks of magic in his fingers as it ran from him and into her. He hadn't even known what he was doing then, but it had felt natural. It wasn't a lot of magic, but it was enough that whatever was broken inside her started to weave itself together. Sunny's eyes opened and landed on him, and she chuckled slightly, humorless.

"Yeah," she said. "No promises."

Eli woke to a face hovering over him, ruffled and irritated, somehow managing to accurately convey all the levels of *I told you so* that were undoubtedly sizzling on the tip of her tongue.

"Oh good, you're not dead," Sunny said brightly. "Now I get to kill you myself."

Eli sat up and looked around. He'd half expected Pam's to be in ruins. It wouldn't have been the first time. Once, close to the start of their friendship, Eli had foolishly brought back the horn of a rolling calf that they'd found stashed in the back shelves of their local library, intending to gift it to Max, since she was always going on about how rolling calves' ivory could be used for spells. Eli was still new to their world then, and while Pam had been gradually unraveling what she called the "gifts of their ancestors," he hadn't yet learned that some gifts were best left unopened. As it turned out, the librarian they'd taken it from was neck-deep in duppy magic; the horn was cursed with such wickedness that it had very nearly destroyed the entire street when they'd left it in a vat of water to cleanse overnight.

The aftermath of that night was burnt into Eli's brain; blackness threaded through the ugly palm-tree-painted linoleum, deep and inklike, broken glass littering the floor, drywall and bits of plaster scattered across it like crumpled paper planes. The three of them had spent days cleaning up the mess, with Pam's critical eye burning into them the entire time. In the end, there had been something satisfying in it. They'd swept up the restaurant, and with it, their horror at the trauma they'd endured. It was a closed chapter. Finished. They'd moved on.

This time, though, there wasn't any mark of what they'd experienced. Eli didn't know how they were supposed to deal with this.

"At least make it quick," Eli said, and he paused to swallow, noting how uncharacteristically gruff his voice sounded. His throat felt raw, like he'd been screaming, but he didn't remember doing so. "It's been a really long day."

Sunny didn't smile. She wordlessly handed him a scrunched-up tissue from her pocket, and Eli realized that it was for his nose, which had apparently been streaming with blood. He glanced down and saw that his whole T-shirt was stained with it. The cost of using that much magic, he imagined. There was also a crack in one of his glasses lenses, which would need to be fixed. This, more than anything, filled Eli with dread; yet another thing he was going to have to figure out a way to pay for.

"You scared us," Max said. She looked okay, if a little worse for wear. There were reddish marks around her neck where that thing's magic had grasped her. Eli looked away, but doing so was mostly futile. The image of her fighting for her life was going to be scorched behind his eyelids for a long time.

"Are you hurt?" Eli asked, and Max smiled.

"You blacked out, and you're asking if I'm hurt." She shook her head. "I'm fine, might be wearing scarves for a while, but whatever. Are *you* okay?"

Eli considered this for a moment. His hands had stopped shaking. The buzz under his skin had finally waned. Sure, he was covered in blood, but that wasn't exactly a rare occurrence in his line of work. "I'm good," Eli said.

Beside him, Sunny snorted in disbelief.

"No, really," Eli insisted. "I feel—*good.*"

It was true. He'd expected it to hurt somehow, but it was the opposite. His lungs felt lighter. There seemed to be less of a weight on his shoulders. For the first time in a long time, he didn't have a headache.

"Sorry," Eli said, trying to unscramble his thoughts. He could only remember fragments. Max. White eyes. The sting as the magic hit his palm. He looked down at his hand, but there was nothing, no marks, no scars. Had he imagined it? "What . . . happened, exactly?"

"Uh, I'll tell you what happened," Max said. "What happened is that your eyes went black, like you were in *The Exorcist* or some shit. Then you went nuclear."

"Yeah?" He looked around at his perfectly untarnished surroundings. He didn't remember, and while this too wasn't unfamiliar, it also wasn't comforting. He hated the dependency that came with not knowing. Unease knitted away at the depths of his stomach.

Max shrugged. Now that she had seen that Eli was certifiably alive and well, she didn't seem particularly concerned by any of this. If anything, she looked intrigued. She made a gesture with her hands as if to signify a sizable *kaboom*. "It was pretty serious. What do you remember?"

"That . . . man?" Eli asked, stumbling over the words slightly. It seemed ridiculous to refer to the creature as such when that obviously couldn't be further from the truth.

Only now did Max's expression waver. She gave a little nod toward the store counter.

It took Eli an embarrassing amount of time before he registered what he was looking at from behind his scratched glasses. Beyond the counter, crumpled like a used tissue, was that thing's remains. It looked like a broken clay sculpture, cracked into even parts. There was no blood, despite it being in pieces, and the gray of its skin had reverted to weathered marble; it was simply as if someone had taken a porcelain doll and dropped it from up high.

Eli stumbled backward and felt the crunch of something airlight and crisp beneath his foot, like a leaf during autumn. Well, Eli thought, trying to swallow back the nausea. At least that answered any notions that the thing had been human.

"That's all that's left of it," Max said. There was grim satisfaction in her voice. "Not so scary like that, huh?"

Eli wasn't so sure about that, but he was pulled from his thoughts when Sunny picked up a broom and thumped him hard on the arm.

"Ow! What was that for?"

"Nice distraction, idiot."

"You said *Old Street*."

"So?"

"*So?*" he mimicked. "I thought that was code for 'make some noise.'"

Sunny made an exasperated sound and whacked him on the arm again. "I meant, like, knock over some shelves, not let off the magical equivalent of an atom bomb in our place of business."

Eli rubbed his arm and glared at her. "I mean, it worked, didn't it?"

"You could have killed us."

"Could have," Eli countered. "But didn't. That's the important part here."

"Seriously?" Sunny said. "What is wrong with you?"

"Do you want an itemized list?"

"Sunny's right," Max said, and Eli opened his mouth to protest, but Max's attention was still on the dead thing. "You see the blue mark on its skin? The white eyes?" He hadn't noticed before, but there were some chalky sapphire-blue dustings around the remains of its arms and torso. They looked like they'd been finger-painted on. "They're like that because someone made them a deal in exchange for their will after their death," Max explained. "Instead of going on to the afterlife, they're given a new body in return for following commands. The marks are a sign that you've severed yourself from your humanity, so you're like a puppet. Back in the day, witches used them to do their bidding."

"So it was sent here by someone." Eli nudged a stray piece of it with the toe of his trainer and then grimaced as it instantly crumbled at the contact.

Max nodded. "Someone powerful."

"There's more to this than you've told us, Maxie," Sunny cut in. She looked deeply irritated by the whole situation, but Eli wasn't too concerned, since that was her default setting.

Max's silence was immediately damning.

"Let me guess," Sunny said. "You promised Pam you wouldn't." Max started to sputter indignantly, and Sunny raised an eyebrow. "Am I wrong?"

Of the three of them, Max was undeniably closest to Pam. Max was the youngest of them all, the baby of their strange little self-made family, which meant that even though she was usually a culprit—if not the architect—of their various antics, she often managed to escape the full force of Pam's wrath by feigning innocence.

Most of it came down to the fact that she was also the only one of them who had any genuine interest in magic. For Sunny and Eli, magic was a means to an end, another way of filling their pockets, as much as waiting tables and answering phones. Max, however, had always treated magic with a kind of reverence. She had grown up in a home where the use of magic was seen as sacrilegious. Her parents saw any kind of magical practice as a remnant of an old world, something that should have been left behind when they immigrated to this country. Assimilation, they called it. A means to survive. But Max had claimed that there was only one word for burying the gifts that their ancestors had so laboriously mastered: *severance*.

It wasn't until she'd started working at Pam's that Max was finally able to explore that part of her ancestry. She'd devoured any information in her path; she would quiz Pam on histories constantly, dissecting any oddities that she found, desperate to soak up every drop of knowledge she could. Pam indulged her curiosity and in return had earned Max's fierce and unwavering loyalty.

Right on cue, Max crossed her arms. "Pam keeps her secrets for a reason," she said.

"Really, Maxie?" Sunny said. "Because she's never shared a single one of those reasons with us."

"You know she's always had our best interest at heart."

"Right," Eli said; this was an old song-and-dance routine between the three of them. "Like that time she sent us to that boat on the Thames and we almost got drowned by river duppies."

"Or," Sunny added, "that time we ended up at that graveyard in Greenwich and Eli almost lost his fingers to a bone witch."

"*Or* how about when we—"

"All right," Max cut in. "Point taken. Look, I don't know everything, okay? Just what I pick up here and there." She looked around, cautiously, like someone might be listening in. "The story is that Osebo's fang can eat magic. They say it's the only weapon on earth powerful enough to kill a god."

"A god," Eli repeated. A chill ran up the back of his neck. He knew, of course, of the Sky-god and Anansi, of Death and his daughters. If you believed the stories, the gods were where all magic came from; they descended to earth centuries ago and bestowed gifts upon a few of their lucky followers, sometimes in thanks, sometimes as revenge. Those were the gifts passed down through bloodlines. Any magic today, of course, had to be inherited, but it couldn't be truly mastered without those same ancestral practices taught by the gods to their ancestors. So while some of the gifts had endured, passed down in leather-bound journals with browning pages or through folk stories relayed in warning, old magic, real magic, the kind rumored to come straight from the vein of a god—that barely existed anymore. "Why does Pam need a weapon that can kill a god?"

Max shrugged. "That's all I know, okay? They say if you touch Osebo's fang, it will devour all the magic in your bones, and when there is nothing left, it *unmakes* you. Turns you to dust. It's an ancient weapon, some kind of mad god magic that was originally used to break curses. That's all I needed to know. Whoever made this—this thing that attacked us, it wasn't an accident. Being able to do magic like that? I mean, this is old magic. Like, *old*, old, not to mention it takes skill."

Pam was always telling them that back in the day, magic was strong enough to topple whole cities and crumble armies, to rewrite the lines between life and death. *You pickney don't know nothing about magic*, she'd chide, and they'd be forced to hear about how, as a child, she was made to stand outside the house each morning, under thick, sweltering heat, instructed to make a piece of straw levitate or else not be permitted indoors. *Magic required discipline,* she'd say. That was why the real art of it was dying out. She'd taught Eli to heal the same way; a pinprick in each of his fingers that he'd spend hours willing closed. A hand over a stovetop so that he could learn how to take away the itch from a burn. Even these small tricks couldn't compare to the ancient magic of the gods, though. Eli wondered what it was they might have gotten tangled in.

"So they'll be back," Eli said.

"They'll be back," Max said, nodding.

The rush was seeping out of Eli's bones, and he felt exhausted. They were all quiet for a moment, the weight of the situation silently dawning on them. Eli took in his friends. They looked worn and battered, and like they needed a good night's sleep. Sunny's eye was beginning to purple.

"Let me take a look at that," he said. "They're gonna start calling you One Eye Enos."

"Very funny. I've been called worse."

"Yeah. By me. That doesn't mean I want to look at it."

"It does look pretty bad," Max agreed.

"Okay, fine," Sunny relented, "but make it quick, and you better pay attention this time. Don't think I've forgotten about that thing with my knee."

"That was one time," Eli protested. Sunny raised a hand to flip him off, but she still collapsed onto the stool and allowed Eli to gently tilt her chin to one side so that he could get a better look.

Usually, the magic of getting skin to knit itself back together was a lengthy process. Pam had taught Eli to think of it as embroidery; painstaking, delicate, one out-of-place stitch and there was a sense of wrongness to the final picture. Like with Sunny's knee—she had a tiny, jagged permanent scar from where he'd lost concentration once. He was careful to focus now as the slow prickle of magic stirred in his fingers. This time, however, as he brought his hand to Sunny's face, there was an unfamiliar surge through Eli. His hand had barely touched Sunny's cheek, and already the skin was losing its pinkish, tender inflammation and the split on her lip was sealing back to normal. The magic poured from Eli more quickly than he could control it, sticky and molten, and he snatched his hand back, wincing as if he'd touched an electrical current.

"Ow! What the hell?" Sunny hissed.

"Shit, sorry."

"What was that?"

"I don't know, I didn't mean to!" Eli looked down at his hand, half expecting smoke to be wafting from it. "It was just—the magic. I couldn't control it."

Sunny ran to a nearby mirror and only stopped scowling when she saw that she hadn't been permanently disfigured. "Yeah, okay," she said. "We're getting rid of it. And as soon as it's gone, we're forgetting about that fang."

"Where?" Max asked. "Pam won't take it, and you can't hand it over to just anyone. It could be dangerous."

"Max's right," Eli said. Sunny's friend Legs would undoubtedly finesse it out of them for a third of its worth, and then sell it on to someone twice as sketchy. It didn't settle well with him. "We probably shouldn't be careless with something like this."

Sunny crossed her arms. "We need to get rid of it, one way or another. We're not going to be safe until it's gone. Plus, it's in you now, Eli. You know what happens if you use too much of a magic that's not your own."

Eli had learned this early on. Stolen magic was caustic to the soul. It might feel good at first, but then came headaches, nosebleeds, a chill right to your bones. More than that, it was addictive. Keep it long enough and it had a way of altering something in you from the inside.

"So you just want to, what?" Eli asked. "Destroy it?"

"Maybe not," Max said. She wasn't looking at Eli. "I know someone who might be able to help us. If Pam found out, she would freak, but with magic like this, we might even be able to bargain for . . . well, for something else."

"Something else," Sunny repeated. "You mean—"

"My memories," Eli finished. He felt the tiniest flutter of something that might've been excitement unfurl its way through his gut. Eli clamped it down. The thing was, they'd been through this before; the agony of being inches from uncovering his secrets, close enough that he could practically feel it against his fingertips.

It was after the last dead end, a lead Sunny had gotten from a friend-of-a-friend who had been looking for someone who vaguely matched Eli's description, that Eli had decided enough was enough. That was around the time that he'd first broached the idea of applying to college. It had been two years by then, and nobody had come looking for him. Nobody missed him. Nobody cared that he was gone. He'd had to accept reality. How many boys who looked like Eli disappeared every day with nobody noticing? How many Black boys had simply been forgotten? His options were clear: he could either torture himself with a past that he didn't remember, that hadn't come looking for him, that he was never going to know, or he could let it go.

Of course, he hadn't really anticipated how difficult that was in reality. The part that was longing for answers, the part that stayed up all hours of the night, searching the depths of the internet for any sign of his existence, the part that caught the eye of every stranger he passed in hope of catching some kind of recognition in their expression. It was still there, despite his efforts to move on.

Sunny knew it. She would stay up with him on the nights when the numbing blankness that haunted his nightmares got too bad and sleep wasn't an option. Max knew it too, since she had been there herself every time a lead had turned out to be nothing more than a door slamming in their faces. It was why Max was struggling to look him directly in the eye as she made the suggestion, why she was even suggesting it at all.

"There's a woman," Max said. "She goes by a lot of names, but in the stories Pam told me, she was called La Diablesse. She's old magic. Older than Pam, even. They say she used to be human once, but she made too many deals with the devil, and now she roams the half world between the living and dead by surviving off deals, granting wishes in exchange for a price, that type of thing. There's not much she doesn't know. With something like this to offer, she could help us."

"No," Sunny cut in sharply. "Absolutely not."

They both turned to look at her, surprised at the finality in her tone.

"Ooo-kay," Eli said, keeping his voice carefully neutral. "And why not, exactly? You just said we should get rid of the magic."

"'Cause it's a bad idea. I mean, you want to throw away a paycheck—real, palpable money—and for what—a pipe dream? That is the dumbest thing I've ever heard."

"You love dumb ideas," Eli protested.

Sunny glared at him, knowing he was baiting her and refusing, for once, to engage. "You're not funny." She pointed at him. "And you're not thinking this through. Say you do get your memories back, find out who you are. Have you even considered what you'll have to give up?"

Eli faltered, not entirely sure what she meant. His eyes fell to Sunny's hands; the thick, gnarled scars that still lined her fingers, jagged and bone-deep, where the last of the magic in her fingers had bled out that day Eli had found her. Sunny never spoke about what happened to her, and every time anyone tried to broach the topic, she would immediately become closed off and defensive. Hearing her talk about it now, even in the abstract, was like teetering on ice.

A thousand questions ran through Eli's head. He wanted to ask if that was what happened to her, and what she'd been forced to give up. He wanted to ask how she got those scars, and why she never spoke about her family. He wanted to ask what it was that she was so afraid of.

"That doesn't matter to me," Eli said. "You of all people should know that by now."

Sunny took a deep breath. When she raised a hand to squeeze the bridge of her nose, it was shaking. "Have you actually stopped for a minute to think about how lucky you are?" she asked. "You've got no baggage. You have a once-in-a-lifetime opportunity to start fresh. Don't you realize how good you've got it? How many people would kill for a chance to start over from scratch? What if you don't like what it is that you discover? What if it's something that should have stayed forgotten?"

Eli released a sigh. He got the feeling they were no longer talking about him, and he closed his eyes. "Look," Eli said. "It was a mistake to take that boy's magic. If this witch can take it off our hands, then we should go to her. This might be our only option."

Sunny turned to Max. The anger radiating from her was tangible, but she kept her voice even. "You think it's possible? She can actually make Eli remember?"

There was an apology there, in Max's eyes, like she knew what it was costing even to suggest it. "I think it's worth a try."

Eli played the scenario through in his mind; he saw himself getting his hopes up, coming tantalizingly close, having it all fall through, and being left empty-handed once again. But he saw some-thing else, too. He saw the tiniest microscopic chance of it going well, of getting answers, of finding himself, discovering his family.

"I'm in," Eli said. "Let's do it."

"Yeah?" Max asked.

"Yeah."

"Sunny?" Max asked, and they both turned to look at her until her eyes rolled skyward.

"I just want to make one thing clear," Sunny said. "When we all die, I'm allowed to say I told you so."

"Seems reasonable," Eli allowed, and he reached forward to pull on one of her braids. It was a guaranteed way to irritate her, but always resulted in the corner of her mouth dragging itself into a begrudging smile, which she did right on cue. Only then did he turn back to Max.

"So, this witch," he said. "How do we find her?"

"Well," Max said. "That's kind of the thing. I don't suppose either of you knows anyone dead?"

CHAPTER THREE

ELI

The guests were supposed to arrive at six o'clock. Of course, in true West Indian fashion, the house wasn't full until way after, frantic phone calls from late attendees dismissed with a kiss of the teeth and a "soon come." Eli only knew this after overhearing some hearty lamenting from a robust, fiftysomething auntie type as she wrestled a vat of curry goat from the boot of her car.

When they did arrive, of course, they all came at once: aunts in their Sunday best, arms full of rice and peas and chicken and macaroni; uncles who greeted each other with loud slaps on the back and complaints about the parking; cousins with babies on their hips whose condolences left lipstick smears across cheeks; nieces and nephews who had grown more than a foot since last time, who no longer required bending down to hug.

Eli, Max, and Sunny had been standing across the street from the small semi-terraced house for something close to an hour, watching the comings and goings of the party. This was Sunny's one stipulation: she refused to step foot inside until they were absolutely certain that it was safe. So far, there was no indication of it being otherwise. It was a nice neighborhood, pleasantly suburban, the kind of area that Eli wouldn't have minded being brought up in if he could have picked.

"You're sure this is the place?" Max asked, for what might have been the third time but felt very much like the tenth.

Beside him, Sunny gave an exaggerated sigh. Her legs swung to and fro from where she was perched on the front wall of some unsuspecting neighbor's house, absentmindedly rolling cigarette papers between her thumb and forefinger. The wall was littered with their stakeout snacks: an empty bottle of Lucozade, some bubble gum, a half-eaten packet of crisps. Eli couldn't see Sunny's eyes—she was wearing sunglasses despite it being overcast—but he was certain they had just rolled in response.

"This is the address that it said," Sunny said. "So unless Eli put the wrong details into Google Maps—"

"—which he didn't," Eli swiftly cut in.

"—then we're in the right place."

The address of the nine night had been posted on a bulletin board at Pam's, between a poster for someone's missing tabby cat and an advert for the local church fete. George Henry, beloved father, grandfather, and uncle. His nine night was to be held close enough nearby that they only needed to jump on the 144.

Across the road, Eli's attention drifted back to the house as another cluster of family members made their way up the path. To an outsider, the three of them probably looked pretty conspicuous. They weren't exactly dressed in funeral attire; Eli owned only one shirt, the uniform he used for waiting gigs, but it was now unfortunately stained with three pea-sized bloodstains after having another nosebleed on the bus ride over. Max had her thumbs hooked through the belt loops of her dungarees, and Eli was struck with the dawning realization that she was dressed like a Minion from one of those annoying cartoons. As for Sunny—well, Sunny was the only one who looked funeral ready, but that was because her day-to-day wardrobe was solely made up of varying shades of black.

"So," Sunny said. She lit her cigarette and took a deep inhale, legs still swinging from her position on the garden wall. "What are we thinking? Stroke? Cancer? Leprosy?"

When Max and Eli stared at her blankly, she nodded toward the celebrations and said, exasperated, "The old man. How'd you reckon he popped his clogs? My money's on something lung-related. Judging by the picture in that obit, Uncle was a frail wisp of a man before he kicked it. Looked like a single lick of wind could have taken him out, so those lungs couldn't have been doing much in the end."

"Jesus, Sunny," Eli said, though any faux outrage was mostly undermined by his laughter. "That's dark."

Max shook her head. Even when Sunny was in a mood, she found a way to be utterly ridiculous.

"Anyway," Eli added. "You're wrong. It's clearly murder."

"Eli," Max chided.

"What?" Eli exclaimed. "I'm just saying." He pulled the wad of bloodied tissue from his nostril and sniffled in relief. "The guests look all, like, you know. Haunted."

"No shit, Sherlock," Sunny said. "It *is* a funeral." The sourness had dissipated from her scowl. Sunny enjoyed when Eli indulged her inherent morbid streak.

"You two are going to hell," Max said. "Besides, you're both wrong. He died of a heart attack. Was fit as a fiddle before it happened, taking his granddaughter to the park. Then out of the blue, boom." She snapped her fingers. "Dropped dead."

"How do you know that?" Sunny asked, though she sounded impressed.

"It was on the internet," Max said. "Honestly, did you lot not do any research before we left?"

"No," Sunny scoffed.

Eli winced. "Were we supposed to?"

It wasn't the first nine night Eli had attended. Somehow, even through the foggy haze of his nonexistent memories, Eli was certain of that much. He could feel the familiar pounding of blaring music from a sound system inside right through to his veins. It was a sensation that felt like home. Something about it chewed away at his nerves.

He checked his phone, hoping for some sort of distraction, only to see that he'd received a bunch of irritated messages from the temp manager at the waiting gig he was now officially late for. Eli shoved his phone back in his pocket and made the conscious decision to not think about it. Besides, he reasoned. What did it matter? There was a solid chance that they weren't going to make it through the day.

"All right," Sunny said after a little while, clapping her hands together. She jumped to her feet and stubbed her cigarette out against the bricks. Eli spared a fleeting thought for the neighbors whose front garden they'd just littered, but it was Max who immediately started collecting their rubbish and shoving it into the depths of her backpack for disposal later. "If we're actually going to do this, I've got something for you both."

"Please," Max said, "don't tell me you brought weapons to a funeral."

Sunny looked genuinely delighted by the suggestion. "You flatter me, Maxie."

She pulled a small cloth pouch from her pocket. Something

rattled inside it, like the jangle of pennies, and she opened it to reveal a twin set of bracelets, beaded with red-and-black pearls like the shell of a ladybug, and threaded on golden string. Eli took one in his hands and plucked the thread like it was a string on a guitar.

"Friendship bracelets?" He couldn't resist smiling. Sunny was wearing a matching one. "Never took you for the sentimental type."

"It's protection," Sunny said as she tightened one to Max's wrist. "Meant to ward off the wicked stuff, evil eye, any kind of bad-mindedness. Anything that wants to hurt you will have a harder time." She shrugged a little awkwardly. "If we're going to attempt to summon a duppy witch, I, for one, would like to come out of this not dead."

Eli slid his bracelet on and felt a warm feeling start to tingle in his wrist and trickle up his arm. It wasn't an uncomfortable sensation. It was like falling asleep in the summer and waking up to sunshine on your skin.

"So who'd you steal these from?" Eli asked, and Sunny shot him a scalding look.

"If you don't want it, I'll take it back."

"That's not what I said. I just meant that shit like this is expensive—"

"Sorry, are you my accountant now? Are you going to start filing my taxes?"

"Oh yeah, I'd love to see that play out. 'Excuse me, Mr. Tax Man, what's the procedure for *stolen goods*?'"

Sunny gave him a cool look from behind her glasses. "Whatever," she said. "Are we gonna do this or what?"

Eli turned back to the house. All they'd seen were some overbearing grannies and a few belligerent five-year-olds. Nothing nefarious seemed to be going on. At least, nothing they were going to find from standing out there all day. Eli watched as another cluster of relatives approached the house, and then made an executive decision.

"All right." Eli shrugged. "Let's do this."

An elderly gentleman was on the front steps, wrestling with two plastic garden chairs through a stubborn front doorway when they approached. Behind him, a sullen-looking child, who couldn't have been more than ten years old—a granddaughter or niece, maybe, judging by resemblance—held the door open for him with increasing impatience.

Eli politely made his presence known with a subtle cough.

"Hi. Hello?" His voice lilted into something he hoped came across as wholesome and neighborly. "Excuse me. I live across the street, and I couldn't help but notice you struggling there a little. Could you use a hand with that?"

The old man was at least a foot shorter than Eli, with a halo of puffy white hair and large, warm eyes that brightened into two thin crescents when he smiled.

"Oh!" His accent felt like rum and gravel. "Didn't see you there. These damn cataracts, you know. Makes everything a surprise." He laughed heartily and adjusted his glasses to get a better look at the three of them. The scornful-looking child beside him gave a big huff under her breath. Eli was willing to bet this was not the first time the old man had told that joke. "Yes, yes, grab this chair for me there please, son. I need to carry it through to the back. Thank you, thank you."

Eli lifted the chair and followed the pounding of the music into the entrance hall. Beres Hammond played on an old sound system, and a whiff of frying food drifted in with the sounds of raucous laughter from the next room.

Eli opened his mouth to ask where, exactly, he should leave

the chair, but the second he stepped into the house, he was struck hard with the strongest magic he had ever felt. He knew that generally places like this—busy places filled with lots of people, markets and airports and hotels—tended to be hot spots for the uncanny. The fabric of the world got worn down to its thinnest, and people's unique peculiarities manifested their own sort of magic. But this. This was like thrusting wet hands onto a live wire.

The house brimmed with it. The air hummed, alive, and Eli felt it all over; it weaved around his fingers like a cat's cradle, clung to the top of his mouth like peanut butter and left a tangy copper taste on his tongue, as if he had been sucking on a penny. It wasn't an entirely unpleasant feeling. There was almost an urge to let it in, to swallow it whole and feel it course through his veins, but the logical part of his brain, the part that sounded eerily like Max's pragmatic voice, told him that perhaps he shouldn't. It felt like too much.

"Just through to the back," the old man said. He didn't seem to be experiencing the same sensation that Eli was, and a glance at Max and Sunny revealed that he seemed to be the only one feeling it.

Eli had to allow himself a few breaths to steady himself before he could continue. He focused on his breathing, in, out, in, out.

"You okay there, son?" the old man asked. He'd turned back when he realized Eli wasn't behind him anymore. There was genuine concern on his face. He was kind, Eli thought, and felt a wave of sympathy for him.

"Yep—yeah," Eli stammered. "This is just . . . I'm really glad we were able to make it."

The old man's eyes brightened. "Well, that's very kind of you. It's just through here."

There was something achingly familiar about the place. Though, Eli thought wryly, it might have just been the undeniable Jamaican-ness that exuded from the house's every pore. Bible quotes framed against mustard-colored floral wallpaper, beaded curtains that had undoubtedly been hanging since at least the 1970s, deep mahogany cabinets that housed untouched fine china on graying doilies. There was a back room with plastic protectors on the sofa that seemed to be off-limits. A spare room where kids were crouched around a game console, climbing over piles of coats. Eli felt not that he had been here exactly before, but somewhere achingly similar. And it was a strange sensation, for somebody who had nobody, really, to feel that he had stumbled upon somewhere he might've belonged.

Family spilled from every seam, laughing, eating, sharing stories. It was in no way a woeful event; nobody wore black, and there were no tears, aside from the few that came from wheezing laughter. Eli was even beginning to think that he might have been wrong about it being a nine night at all, when he passed a huge black-and-white portrait of an extremely distinguished unsmiling old man. Beside that were smaller photos, holiday Polaroids, and printouts from a photo booth from when George was a teenager. There was a strange assortment of bits and pieces: a lighter, some vinyl, a well-worn watch, a bronze flask. Things that had been precious, once.

Eli felt a hand clasp his shoulder and he looked around to find the old man smiling at him. "George never believed any of that duppy nonsense," he said. "Those were his words. Thought me a fool when I left out gifts after our mother passed. I tell him, don't you think it makes the journey a little less arduous to think that afterward you'll have somewhere to go? He just kissed his teeth, told me *when I die, leave me pon mi bed and let the maggots tek me.*" He laughed fondly. "He was a fool."

"You're his brother?" Eli asked carefully.

"I am," the old man said. His mouth curved into something rueful. "Levi."

Levi shook his hand in that sure, firm way that Eli hadn't quite learned to replicate yet. Eli could tell that the man used magic, or at the very least had for a good portion of his life. It was something in his posture, like the weight of it had worn him down. Eli saw elderly witches down at Pam's all the time, whose magic had now dried up, their skin sallow and puckered and their hands knotted from years of spell casting; but they had an air to them, traces of it on their fingers like ink stains. Power that hadn't quite receded.

"Eli," Eli replied. "It's nice to meet you. This is all so . . ." *Nice* didn't seem like enough of a word to convey what this was. He wanted to say that the love he felt here was tangible, that it was clearly threaded into every element of the day, that he yearned right down to his very core to be part of a family like this. "I think it would make George very happy."

Levi's eyes softened. "That's very kind of you to say, Eli. Course, my brother has never been happy a day in his life. He was a miserable old fool, right down to his very last breath." His hand clasped Eli's as he chuckled. "Eli," he repeated, and looked over to where Sunny and Max were hovering nearby, the picture of nonchalance. His eyes brightened with unfounded recognition. "Forgive my manners!" he exclaimed. "You must be one of Brenda's three, yes? Eli, Simone, and, uh, Joanne, was it?"

"Just Jo," Sunny corrected him. The lie slipped from her so swiftly and convincingly that Eli couldn't help but cast her a cutting look. It felt wrong to take pleasure in conning a man who was grieving the loss of his recently deceased brother, not to mention someone who had been nothing but welcoming to them so far.

Sunny stuck out a hand and Eli watched as Levi's gaze landed on the jagged scars lining her fingers. It was only momentary, barely even the space of a heartbeat, but it was long enough that Eli noticed his hesitation and that he knew Sunny did too. Most people had that reaction to Sunny. Even those who knew nothing of magic tended to be wary around her, like they could sense something was missing, even if they couldn't discern what exactly it was. It was like seeing someone who didn't cast a shadow. The people who did understand were even more cautious because they were able to quantify what she'd lost. Those people tended to respond to Sunny with one of two emotions: fear, which only succeeded in irritating Sunny to no extent, or pity, which somehow only managed to enrage her further. Sunny had never been ashamed of her scars, though. She wore them like accessories, styled them with gold rings and bracelets and painted nails. When she saw Levi notice them, her mouth curved into a knife's edge.

"Of course, Jo. My mistake." Levi took her hand with a smile. "Brenda talks about you three all the time, and how much trouble you cause her. Well, you're all very welcome here. There's plenty of food and drink, so make yourselves at home. You are old enough to drink, yes? I don't want Brenda on my back now."

"Oh, she's not so bad," Sunny smiled, saccharine sweet. "She's loosened up in her old age."

"I'll believe that when I see it!" George hooted, and Sunny's laughter didn't even have the decency to sound hollow when it joined in.

"That's, uh, very kind of you," Max said politely. She, at least, seemed to be as uncomfortable as Eli with their facade.

Levi gave them another smile, warm and unearned, before drifting away, and Eli felt his stomach twist with nausea.

"What's with you?" Sunny asked as soon as Levi was out of hearing distance. It came out half garbled, mid-chew. She had, of course, managed to find her way to the food in the short time that they'd arrived. "You look like you smelled something nasty."

"I could be asking you the same thing, *Jo*," Eli countered. He hadn't meant to sound so petulant, but the lies were beginning to feel bitter on his tongue.

"Oh," Sunny said. "My bad. I offended your delicate sensibilities. Would you have preferred that I tell him the truth? Uh, yeah, Levi, don't mind us. We're just crashing your brother's funeral because we need to use his ghost to contact some duppy witch. I'm sure that will go down well." She paused and squinted at him. "Your nose is bleeding again, by the way."

Eli grabbed the tissue that Max offered him reflexively and tried to hide his scowl. "You just . . . you didn't need to have so much fun with it."

"With what?"

"With *lying*." He couldn't believe he was having to explain this.

"Lying wasn't for fun. That was just a necessity. Taking his wallet"—she wagged a finger—"now that was the fun part."

"Sunny," Eli said, low. "Please tell me you didn't."

Sunny threw her head back and laughed. "I beg you, relax," she said. "I'm joking. You're so uptight sometimes."

"Guys," Max said, silencing them with a clap of her hands. "Can we not do this now?"

Eli looked up and realized the root of her concern. The little girl from before, Levi's maybe-granddaughter, was hovering nearby, watching their exchange with the same placid sort of intensity that all children possess before they've been socialized to know that intensely staring is something that might be considered rude.

"Look," Eli said, lowering his voice to a hush as he turned back to the others. "We need to be careful. The magic here isn't like anything I've ever felt before. It almost knocked me out when I walked through the door."

"Eli's right," Max said. "Let's try not to draw any unnecessary attention to ourselves." This was said with a meaningful look at Sunny, who flung her arms up dramatically.

"You know your lack of confidence in me is really offensive," she said. "I would just like to point out that I did not want to be here in the first place. Plus, which one of us was gurgling back stolen magic less than half a day ago?"

"Yeah, all right." Eli waved a hand. "Let's just find the duppy and get the hell out of here."

Sunny flashed him a smile that might have been innocent, had it been on anyone else. "That's the least stupid thing you've said all day," she said.

All around the house, stories of George passed from mouth to mouth. It didn't take much detective work for Eli to get an idea of the man. He had barely taken two steps before a warm old auntie handed him a paper plate overflowing with food and wrangled him into conversation with such fervent familiarity that it felt as if Eli had known her his entire life.

He learned that George had worked as an electrician for over fifty years. That he was a drinker, a bit of a crook, and it seemed he was, despite his eternally somber disposition, universally beloved. The tales spun like yarn: the time George bought a train ticket to Kingston Station thinking it would take him home to Jamaica, the time George miswired his ancient sound system and almost burned down the whole street, the time a teenage George was caught red-faced by the father of his then-girlfriend and forced to walk home buck-naked with nothing but a hand towel and a smile. There were other murmurs too, mutterings about George being caught up in things he shouldn't have been, but those were met with a quick side glance and rapidly brushed under the table, only to have the conversation ushered on.

Hearing it all brought a strangely nostalgic sensation to Eli. He saw fragments of it in the back of his mind like scenes from a film; the sensation of being a child and sitting on somebody's lap—a grandmother, maybe—an arm tucked around his waist to hold him steady while the grown-ups around him shared drinks. The distant awareness of growing tired enough to eventually slump against a shoulder, restless until he was lifted carefully onto someone's hip and carried up to a spare room to sleep.

It was this, possibly, that made him hyperaware of the shadow that followed them as they searched for signs of duppies around the party.

"Looks like you've got a fan," Max said, nodding toward where the little girl from earlier was still hovering a short distance away, watching his every move.

"I noticed," he murmured.

Eli hesitated, wondering how to strike up conversation with a little kid. Earlier he'd placed her at around ten, but now he'd probably guess a little younger. Before he could stutter out a fake, child-friendly greeting, however, she beat him to the punch.

"I like your bracelet," the girl announced as soon as Eli was in hearing distance.

"Uh, thanks," Eli said, sparing a glance at Max and Sunny, who were watching with amusement. The little girl had her hair in two perfect little puffs, tied up with cherry-red scrunchies. "I like your hair."

"My sister did it," she said. "She's a hairdresser. She can do twists, too. Like yours."

"Oh," Eli said idiotically. "That's cool."

"Are you looking for Uncle George?" That startled him. The girl's large brown eyes gazed up at him suspiciously. Her face was too somber for someone who probably hadn't yet learned the word.

"How'd you know that?" Eli asked.

The little girl shrugged. *Wow*, Eli thought, *kids could be creepy sometimes.*

"What's your name?" Eli asked.

"Tia," she said.

"Well, Tia." Eli bent down so that he and Tia were the same height. "You know it's kind of rude to eavesdrop, right?"

"What's 'eavesdrop'?" Tia asked.

"Eavesdropping means listening to someone else's conversation without permission."

"Oh." Tia at least had the self-awareness to look a little guilty. "Does it count as eavesdropping if the people are talking very loud?"

"Yeah, okay." He supposed he couldn't really fault that. "Good point. Look, as a matter of fact, I am looking for your uncle George. Do you know where he is?"

"He's dead," she said, sounding entirely unfazed by this revelation. Eli winced at her volume and glanced around quickly to see if anybody had overheard. Of course, he didn't have to worry about that here. There were signs of magic everywhere if you knew where to look: Wards on the doors and windows that tickled the hairs on your arms if you passed them. Hastily jotted spells stuck to the fridge door with magnets. Generally, magic wasn't something used in the open. It hadn't been for centuries, ever since their ancestors were enslaved and severed from their gods. Keeping the secret of magic became necessary to avoid persecution or theft. There had always been places like this, though. Safe places where they could exist in peace. Eli looked around; one auntie was lighting candles on the windowsills without using a match, another waved their hand and let the music drift out into the hallway, where there were no speakers. It was not uncommon to talk of the dead in places like these; still, it was a little jarring to hear it from a child.

56

"He's upstairs," Tia continued blithely. "I think he's hiding. Uncle Ian says that you're supposed to keep the body on the bed for nine days, with the mattress pushed against the door to keep the evil jumbies out. Auntie Angela says Uncle Ian talks nonsense and that we shouldn't listen to him until he learns to pay his rent on time and stop asking her for money. He's still up there, though. Uncle George, I mean. He gets lonely."

"Upstairs," Eli repeated. That was a lot to digest. "Do you mean— like, his body?"

Tia gave him a look that could rival Sunny in terms of sardonicism.

"No," Tia said, witheringly scornful. "That would be nasty. 'Sides, he would be, like, a mummy by now. We learned about those at school. They take out your organs and brains with a hook, and then they put them in jars and stuff. I mean his ghost."

Eli felt a little chill run down his spine. Children had always been more attuned to being able to see between worlds, so it wouldn't be outside the realm of possibility. "You saw his ghost upstairs."

"Uh-huh. I wanted to play with him, but I think he's kind of sad 'cause we moved all his furniture around down here. That's what you do, Uncle Ian said, so that the duppy gets confused and goes away. Uncle George is still there, though, but now he's just grumpy. Can I have a Capri Sun?"

Eli blinked. He was getting whiplash from this conversation. "Yeah, sure, I can get you a Capri Sun. But, listen, um. Do you think you could show me where exactly your uncle George is?"

Tia looked at him suspiciously. "And then afterward you'll get me a Capri Sun?"

"Yeah, sure. I'll get you all the Capri Suns you want."

She stuck out her little finger, somberly. She was wearing sparkly nail varnish. Eli wondered if this was what it felt like to make a deal with the devil. "Pinkie promise?" she insisted.

Eli felt Max elbow him, and he relented. "Okay," he said, crossing his little finger with hers. "I promise."

It was obvious from the moment they stepped into the main bedroom that nothing had been touched since George had passed. The air was stale, but his suits still hung, crisply ironed, in the wardrobe. His books—strictly one King James Bible and a collection of almost-identical business how-tos by smiling middle-aged white men—remained on the shelf. The room even still smelled like his cologne. The only things that had been changed were the mirrors. They'd each been covered with a thin white sheet, the sign of a spirit being present.

Eli had sent Tia away with the promise of all the Capri Suns her little arms could carry, so now only Sunny and Max remained.

The door clicked shut behind them, and there was silence.

They weren't alone.

The figure sitting on the edge of the bed wasn't the imposing man in the portrait that Eli had seen. He wasn't particularly unsettling, either, as one might imagine a dead person to be. His shoulders were slumped, the small tufts of his hair gray. He was dressed in what Eli assumed were his burial clothes, and he was drinking what looked to be a glass of rum. He looked tired.

Sunny's hand shot out to stop Eli before he could take a step forward. Her eyes said *Don't be an idiot*, but then again, they always said that, so Eli shook off her grip.

"George?" Eli asked softly.

George looked up, no hint of surprise behind cool eyes. He took in the three of them but only raised an eyebrow, vaguely challenging. The gesture reminded him of Pam and the quick, assessing way that she would always inspect them when they came back from a job, so much so that it almost made Eli want to smile.

58

"You come for the rest of me?" George asked.

Max instantly began poking around the room. She picked up a few pots and sniffed, wrinkling her nose. It was a little brazen, even for her, but George only looked amused. "Your friend know what we used to do with t'iefs, back a yard?"

The magic was duller in here, but Eli could still feel it, lightly dancing on the hairs of his skin. With the door closed, it had faded to a distant throbbing baseline along with the music.

"Nothing good, I'm guessing," Eli replied.

"Mm," George said. "Certainly nothing good."

"I'm Eli. This is Sunny and Max."

George sighed, took a sip from his glass, and eyeballed them speculatively. "One girl that cyaan hold magic, another that sells it for coin. Interesting company you keep."

"Wait," Sunny said, eyes sharply narrowed. She hadn't moved from where she was frozen by the door, and Eli was willing to bet that she wouldn't, either, unless it was to bolt back through it. "The duppy. He's here? You see him?"

Eli glanced back to where George was taking another swig of his drink, watching the theatrics with interest. There was an odd quality to him, flickering and pale, like he was at the bottom of a swimming pool, but he was undeniably there.

"You mean you can't?" Eli asked.

"No, Eli," Sunny said stiffly. "I don't see anything."

"Max?"

Max put down the photo frame she was holding and now had the sense to look shamefaced. "I thought we were alone."

"That will be the duppy magic you got in you," George said. He gestured to the half-empty bottle on his bedside table; Appleton rum, aged twenty-five years. "You want?"

"No thank you," Eli answered cautiously. There was stupid,

and then there was knowingly walking into Hades and filling your pockets with pomegranate seeds.

"Suit yourself." George shrugged and took another swig.

Eli glanced at Max and Sunny, who were still eyeballing the room in disbelief. He sighed. It was going to have to be him, then. He took a reluctant step forward.

"What happened to you, George?"

George turned his head to the left. Eli almost thought he was being dismissed, but then he realized what the old man was looking at. It was a small oil landscape of a rain forest in Jamaica. It was painted in swirling reds and greens, like something from a fantasy. Eli had seen a similar one before, but he couldn't place where.

"You ever hear the story about the man with one rib?" George asked.

Eli was used to this. Patrons at Pam's tended to be the same way. You would ask a simple yes-or-no question and end up sitting around the table for hours, poring through entire life stories, laughing through anecdotes recycled through generations of bloodlines and across oceans and continents.

Eli risked a glance back at the others, but they were only watching him. "No, I haven't."

"Well, I'll tell you it, then. He was special, you see. He had a very special magic. Through his pain, his blood, he had the ability to grow. At first, it was a small thing here and there: A flower. A teaspoon of honey. A piece of fruit. But the more he gave, the more it would blossom. In time he got so good at using this magic in him that once a month the man would go into his back garden and he would open a vein, and from it would come life. First it gave him food, crops as tall and as far as the eye could see, enough to feed him for the next month. Then it gave him wealth, and with that he built himself a home, where he lived comfortably. After that, it gave him a son, and a daughter, and a wife to be their mother. And he would bleed, and they would all eat. He was scarred, yes, all the way up to his elbows, but every night he and his family went home to their big, big, everlasting house, and they would sleep with their bellies full, and they would be happy, and it would be worth it.

"Of course, his old friends from the village eventually caught wind of his happiness, and they wanted to know: How is that you eat so well? How can you afford all this? Times were hard, you know, and the man was not a selfish man, so he told his friends: Don't worry. I'll make sure we all eat. So what if he had to bleed a little more? What was a little sacrifice for those he loved?

"Word spread of his doings. Soon he was feeding his family, and the next family over, and the family next to them. The greener his garden got, the more people talked, until everywhere the man turned, there was someone hungry waiting with their hand out. And he would bleed for them, because how could he say no to someone hungry? No one knew what it took to fill their stomachs with such wealth, so nobody bothered to question the generosity. Why would they? They were all eating well, better than they'd ever eaten before.

"Eventually they stopped bothering to find food for themselves. They grew reliant on him. It became something they expected. And naturally, the more stomachs to fill, the more blood was required. Soon the sacrifice went from monthly to weekly. From weekly to every day. From every day to every morning and every night, until it was multiple times a day that the man would go outside to bleed himself dry. As I'm sure you can guess, it wasn't long before the man ran out of blood to give. He was not infinite. No man is. So when his veins were empty, when they'd sucked his marrow dry and there was not a drop more to give, he turned to other things. A tooth. A finger. A toe. An ear. And when he ran out of those, what else did he have to give but to reach inside his chest and pluck out—"

"A rib," Eli finished.

"Exactly."

George gave a toothy grin, and the rum sloshed in his glass.

"So what happened?"

"Eh?"

"To the man. What happened in the end? That can't be it."

George kissed his teeth. "What you think happened? The man dead. He only got so many ribs."

"And the family? His friends? All those people he was expected to provide for?"

"They found a way to eat, of course. They always do."

"So it was all for nothing."

George shrugged.

"That's a terrible story," Eli said.

"Yes," George said. "It is."

Eli frowned. "It's you, isn't it," he said. "You're the man with one rib."

"Well," George said, and there was that grin again. "In so many words."

"Is he gonna help us, or what?" Sunny murmured. She was looking at her nails, but Eli could see the worry in her shoulders.

George laughed, loud and infectious. It must have been something, Eli thought, to hear that laugh when he had been alive. "You've been looking for Osebo's fang, haven't you?"

Eli blinked, surprised. "You know about that?"

"You're not the first," George said easily. "I can help you and your friends, but are you sure you want me to? This is big man's magic, you know. Not the kind of lickle parlor tricks you pickney like to play with."

"We're sure," Eli said, with as much resolve as he could summon.

"And what I get in return?" George asked.

Eli fell quiet, stumped. He wasn't sure how to answer that.

"What's he saying?" Max asked from behind him.

"Well," Eli said. "He wants to know what's in it for him."

Max nodded and turned vaguely in George's direction.

"Your family," Max said to the space at large. George tilted his head, bemused. "They've already said a prayer for you. They played your song. They danced for you. They've honored you and said their goodbyes. You shouldn't be here. You should have crossed over by now."

"Hm," George said. "Yes. I suppose she's right."

"So maybe that's how we help you," Max continued. "Open the door for us, and we'll open one for you. Help you to pass over."

George sighed. "There is no passing over for me, I'm afraid."

"Why not?" Eli asked.

George raised his head to take them in properly. Eli knew this look: he was being sized up. Eli wondered what he seemed like to a man like George, who had lived through such a drastically changing world and was now watching it from the other side. It couldn't have been much. Eli was scruffy on a good day, with short twists and scrawny arms. He didn't own jeans that didn't have holes in them, his one shirt was covered in bloodstains, and his jacket—two sizes too big—was secondhand.

George didn't seem concerned about any of this, however. His eyes drifted to the space over Eli's heart and then narrowed, as if he could see through right to the root of him.

He must have passed George's invisible test, because the old man heaved a heavy breath. Resigned, he reached up to the neck of his shirt and dragged it downward, just past his collarbone, to reveal a series of thick, gnarled black scars—claw marks—across his chest. Eli stared, wordless with shock. Right over the place where his heart had once beaten, something had torn at the magic inside him, frenzied and vicious. A piece of him had been ripped away. His magic. His soul. It was completely gone. Eli remembered what Max had said. That there had been people missing all over. That they'd been found dead with their magic ripped from their chests.

"We'd heard it was your heart," Eli said numbly. "You made a deal, didn't you?"

"A pact," George corrected him. "Sworn in my blood, twenty years ago. The same kind of deal you're about to make, I imagine. Though I hope you don't come to regret yours as I did."

"That's why you're stuck here," Eli realized.

George smiled tiredly. "Yes, well, it's not like I've ever been one for a party. It's this." He tapped his chest, the ruins of skin, the hole in his heart. "It's the part that's gone. I can't pass over without it. And as long as they're here"—he nodded to the hallway, where the distant sounds of rambunctious laughter from his family flooded through the crack under the door like sunlight—"tying me here with their memories, it's where I'll be."

"But what happens when the nine nights are over?" Eli asked gently. "Your family love you, but they can't anchor you forever. Eventually your brother will close that door, and then we won't be able to help you. Nobody will. You'll be trapped, until there's no one left to remember you anymore."

"They're safe," George said. "That's all that matters to me. If that's the price I have to pay, I'm okay with it." He took a swig of his rum. "I think that's cause enough for a drink, don't you?"

"I'm sorry," Eli said. He meant it.

George shrugged. "*Sorry* is a sorry word. You want some advice?"

"Not really."

George cracked a smile. "Some doors are locked for a reason."

He gave him another scrutinizing look, then clapped his hands together like a schoolteacher trying to rein in an unruly class.

"Okay," George said. "Come. I'll take you where you want to go."

He hopped up, spryer than Eli expected him to be, and crossed the room to pull a sheet from where it was draped over a floor-length mirror. Eli found himself confronted by his own reflection. There were large bags under his eyes, and the bloodstains on his shirt made it look like he'd lost a fight. Eli didn't focus on that, though. His attention was on the mirror. There was something under the surface.

"You'll find her through there." George nodded.

Cautiously, Eli reached out to touch the glass. It was cool against his palm and puddled under his fingers like water. The magic prickled against him like thorns, like he wasn't quite welcome. "And I can come back, right?" Eli asked.

"If you're quick," George said. "The door won't be open long."

Eli glanced toward Sunny and Max. He briefly contemplated explaining this minor fact to them but decided against it. Better to ask for forgiveness than permission, and all that.

"Thank you," he said instead to George. He reached out to shake George's hand, cordial, like they were at the end of a job interview. Eli half expected to float straight through him like mist, but it was just a hand: cold, but not inhumanly so, solid and worn with age.

"I suppose there will be no talking you out of it," George said. Eli didn't think he was imagining the disappointment he heard.

"Sorry." Eli shrugged.

"Very well." They could still hear the distant *thud-thud-thud*ding of the party downstairs. Surely, Eli thought, the world couldn't be this cruel; to force a man to spend eternity trapped in a room upstairs while below his feet was a party with everyone he loved. "Can you believe there are eight more nights of this nonsense?" George asked.

Before Eli could contemplate any further, he stepped forward, took a deep breath, and walked through the mirror.

CHAPTER FOUR

ELI

The first thing that struck Eli was the weight of the air. He had only blinked, but suddenly humidity clung to his every pore. It was thick and heavy, like the sky before a thunderstorm. His forehead prickled with sweat, and he could feel his shirt stick to his body, so he rolled up his sleeves.

He was alone. George was gone, as were the distant pounding of music and the sounds of the party from below. This room was a mirror image of the one he'd just left, and it was immediately discombobulating, like he'd entered a fun-house version of reality. Eli moved to look outside the bedroom window, and he found that the street below was silent too. There were no partygoers drifting to and from their cars, no nieces and nephews perched on the front wall outside, knees dangling as they avoided their parents. No Sunny. No Max.

It occurred to Eli belatedly that there was a very high possibility that he might've just died—it had probably been extremely stupid to trust the dead, and he was undoubtedly never going to hear the end of it from Sunny—but he put his hand against his heart, and sure enough, there was its familiar beating.

So, alive, then. At least for now.

Eli wasn't sure how he felt about that, but he pocketed the feeling and shoved it deep down to where he could deal with it later.

He didn't see it until he turned around. Maybe it was that the general oddness of the magic surrounding him had numbed his senses, but he felt stupid for not noticing it immediately. Almost the entirety of the room had been engulfed by the trunk of a tree. It was a monstrous-looking thing, the width of a double-decker bus, with swooping, gnarled branches that spiraled through the ceiling and walls, far higher than he could see.

He knew this tree, was the thing. Knew the stories that bloomed from it like leaves. Stories of devil men that lived inside its hollow, of witches that climbed its branches in hopes of flying back to the motherland, of slaughtered slaves whose spirits stood guarding hidden treasures buried beneath its roots.

It was a silk cotton tree—a duppy tree—but it wasn't supposed to be here. Not *here*, here, trapped in the bricks of some terraced house in the dull grays of London, where magic had long been stolen and forgotten, diluted by dank city air. It was supposed to be an ocean over, where the earth was red and the rain was warm and where spells, like stories, were as common as sunshine.

Eli moved as close as he could get without touching it, but even with his neck craned as far as it would go, he still couldn't see to the top of its branches.

Something about the tree was calling to him, drawing him in. It felt natural to reach out and trace the ragged trunk with the tips of his fingers. Magic pounded from it like the beat of a drum.

"Hi," Eli murmured. He felt like he had just stumbled into an old friend. "Where have you come from?"

A slight breeze fluttered through a window that Eli hadn't realized was open, and white fluffs of cotton burst from one of the buds dangling from a branch above him. It drifted down, down, down, like flakes of snow, and he caught one in his hand, letting the softness dance lightly against his palm. It was as light as cotton candy. Eli smiled in wonder. If he was being self-indulgent, he would've said that it was almost like the tree was trying to speak to him.

Hello, it might've said. *Welcome home.*

As if summoned from Eli's mind, a woman stepped out from the shadows of the trunk. She was taller than Eli by at least a foot or so and wore a long, tattered white dress, silky and light. Her face was hidden by a large, swooping brimmed hat, and there was an odd angle to the way she stood, as if her dress was covering limbs that weren't fully human.

Max had warned him about that. *According to the stories,* Max had told him, *La Diablesse wears a long white dress to hide her true monstrous form.*

Monstrous form? Sunny had snorted. *Sounds like me in the mornings.*

The point is, Max had continued, *if she ever reveals her true face, you run. She'll drag you into the trunk of the silk cotton tree and feast on you. Nobody who's ever seen it has survived.*

"Hello, Eli," she said. Her head was tilted. There was something animalistic in her movements, something that had Eli stepping backward.

"Hi," Eli greeted her. His instincts were ringing. His fingers found the beads of the bracelet Sunny had gifted him. The magic from it murmured in encouragement, enough to quiet his nerves a little.

"Why have you come here?" the woman asked. She sounded genuinely curious. She swayed toward him, a slight dance in her step, her dress bunched in a fist and held to the side, as if she were wading along the shore of a sandy beach. Her face was shrouded in shadow.

"To make a deal," Eli said. "I was told that's something you could help me with."

"A deal," she repeated. Her footsteps made a strange scuffle as she circled him. *Step*. Drag. *Step*. Drag. Eli averted his eyes, wary of what he'd find if he was to look down. "And what were you hoping to gain, Eli?"

She spoke his name strangely, as if it was a joke.

"I'm looking for something," Eli said. "My memories were taken from me. At least, I think they were taken. I don't know. I don't have them. I want to know who I am."

"A boy without an identity," she said, and there was that sound again: *Step*. Drag. *Step*. "You're not the first of us to have your own history taken from you, nor will you be the last. That's what makes our story. And you know, that's all we had once, our stories. When they took everything from us, when they stole us from our homes and slaughtered our families and made us give up our gods, that was all we had left. It's the eternal question: Who are we, without what we come from? I suppose it's the paradox of our people."

Eli had no idea what that meant.

"So . . . you're not able to help me?" he asked.

"So pessimistic." He caught a flash of a smile through the shadow. "I can show you who you are."

"For a price," he surmised.

"Yes, *Eli*," she said, and there was that tone again, like he was the punch line of an untold joke. "For a price."

"How do I know that it's real?" Eli asked, because he knew a con when he saw one. He could easily see this playing out: Eli giving her what she wanted, and her filling his mind with fabrications. False memories, forged images, maybe, that would drive him mad and bring him straight into death, which was likely what she intended in the first place. Then she'd take the magic from him and leave him with nothing. He wasn't going to fall for it. "How do I know that I'll really remember?"

She lifted her head, the tiniest motion, but it was enough that Eli caught a quick glimpse of her eyes: perfectly golden, the color of molten lava.

"Do you have so little trust?"

Eli gave her a smile, the one that usually got him out of trouble. "It's nothing personal."

She laughed, and wind fluttered through the tree, sending more buds of cotton fluttering through the sky.

"Very well," she said. "I'll bite."

She stepped forward to raise a hand to Eli's cheek and let her finger trace his jaw. Her touch was a quick sting, white-hot like the lick of a flame, and Eli had to forcibly keep himself from recoiling.

It came to him gradually. The tiniest hint of a memory, triggered by the touch, that edged its way into the back of his mind. He remembered, suddenly, standing in a park and looking up at the sky, just like now, as snow drifted down on him.

Where does snow come from? he asked. He was a child, and there was a hand holding his. It was worn from years of use. Warm, stable.

It's magic.

It's not, Eli insisted, petulant. He knew magic. Magic was the smell of burning incense from his grandmother's room, and the soft song of a lullaby he'd catch sometimes through the walls. It was salt strewn across windowpanes and the kiss on his forehead as he was ushered away from grown people's business. This wasn't magic.

It is to me, the voice said. She waved a hand and the snow fell heavier, coating the ground in a thick carpet of white. *You know, we don't have snow where I come from.*

I know that, Eli grumbled, put upon. And he did know. He knew everything about the home he had never been to. He knew about the sweltering heat and the thunderous rains during the summer. He knew about the sweet and succulent flavors—not like here, he knew; here was just a pale imitation of what was there. He knew the stories of the dead, of thieves, tales of badmind countrymen getting their ears nailed to burning barn doors. He knew it all.

In the memory, he felt a hand on his chin, guiding his head up and out of his sulking.

There's magic everywhere. You just have to look a little harder. Try again, the voice said. *Can you see it now? Where do you think it comes from?*

And he did see. He could picture it. Far above them, he envisioned a woman somewhere, with sleeves pushed up to her elbows and sweat dampening her brow from hours of bending over a kitchen counter. He pictured her kneading dough, and every time she flipped it, beat it with the heels of her palms, the flour would sprinkle down, down, down, like wads of silk cotton from a tree, until it reached them on the ground. Snow.

He said as much out loud and was met with hearty laughter.

Your imagination, he was told, *is something special. Promise me you'll never forget that.*

Promise, he said. He meant it too. He meant every promise he made to her.

Eli blinked and the memory was gone. He was standing once again with the witch, in the bedroom of a dead man, beneath a silk cotton tree. It took him a few moments to get his bearings.

"What—what was that?" Eli couldn't catch his breath. He could still feel the ghost flecks of ice on his skin. He needed to see it again, to take it in. Who was the woman in his memory? Was she family? Was she still alive? Did she miss Eli? Eli couldn't stomach it. He had

71

been loved, once. Maybe he was still loved. The realization left him reeling, and he felt very small and gnawingly trapped.

"Consider that a gift," the woman said. "A taste of what could be. A memory of yours, returned for you."

"It wasn't—it wasn't enough," Eli said. His voice cracked and he found it difficult to catch his breath. "I need—please, there has to be more."

"The next one will require a price," she said. She was gentler than Eli expected her to be, kinder than the situation really warranted. Eli couldn't see her face, but he was sure if he could there'd be sympathy there. It made it worse, somehow. Like cauterizing a wound. It made him wonder what had happened to her for her to end up this way. Stuck in this in-between world, feeding off misplaced bargains made in desperation.

Eli took a moment to steady himself, but he felt like he wanted to crawl out of his skin. He let his breath even out and wiped the damp away from his cheeks. "Okay," he said. "Okay. Yeah, all right. Name your price."

She reached out a finger and let it hover over the place where the stolen magic had entered his chest.

"I want your magic," she said. "All of it."

"All of it?" He'd been expecting to hand over a portion, of course. It was why he was here, to rid himself of the stolen magic. But a person was born with only a finite amount of magic in their soul, depending on the strength of their bloodline; anything else had to be borrowed or bartered. This was not the first time Eli had received the offer of selling his magic. It was, however, the first time he'd truly considered it. "What will you do with it?"

"If you want an answer to that question, I'm afraid I will have to raise the price."

Eli hesitated. He wasn't entirely sure she could be trusted, but he couldn't turn back now. Not when he was this agonizingly close to answers. This was their way out. All he had to do was say yes, and then he would have them.

"Be sure," she said. "Once it's done, it's done."

Eli took a breath. He could feel the magic coursing through him even as he stood there. It should have been an easy decision to make, but the exhilaration he felt in that moment, he imagined, was like the moment before free-falling from a cliff edge. Eli raised his hand, ready to pluck the magic from his own chest in the same swift movement he had so many times before and hand it over, but before he could, something dawned on him. The room had inexplicably and suddenly grown very cold. Hadn't it been humid enough to leave sweat on his brow just a few moments ago? Now, he exhaled, and his breath puffed into ice. He glanced down to find that his arms were lined with goose pimples. That he was shivering.

Eli looked at the silk cotton tree and saw that some of the buds were flaking like ash and floating away, as if it were the dead of winter. He turned to the woman, but even she seemed mildly startled by the discovery. Something about her had changed, a spell around her broken.

Before Eli could question anything, she lurched forward, inches from his face.

"Quickly," she said, the niceties fading like the cotton from the tree. "We don't have much time. Give it to me."

"What's going on?" Eli asked. Flakes of ash floated around them. It was the magic of the tree; it was deteriorating.

"She is coming," she hissed. "Do it now."

Eli stepped back. This was wrong. He'd been stupid to come here, to be prepared to hand this over. He needed to go.

"Who is coming?"

"The one that keeps me here," she whispered. The silky sweet tone of her voice had soured; her voice had lowered to something hushed and urgent.

"I thought you sold your soul to the devil?" Eli said, stumbling backward slightly.

The witch laughed, humorless. "Not the devil," she said. "She's worse. She cannot have the magic. She cannot find the fang. Give it to me, or I will tear it from your bones."

"No," Eli said. "I'm good, actually."

Her head raised slightly, and he caught a glimpse of her eyes; they were no longer golden but a milky white, just like those of the creature that had attacked them in Pam's. He remembered what Max had told him. This was a sign that she'd dealt away her will to another. That she was doing somebody else's bidding. Eli edged away, but she reached out and seized him around his forearm before he could escape. As soon as their skin met, however, she shrieked, her hands as red-raw as if she'd clutched a hot iron. It was Sunny's bracelet, Eli realized. It had protected him.

That seemed to be the final straw. All of a sudden, she was rising: up, up, up, one foot, two feet, three, until she was tall enough that Eli had to crane his neck to look at her. In minutes she had all but engulfed the room, and then it was no longer a *she*. It was feathers and teeth, wings brittle and jagged as bark, talons like hooks. There was an odd scent to it, burning, pungent enough to make Eli gag. It smelled the same as the creature that day in Pam's. It smelled of death.

"Do you know what will happen if her magic is returned?" it snarled. "Do you know what it's worth? What you were willing to give up, for something so small as a memory?"

Eli froze, heart pounding in his chest. He wanted to run, but he was too terrified. He couldn't move.

"It'll be easier for all of us if you don't fight it," the thing said, and it opened its mouth wide enough to eat him whole.

Eli had a fleeting moment to think, *What have I done?* before something swooped around his waist and heaved, knocking the air out of him and sending him hurtling backward. Eli landed hard on the ground, elbows grazed, disoriented from the force and blinking the confusion out of his eyes.

"Wh-what—"

"Stay down," said the voice. In one solid motion, the figure raised a palm, like he was greeting an old friend, and the creature was sent swooping, gracelessly, straight back into the gnarled depths of the tree. The last Eli saw of it was its fingers, outstretched toward him, as if it could crawl its way out of the dark.

When his vision came into focus, Eli found himself staring up at a familiar face. It took him longer than it should have to realize who it was. The first thing that he noticed was the golden pendant around his neck, a snake wrapped around a dagger. Eli's stomach knotted with dread at the realization.

"Oh," said the boy whose very magic Eli had just tried to barter away. "There you are."

BEFORE

CHAPTER FIVE

MALCOLM

The thing about magic was that, like blood, it had a way of getting stuck underneath your fingernails. Malcolm had a bad habit. When he was bored, he tended to pick at it, sculpt it between his thumb and forefinger like a wad of Blu Tack until it became something tangible.

The act of magic, for Malcolm, had always been a little like scratching at a scab. It required a sacrifice, and it wasn't a sacrifice unless it hurt. So Malcolm would sit and absentmindedly roll magic between his thumb and forefinger, a little like rolling cigarette papers, and in the same moment, he would endure the sting of it; the trickle of blood that would run down his wrist as a result; the crack of the tooth he'd have to spit down the drain; a clump of hair for something minuscule, a broken bone, maybe, for something more.

Like now, for instance. Even as he rode his bike through his city, the sun setting above him, Malcolm's fingers were still stained with magic from the night before. He felt drained, as if he'd done a strenuous workout, and he could feel the last of it buzzing pleasantly in his veins.

For some reason, Malcolm had always found magic easiest on heavy, humid nights like this, when the air was sticky and the sky was streamed with red. *It's because it feels like home*, his mother had told him when he'd mentioned it to her once. She herself had always had a particular fondness for thunderstorms; more than once Malcolm had caught her standing alone outside, completely unbothered as the rain pelted down around her, calling on lightning like it was an old friend. Malcolm didn't share the same nostalgia for cloyingly thick air and warm rain that his mother did, mostly because he hadn't ever been to the home she was referring to, but also because the sound of thunder had always scared him a little. All he knew was that nights like this, when dusk washed the sky with peaches and oranges and the streets were left a sickly sweet color, like the flesh of an apricot—those were his favorite. He rode through the scarcely lit entwining roads with lightning at his fingertips and a trickle of blood at his nostril, and above him, the sky turned the color of a grapefruit's insides.

It had been a warm day for London, but now a chill settled in the air. He stashed his bike, padlocking it to a lamppost, and then, with a furtive glance around to make sure nobody was looking, hefted himself up into a nearby tree the way he used to as a kid when he was hiding from his parents. Perched at this height, Malcolm had a perfect eyeline of the sun setting across the city. It was small enough that, had he wanted to, he could have reached out with his thumb and forefinger and squashed it flat.

There was a comforting loneliness to this time of day. Further along the street, a kid skittered past on a skateboard. A fox, a few yards away, darted between the neighbors' gardens in a hunt for scraps. Malcolm caught sight of an elderly white man sitting in the dark of his home across the street, his face illuminated by what looked like a football match. Someone scored, and the man raised his fists triumphantly.

Malcolm ignored all of it. They weren't what he was here for.

The family at number twelve were tediously inconspicuous. From this height, Malcolm could see them sitting around the table eating a roast dinner, though the youngest kid, toddler-sized, was gradually turning his potatoes into a Jackson Pollock painting. Occasionally, Malcolm would catch a burst of laughter from the mother and father, and the man would press a kiss to his wife's cheek or the crown of his daughter's head. It was nice. Warm, if artificial, like something out of a sitcom. There was no magic here that he could sense, but it still felt peaceful.

Malcolm thought of his own home, and how it resembled nothing like this. He thought of the tiny two-bedroom council flat he and his mother kept in Edmonton. The gas oven that didn't work unless you cajoled the flame into lighting with a whisper. The threadbare sofa the two of them spent most of their evenings on, dinner balanced on their laps as they shouted answers at game shows.

Eventually the front door of number twelve opened, and the man from inside came out and lumbered his way down the pebbled path to dispose of two well-stuffed black bin bags. He carried them to the end of the driveway and, with a glance back at the house to check his wife wasn't looking, pulled a cigarette from his back pocket. Malcolm watched for a few moments as the tension gradually depleted from his shoulders with every exhale.

He shouldn't have been imposing, feet shuffling in oversized sliders, his work shirt ruffled from play-fighting with his kids, but even from up where Malcolm was perched above him, he looked like a formidable man: wide-shouldered, square-jawed, arms thick from a lifetime of heavy physical work.

The man finished his cigarette, then stumped it out with the heel of his shoe. It was only then that he cleared his throat.

"Malcolm," the man called easily. His hands were stuffed in his pockets. He didn't bother raising his voice. "Come down. I know you're there."

Malcolm didn't flinch, but it was a near thing. He winced and swung down to land with a thud, pulling down the hoodie from his head.

"Hi, Dad," Malcolm replied.

His father ran an assessing eye over him, taking in the tips of his scuffed trainers and slowly roving upward. Malcolm watched him map each and every way in which Malcolm was a disappointment: his mismatched socks, his ripped jeans, his battered puffer jacket, the frayed backpack on one shoulder, his newly earned busted lip.

The last time they'd seen each other, Malcolm had been twelve years old and still had to crane his neck to look up at him. Now he and his father were the same height. It was an odd, lilting feeling, to be able to look at the man eye to eye. He hadn't changed much. There were speckles of gray in his beard that Malcolm didn't recognize and a few lines around his eyes that were new, but he still had the casual air of confidence that Malcolm remembered, the set to his jaw that always made Malcolm want to stand up straight.

"You're late," Casper said. His eyes trailed over Malcolm. "And you've grown."

It was a loaded statement, one that Malcolm didn't know how to respond to without acknowledging the gaping absence between them, so he let his eyes fall to the gravel beneath their feet, where the crumpled cigarette was crushed into the pavement. "Yeah," he said. "Sorry. Had to wait for Mum to fall asleep."

"Hm." Casper sniffed. "And how is your mother doing?"

From anyone else, the question might have sounded perfectly perfunctory, but Malcolm knew his father; somehow, he always sharpened even the most innocuous question in order to slice him open at his softest parts. Malcolm's hand moved to the pendant he always wore. It was his father's, the one keepsake Malcolm had kept of his after he left: a golden pendant with a snake wrapped around a dagger. Usually, Malcolm was careful to keep it tucked inside his T-shirt and out of view, but he had the habit of playing with it when he was nervous. He watched Casper's gaze drop to it, but if he recognized it, he didn't mention it.

"Mum's okay," Malcolm answered, stilted. "Same as always."

"And she hasn't had any more . . ." A pause. "Incidents?"

Incidents. That was a funny way to describe his mother almost accidentally burning down their home one night in a frantic spiral.

"She's fine," Malcolm repeated, unable to keep the edge from his voice.

Casper just raised his eyebrows, like Malcolm had told a particularly funny joke. "Well, I didn't call you down here just for small talk. I know you must be busy." He flashed another one of those smiles, like Malcolm wasn't drowning in the responsibility of maintaining his part-time job, floundering through his second attempt at sitting his A Levels after failing the first, and making sure that he and his mother didn't go hungry. "Did you bring what I asked for?"

"Well," Malcolm started, and then paused. He'd been practicing how to phrase this part on his way over, but now that he was facing his father's furrowed brow, he suddenly became incapable of forming the words.

In hindsight, it was difficult to determine where, exactly, things had started to sour. Perhaps it was when his father had called him the night before, and he'd made the mistake of answering. It was the first time he'd heard from his dad in almost six years. Six years was a long time to not have a dad. It was six years of missed birthdays, missed Christmases, missed parents' evenings and doctor's appointments and barbershop trips. Six years of awkwardly laughing off the topic whenever anyone mentioned his father. Of having to make up excuses for his absence.

There were plenty of rumors of what had happened to Casper King. Even after so much time, Malcolm would still catch whispers now and then. A lot of people in the magic world assumed he was dead, that the wicked, rotten death magic he'd infected North London's bloodstream with had finally seeped into his own bones and poisoned him from the inside out. Others dismissed that as implausible: after all, everybody knew Casper as the duppy king, and how could you kill a dead thing? Malcolm might've assumed that his father was dead too if it hadn't been for the monthly child support that arrived in his mother's bank account, but even that had subsided when Malcolm had finally hit eighteen.

The truth was, Malcolm had long since accepted the reality of the situation. His father hadn't disappeared in a puff of smoke like the rumors said. He hadn't been strung up by vengeful duppies or dragged into the Thames by Mother of Waters. Casper had simply grown tired of his family; he'd aspired for a better life without them, so he'd packed up his bags one day and left. Malcolm was now old enough to understand that. He didn't delude himself with fantasies that his father was desperately longing to return.

Yet when Malcolm received the phone call that evening, he'd seen his father's name flash across his phone, and something had lurched in his stomach. He'd come to the sobering realization that, despite everything, there was a small part of him that hoped his father had grown out of his distaste for parenting. That maybe reaching out to him after all this time meant that they could go into the relationship anew, something with a little less pressure—become friends, even. As he'd watched the phone ring, Malcolm made a decision: if his father was calling to reconcile, Malcolm would accept him. Not *forgive*, no—how could he? It was one thing to leave, of course, but another entirely to not come back—but he would hear him out. He would be open. He would consider letting go of the sickly, bitter resentment that he'd harbored for all these years, and he'd be willing to put the past behind them.

So despite common sense telling him otherwise, when Casper had called, Malcolm had answered. Only, there had been no apologies, no hellos, nothing to acknowledge the years of silence. "I've got a job for you," Casper had said, and Malcolm knew instantly that nothing had changed.

The task had been simple: there was a seer man by the name of Jem who frequented a pub by Camden Lock, an old friend of Casper's who owed a decade-long favor that Malcolm's father finally intended to cash in. The seer man had come into possession of an ancient fang said to be powerful enough to kill a god. All Malcolm had to do, Casper had told him, was go to the alleyway next to their regular pub in Camden and retrieve it. The seer man was expecting Malcolm (as seer men often expected most things), so it was simply the matter of turning up on time and bringing his two hands. Scut work, Casper had called it. Impossible to screw up. Casper would have gone himself, of course, but there were too many eyes about and *this*—this part he stressed several times—had to be kept quiet.

"Why me?" Malcolm had asked, because out of all of the questions he had, this seemed the least likely to hurt.

"Because, Malcolm," Casper had said, like it was obvious. "We're blood."

So Malcolm had gone to the address his father had texted him, and he'd met the seer man, who had long white locs and faded tattoos up each arm. Jem looked less like a seer man and more like he could rent you a van for a good price, but the magic on him had smelled bitter and synthetic—tangy, even.

"You're Casper's pickney?" the seer man said, and Malcolm had confirmed that he was, that he was here to collect Osebo's fang. "You look like your father," Jem said, and that was the last thing Malcolm registered, because the next thing he knew, the man had pulled out the ancient, curved fang and come hurtling toward him.

He should have died. In fact, there had been a moment that Malcolm was certain that he *had* died. Osebo's fang was said to be able to eat through all magic, that it was powerful enough to kill even a god. But sometime later, he'd woken up, not a scratch on him. He had no idea how he'd survived. The seer man was gone. All he knew was that he'd been sent to retrieve Osebo's fang, and he'd failed.

Once Malcolm had finished stumbling over his explanation, Casper raised his eyebrows, the first indication of surprise. "Well, that's certainly unexpected," he said. "Jem is a lot of things, but he was never stupid. What about the fang?"

"Gone."

"And your magic?"

Malcolm faltered. He hadn't entirely been expecting his father to notice that. When he'd woken in the alleyway, Malcolm had realized instantly that something was missing. His magic had always had a heaviness to it, and as he'd pulled himself to his feet, he'd stumbled a little, feeling off-kilter. A piece of it was missing. Shame had hit him first. He'd been stupid enough to walk straight into a trap and too weak to defend himself. Then he'd realized that he would have to admit this to his father, and his stomach had felt tight with nerves. He'd fleetingly hoped he could find a way of getting his magic back before his father found out, but he now realized that had been naive. His father measured people's worth by how much magic ran in their veins, by the bloodline they'd inherited. Of course he'd recognize it lacking in his own son.

"I'm working on it," Malcolm said.

Casper sighed and closed his eyes. Malcolm watched his father bristle, various cogs running through his mind. Malcolm wondered if Casper had even expected him to be successful at all. The thought bothered him more than he expected.

"In that case," Casper said, "I've got another job for you."

And there it was. Malcolm wondered how he did it. Waited until his son was at his most ravenous before he dangled scraps of meat. The bruises across his stomach hadn't even begun to yellow yet.

When Malcolm didn't respond, Casper stared at him. "You're not interested?"

Malcolm hesitated. Everything always came with a price, with his father. But the fact of the matter was, his mother was getting worse. Just the day before, he'd found her wandering in the middle of the street in her nightgown, mind too jumbled to find her way home. Malcolm knew it was his responsibility to step up for the both of them. Malcolm's father knew it too.

"What's the job?" Malcolm asked.

His father smiled, and there was something cutting enough in the gesture to draw blood. He pulled the car keys from his back pocket and tossed them to Malcolm in one deft motion. Malcolm caught them, fumbling slightly, and frowned in question.

"A chance to redeem yourself," Casper said, and nodded toward the car. "Open the back."

Malcolm glanced back at the house. The kids weren't at the table anymore; their mother must have shepherded them up to bed. Malcolm could picture them in their matching pajamas, nudging each other, singing and giggling. He wondered if they even knew his name.

After a breath, he opened the boot.

Slumped in the back of the car, like a sack of rotting potatoes, was a dead man.

"What the *hell*," Malcolm hissed, immediately staggering backward.

His father had moved to hover behind him, and the two ended up colliding. "Is this some kind of joke?"

He covered his mouth with the crease of his elbow and determinedly looked anywhere but at the car boot. He could feel the nausea stirring at the bottom of his stomach, but the thought of vomiting in front of his father was shameful enough to be sobering. He pushed himself away, disgusted and furious. "The hell is this?"

"Lower your voice," his father said. He brought a firm hand to Malcolm's arm and forcibly turned him back to face the corpse. "Calm yourself and take a closer look. You recognize him?"

Resentfully, Malcolm forced his eyes to take in the body. The dead man looked to be a similar age to Malcolm's father. His skin had turned a speckled gray-blue, bruised and marble-like in parts. It took Malcolm a few seconds to register what exactly he was looking at through the darkness, the shock making it difficult to concentrate, but then he realized. He drew in a sharp intake of breath. "Is that—"

"Yes." His father sighed. "You remember your uncle Erwin."

Had Malcolm eaten a substantial meal that day, he undoubtedly would have thrown up straight onto his father's neatly paved driveway. As it was, all he'd had was a piece of toast and a dry bowl of cereal, so instead, he ended up crookedly bent over at the waist, heaving into the crease of his arm. It was a visceral reaction, and his already bruised ribs ached as he retched. His father hovered silently the whole time, arms crossed as he waited for him to finish. When Malcolm was done, he wordlessly handed him a handkerchief.

"As you can tell," Casper said, "this isn't ideal."

Malcolm cast his father a look of disbelief. Erwin had been the man's best friend once. They weren't actual blood, but they'd grown up together, went to the same school and church together, and their families had rented rooms from the same racist landlord. *Erwin's your uncle*, he remembered his father telling him once. *And because he's family, that means you must treat him with respect.* All it really meant was that throughout Malcolm's childhood and under the guise of family, Erwin had never felt shy about borrowing wads of money from Malcolm's parents that he never intended to pay back.

Malcolm hadn't seen the man since he was a kid, when he'd disappeared from Malcolm's life the same time his father did, but his only memories of Uncle Erwin were ones of general torment: of being mocked for having long hair, for his general disinterest in sports, for his preference to stay by his mum's side rather than hang out with the other kids on their estate.

"What happened to him?" Malcolm asked. He stood as far back from the car as he could, and it still felt too close.

His father waved a dismissive hand. "If I had to guess, I'd say it looks like the magic was clawed out of him."

It was true, though Malcolm would have said it looked more like an animal attack than a person. The gashes were deep and wide across his chest. They even went across his forearms, like he'd put up a fight. "You think someone did this to him?"

"Well, he certainly didn't do it to himself."

Malcolm couldn't look away. He found himself racking his mind for a pleasant memory of the man, but all he could think of was the time Erwin had been roped into helping Malcolm and his mother move into their flat in Seven Sisters a little while after the divorce. Erwin had turned up stinking like a brewery and then spent the day barking slurred orders in Malcolm's direction. At one point, Erwin had tripped and fell into Malcolm's mum's fine china cabinet—an heirloom all the way from Jamaica—and the special gravy jug that they only used at Christmastime had been smashed to smithereens. He'd blamed Malcolm for it. Malcolm had been grounded for a week.

"Are you listening to me?"

"Huh?"

"I said," his father repeated, enunciating as if Malcolm was an infant, "we need to find out who did this."

"Yeah," Malcolm agreed. And then the words caught up to him, and he realized his father was still watching him expectantly. "Wait, you mean you want me to—"

"Wake him."

Malcolm froze. Was this another of his father's jokes? He looked down at his uncle's slack jaw and ashen skin. He would start to smell soon, surely. His limbs were probably already stiff. How long was it before flesh started to rot? Malcolm remembered one time when he was still a kid, an old man in their building had passed away, and it wasn't until Mr. Aviv on the third floor called the landlord complaining about the smell that they realized he'd been dead for days. It had caused a stir throughout the whole of the estate, kids making up ghost stories to taunt each other with and claiming to see the old man's duppy walking the hallways at night. *I reckon Malcolm King had something to do with it*, he remembered overhearing one kid snicker to a circle of assenting murmurs. *He's always been a freak.*

His father appeared to be serious. Malcolm shifted under the weight of his gaze.

"How did you—"

"I hear the stories," his father said airily. "Didn't I always tell you that death works differently on us?" Malcolm wasn't necessarily surprised. Word spread like wildfire in their ends, and the word about Malcolm was simple: he was to be avoided. But something about his father's flippant tone of voice stuck with him. Had he been looking out for Malcolm after all? Was he secretly checking up on him for all these years?

"I don't do that," Malcolm said. "I can't—I'm not . . . like you."

"You need to put your feelings aside, Malcolm," his father sighed, and Malcolm dropped his eyes. He knew this was another trait his father had always disliked about him, ever since he was young. *Soft*, his father used to joke to his friends. *You know, I don't know how I ended up with this one. I've seen melted butter harder than him.* Now that he was older, Malcolm understood why his father would get frustrated. Once upon a time, the man had been Casper King, the duppy king of North London. He orchestrated the dead with a wave of his hand; he molded death like putty. Now, Casper's magic was mostly gone. It would be enough to make anyone angry.

"I don't think I can do it," Malcolm mumbled.

His father cocked his head to one side as if Malcolm was a riddle he couldn't crack.

"Don't you want to help your mother?" Casper asked. He sounded genuinely curious, as if the idea of wanting to help anyone was alien to him.

Malcolm felt the magic prickle in his fingers, waiting to be released. It would be easy, Malcolm was sure, with this anger in him. With the sky purpling above him like an old bruise. With the imprint of gravel from the alleyway floor the night before still ingrained on his palms and his ribs still tender from the beating.

His father watched him carefully. What Malcolm should have told him was that he owed his father precisely nothing. He should have told him that this was his mess, that neither Erwin nor Casper deserved a single moment of Malcolm's time, that he wasn't going to spend another summer trailing after dead things while other people his age were off going to parties and applying to university. But of course, he couldn't. Not when his mother was at home, relying on him.

Malcolm turned to look his father dead in the eye. "If I do this," he said, "what will you give me in return?"

His father smiled, and it was the first genuine smile that Malcolm had seen him wear in a long, long time.

CHAPTER SIX

MALCOLM

Malcolm discovered what he could do like this:

He was ten years old, and there was a dead spider on his windowsill. It was sprawled on the hard shell of its back, four pairs of legs angled jaggedly up toward the sky. Malcolm watched it for a moment, feeling morbidly curious about its existence. He'd learned at school that house spiders only lived for around a couple of years, a short, fleeting life, during which they mostly existed as a nuisance. It was a familiar concept for Malcolm, who had always been big, tall, slow at talking, and constantly muddling his words. His father had always made it clear that his existence had very much been accidental. *A surprise*, his mother would swiftly correct him, with a cutting glare in his father's direction, but even then, Malcolm knew a platitude when he heard one.

This spider was around the size of Malcolm's thumb. If his mother had caught sight of it, she would undoubtedly have shrieked and demanded he fetch the dustpan and brush. Malcolm was forever removing insects from her presence, which was something that always made him laugh, since she miraculously lost that same sense of squeamishness when it came to stewing cow foot or sucking the jelly from the eye of a fried fish. Plus, spiders were different. His father had always been adamant that he not hurt them. *You should never hurt a spider, you know,* he remembered his father telling him. *How else you think Anansi sends us messages?*

He'd been thinking of just that, the first time. He had simply reached out to pick it up, to carry it out of the house and away from his mother. Then his fingers brushed the leg of the spider and just as he was thinking, *Tell Anansi I said hello,* he felt the indisputable sensation of magic.

He knew magic felt different to everyone. His mother always described magic as something musical, that rhythm that allowed your body to move to a beat. He'd seen people draw magic from the heat of rage and anger and blood, who couldn't summon a spell unless they were drowning in it. For Malcolm, it had always felt like electricity. Magic was white noise to him, a peaceful ever-present rumble that existed at the corner of his brain. It was like brushing your hand over a television screen and feeling the friction crackle against your skin.

He had felt it prickle that day, the wiring in his veins. There was a quick jolt, and then, in the space of a single heartbeat, the spider twitched. He remembered lurching backward, stunned. The spider had gone from stiff and unmoving to scrambling upright onto its eight now-scurrying legs.

He'd stared down at his hands for a long time, as if they might offer some explanation, but they looked as they always did: dark-skinned, bony, and a little smudged with dirt. Yet it was undeniable: seconds ago, the spider had been dead, and now, it wasn't.

He'd told himself it was a fluke, at first. The day-to-day magics he knew were small, mostly inconsequential things: sticking your finger in a pot of water and watching it boil, clapping your hands and lighting every bulb in the vicinity. These were small tricks, little secrets passed on from the ancestors who lived in their bones. Life and death, however, was something else entirely. You don't mess with duppy magic. It had been drilled into him for as long as he could remember. Malcolm, who already stuck out like a sore thumb, who was constantly the butt of everybody's jokes just for being big and slow, whose father's name was constantly whispered by the kids at school, had known at that moment that this was added attention he did not need. Not when surviving seemed to be hard enough as it was.

So he dismissed it. He packed it away in that small part of him that kept hold of the names the other kids called him, the scraped knees that came from being pushed over, the looks of resignation he'd catch from his father when Malcolm said the wrong thing—and he ignored it.

Or at least, he tried to. At nighttime, when it was just him, lying between cool sheets and ignoring the sounds of his mother quietly sobbing in the next room, he'd poke at the idea. Was it just a one-off? Was it something he could do again? Was it even something he should try?

He would often think of the dot of blood that landed on the center of his palm that day, of how he'd raised a hand and found that his entire nose had started dripping with it, enough to stream through his fingers and run down his arm. He'd remember how he'd followed the spider, his fist still cupped around his streaming nose, heart pounding in his chest the entire time. He'd think of it skittering across the windowsill, and then along the wall, weaving haphazardly along the cracks in the floorboards until it finally disappeared into a crack in the plaster, and he knew, knew in his core that he was on the verge of something.

But more importantly, he'd think of his father. His father had only been gone for a few months at that point, but on those nights, Malcolm would be overcome with the sudden urge to tell him about this discovery. He'd think about how excited he would be. How it might be enough to make him come home. And Malcolm knew it, even at the age of twelve. This—this was the way he would be useful.

Malcolm reached for his dead uncle's wrist, the skin cold to the touch. At first there was nothing, but he closed his eyes and blocked out the weight of his father's gaze bearing into the back of his neck, and eventually he began to feel his fingers prickle. It was gradual, the fear numbing the thrum of the magic in his veins, and if he didn't think about it too hard, he could almost pretend it was just pins and needles. Eventually, just like it had that very first day with the spider, he felt something flicker into fruition beneath his fingers.

"I'm not going to be able to hold this for long," Malcolm warned his father. Already, he could feel the rush of it slipping through like grains of sand. If he was going to be able to pull this off at all, they would only have a few moments. He tugged on it—an essence, his *life*—but it was slippery and resistant. Every time his fingers got near, it would sting him, and Malcolm had to forcibly stop himself from backing away.

"Hold on," his father said. "You're almost there."

A trickle of blood dribbled from one of Malcolm's nostrils. His hands felt like they were being licked with flames, but his father was right. It was a flutter, ever so slight, a faint pulse that Malcolm could carefully drag out with his fingertips.

A heartbeat.

He took a deep breath, counted to three, thought of his mother, and—

Uncle Erwin opened his eyes and sat up, limbs flailing, gasping for air as if he had just broken through water. His eyes were those of a dead man, pale with cloudy pupils, and there was still the odd, stale hue to his skin, but he was awake. He was breathing. He was *alive*.

"Cas," Erwin gasped, eyes flitting between Malcolm and his father. He clutched his chest, as if he'd been running. Malcolm watched the heave of his rib cage, a little wondrously: up, down, up, down. Erwin was alive, and it was his doing. "Cas, that you?"

Malcolm kept his fingers firmly locked around Erwin's wrist, scared that if he let go for even a moment, the spell might just break.

Back when Malcolm's magic was only just beginning to become what it was, he would trail the garden for dead things to practice with. He'd tried plants first, a few wilted flowers from his mother's garden, but they remained brown and limp. Then he'd moved on to the more or less sentient: squashed slugs and snails he found curled against watering cans, flies caught unmoving in webs, an unlucky field mouse that had been struck by their neighbor's wicked cat. He touched them all, and the results were always the same. He could bring things back, but if he didn't concentrate properly, if he lost thought for even a second, they would aimlessly scramble around for a few moments, confused and bewildered, until they inevitably froze, stumbled, and fell, dead again. Irreversibly so.

He had never tried with a person before.

Erwin blinked rapidly. There was an odd jerkiness to his movements that made him look as though he was being puppeteered. Rigor mortis, Malcolm realized. It hadn't quite left his limbs. "Cas," Erwin breathed. "It is you. I knew you would come for me."

Malcolm felt a wave of sympathy for the old man. Erwin believed that Casper had woken him out of some sense of loyalty, when Malcolm saw it for what it really was: an act of desperation.

"Of course I came for you, Ernie," Malcolm's father said easily. It was an old nickname that Malcolm hadn't heard for years. A name from their childhood, where nicknames had a tendency to stick to you like a shadow. "I said I would, didn't I?"

"Yeah, yeah. Suppose you did." Erwin kept glancing around a little frantically, as if trying to grasp his surroundings. Malcolm looked down at where his hand still encircled the old man's wrist. He could feel Erwin trembling against him.

"Hey," Malcolm murmured. He kept his hand around Erwin, but loosely, so as not to spook him. It was odd for Malcolm. In many ways his uncle had always been a looming, menacing figure in his memories. Now, he simply looked like a frail old man. Malcolm crouched down so that they were eye level and spoke to him the way he would speak to his mother sometimes, when she woke him up in the middle of the night with her shouts. "Hey, it's okay. You're all right."

Behind him, Casper looked away, a little awkward. "You remember my son," he said, with a wave in Malcolm's direction.

Erwin laughed, and there it was. That brutish, mocking noise that used to fill Malcolm's childhood with dread. "Of course," Erwin said, and almost sounded pleased to see him. "Little Malcolm. Boy, Cas, if he doesn't look the spitting image of you."

He raised a hand, as if to push his glasses further up on his nose for a better look, and then caught himself midway when he realized that he wasn't wearing them. Dead men, of course, didn't need glasses. "So," Erwin said. "I really am dead."

"You are," Casper said.

"It's funny." Erwin twitched as if to scramble upward—he was still sprawled in the boot of the car—but Malcolm's hand tightened, steadying him. "I don't feel too dead, you know?"

"Well," Malcolm's father said dryly. "You look it."

Erwin grinned and a fly buzzed its way out of his mouth and crawled across his bottom lip.

Malcolm snuck a glance in his father's direction, but Casper's face was completely blank. Malcolm had vague memories of them hollering at each other over games of dominoes, voices slurred over too many glasses of rum. Of them standing over the barbecue during the summer, playfully bickering over the best way to cook ribs. Malcolm had never had a friend like that, but he imagined this couldn't be easy.

"Tell me who did this to you," Casper said, and Erwin gave a laugh as coarse as sandpaper.

"Come on, Cas. Who do you think?"

Casper's expression hardened. "It can't be."

"Well, it is," Erwin replied. He coughed and something black and tarlike landed on his closed fist.

"It's not possible," Casper said. "It's been over a decade."

"Almost two," Erwin agreed. His movements were beginning to be clumsy, as if he were a rag doll. Malcolm tightened his grip, tried to will more of the magic from his fingertips into his uncle, but a cold bitterness had begun to settle in Malcolm's own bones. He was drying up; he couldn't hold on much more. "We said it would be long enough."

"It should have been long enough," Casper snapped. "She should have starved to death by now. She should be nothing but ash and bone."

"Well, she certainly isn't that," Erwin said tiredly. "You think we miscalculated?"

"No," Casper said sharply. "We didn't."

"She is powerful," Erwin agreed. "But not *that* powerful."

"So someone's been feeding her," Malcolm's father said. He began to pace. Malcolm tracked his movements. He'd never seen his father like this before. Unnerved. Scared, even.

"Is it possible?" Erwin asked.

"Less than ten people on this earth know where she is," Malcolm's father said, but that wasn't a no.

"So someone has betrayed us," Erwin said.

"It seems that way."

"We know what she wants," Erwin said. "It's the same thing she's always wanted: me, you, all of us, dead. If someone tries to free her now, they'll succeed. She's the strongest she's ever been, and now look at us. You're dried up. I'm dead. There's nothing stopping her anymore. And it won't just be us she'll be after, Cas. If she gets free, she will suck the magic of this entire city down to the marrow. Nobody will be safe."

Malcolm glanced at his father for an explanation, but the old man was simply grimacing, his mouth twisted into a hard line.

"Did you hear about George?" Casper said. His voice was low. If Malcolm didn't know him any better, he would have thought that he sounded guilty.

Erwin's head slumped into an attempt at a nod. "They got to him too. I can feel him. . . ." He gestured vaguely. "Over here."

"If you're right," Casper said, voice hard, "it's me she'll be coming for next."

"Hm." Erwin slumped a little, his head fighting a losing battle with gravity. He began to blink slower and slower, and this gesture, at least, was a little more familiar to Malcolm. He looked drunk. "Only the magic of a god can kill a god. So unless you have one of those up your sleeve, I'm assuming you have a weapon."

"I'm working on it."

"Then you know who you will have to speak to."

Casper sighed and cursed under his breath. There was something unfathomably teenage about the gesture, in the slump of his shoulders, his hands stuck in his jeans. It only occurred to Malcolm then that his father had never really grown up. Casper had met Malcolm's mother when they were teenagers, and they'd had Malcolm shortly after, so he'd never really gotten to grow into becoming a man by himself. She had always taken care of him. It was odd for Malcolm to see himself mirrored in this person, when he himself had never had any choice but to grow up as quickly as he could.

"She won't see me," his father said. "She banished me, remember?"

The men shared a wry look.

"Well," Erwin said, and his eyes drifted to where Malcolm was hovering. "You may be banished, but *he's* not."

They both turned to look at Malcolm, and Malcolm immediately wished he could shrink into the shadows. Casper cussed under his breath.

"Well, good luck with that," Erwin said, and he laughed that brittle, brutish laugh once more. "Sounds like you'll need it." It was the last thing he said before his head sank backward, jaw slack. It was like watching a balloon deflate. His chest sagged, fingers loosened, the final beats of his pulse fading under Malcolm's grip. Then, just like that, he was gone.

As soon as it was over, Malcolm felt a tremendous heaviness hit him. It was like he could suddenly feel the weight of every single bone and organ in his body. There was a coldness in the tips of his fingers that had spread all the way up to his elbows, and he felt hollow all the way through.

Casper let out a frustrated huff and slammed the boot shut, hard enough to make the car rattle. He kicked it, then kicked it again. When the alarm started to chime, lighting the whole street with flaring red, he kicked it once more. One of his sliders went skittering across the driveway from the force of the action, but neither he nor Malcolm acknowledged it. When he was done, he turned back to Malcolm, wiped the sweat from his brow, and straightened his shirt from where it had ridden up.

"So," his father said quietly, as if not to wake the dead. "It appears I have another job for you."

CHAPTER SEVEN

MALCOLM

"We closed," said a husky voice, before the bell hovering over the door even got the chance to signal Malcolm's presence.

Malcolm stood in the doorway of Pam's West Indian Takeaway. His father's voice rang in his ears; *a magical hideaway* was how he'd described it. To Malcolm, it simply looked like any other sticky-floored diner.

"The sign says open," Malcolm said, nodding toward the door.

The old woman standing behind the counter was small and stout, barely reaching the height of Malcolm's shoulder. She had a cloud of wispy white hair, a cane that she rested heavily on, and one working, scowling eye. Behind him, the sign hanging on the door at once rattled and flipped swiftly from OPEN to SOON COME. Had that been her? It was difficult to tell. He hadn't seen the woman move, but a lot of these old buildings had magic weaved into their bones and tended to have a mind of their own.

"You cyaan read?" Her attention was on the newspaper spread across the counter in front of her. She appeared to be doing a cross-word. "I said we closed."

Malcolm resisted a smile. Casper had warned him about the old woman's ill temperament. Today seemed to be no exception.

"It's . . . Pam, right?" Malcolm edged forward, hands stuffed in his pockets. He felt the familiar ghosting of magic as he entered, dusting the hairs on his arms beneath his hoodie. It wasn't quite uninviting, but it certainly wasn't welcoming, either.

The old lady didn't look up, but her pencil did momentarily still from where it was scrawling answers across the black and white squares. "And who's asking?"

"My name's Malcolm. My"—he stumbled slightly around the word—"my dad sent me."

"Yeah?" She sniffed. Still no proper acknowledgment of his presence. "And what he want?"

Malcolm hesitated. This was the part where Casper would lie. He'd slick-talk his way into getting what he wanted, and he'd do it without revealing a single piece of himself. That wasn't Malcolm. Even if he had wanted to lie, Malcolm's face always had a way of betraying him. "He thinks you can save his life."

Those hadn't been his father's exact words. "She's a cantankerous old crow" was what Casper had actually said. "She'll want you to humble yourself, which you will, if necessary, because she is our only chance. I don't care what it takes. Get on your knees if you have to."

"Right," Malcolm had replied. Truthfully, he'd hoped his involvement would end after waking his uncle Erwin. This was the most contact he'd had with his father in years, and the weight of his presence was starting to feel abrasive.

"Pam and I—well, we had some disagreements," Casper had told Malcolm airily. "She made it clear that I'm not welcome in her establishment. She'll likely make it as difficult as possible for you, but I'm being serious, Malcolm. I need you to not come back empty-handed."

"Okay," Malcolm had said. "How do I do that?"

Casper had made a weary, put-upon noise, but a second later, he'd pulled a coin from his pocket and tossed it to him. It was thick and gold, larger than a two-pound, and older than any currency Malcolm had ever seen. A spider was engraved into either side. It looked like it should be in a museum.

"Show her this," Casper said. "But don't give it to her. Not yet. She'll understand what it means, though."

Now, Pam raised her chin to finally take in where Malcolm was hovering before her. She fixed him with a stare that he felt right down to his toes. Pam only had one working eye, the other milky-white and sightless from a deep, jagged scar. Casper had laughed as he told Malcolm about it. Allegedly nobody knew exactly what had happened to her eye, but the stories ranged, everything from car crashes to curses to self-mutilation. Malcolm's father had mentioned he suspected that Pam had simply lost it scrapping in a bar fight, and Malcolm had figured it was another one of his tall tales. Upon meeting her, though, the image stuck with him. Pam did seem to have the bones of an alley cat through and through, and if she really had lost the use of her eyeball in a brawl, he shuddered to think what the other person had walked away without.

"Save him," Pam repeated, her voice lilting an octave higher. "And why, pray tell, would mi wan fi do that?"

"Well—"

"Not to mention why, if your father need me so bad, he hasn't come himself? Him legs mash up?"

"No—"

"What about him head? There something wrong with that?"

"Well—"

"So, explain to me."

Malcolm hesitated, and then after a moment he pulled the gold coin from his pocket and held it out to Pam. "He said to show you this and you'd know what it means."

Pam narrowed her eyes. She shuffled around the counter until she was standing before Malcolm to get a better look. It was a slow process; her joints creaked and groaned like the bones of an old ship. "That witch is older than time." His father had laughed. "Rumor is that she simply emerged from the ocean floor one time, walked out of the water, and started cussing everybody out." Malcolm didn't know whether to believe that; it was always difficult to tell what was real with West Indians, who collectively lacked the ability to be serious about any and everything, and who would embellish ceaselessly, simply for the sake of a joke.

Watching her now, however, it wouldn't have been a stretch to believe it. Pam could very well have even been as old as the sea, for all Malcolm knew. She certainly carried a tempest on her shoulders.

"Your father is Casper King."

"Yes," Malcolm said. "And he needs your help."

He could see Pam looking at him with something new, reevaluating him. "I know your father from he was a pickney," she said.

"Yeah?" It was difficult to picture his father young. People often said that the two of them looked alike, but Malcolm could never see it.

"Yes," Pam said. "And he been a lowlife, piece-of-dirt pain in mi backside ever since."

A burst of laughter came from Malcolm before he could stop it, and something softened around Pam's eyes.

"That man has brought nothing but pain and destruction into my life," she said, though she didn't sound angry about it. If anything, she simply seemed curious. "Why on earth does he think— *Oh.*" Something like understanding dawned in Pam's eyes. "Let me guess. She's back."

Malcolm opened his mouth to answer, but before he could, the old woman had turned on her heel and hobbled back toward the kitchen, leaving no time for protest. "You hungry?"

Malcolm hesitated. "Uh—"

"You don't look like you eat." She piled spoonsful of food into a Styrofoam box before Malcolm could protest: rice and peas and plantain and chicken and fritters. "Your father nah feed you?"

"Uh, w-we," Malcolm stuttered, "we're not really . . . like that."

"Well then." She slid the plate across the counter toward him. "Eat, then we will decide. And put that coin away, unless you plan on using it."

Malcolm wasn't used to unwarranted kindness, and he didn't know how to accept it, least of all convey his thanks. But then Pam set about making herself busy behind the counter, leaving Malcolm with no other choice but to sit down and tuck in.

They were quiet as Malcolm ate. Pam would occasionally turn to bark a series of rapid-fire orders over her shoulder to the workers in the kitchen, but Malcolm didn't see them, and the most he heard in response was a visceral kiss of someone's teeth. Malcolm didn't pay them much attention; he hadn't realized before how hungry he was, but Pam had been right. He was starving.

"It's the magic, you know," Pam said, without looking up. "Making your belly rumble so. It will nyam right through you if you let it." She glanced at him a little speculatively. "Casper tell you where his magic come from?"

Malcolm paused midchew, fork still in hand.

"The story is that he won it," Malcolm said, after a long moment. He was certain he was being tested. "From the daughter of Death."

"Won it, hmm? Like Anansi the Spider, who won all the stories of the world from the sky god. Casper did always like those stories as a boy. His favorite was the one where Anansi accidentally dropped his bowl of knowledge from a silk cotton tree, spreading it to man. Used to make me tell it to him over and over, make me do the noise when the pot hit the ground—*clank!*—and he'd clap his hands every time." She shook her head, but there was that same softening of her brow, which Malcolm was coming to realize meant that she was amused. "By the sounds of it, he never changed one piece, that man."

"It's not true?" Malcolm asked.

"That Anansi gave us knowledge?"

"That my father earned what was his."

Pam gave him an unsympathetic look. "What you think?"

Malcolm's eyes fell to the lines of his hands. He had so few childhood memories of his father that the rare fragments he did possess seemed to form the man's entire personality in Malcolm's mind. One always arose: his father firmly holding Malcolm's hand between his own, telling him, *Don't move* as he took a pair of tweezers and plucked a nasty, jagged splinter from underneath his thumbnail. It had gotten lodged there after Malcolm had been pushed into a pile of wood chips on the playground by some kid on his estate. He vividly remembered the sting as the splinter was plucked from his skin and the grim determination on his father's face, mixed with ever-present disappointment as Malcolm cried out in pain. His mother asking: *What happened?* His father casting him a quick, sideways warning look before swiftly answering for him. *Nothing, he just fell.*

"No," he said, thinking of his mother, of his uncle Erwin, of the bruises on his ribs from the night before. "He's definitely not honest."

Pam smiled but didn't say anything further, and Malcolm let himself fall quiet as he made his way through his plantain, chewing thoughtfully. It was sweet and crispy on the outside and fluffy in the middle, just like he liked it.

"Your father tell you he won his magic fair and square? That's a lie. The truth is he t'ief it. T'ief it from the daughter of Death, lef her empty and cold and bitter. When he couldn't deal with her anger, he lock her up where no one can find her. She's been after his blood ever since. Course, he *used* to be strong enough to ward her off."

Malcolm didn't say anything, but he didn't need to. Pam gave him a sad, knowing smile.

"You have it too," she surmised.

"I'm not—like him," Malcolm faltered.

"I see that," Pam said, with an airy wave of her hand. Pam's accent must have softened after years of being away from home, but there was something in the way it slipped through a little in the syllables, particularly when angry, that felt comforting. "But we all carry more of our parents in us than we want to. So," she said. "Casper. His magic must be almost gone by now. I suppose he relies on you to do his dirty work?"

"Something like that."

"What has he got on you?" Pam asked, lightning quick.

Malcolm paused. "My mother," he said. "She's not well."

Pam shook her head again. "I warned him this would happen. I told him. But Casper . . . he doesn't listen. He never has."

He suddenly found himself thinking of his mother and the night his father left. He remembered the sweet smell of frying plantain greeted him as he stepped through the door after a long day of school. His mother in the kitchen of their flat, standing over the oven. Her hair was wrapped up in a satin headscarf, and she had her back to him, swaying to and fro to the gentle sound of crooning 1970s reggae from her ancient radio. He remembered her turning her head as he entered the kitchen, to take him in, quick and assessing, the way she always did. The sizzle of the pan. The angular shape of her back. *Grab a plate, this will be done soon,* she'd said. *We're not waiting for Dad?* Malcolm had asked. He remembered that moment was the first time he'd ever really thought of his mother as seeming old. She wasn't the same woman who would hoist him up on her shoulders, who would chase him around the garden, swinging him under her arm. *Your father won't be coming home again,* she'd said, and that had been that. They'd never mentioned it further.

"He thinks you can help him."

There was the tiniest hint of discomfort in Pam's expression, a tightness in her brow. "When I heard about Erwin, I knew they would be coming for him next. Casper and them thought they could lock the door on her and throw away the key, but I told them. As long as she has claws, she'll be scratching to get out. She won't be free until each of them are dead."

"Maybe we should just let her out," Malcolm said. He meant for it to come out as a joke, but the expression Pam gave him was grave.

"If she is still alive, then that means that she has been sitting in wait, hungry and bitter, for almost twenty years. If she is set free and restores her magic, there will be no stopping her. Nowhere will be safe. Not just for your father, for all of us."

"Oh," Malcolm said, and Pam shot him a scathing look.

"Mm," she said. "*Oh.*"

Malcolm shifted in his seat. He was unsure whether to broach the next subject. His father had warned him not to show his cards, but he had a feeling that the only way he was going to get what he'd come for was by being truthful. "Casper sent me to look for something," Malcolm said. "He said that only the magic of a god can kill a god, so he needs a weapon. He said it was called Osebo's fang."

Malcolm blinked, and then Pam was right in front of him, her face alight with fury.

"Lower your voice," she hissed. "You must not repeat those words to anyone, you understand me? *Nobody.*"

Malcolm nodded, feeling chastised, and Pam kneaded at her temple like a headache was forming.

"Did he tell you what it does?"

"He said that it eats magic. That it can break any spell."

"Not only that," Pam said. "It *unmakes* things. That's why it can kill a god."

Malcolm thought back to the night in the alleyway. The force as he'd felt something razor sharp plunging through his stomach. He should have died that night, but something saved his life. Whoever saved him, why he was saved, it must have been for a reason.

"Come," Pam said, snapping him from his thoughts. "Let me show you something." She hobbled to the middle of the room to squint at something on the floor, then ushered him over.

Malcolm wasn't sure what she was looking at, but he moved to stand by her.

"You see that? On the floor?"

"Uh—"

"Look closer."

Malcolm crouched low and squinted. There was a small dusting of something red on the tiles, almost like sand. Clay. "What is it?"

Pam squatted down with a grunt and ran her index finger against it.

"When I heard whispers that Death's daughter was stirring, I sent my assistants out to retrieve the weapon, but that was over a day ago. They haven't returned yet. But this, this shows me that *she* has been here, so they must be close. If you want to save your father's life, you'll need to find them before she does."

"Okay," Malcolm said, and not for the first time that day he wondered what, exactly, he had gotten himself into. "Where can I find them?"

NOW

CHAPTER EIGHT

MALCOLM

Malcolm wiped the splatter of black blood from his face with the sleeve of his hoodie, grim-faced. There was a second when he just stood there, hand raised from where he'd sent the monster flying back into the tree. His fingers trembled with leftover adrenaline, and he stared at them, willing them to still. There was magic on his fingers, powdery and silver at the edges. He could still see the faint light of it in his veins. It had been a long time since Malcolm had used that much of his magic at one time. So he forgot, sometimes, the thrill that came from having it at his fingertips.

Belatedly, he realized that Eli, the boy Pam had told him about, was still behind him.

"Don't take another step," Eli warned.

Malcolm raised his hands, palms outward. Malcolm had a few inches on Eli heightwise, and he was broad and tall where Eli was sharp-boned and slight, but there was something about him, in the tilt of his head and his narrowed eyes. He meant it.

"It's Eli, right?"

"Who's asking?" Eli's voice was low and measured, and he was angled tight, like at any moment he was going to snap. Malcolm had known people like that before. It wasn't the loud, rowdy ones you had to be wary of. It was the ones standing behind them, careful and calculating, who were the real danger.

"My name's Malcolm King. Pam sent me. She said you might have Osebo's fang."

At the mention of Pam, something in Eli's posture loosened, but he didn't back down. He nodded at the tree behind him. "How'd you get here?"

"I, uh." Malcolm looked around at his surroundings. "I came through the door." At Eli's blank expression, Malcolm huffed a laugh, a little sheepish. "Death works a little different for me."

Eli stared at him, his expression dubious. Then it must have clicked, who Malcolm was and what that meant, because his eyebrows shot up. "Wait," he said. "Malcolm King. You related to Casper King?"

This was a dilemma that Malcolm often found himself faced with. Did he claim his father, the man who had walked out on him when he was twelve? Or did he shrug him off as the stranger that he'd become? There had been times when he was cornered by a group of older boys at school, about to have his teeth kicked in, that he'd resorted to using his father's name as a weapon. There was strength in it, like armor, to be a King. Fear in just the knowledge that what ran through Casper King's blood also ran through Malcolm's. Other times he felt like he might suffocate underneath the weight of his legacy. He would feign innocence, claim the name a coincidence, just so that he'd stop getting those fearful, slanting looks that people would give him when they knew of his heritage. It was a shadow that loomed over him, one that he often wished he could sever from the soles of his feet like Peter Pan's shadow.

"Yeah," Malcolm admitted after a long moment. "He's my father."

"*Shit*," Eli said feelingly. His eyes widened behind the frame of his glasses, and for the first time, he looked uneasy. "You're the son of the duppy king."

"It's . . . complicated."

"But you have his magic." That part wasn't a question.

"Yes."

Eli was quiet, as if measuring his options. Malcolm read it across his face; he knew what it looked like to be backed into a corner. He saw Eli contemplating making a run for it, then briefly considering putting up a fight. Neither of them would win in either of those scenarios, so after a long moment, Eli lowered his hands. Allies, then. At least for now. "I don't have it," Eli admitted. "The fang, I mean."

"Oh." Malcolm hadn't thought about what would happen if that was the case. He'd counted on Eli handing it over, so that he could go back to his father with answers. "But Pam said—"

"Someone beat us to it."

"Okay." Malcolm took a moment to digest that. "Who?"

Eli shot him an acidic look. "What is this, twenty questions?"

"No, I just—"

"How'd you even stop that thing?" Eli was looking at Malcolm's hands as if he was holding a weapon. It was the same way the kids who knew who he was looked at him back at school; like Malcolm had just set his foot on a trip wire. "I've never seen magic like that before."

"Uh." Malcolm scratched the back of his neck, uncomfortable. "I don't know, instinct?"

"People's instincts are usually to run away from monsters," Eli said.

"Well." Malcolm shrugged a shoulder. "*Monster* is subjective."

The corner of Eli's mouth quirked a little, like he was about to smile and then decided against it.

"You've seen something like that before," Eli said. "That creature, I mean."

"Heard about it," Malcolm said, and he had; mostly through his father, who had made many deals during his lifetime in exchange for all the power and riches possible. "They live in the kind of half world between the living and the dead and tend to pick on spirits before they can move on, see what bargains they can make and stuff." Eli stared at him blankly, and for some reason, he felt compelled to keep talking. He felt fidgety and nervous. "It works for her, so it won't be gone for too long. I just hope we stopped it for a while."

"Her?" Eli asked.

"The daughter of Death."

Eli went very still. "So that's what this is all about. The fang, the deaths, the monster, everything."

His attention shifted back to the silk cotton tree, like he expected the creature to come lunging out again any moment. Malcolm used the distraction to take him in. There was something familiar about him, Malcolm thought. He tried to recall if they'd met before, but his mind came up blank.

"Hey. You're bleeding," Eli said, pulling him from his thoughts.

Malcolm looked down at himself. Sure enough, there was a circular red stain on his shoulder, spreading through the thin polyester of his T-shirt. Well, that explained why his right arm was hanging limply by his side, and why he was feeling increasingly light-headed. That thing must have nicked him with one of its claws. Malcolm prodded it, experimentally, and winced when he found that, yep, that definitely hurt. It didn't help that magic took a toll on his body anyway.

"Oh," Malcolm said. "Yeah, guess I am."

"That looks bad." Eli frowned.

Now that he was aware of it, his arm was beginning to throb painfully, and there was an unpleasant, dizzying tingle in his fingertips. Malcolm raised his chin, determined not to let it show. "It's okay. I've had worse."

"Yeah, that's not reassuring," Eli said. "Maybe you should sit down. I can heal it for you."

Malcolm looked up, surprised. Pam hadn't said anything about healing magic. It was one of the rarest kinds of magic out there; most healers had died centuries ago, in the bellies of ships and at the hands of enslavers. He didn't even know that magic like that still existed. "You can do that?"

"It's the least I owe you," Eli said, and there was something complicated and unreadable on his face.

"No," Malcolm said, but his body seemed to be disagreeing with him. "Um. Actually, we should probably get out of here. You won't have very long if you want to return to the other side. Plus, she'll be back."

Eli's eyes snapped toward the tree, weighing the danger, then back to Malcolm. Malcolm was taller than most people—tall enough that he rarely blended in, that he walked with an ever-present hunch in order to skulk out from beneath the eyes that constantly followed him. He remembered a teacher calling him "mean-looking" once, and for some reason, it had stuck with him. He'd always been quiet. Even as a kid it was something that had isolated him from others, but it wasn't until his teacher had highlighted it that he'd realized how his shyness could be interpreted by other people; that he could be intimidating just by saying nothing. That people would be afraid of him simply for the way in which he existed. Standing there, with a good few inches on Eli, Malcolm found himself hyperaware of it.

Eli, though. Eli didn't look frightened. Eli looked *curious*.

He felt the room start to tilt sideways and suddenly, there he was, slumped against Eli.

"O-*kay*," Eli said. "I need you to concentrate on staying awake so that we don't die here."

"Right," Malcolm said, but the room was spinning. It was funny, watching Eli struggle to hold up Malcolm's weight. He was, like, kinda short. "Dying. Bad."

"Malcolm."

"Huh?"

"You're crushing me."

"Oh. Sorry."

Malcolm looked down to find that the blood had run down his sleeve to his fingertips. It was an odd sensation, to feel your own blood outside of your body. It felt distractingly warm.

"Have we met before?" Malcolm blurted. It came out a little more slurred than he'd anticipated.

"No," Eli said as he ushered him toward the mirror. "No, we definitely have not."

Malcolm woke, feeling like he was swimming. The first thing he registered was voices.

"All I'm saying is," said someone unfamiliar, somewhere above him, "he turns up here out of the blue, the son of some creepy duppy whisperer, and we're just supposed to trust him? How do we know he's not an opp?"

"Sunny," another voice sighed, chiding but also amused. "Be nice."

There was a scornful cackle in response. "This is me being nice."

"He saved my life," someone else said, and Malcolm recognized that voice. The low, ever-serious tone of it. That was Eli.

"So what?" The first girl—Sunny—snorted. "Who here hasn't saved your life? Raise a hand."

"Wait—shh. I think he's waking."

"Malcolm?"

Gradually, Malcolm's vision came into focus. Pam was sitting by his bedside frowning down at him. Beside her was Eli, and next to him were two girls he didn't recognize. The first was tall and willowy, stood with her hip cocked to one side. She had long, pastel-colored braids, and she wore a battered T-shirt that read FOR THE ANCESTORS in the colors of the Jamaican flag. The other girl, peering at him through wide, wire-frame glasses, was about a head shorter, round, and freckled. She was dressed somewhere between a librarian and an eccentric primary school teacher.

"Hi," Malcolm said, feeling distinctly awkward.

He took in his surroundings. He was on a small bed in a crowded room. Someone had draped a checkered blanket over him, and there was a steaming mug of tea on the bedside table. The only light filtered in from a single, smudged window, making the floating dust particles in the air dance. There was a rug, clearly secondhand, and a wooden desk chair, also secondhand, but the thing most noticeable about the room, undoubtedly, was the plants. They were anywhere and everywhere, on every possible surface that could shelve them and balanced precariously against the things that couldn't. Rapunzel ivy draping from bookshelves and rows of lilies along dusty windowsills. Ceiling-tall ficus and ferns in terra-cotta pots.

Pam's sleeves were pushed up to her elbows. She reached forward and touched his forehead with the back of her hand to gauge his temperature, the way Malcolm's mum used to do when he was sick. Whatever she felt must have satisfied her, because she nodded and handed him a glass of water, eyebrows raised until he obediently took a sip. "How are you feeling, young man?"

"Uh . . . I'm okay," he said, voice a little gruff. He eyeballed his audience, conscious of their gazes on him. "Where am I?"

"You're in Elijah's room above the diner," Pam said. "You were injured, so he brought you here to rest. He healed you."

He risked a glance at Eli, who looked embarrassed. "It's what the plants are for," Eli said, scratching the back of his neck. "They help."

Reality caught up with Malcolm, and he immediately went to sit up, wincing when the dizziness caught up with him. "I should go. My mum—"

"Is fine," Pam said calmly. "Maxine, get the boy some food. You can't see he's nothing but bones?"

Max, the small, curly-haired girl, hesitated. They were all staring at him with varying degrees of curiosity except for the tall girl with the braids, who was openly glaring.

"*Now*, Maxine," Pam snapped, and the small girl jumped to attention and scurried out of the room.

"That was Max," Pam said, when Malcolm stared after her. "She assists me in business. This is Sunny." She gestured to the remaining girl, whose eyes were still running over him like she could see right through to his core. "And of course you know Elijah."

"Um, yeah. Hi. Look, thank you. This is—this is really nice of you," Malcolm said. "But I should be going."

"Malcolm," Pam said sternly, and it was that tone that was drilled into him to obey. The one that brooked no argument. The urge to respect his elders. "The only thing you should be doing is lying down. You'll be no help to anyone unless you rest."

"Plus, it would look, like, really bad for us all if you were to die on our hands," Sunny said. "Even just logistically speaking." Pam cut her a scathing look and opened her mouth, ready to cuss, but Eli swept an arm around Sunny's shoulders and hauled her toward the door.

"How about we give you both some privacy?" he said, but Malcolm didn't miss the fleeting look Eli slid his way. It was still curious, somewhat wary, but there was something else there too.

Mutual amusement. A little tug of camaraderie. Malcolm was still dissecting the feeling when the door shut.

"Any more pain?" Pam asked.

Malcolm looked down at himself. He was too tall for this bed; his socked feet poked out at the end of the blanket, but it was funny: this was the most comfortable he had been in a while. He wriggled his hand experimentally. There was still an odd tingling under his skin, that pins-and-needles sensation again, but the pain was gone. When he brought his fingers to the skin knitted over his shoulder, it was perfectly healed and smooth. There wasn't even a scar. "No," he said, unable to keep the awe out of his voice. "No pain."

"Elijah's magic . . . it's different," Pam said, though she didn't make it sound like a compliment. "It was one of the very first kinds of magic there was, you know? Healing. One of our very first gifts from the gods. They say that it comes from the veins of the Earth Mother herself. Eli is still learning. You'll be stiff for a few days, but the hurt should stay away. Try not to get any more blood on you, though. It will remind the skin it's not supposed to have healed yet, and it will open back up."

"Right," Malcolm said. "No blood. Got it."

Someone had left his phone on the table, and he picked it up. He had a missed call from his mother and a text from his father: *Call me.* Malcolm shot his mother a quick text—*Be home later. Don't need dinner. Don't forget to take your meds. Love you*—then put it away, screen down, so that he couldn't see it. He wasn't quite ready to deal with his father just yet.

"You've had a tough few days," Pam said. She seemed to have a way of doing that. Reading right down to the core of him. He wondered if this was why his father had such a problem with her. Casper, who had always worked so hard to be unknowable. Pam had probably seen through him like cling film.

"I'll be fine."

"I'm sure you will." It might've sounded patronizing coming from anyone else, but Pam sounded sincere. "You seem to be a fighter, like your mother."

"You know my mother?" Malcolm asked, surprised. He was used to people knowing his dad. He was forever getting stopped in the streets by well-meaning neighbors who would throw their arms up in the air to exclaim, *Malcolm? Woi, if yuh nuh luk like yuh fadda!* His mother, however, had never been much for socializing. The only people who did know who she was, did so for reasons that Malcolm would very much like to forget.

"It's been a while," Pam said. "But I always like her. Quiet, not like your father, that's for sure, but kind. Smart, too. There was always something running through that mind of hers. Plus, she didn't stand for anybody's nonsense, least of all his."

"Yeah," Malcolm said. He was feeling very sleepy, and it was relaxing here. He could feel himself being lulled into contentment. "That sounds like her."

"You shouldn't worry so much about her," Pam said, squeezing his shoulder. "It's her job to worry after you, not the other way around."

Malcolm looked down at his hands. "She forgets," he said, though even that slight admission felt like a betrayal of her. He wasn't sure why he had volunteered this information willingly. Malcolm wasn't a talkative person, but there was something about this place. Things didn't feel difficult here. He got the feeling that no matter what he stuttered, Pam would probably understand.

"You have a question," Pam said, and Malcolm looked up, surprised, to find Pam amused by his confusion. "I can smell it. You should ask it, unless you want me to pull it from you."

"You can do that?" Malcolm frowned.

"You wish to find out?"

In his pocket, Malcolm still had the golden coin that his father had given him. He pulled it out now and held it between his thumb and forefinger. "What is this?"

At the sight of the coin, Pam sighed. She put a hand over his closed fist, so that she didn't have to look at it. "It's not an interesting story," Pam said. "A long, long time ago, I was trapped, a little like the daughter of Death. Casper set me free and saved my life. Now I owe him a debt, bound to this coin. He has been holding it over my head for many years, refusing to cash it in. It's another of your father's games. I'm sure you've been an unwitting participant in a few of those yourself."

"You could say that."

Pam smiled, a slight curve of her mouth that transformed her whole face. The lines in her skin ironed out and she immediately looked decades younger.

"What did he do to her?" Malcolm asked.

Pam eyeballed him curiously. "To who?"

"To Death's daughter." He picked at a stray thread on his sleeve. "He tricked her, didn't he? She must have trusted him, for him to get away with something like that. To hold such a grudge after all these years."

Pam inspected him, her one good eye reading him like the pages of a book. He thought he saw understanding there, but it may have just been wishful thinking.

"It was the same thing that happened to all of us," Pam said. "We came here because we wanted better lives, but we were sold a fairy tale. This place, it's a sickness. It creeps into your bones and gets you hooked until you can't leave. Not even if you wanted to. Your home becomes this . . . this distant memory, and you adapt to survive. We all did. Sometimes that meant making yourself smaller, diluting yourself, packaging yourself into something malleable, you know?

Something easy to swallow. And other times, it means selling little pieces of yourself. Just so that you can eat. What they don't tell you, though, is that every time you deal away that piece, something chips off inside. Tit for tat. That's what happened to Mercy."

"Mercy?" Malcolm asked, surprised.

"That was her name back then," Pam said. "She was young, and she made a deal to survive. She gave your father a little piece of her magic. And then another. And another. But the more she gave him, the more he wanted, until there was nothing left to give. Not her beauty, not her youth, not her wit. Then there wasn't even any girl left, beneath the flesh, in the end. Just hunger, raw and simple. Hunger and magic."

"That's what she does," Malcolm said, thinking back to the conversation between his father and Erwin.

"She devours," Pam said. "He took what made her strong, and she has been ravenous ever since. Eventually her hunger outweighed his, so he stopped her the only way he could. He locked her away."

Malcolm pulled at a stray thread on the blanket. Something dawned on him.

"She loved him," Malcolm realized.

Pam sighed, a long, weary sound. "Yes," she said. "She did."

"Did you know her?" Malcolm asked. "Before, when she was just a girl? When she was *just* . . . Mercy?"

"Don't be mistaken," Pam said. "She was never just a girl."

It was dark by the time Malcolm made his way downstairs to find Eli and Sunny sitting in the back room of the diner. It smelled faintly of fried food down here, and there was an old rerun of *Desmond's* playing on a fuzzy-screened TV. Eli was cross-legged on the floor in front of Sunny, chin tilted back as she methodically rewound his loose twists, twining the hair between her fingers with fresh coconut

124

oil, soft from the microwave. Their faces were illuminated by the cool lights of the screen. It was quiet aside from the sound of the laugh track from the television and the occasional grumble from Eli as Sunny pulled a strand of his hair too tight. At his arrival, they both turned to look at him, neither saying anything.

A whole day had passed. Pam hadn't been lying when she said that he'd needed the rest, but now Malcolm realized that his brain was not yet awake enough to form a greeting.

It was Sunny who broke the silence.

"Well, come and sit down, Grim," she said with a roll of her eyes. "You're letting in all the cold air." She scooted slightly to one side of the threadbare sofa, which Malcolm took as an invitation. "You look less dead."

"Thank you?"

"You're welcome." The look she gave him might've been openly hostile if it weren't for the way her mouth was angled into a smile. She was delighting in the discomfort of the situation, Malcolm realized. She was going to make absolutely zero attempts to remedy it. "So, your dad's really the duppy king?"

"Uh." He risked a glance at Eli, whose attention was on the TV. "Yeah."

"Too bad."

The sounds of the television hung between them, and Malcolm used the lull in conversation to take in his surroundings. The room seemed to operate somewhere between a staff room and a living space. They were surrounded by piles of dog-eared books and half-finished snacks. Someone's sticker-covered laptop was open on an empty Word document that just said *IDEAS: ????* There was a work schedule up on a whiteboard, but there were photos, too. Some of Eli, Sunny, and Max, some of people Malcolm didn't recognize.

Malcolm's attention was snagged by an old oil painting of a

Jamaican landscape just above the television. The view in the painting overlooked a cliff edge of the island, the sky and ocean a crisp royal blue. Malcolm recognized it: Lovers' Leap, St. Elizabeth— where, according to legend, two runaways escaped slavery and jumped to their deaths rather than return to captivity separated. Malcolm's mother had a similar painting in their flat, a gift from his father. He'd always been told that it was custom-made by some underground artist back home, but now Malcolm realized that his father had probably forgotten to buy a gift for his mother and simply picked it up at the duty-free shop.

"Hey," Sunny said. Her braids were flung over one shoulder and her palms slick with coconut oil. Her fingers didn't stop the twisting motion, but before Malcolm had time to protest, she was guiding his hands toward a section of Eli's hair. "Since you're here, you might as well make yourself useful."

"I don't think . . . ," Eli started to protest, but Sunny flicked him on the head.

"No one cares what you think. Grim, hold this out of the way for me. I'm running out of hands. Lij, man, stop moving."

"I'm *not*."

"Why would I say it if it wasn't true? Keep your hand there, Malcolm, don't block the light."

Malcolm knew this role. It felt like half of his childhood had been spent hunched between his mother's knees, head tilted to one side while she braided the coils of his hair into submission. His father passing by the doorway: *You should just cut it off*, he'd grumble. *You look like a girl.* It wasn't until after he left that Malcolm had taken the clippers he'd found in his father's leftover belongings and shaved his head completely. His mother had taken one look at him and sighed. *You look like him* was the only thing she'd said. They'd never discussed it further.

Eli's hair between his fingers was a lot softer than he expected. It was also lighter up close; the very ends had a bronze tint. His hair wasn't long at all, but Malcolm watched Sunny expertly wind the tight coils of his hair into short twists. It was as he was following the motion that her fingers caught his attention: there were black scars lining each of her fingers, like a tar-stained lung. Malcolm had heard of this happening before. This was what magic looked like when it had rotted from the inside, when a spell turned sour. He wondered what Sunny must have been messing with to bear scars like that.

"Ow," Eli complained as Sunny picked a parting with a wide-tooth comb.

"Stop being such a baby," she snapped. Then to Malcolm she said, almost apologetically, "Ignore him, he's tender-headed."

"First of all, I am not. You're just heavy-handed. And second of all—"

"I've got more books," Max announced, charging into the room with a small tower of dusty leather tomes in her arms. She didn't even blink at the scuffle, deftly stepping over Eli's sprawled legs to hand him a book.

When she saw Malcolm sitting there, she paused and readjusted. "Oh. Hello." The books tilted a little, and Malcolm rushed to steady them before they could tumble to the floor.

"Hi," Malcolm replied, wishing he could shrink out of existence.

". . . Hi," Max repeated, and then they were just staring at each other.

Sunny made a sound that might've been a laugh if she wasn't forcibly smothering it. "What'd you find, Maxie?"

"Well, um. Not as much as I'd like," Max said. "Mostly folktales."

"Let's have a look," Eli said. He straightened his glasses, pulled the book onto his lap, and began to read out loud. "*And from Brother Death came three daughters: one that could twist time, one that bent* bone and blood, one that walked through dreams. The sisters lived in harmony, but there were rumors of another daughter, begat in secret: a daughter born into hunger and thus cursed with an insatiable appetite. According to legend, she was the only sister, having been human born, that could travel across oceans (for the oceans belonged to Mammy Water, and no god would ever cross her). Because of this, her sisters hated her and tormented her for years. More notably, she was the only one of her sisters to inherit her father's magic: power over the dead." Eli squinted down at the book. "This is her?"

They all leant over his shoulder to look at the page. There was an illustration of a woman, veiled in black and gold, a snake wrapped around her wrist. Her hair tumbled down, almost floor-length. Behind her, unmistakably, was the branch of a silk cotton tree. At her feet were a series of monstrous creatures representing the world of the dead, bowing and deferential.

"I did some digging, and there are mentions of her going centuries back," Max said. "I'm talking massacres, wars, famines, everything. There's a story where marooned enslaved people were losing on the battlefield during an uprising. Then the daughter of Death appeared and suddenly all the dead around them rose, picked up their weapons, and rejoined the fight. The Maroons won. She's had followers ever since, people handing over their souls for her to eat. Lesser witches doing her bidding, like the one Eli met at the nine night. It's all just stories, though. Seems like history lost track of her once she left home."

"What can you tell us about her, Malcolm?" Sunny asked, and all three heads swiveled in his direction.

Malcolm blinked, caught off guard. "Uh. Not much. There were a group of them. Casper and seven others. Almost twenty years ago, they locked away the daughter of Death, trapped her away in the world between life and death. She wants the fang because it's the only thing powerful enough to eat through the magic locking her away. But it's also the only weapon that might be able to kill her."

"So that's why they all want it," Eli said, turning to the others. "That's why Pam was acting so weird about finding it."

"Well, bad news on that front, 'cause I have no idea where it is," Max said. "None of our usual tracking spells are working. It's like it's poofed into thin air."

Sunny wiped her hands on the towel draped over Eli's shoulder, then leant forward to read through the page. "I don't see why your usual tricks shouldn't work. You showed this to Pam?"

"I believe her exact words were," Max said, and her voice rose in a nasally, high-pitched impression, "*Wah mi luk like tuh yuh? A Tom-Tom?*"

They all laughed, and Malcolm looked between them all, unsure whether he was fully permitted to join in.

"It must be whoever has it," Eli said. "They must be, like, cloaking it somehow."

Sunny raised a perfectly arched eyebrow. "That's possible?"

"Well, there was that time—"

"—in Tottenham, yeah. I remember."

"And we—"

"With the salt? Yeah, won't work, tried it."

"It had to be sea salt. The big grains."

"I tried it. Sea salt. Table salt. Nada."

"But what about with with—"

"Cerasee? Yeah, tried that, too. Nothing."

"Shit."

Malcolm watched the seamless way they communicated, feeling equal parts awkward and detached. The three of them seemed like siblings, the way they unhesitatingly invaded one another's spaces and constantly talked over one another, viciously bickering one second and howling with laughter the next. Malcolm had never had that. His own siblings didn't know he existed, and any friends he used to have had quickly disappeared after the incident with his mother. For most of Malcolm's life, it had just been the two of them, and they had always treated each other with extra care, like they were perpetually scared the other would shatter if they applied too much pressure.

"Well," Eli said. "Malcolm, any thoughts?"

They were all looking at him expectantly again. "Me?"

"Yeah," Max said gently. "We're kind of out of ideas here. Pam said . . . you were out looking for the fang?"

"Yeah. Casp—my dad sent me out for it." Malcolm squirmed slightly at the memory. "Told me to go to that pub opposite Camden Lock. A friend of his, this old seer man, allegedly had it in his possession. But when I got there, I introduced myself, and he just . . . he lost it. Swung at me, caught me off guard. He was strong . . . stronger than any human should be. He got me down, shoved the fang in my stomach."

The three of them stared at him silently.

"The fang," Eli repeated. "It actually touched you?"

"Just for a moment, but yeah, hit me right here." He put a hand over his T-shirt, where the small, raised scar at the base of his gut was. If he closed his eyes, he could still feel the ghost of it, slow, thorny, like dozens of little needles.

"Wow," Max said, though she didn't sound concerned by the revelation, or even particularly sympathetic. She sounded impressed. "That's—wow. You realize you should have died? Like, the fact that you're even alive— The fang comes from a god. A normal person would have died."

Malcolm bit back a flinch. *Normal.* She was right, was the thing.

Normal people didn't raise their uncles from the dead.

"It's just—this is *cool*," Max continued. "You were hit with a weapon designed to kill a god, and you lived. If that fang had stayed in you even seconds longer, you probably would have had no magic left. The fact that you survived is . . . well, it's unheard of. You're kind of a walking miracle, Malcolm King."

"Oh," Malcolm said, because he had no idea what to say to that. He'd been called a lot of things, but never a miracle. "Well . . . thanks. My dad always said that death just works a little different on us."

"But about this seer man," Eli said, pulling them back on topic. "Any idea where he went?"

"No." Malcolm felt the shame prickle at the back of his neck. "I blacked out. Most of it was a blur. The only thing I remember is that there was a weird smell. It was like . . . I don't know, burning or something."

And there it was again. Another one of those meaningful three-way looks that Malcolm couldn't parse.

"Burning," Eli repeated. "Like smoke?"

"No," Malcolm said. "It wasn't woody . . . it was, like—"

"Metallic," Sunny finished.

"Right." Malcolm nodded. "Like car fumes. How did you know that?"

Sunny sighed heavily and cussed under her breath.

"You don't think—" Eli said.

Sunny shrugged. "It's the only thing that makes sense."

"We should have clocked it before," Max sighed. "But if one of them has the fang, then . . ."

"Yeah," Sunny said. "This complicates things."

"I'm . . . not following," Malcolm said.

"Your seer man," Eli said. "What was his name?"

"Uh . . . Jem. That's what my dad called him. Jeremiah, I think. I don't know his last name."

Max typed something into her phone, and a few seconds later she held it up to show Malcolm the screen. "This your guy?"

It was him. Malcolm had only seen the seer man briefly before he was attacked, but the face was seared into his mind. That same face stared back at him; white locs, dark eyes, graying tattoos.

"That's him," Malcolm said.

"Yeah," Max said. "Jeremiah was found dead last week, his chest clawed out."

"Last week?" Malcolm felt sick. "But . . . that's not possible. Who did I meet in the alleyway?"

Max stood up and ran from the room, returning a few moments later with another book: this one was a ratty moleskin, bound with a string. She flipped through a few pages, then stopped and handed it over to Malcolm. He was looking at a crudely drawn wolf-man creature; it had a large chain around its body.

"*A lagahoo*," he read dubiously. He'd heard stories, but that was all he thought they were. Evil shape-shifters that roam the night; that could go from being as small as an insect to as large as an elephant within the blink of an eye. They could steal the likeness of any creature, living or dead. He scanned the page quickly, conscious of the others' eyes on him. After a minute, he turned back to them. The description matched, was the thing. The distinct smell of metal. The inhuman strength. "They're real?"

"We ran into a few a little while back," Eli said, wincing. "It got nasty."

"Lagahoo magic shifts around them. If one of them killed Jem and then took the fang, it would explain why we can't track it," Max said.

"So we get the fang back from the lagahoo, and we can stop the evil duppy witch from escaping from her grave and killing us all." Sunny didn't exactly sound enthused by the prospect. "Sounds like a plan."

"I don't have a better idea," Eli admitted. "What do you think?"

Malcolm realized with an odd jolt that, once again, they were looking at him.

"Oh." He felt exposed, sitting there in the dimly lit room with the three of them looking to him for an answer. Max sat in a chair with her socked feet on the coffee table. Eli had an open packet of Starbursts on his lap. This was their natural habitat, and here Malcolm was, being asked to take up space in it.

"Do you think we could actually do it?" Malcolm asked. "Stop the daughter of Death?"

"Your dad did," Eli said lightly. "At least, that's what Pam said."

"I'm not him." He meant for it to come out as certain, but his voice wavered slightly at the end. It felt important that they know that, somehow. Like he wasn't setting them up for disappointment.

"Yeah, thank God for that." Sunny snorted. "No offense."

"None taken," Malcolm said, and he had to bite down on his lip to keep from smiling.

"Look," Max cut in. "This is serious magic, but I think it's possible. It will take all of us, though."

"Well, I'm in." Eli shrugged. "Obviously."

"I guess that means I am too," Sunny said with a sigh.

"We'll have to be careful," Max warned.

Malcolm shoved his hands into his pockets. He looked around at their faces, at this odd little mismatched group they'd assembled, that had so easily opened its doors for him.

"Okay," he said. "Let's do it." And then a thought occurred to him.

"Though, um, where exactly do you go looking for a lagahoo?"

Sunny groaned heartily. "Please," she said. "I beg. No more research."

"No need," said Pam, who had appeared in the doorway, crouched over her walking stick. Malcolm didn't know how long she'd been hovering there, but he got the sense that it may have been a while. "If the lagahoo has taken the place of Jem, I know exactly where it will be."

CHAPTER NINE

ELI

"Not far now," Max called over her shoulder.

Sunny and Eli exchanged another withering look. For almost an hour, they'd been following her around the winding, narrow streets of Brixton Village. Eli hadn't realized that it was the weekend until the exact moment they'd stepped off the bus, when they immediately found themselves suddenly having to wade through crowds of people. It wasn't often that he went south of the river, or really outside his postcode, and he was already beginning to regret it.

Eli concentrated on the gentle thud of Max's footsteps in front of him as she led them around the cobbled pavement. Despite his best efforts, the past few days were beginning to catch up with him. He felt hollowed out, like somebody had scooped out the meat between his rib cage with a spoon. His skin felt like sandpaper, and his limbs ached tirelessly. Plus, the intermittent bleeding had expanded from just his nose; he'd woken that morning to find his ears crusted with blood. Then, before they'd left, he'd spent almost an hour retching over the bathroom sink, leaving the white porcelain painted with flecks of red. It was obvious that his body was not equipped to handle this kind of magic, yet it stubbornly refused to leave him. He'd stared at himself for a long time in the bathroom mirror. *Come on*, he'd tried to reason with it. *Let me go.* He'd tried to pluck it from himself, just as he had with Malcolm, but the magic was hungry. It wasn't going to let him go until it had finished eating.

Sunny seemed less bothered by the recent happenings than Eli was. She had always been at her most comfortable when she was out and about, weaving through the cracks in the world. She wore these ridiculous cat's-eye sunglasses balanced low on her nose, and every so often her hand would dart out to swipe something of interest as they passed a market stall. Sometimes she'd just study it, the perfect image of a curious tourist browsing the offerings, before returning it to its place with a smile at the market person. More often than not, however, her hand would dart into her pocket as swiftly as a cat, and she'd speed away before Eli could protest.

"What did you say?" Eli called over the hustle and bustle of the market. He was aware, distantly, that Sunny had been grumbling about something, but his attention had drifted to a billboard across the road that was advertising a local college. APPLY BY JULY TO START YOUR FUTURE! the advert read, and Eli was hit with the sobering reminder of his own college application, which remained unfinished on his laptop. It felt like light-years away.

"I *said*, you're not going to pass out again, are you?" Sunny repeated.

Eli snorted. "No, I'm not going to pass out."

"Well, just give me a warning," Sunny said. "You know I don't have the upper body strength to catch you."

Eli laughed outright at that. Sunny had a way of doling out cruelties the same way other people gave flowers.

Malcolm looked between the two of them like they were a

riddle he couldn't quite crack. This seemed to be a recurring theme, Eli noticed. Malcolm didn't offer up conversation unless directly prompted to, and even then, his answers tended to be monosyllabic at best. He couldn't have been more different from the three of them, who mostly communicated by shouting over one another incoherently at all given times.

"Ignore her," Eli said. "Hot weather. Gives me nosebleeds. It's a thing."

He wasn't sure when to bring up the whole *Remember that night you got jumped in an alleyway? Yeah, actually it was me that saved your life and stole your magic* thing, but right then didn't exactly seem like prime time.

"Sure," Malcolm said with an easy smile, and Eli immediately felt the lie sour in his gut.

"Hey, Max," Sunny called ahead, distracting them. "Seriously, how far is it now? Didn't realize I should have been doing stretches before we left."

"Oh," Max said. She looked up from where she'd been intently gazing down at her map, as if she'd suddenly remembered that the three of them were trailing her. This did happen from time to time; Max sometimes got so deep in puzzles that they'd have to fish her out. "My bad. It's just . . . I don't get it. It should be right here." She stopped walking. Circled left. Circled right. Looked up, confounded. "This stupid map doesn't make any sense."

"When you say 'here,'" Eli said. "You mean . . ."

"As in this very spot," Max said. "Under our feet."

"Oh," Eli said unhelpfully. "Maybe it was, like, gentrified out of existence?"

"Yeah," Sunny agreed, "are we sure it hasn't been turned into one of those quirky little cereal restaurants that white people love?"

Max gave them both a resigned look.

"I'm, like, ninety percent sure that Pam wouldn't send us to a cereal restaurant in search of the fang from a leopard god."

"I wouldn't put it past her," Sunny muttered.

"Maybe," Malcolm suggested meekly, "it would be helpful, uh, to go through what Pam said? You know, again."

"Well." Eli put on his best imitation of an aging Jamaican auntie. "She said: *Follow the directions to Brixton's heart. Once you are there, the door will find you.*"

"As vague and unhelpful as the first time we heard it," Sunny said.

"Well, it's got to be around here somewhere." Eli shrugged. "Unless we're following her directions wrong."

"We're not following her directions wrong," Sunny and Max said in perfect unison.

Max unfolded the map out in front of her, blocking the pathway of several grumbling tourists who were forced to walk around her.

"I still think it was back that way," Eli said. "Maybe we should vote on it."

"Okay," Sunny said. "All in favor of ignoring Eli and going the actual way the directions said?"

Three hands raised—one hesitantly.

"*Hey*," Eli protested.

"Oh look, the vote's spoken."

"Wait!" Max blurted, ending the debate. Before anyone could question her further, she was speeding away in the opposite direction.

"*O*-kay," Eli said. "Guess we're off again."

They took a sharp turn, passing another shabby coffee shop and a fruit stand, and ducked through a stall draped with an array of printed dashikis, ignoring a market worker's squawk of protest. Max lifted the sheet of material from the back of the next stall, ushered the three of them blindly through despite their grunts of objection, and then stopped.

"Okay," Eli said. He blinked once, twice, three times, but nope—it wasn't his imagination. He looked around, but he couldn't catch his bearings. "Okay, yeah, that for sure was not here before."

They stood at the mouth of an alleyway, and there, at the far end, was a door. It was black, sleekly painted, and wholly inconspicuous. There were no numbers or letters indicating a street address that Eli could see. They probably wouldn't have even registered it had they not ducked under the back of the market stall. Eli glanced back at the others, but they looked just as perplexed as he felt.

God, Eli loved magic sometimes. Every time he thought he had unraveled all the hidden treasure troves of his city, he stumbled into something like this and lost his breath all over again.

"This is the place?" Sunny asked.

"Looks like it," Eli said, with a wary look around. The door belonged to a four-story Georgian town house, the kind you'd normally only see on a postcard. It was completely out of place here. There was a stillness that was disconcerting, but he shook the feeling off.

The alleyway was narrow enough that they had to walk single-file. Eli kept his palms against the cool brick walls on either side of him, partially to steady his balance, partially to ground his nerves. It was quieter, away from the hustle and bustle of the crowds. Silent, almost, aside from the crunch of their feet against the gravel. Eli looked at the sliver of gray sky above him. It would rain soon. They would be glad, at least, to be inside.

There were three steps up to the entrance, which was bracketed by a peeling, rusty rail banister. Now that they were closer, Eli got a better look at the door. He was right that there was no house number. Instead, a small golden carving of a spider was engraved above the knocker. The wood of the front door had been splintered somehow, broken along the right-hand side, where someone had kicked it down. He nudged it with the toe of his trainer, and it eased open with a creak.

"Wait," Max said, stopping him with a light hand on his elbow. She crouched down to squint at the doorstep. Something white and powdery lined the floor of the entranceway. Max prodded it experimentally and then stuck her finger in her mouth, ignoring the others' protests.

"Salt?" Sunny asked.

"Even better," she said. "Sugar. Sign that a lagahoo has been nearby. This is definitely the place."

"Okay then," Eli said. "Everyone ready?" He was met with various mumbles of assent. "Then, like we discussed."

On cue, each of them rolled up their sleeves and held out their arms, palm down, as was expected. Malcolm raised a hand and summoned a shard of magic at his fingertips. With a small wave of his fingers, identical gashes slit a perfect line across all four of their arms. It was just thick enough to draw blood, and to sting, painfully, like a paper cut, causing them to each let out yelps of surprise.

"*Cool*," Max said, because she was morbid like that. "Remember, scars can be faked, so as long as we're bleeding, we'll know it's us. If you have any doubts, check the arm, okay?"

"And if it's not there?" Eli asked.

"Uh," Max said. "Well, if it's not there, then you're not speaking to one of us. So . . . in that case, you should probably just run."

A glance toward the others revealed that they were just as unenthused by the idea as he felt.

"Great," Eli said, and turned to the door when nobody else made a move to do so. His arm really did sting. "Here goes nothing."

There was very little light inside, so Eli pulled his phone from his pocket to use as a torch. It took a few moments for his eyes to adjust to the dimness and register what he was looking at. What first struck him was the sheer number of things. The ceilings were high, like the place might've been something grand before it had been left to fall into disarray, but now there was clutter everywhere. There were mountains of weathered books and outdated magazines, glass displays filled with tribal masks and porcelain dolls. The uncanny was haphazardly stuffed in between the canny; on one shelf he spotted vials of something black, liquid, and undeniably magic; on another there was a box of workout videos on VHS and a row of old, rusty bells. He took a single step forward and something caught beneath his foot, making him jump. He squinted through the darkness: shed snakeskin. He sincerely hoped that whatever that belonged to was no longer around.

By some kind of unspoken mutual agreement, the four of them knew to be quiet. There was something off balance. As soon as they'd opened the door, a chill had hit Eli, as if he'd stepped outside on a winter's day. It started in his fingertips, prickling and ice-cold, and gradually crawled further up each arm with every step he took.

He passed a wilted flower on a nearby shelf, and without thinking, reached out to touch it. His fingers had barely grazed its browned leaf before the magic shot through him, uncoiling the curled stem and turning the brown areas green until it had flourished back to life. From the corner of his eye, he caught Malcolm watching, a startled, wary look on his face, but neither of them said anything.

"Look at all this stuff," Max whispered, though Eli still recognized the delight in her voice. She flipped open the lid of a jewelry box and a tiny ballerina twirled to a lullaby. Everyone jumped at the sound apart from Max, who looked delighted. "It's like a museum. Is it weird that I kind of love it here?"

"Yes," Sunny said flatly. She snapped the box shut. "It's weird."

Eli agreed; he felt uneasy. The whole place felt cold. Like walking through a mausoleum. When he put a hand to the wall, he was greeted with the faint pulsing of magic. It was chipped and peeling underneath the wallpaper, like someone had tried to burn it away, but he could still smell the remnants of it. He crossed the room to open the curtains, knowing that even the smallest amount of sunshine was as good a protector as any, only to find that the windows had been barred over with panels of wood. Eli put his hand to one and pulled, but it was wedged tight. Someone had not wanted to be disturbed.

"You think the fang's actually here?" Malcolm murmured.

"Could be anywhere under all this mess. I mean, look." Sunny picked up a tiny potted plant that from afar looked like a cactus but upon closer inspection seemed to possess tentacles. "What even is this?"

"It's here," Eli said. In the corner of his eyes, he felt Malcolm eyeing him again, speculative. "I can feel it."

Max stuck her head around the corner into the next room. She was illuminated by the blue light of her own phone, and the angle of it on her cast a huge shadow across the wall. "Doesn't sound like anyone's home."

Eli brushed his fingertips against the glass of one of the displays, expecting to find dust, but it was smooth. Recently polished. "I don't know about that," he said.

Wordlessly, they split into separate rooms. Max and Malcolm took the door to the east, and Eli left them pulling open cupboard doors and fumbling through old pots and pans. Sunny headed through some French doors and ended in a long hall filled with displays covered in dusty white sheets.

Eli followed the feeling in his chest and rounded the corner. He ended up in what looked like an office. There was a thin vibration in here, a peculiar kind of magic, just vaguely registering on the periphery of Eli's consciousness. It felt off, amid the coldness of everything else. He couldn't put his finger on where it came from, so he started to look around.

It was a slow process. He found an old box of matches and lit a nearby candle, casting the room in warm orange light. Then he started going through each drawer. The contents were largely nothing of consequence: utility bills, faded phone books, and receipts from shops he was sure had long since closed.

He picked up a stack of dusty photos from a side cabinet and flicked through it. They were mostly portraits of unsmiling elders, with a few candid Polaroids from what looked like some pretty live parties back in the day. One caught his attention: a group shot of young people, some of them not that much older than him, crowded around the front step of what looked like this very house, only— gathering by their baggy plaid shirts and high-top fades—it must have been at least twenty years ago. On the back was a scrawled annotation: *House of Spiders*. He pulled the torch from his phone closer so he could get a better look. There was something familiar about a few of the faces—the thin, sinewy man with a speaker box under one arm, and the tallest one, hands stuffed into his pockets, casually confident—but he couldn't put names to the faces.

He put this aside but paused when he noticed a stack of papers at the bottom of the drawer. They were handwritten, almost incomprehensibly so, scrawled in a combination of Patois, shorthand, and symbols Eli didn't recognize. He knew a spell when he saw one, though. Dozens of them, in fact; some hastily scribbled on scraps of paper, some spreading across multiple pages and weaved together with a piece of string. It reminded him of the recipe journals Pam kept stashed above the diner. He and Sunny were fascinated with them; how they seemed to be both obscurely detailed and yet utterly unfathomable in every single way. No direction of quantities of ingredients, no determination in time. It assumed pre-existing knowledge that was entirely impossible. *Tek handful. Maybe two(?) Use Angela's method. Put in oven till it cook.* These instructions looked to be written in the same manner.

"What are you doing?"

Eli looked up. Sunny was in the doorway, her head tilted curiously.

"I think I've figured out what this place is," Eli said.

"Yeah?" Sunny quirked an eyebrow. "What's that, then?"

"Well, I'm thinking it was some kind of sanctuary back in the day. For people like us. It's hard to recognize it with all the crap rammed in here, but look—that's here, see?" Sunny came over as he passed her the photographs, and she flicked through, frowning.

"Maybe," she said placidly.

"*Maybe,*" Eli mimicked with a mocking face. "Look. The house in this photo looks exactly like where we are. The street's different, but there's the same spider mark on the door. And if the building moves . . . It would make sense why this place is only visible to locals, why we couldn't find it, why it had us running around in circles for ages."

"You think it needed to figure out if we were trustworthy," Sunny said.

"Exactly." Protection like that meant that it was more difficult for the magic of this place to be harvested and mangled or watered down and sold. It was clever. Whoever had formed this place knew exactly what they were doing.

"And are we?" Sunny asked.

"Are we what?"

"Trustworthy."

Eli glanced at her somber expression and laughed, taking the papers back. "I mean, I can only speak for myself."

It was as he glanced down that it caught his attention. Sunny's hands looked as they always did, right down to the black scars that knitted their way around her fingers, but something was missing. Scars could be mimicked, Max had said. Blood could not. There was no slash across Sunny's arm where Malcolm had marked each of them.

He felt a lurch of panic in his gut, but forced himself to take a breath, to release the tension that had formed in his shoulders. He didn't take his eyes off the imposter.

"Hey, Sunny," he called over his shoulder, loud enough for his voice to carry over into the rooms nearby, where he'd left his friends. He kept his voice light and easy. "You good?"

Then he heard her from the next room over, disgruntled, a little bullish but undeniably her. "Why wouldn't I be?"

Eli stared at the imposter. The imposter stared back.

This close, the likeness was uncanny. Every detail on the doppelgänger was the same. The pristine baby hairs that Sunny painstakingly styled each morning. Her dark brown, almost black eyes. The little scar she had, just above her eyebrow, from the time she claimed she'd fallen out of a tree as a kid. It even had the same small brown coffee stain on the bottom of her T-shirt from where Sunny had spilled her drink that morning. She'd been pissed since it was one of her favorites. She'd bought it at Afropunk, and it said VEXED in capital letters across the chest.

Eli had never met a lagahoo in person. He'd stumbled across a few—it was hard not to in their line of work—but always at a distance. *We don't business with them* was how Pam would put it. Anything that could change its face in the blink of an eye had to be considered dangerous. He'd heard stories about the creatures walking off with newborn babies in their arms, of them emptying entire bank accounts with the account holder being none the wiser. Plus, there of course were the age-old barbershop conspiracy theories that certain famous people throughout history had disappeared and been body-swapped by the creatures. Eli tended to take those with a pinch of salt.

What the stories didn't mention, however, was how quickly they could move.

Eli had barely taken a step toward the door before the lagahoo lurched forward. All at once, it wasn't wearing Sunny's face anymore; its skin shifted and molded like wet clay, and then it was a boar, snarling and fanged, breathing inches from Eli's face. Eli edged backward, arm raised to shield himself, but it was futile. The beast was almost as tall as him, with long, curved tusks, and this close, Eli could feel the damp heat of its breath fogging up his glasses.

Eli backed up until he hit the wall. In this form, the lagahoo was tall enough that Eli had to crane his neck upwards to look at it, but he kept his feet planted, determined not to be cowed. He felt the faint needle of magic in his fingers and under his feet. The earth stirred, waiting to be summoned.

"Who are you?" Eli asked.

The lagahoo quickly shifted back into Sunny's form. Eli could smell the magic on it, burnt and coppery.

"I could ask you the same question," the lagahoo replied. "You're in my home."

"Yours?" Eli laughed. "This isn't yours. I can still feel the magic in the walls. You stole it from the witches that were here before you. The ones in those photos."

"What does it matter?" the lagahoo sighed. "Most of them are dead now, or will be soon."

It sounded so defeated by this realization that a switch flicked inside Eli's head, and he was forced to reassess. "Look," Eli said. "I'm not here to cause trouble. I just want to talk."

Eli blinked, and the creature was no longer Sunny. It wasn't a boar, either. Eli was looking at his own face.

"Funny," Eli said, rolling his eyes.

"*Funny*," the lagahoo echoed, and that was evidently another thing that the stories neglected to mention. They were *annoying*.

It was strange, taking in his own expressions from this angle. It was like looking in the mirror, only with the odd sensation that his reflection was peeking straight back. If he tilted his head, his reflection should tilt his, too. Instead, the lagahoo was tensed, shoulders bent inward, as if bracing itself for a blow. It looked tired, Eli thought. He knew the feeling.

Right on cue, Eli felt his nose start to dribble with blood. He brushed it away with the underside of his wrist and willed some magic into his core to stop the bleeding. The lagahoo caught the motion and frowned.

"You're a healer," the lagahoo said, with Eli's own voice.

Eli said nothing, not wanting to give anything away. Finally, the lagahoo seemed to relax and stepped backward. Its gaze ran over Eli.

"It's been a long time since I've met one of you."

Eli frowned. "One of me?"

"Of the earth."

"What?"

It was difficult to concentrate. He could still feel an odd buzzing sensation under his skin, a wrongness in the room. He'd thought, maybe, that it was the lagahoo doing it, but no. There was something else here.

"There's magic in you that shouldn't be," the lagahoo said, lip curling. "It's rotten. It smells of death."

Eli shrugged, tried to look braver than he felt.

"That magic is eating you from the inside out," the lagahoo said, head inclined to one side. "It's probably only due to the fact that you can heal that you're still alive. Where did you get it?"

"I think you know where I got it from," Eli said.

The smile fell off the creature's face. Its gaze skittered around, wary. "He's alive?"

"No thanks to you. What did you do with the seer man?"

There was something animalistic underneath the lagahoo's skin, as if it hadn't quite shaken its previous forms. Eli wondered what it looked like, really, underneath it all. Every story was different. Some people believed that they didn't have a true face; that they were cursed to forever be unseen.

"That boy, the duppy prince. He has death in his veins, which means he is dangerous. I couldn't let him walk away."

"What did you do with the seer man?"

"The seer had the fang," the lagahoo said. "He was weak. He intended to sell it to the daughter of Death in return for his life. I couldn't allow that."

"And now he's dead," Eli said. "Was that you too?"

There was a twitch above the lagahoo's eyebrow that Eli recognized as irritation. "There's no point in killing a man who has angered the daughter of Death," he said. "She'll come for all of them."

It didn't make sense. Eli frowned, running everything he had learned through his mind. "Is that why you wanted the fang?" he asked. "To bring it to her in exchange for your safety?"

The creature scowled. It was odd to see the expression on Eli's own face. Funny, even. "*Her*," it hissed. "Never. The fang is the only weapon powerful enough to kill a god, to unmake magic. To break an unbreakable spell. I would die before I let it fall into her hands."

"Then why?" Eli said. "Why take it?"

The lagahoo was quiet for a long moment before speaking. "Do you know what a blood pact is?"

"Sure," Eli said. "It's a way of binding something."

"Or someone. If the stories are true, Casper King and seven others used a blood pact to lock the daughter of Death away somewhere in the worlds between life and death. They sealed the door with a spell that meant it would never be opened without all eight members' blood. They were cocky enough to think that it meant they'd be untouchable, that nobody would ever be brazen enough to come for them. The daughter of Death survived off the magic of others, so they locked her away where she couldn't feed on anyone. I suppose they thought that by the time they had grown old, she would have already starved without her magic, so they would never have to deal with the consequences. But they were wrong. She didn't starve. Somehow, she's still alive. Not only that, but she's also hungry and bitter. The only thing stopping her from walking free is the pact of the eight people that put her there. Seven of them are already dead."

"Did you know them?" Eli asked.

"Not personally," the lagahoo said. "But everyone knew of them. There was a time when they wielded some of the most powerful magic in the world. People would come to them if they needed something. They were a force to be reckoned with."

Eli looked down at the photo in his hand, and the thought occurred to him: *George*. Of course. He must have been one of them. The seer man must have been another. Malcolm's uncle, too.

"I've watched and I've waited," the lagahoo said. "And I've searched for that fang, knowing that one day it will be needed to stop her. If the daughter of Death is let loose, if she gets her magic back, the damage she causes will be immeasurable. She cannot be freed. And since the fang is one of the only things that can stop her, I would die before I hand it over."

Understanding crept over Eli as he took in the lagahoo's words. He was able to recognize it, now that it was being mirrored to him in the tic of his own jaw, the furrow of his own brow. The lagahoo wasn't just angry. It was afraid.

"What did she take from you?" Eli asked, and the lagahoo looked surprised before it quickly composed itself.

"Everything," the lagahoo said.

Something deflated in Eli at that. He felt the tension bleed out of the room, instead replaced by a tenuous understanding. "Where is the fang now?"

"It's gone. I've taken it far away where no one will ever find it."

But that wasn't right. Eli hadn't been able to place it before, the odd vibration that had been in the back of his mind ever since he'd stepped into the house, but he was able to decipher it now.

"I don't think so," Eli said. "It's still here, isn't it? You wanted to keep it close to you."

The lagahoo said nothing, and Eli knew he was right.

House of Spiders, they'd called this place. He was going to have to crawl through the cracks.

He followed the vibration until he was right against the wall of the study. It was exposed brick here, like the wall was an extension, and Eli put his hand to it. It was here, Eli knew it.

He crouched down, and there—just by his foot. One of the bricks was loose. Eli pried it out with his fingers and let out a little exhalation of breath at what he saw.

It was about the size of Eli's forearm, dusty and browning, wrapped in a rag. It was brittle and twiglike, only carved sharply at one end into the point of a canine. It stank of rot, like dead meat that had been left to fester in the sun. Underneath that, though, was the tang of magic strong enough to be nearly palpable. When Eli inhaled, he tasted it, sharp and acidic at the back of his tongue. There was something unnerving about it. Something that made him want to take a step back.

He didn't. Careful not to touch it, he opened his bag and lowered it in. He turned to the lagahoo, who had backed up as if Eli was holding an explosive.

"I don't want to have to hurt you," the lagahoo said. "Not knowing what you are. But if you had any sense, you would return that to the wall and walk out of here right now."

"I can't do that," Eli said. "Don't you know what will happen if she gets to this first?"

"And what about him?" the creature demanded. "The son of Casper King. He can't have this."

"Malcolm isn't his father," Eli said, feeling oddly defensive.

The lagahoo laughed. "You think that now, but I've seen what magic like that does to a soul. It corrupts you and breaks you until there's nothing inside." Its smile faded, no doubt realizing that the same magic ran through his veins, too. "Do you know what the daughter of Death has done to people like me? I've heard stories of her peeling the skin from one of us. Heard she captured a lagahoo years ago and kept them locked up, a chain around their neck to stop them from changing. And Casper? He was the one telling her to. You're willing to put power into the hands of someone like that?"

Eli didn't know what to say to that. He found himself thinking of the first day he and Malcolm had met, when Malcolm had saved him. How he'd raised his hand and sent the witch tumbling into the depths of the tree like it was nothing. He thought of how the fragment of magic had felt in his palm. Of what Malcolm would think if he'd found out that Eli had taken it.

"Malcolm's not like that," Eli said. "We're just trying to stop anyone from being hurt."

"You're a child," the lagahoo said. "You don't know what you've got yourself into."

Eli hesitated. The fact that they'd just planned to hand the fang over to Pam suddenly felt infantile. He didn't know, really, what Pam had in mind for it. If she intended to sell it or use it for her own gain. This had all started out as just a paycheck to Eli, another means of survival. Now, with the lagahoo in front of him, he realized that this was something more. He had a responsibility to make the right decision. It wasn't enough to just muddle their way through blindly, not when people would get hurt. Eli didn't get a chance to respond, however, because it was at that exact moment that he heard voices from outside, coming up toward the front door.

"What was that?" Eli asked. His breath had turned to puffs of ice. He looked down at his arms and found that his skin had risen to goose pimples.

"No," the lagahoo said, rushing toward the window. It peered through the gap in the wooden panels and hissed. "No, no, no. This shouldn't have been possible. The house is hidden. It's *protected*. They were never supposed to find me here." The lagahoo spun, expression darkening. "You led them here."

Eli looked down at the fang, and then up at this creature with his own face.

"We need to go," Eli said. He didn't waste any time arguing. He zipped up his backpack with the fang inside and ran for the door. When he looked back, the lagahoo was gone.

CHAPTER TEN

ELI

There were at least three in total. That was what Eli counted when he pried away a corner of the wooden panels barring the windows to squint through the foggy glass outside. They moved up the alleyway and toward the house like mourners in a procession. Three, with identical gray skin and dark suits. They were fractured and peeling in places, as if they'd been haphazardly thrown together in a hurry; one was missing an upper piece of its skull, the other its jaw, but all of them were lined with fractures. Dead, soulless things whose minds didn't belong to themselves anymore.

He returned to the main rooms, where his friends were still picking through boxes. Malcolm perched on a spinning chair behind a desk, rifling through drawers. Max's head popped up from behind a sofa, and Sunny paused in the doorway between the two rooms, hands on her hips.

"Time to go." He clapped his hands. "Now."

The good thing about his friends was that even with the fear of impending death, he could count on them. Immediately they were on their feet looking for exits. They were used to running and knew that even one moment's hesitation could be the difference between life and death. If Eli had more time, he would have taken a moment to think about how objectively tragic that was.

"How many?" Sunny asked, though she was already moving, stuffing things into the little leather bag she wore across her front. Eli didn't know if the things she was taking were of use to them, or just things that looked extra glittery to her magpie eyes, but he didn't think now was the time to ask.

"Three at least," Eli said. "We can't go out the front."

"Back door's a no," Malcolm said from where he had peeked through a gap in the boarded-up doors. Eli moved to look over his shoulder. In the distance, he could see black smoke rising at the back of the garden like smog, just as it had that first day at Pam's. He didn't know how many of them were coming, and he didn't really want to find out. "Doors are warded against magic. Walls too. We need a window."

"Over here," Max said from the kitchen. They followed her into the room without hesitating, Malcolm dragging furniture in front of the door behind them to buy them some time. There was a small window high in one of the walls that hadn't been boarded over. Someone must have figured it was too small to be any threat, but they didn't count on a bunch of underfed teenagers meandering in and out. The window opened outward on a latch into what looked like a narrow alleyway on the side of the house. Eli winced. It was going to be a tight fit, but it would have to do.

"I'll go first, check it's clear," Sunny said. "Give me a boost?"

Eli and Max weaved their fingers together and held them out by their knees, forming makeshift steps for Sunny to lift herself up to the window. She swiftly pulled herself through, folding her long legs after her and twisting her hips with ease to scoot through the gap.

Sunny landed deftly on the other side and then disappeared. Eli spared a thought for the lagahoo. It could have been anything, gone anywhere by now: a mouse weaving through the cracks in the floorboards, a moth fluttering through a vent in the wall.

Sunny reappeared, grim-faced. "There's a way out around the side of the house. It will lead us back where we came in. We can cut through, but we'll have to be quick."

"Okay." Eli nodded. "Max, you go next, you're the smallest."

Max raised an eyebrow. "Uh, the shortest maybe. Definitely not the thinnest."

"*Max.*"

"All right, all right. Help me up."

Sunny caught Max under her armpits as she wiggled through, legs first, softening the fall slightly.

"Come on, Eli," Max said, once she'd readied herself. "You next."

"Oh," he said. "Malcolm, you should—"

"Nah." Malcolm nodded. "You go."

"Today would be nice," Sunny snapped, and Eli glared at her but didn't waste any more time arguing. He passed his backpack, where he'd hastily stuffed the fang, through the window to Sunny, and then removed his glasses, passed those through too, and stepped up onto the open palm that Malcolm offered. Malcolm was surprisingly strong beneath him, and Eli was lifted through the gap with relative ease. It was a tight fit; his hip knocked the corner, hard enough that he would probably find a bruise there later, and he had to rotate himself slightly to get through. He was in no way as graceful as Sunny, but he curled himself up tight, careful not to knock his head.

He'd done this before. As a child, maybe. Been lifted into trees and fumbled up jungle gyms. There was a memory somewhere in the periphery of his mind. A blurry face quirking an eyebrow at him from above, all challenge. *Come on, Lij. You scared?*

He was halfway through, one leg in and one leg out, his chin tucked tightly against his chest as he lowered himself through, when he heard the creak of the front door from further inside the house. Eli froze, midair, exchanging a wordless look with Malcolm. The creatures were inside, which meant that the front would be clear for their exit. They needed to move before any more came.

"It's okay," Malcolm whispered, "just hurry." Before Eli could protest or worry about maintaining his balance, he was hefted through. He lost his balance and ended up falling hard against Sunny and Max, the three of them landing on their elbows and grazing the palms of their hands against the gravel.

"Ow—"

"*Damn it.*"

"Are you okay?"

"Yeah, yeah, fine." He stood up, brushing the dirt from his palms, to find Malcolm closing the window between them. Still very much on the other side.

"The hell are you doing?" Eli hissed. His ankle throbbed slightly—he'd landed at a weird angle—but he pushed the thought away.

"I'm not gonna fit," Malcolm said. He didn't sound surprised by the revelation, and Eli was struck with the frustrating realization that Malcolm had probably planned this from the beginning, as soon as they'd suggested using the stupid window. Malcolm was noticeably bigger and taller than the rest of them, yeah, but Eli had figured that they would find a way to pull him through, if it came down to it. They didn't leave anyone behind.

"Sure you are, come on. Climb up, we'll help you."

"We don't have time," Malcolm whispered. "I'll find another way out."

"What? No, Malcolm," Eli snapped. "We don't leave people behind."

"It's all right." His voice was infuriatingly calm. "I'll be fine."

"Hey," Max whispered. She'd moved to the edge of the alleyway and was pointing a little way around the corner, by the ground. "Tell him to get to the basement. There's a bigger window he can get through that's not boarded up."

"You hear that?" Eli asked through the glass, and Malcolm nodded. "Good. We'll wait for you."

"You don't need to—" Malcolm protested.

"We're not leaving," Eli insisted, jaw set. It was the least they owed him.

Malcolm shook his head, but the corner of his mouth lifted slightly. "Fine," he said. "But if I'm longer than ten minutes, you should go."

"If you're not out in ten minutes, we're coming back in."

Malcolm huffed but nodded. Before he could go, however, Eli hit his palm against the window. "Wait. To keep you safe." He gestured for Malcolm to open the window a crack and, when he did, Eli slipped the little red-and-black beaded bracelet that Sunny had given him through the space. Malcolm took it, an odd, unreadable look on his face.

"Try not to die, yeah?" Eli said.

Malcolm smiled, but Eli watched him slip it onto his wrist. "No promises," Malcolm said.

The three of them dropped underneath the window to wait, the brick cool against Eli's back. Inside, Eli could just about make out the sounds of figures moving around. Clatters as they pulled open cupboards and tossed things aside.

Eli couldn't focus on anything past the footsteps of the creatures inside and the harried breaths of his friends on either side of him.

He tried to think about his breathing, but the worry kept distracting him, sickly and insistent. Ten minutes, he'd told Malcolm. Ten minutes, and then he was going after him.

He looked at the clock on his phone as the moments ticked by.

What if she'd already gotten to him? What if they were already too late? Nobody else was going to know Malcolm was gone. Nobody else was going to miss him. Eli, more than anyone, knew what it was like to have nobody look for you. He wasn't going to let the same thing happen to somebody else.

Max took his hand and squeezed, and Eli forced himself to focus on that instead. On the warmth of her fingers and her chipped nail varnish, on the half-smudged ink reminders that she always jotted across her palm.

"He's back," Sunny said, and sure enough, there was Malcolm, all hulking six feet of him, climbing out of the basement window. He was gasping for breath and there was dirt on his cheek, but he looked unharmed.

"Thank God," Max said, and she reached up to hug him. She was still holding Eli's hand, and it got tangled between the crush of their bodies. Malcolm looked thrown by the sudden contact, but he reluctantly bent over to squeeze her back.

"Cutting it a bit close," Eli said, releasing Max's fingers to dust the gravel from his palms. His heart hadn't stopped thundering yet. "You good?"

"Yeah. Fine," Malcolm said. He wasn't looking at them, though. His concentration was still on the house. "We need to go. You have the fang?"

"It's in my bag."

Max exhaled a breath of relief. Sunny, meanwhile, had a face like thunder. "Great, so at least if we die, it won't be for nothing. Can we go now?"

"Yeah," Eli said, "let's go."

They followed the narrow passageway along the side of the house, stepping over discarded bottles and stray bin bags, careful to keep up a quick pace. Eli felt the grind of gravel under his heels and a graze against the back of his knuckles as they brushed a wall, but he ignored it. The end of the alley was blocked by a gate. It was rusted shut, but Malcolm pushed his way to the front and kicked it, hard, with the sole of his shoe. After three attempts the door opened with a groan.

"Wait," Sunny hissed once they were through. To their right were the steps leading up to the front door, where he could hear movement inside. Left was the first narrow pathway that they'd come from, their way back to the indoor market. They waited until the voices drifted further into the house.

"Okay," Eli said. "Now."

They ran faster than they'd ever run before, slowing only when they reached the fruit stalls and crappy tourist memorabilia.

"Keep moving," Sunny said, and before Eli got a chance to breathe, they were running again. They flew through the stalls, weaving through crowds of shoppers and narrowly skirting displays. Eli could practically taste his lungs with every inhalation. His muscles prickled with exertion. They passed by a terrible busker butchering the same Bob Marley song they'd heard on their way in, and Eli wondered how much time had passed. If any had passed. *Time magic.* Eli would never wrap his head around it.

"Watch out!"

Eli felt himself pulled deftly to one side just as something ice-cold shot past his face, narrowly grazing the tip of his ear. Behind him, a clay pot shattered and fell to the ground. Eli raised his head to find Malcolm watching him with wide eyes. They'd been followed. Eli turned and caught a glimpse of the dark-suited creatures pushing their way through the crowd. They were gaining on them. Before Eli could protest, he found himself being dragged behind a stall of secondhand books and out of the line of fire. He peeked his head around to see creatures run past them, and further into the market.

"We need to keep going," Malcolm hissed.

Eli brought his hand to his ear, which now felt like ice. How had he never noticed the sound that magic made before? There was a cold sleekness to it, like the metal edge of a knife. Like he could run a finger down it and draw blood. The image of the pot shattering looped in his mind. A few centimeters to the left and that could have been him.

"Are you listening?"

Something was gnawing at the edge of his senses. A faint ringing, a distinct feeling of something being not-quite-there, that Eli recognized as magic. It was the fang. Eli could feel it from his backpack. It was making any magic around it burn hotter, like flinging petrol into a fire. He'd noticed before that Malcolm had this odd sense of steadiness about him, an unmoving calmness. Truthfully, Eli had noticed it because it was something he envied. Eli was constantly wrestling with his anxieties; he felt like he could vibrate out of his skin at any given time. Malcolm seemed to be the opposite. The magic surrounding Malcolm seemed to feel different now. The fang was acting as a magnifier. Something was wrong.

It was pure intuition that made him reach out, take Malcolm's arm, and flip it over to where the cut lining his skin should be. The cut on Eli's own arm had stopped bleeding, but it was still red and a little itchy. He'd been rubbing his thumb over it, resisting the urge to make it go away. The skin on Malcolm's wrist was smooth and unblemished. Eli felt a chill settle in him.

"Where's Malcolm?" Eli asked steadily.

The lagahoo took its hand back and didn't even have the grace to look shame-faced at having been caught.

"I don't know."

"What do you mean you don't know? What did you do with him? Is he still in the house?" No reply. "Did you hurt him?"

Nothing.

Eli felt a spike of irritation through his core.

And then it was like that day back at Pam's. Eli felt the last grains of his patience slip, and the magic swooped from him, Dalíesque, and shoved the lagahoo hard against the wall. "Where is he?" Eli repeated, stepping forward. The magic in his fingertips started to burn, but for once, he didn't try to fight it. It felt *good* to use it like this. It wanted to be released; he could feel it. It was hungry.

The lagahoo blinked in surprise. Eli watched it squirm, trying to wriggle from Malcolm's skin into another, something that could fight Eli off—a leopard, maybe, or a vulture, something with claws—but Eli's magic was a steel trap. The lagahoo wasn't going anywhere.

It wasn't really that different, the magic of making and unmaking. Healing was stitching things back together, but Eli also knew how to tear things apart. He plucked, now, at the seams of the lagahoo. He felt the magic strain against it like granules of sand.

"Talk," Eli demanded.

"He was still in the house when I escaped," the lagahoo said. "There were too many of them. They got him."

Eli felt himself bristle with frustration. "How do I find it again?"

The lagahoo frowned, looking genuinely baffled. "Find it?"

"The house," Eli snapped. "It moves, right? There's got to be a pattern or something, a way to get back."

"The House of Spiders can only be found if it wants to be," the lagahoo said. "Or if someone leaves a trail, which *you* obviously did, inadvertently or otherwise. To go back now would be a death wish.

Don't you understand what those things are going to do? The fang is one of the only things on earth powerful enough to open the door between worlds and let the daughter of Death crawl through the cracks. They'll kill anyone in their way."

"Malcolm could be dead."

The lagahoo stared at him, looking genuinely puzzled. "You really care? Even knowing what he is?"

Eli sighed and allowed the magic to drop limply, like the ties of a rope, and the lagahoo fell to the ground, gasping for breath. Maybe it was because it was still wearing Malcolm's face, but Eli immediately felt guilty. He'd lost control. The magic . . . it had lit something in him. He looked down at his hands, which were trembling slightly. A droplet of blood bubbled at his nostril, and he wiped it away with the corner of his sleeve.

"You should go," Eli said quietly. "Before they find you."

The lagahoo scrambled to his feet, not wasting a moment.

"Wait," Eli said. "Not with his face." And then, guiltily, "Please."

The lagahoo cast him a strange, unreadable look. It looked as though it was about to say something, but instead, it just shook its head and continued down the alleyway, hands stuffed in its pockets like it was on a leisurely stroll. Eli watched it step into the open, and then it was no longer Malcolm; it was just a forgettable-looking white man, collar popped up, shoulders hunched, blending into the crowd.

Eli pulled out his phone and saw that he had a text from Sunny.

u safe?

Yeah

i'm with max. come pam's

Eli stuck his head around the corner to check that the coast was clear, and then, hastily, he jogged back toward the house. He had barely taken three steps, however, when he felt something tighten behind his rib cage, like all the air was being ripped from his lungs. Eli started to cough, but he couldn't catch his breath. He bent over, wheezing, and a few passersby cut him with sharp looks. He looked down at his hands for some explanation as to what was happening and found that his knuckles were cut and bloodied. There was blood and dirt under his nails, like he'd been digging. His body wasn't responding to him, because it wasn't his magic that it was reacting to. It was the magic he'd taken from Malcolm. Something was happening on the other end of it.

CHAPTER ELEVEN

MALCOLM

Malcolm was cocooned somewhere small and damp. The air was dank and earthy, and he was enveloped in complete darkness. When he lifted a hand in front of him, it hit a panel of musky wood. Terror rose in his chest. A casket. He was in a casket below the earth.

Immediately, he pounded his fists against the surface, determined to find some way to get out, but as he did, a slow trickle of soil crumbled through the cracks of wood above him and landed on his mouth.

He reached for the magic in him, but everything here felt numbed; even his yells sounded muted. He hit the wood, then hit it again, desperate for it to buckle or break, anything. Distantly, he became aware of pain splitting his knuckles, but his head was clouded by panic. He had to get out. He couldn't die here. Not after everything. He ignored the splinters and cuts and punched harder, frantic—

Malcolm wrenched forward with a gasp and remembered, haltingly, that he was not in a coffin. He was still in the House of Spiders, now bent over and retching as he tried to remember how to breathe.

"Did you see it?" came a voice behind him.

Mercy stood by the window. It had turned dark outside since they had arrived, and Malcolm watched the night bounce off her skin. It was easy to believe that she came from the bloodline of gods. She was at least as tall as Malcolm was, with sharp, angular features and high cheekbones. Her hands and arms were painted up to her elbows in sapphire-blue, and she was still draped in the gold jewelry she'd been buried in.

The first time Malcolm had met her, he'd been struck by how she was simultaneously nothing and everything like the stories made her out to be. They'd met several times since then, just enough that Malcolm had started to notice little imperfections: the soft, uncombed edges of her hair, the chalky paint on her arms smeared around the tips of her fingers and faded over her nails. There was something oddly human about it.

"I—yes. I saw," Malcolm said. It was difficult to concentrate. While they were still in the House of Spiders, it was not the same House of Spiders that the others had left him in. They were once again in the in-between world, neither living nor dead. It wasn't ideal. Malcolm worried that he'd been summoned to this place too many times. If he stayed there much longer, it was going to grow roots in him.

"I've been wanting to show you that for a long time," Mercy said. "But I didn't want to scare you. Something tells me you're strong enough now, though." Her eyes raked over him. "You seem different."

"So do you." Back then, Mercy had been wan and ghostlike. There was a certain solidity to her now, more flesh and bone. She'd fed. "What was that?"

"That was a memory of where your father first left me," Mercy said. If she was hurt by it, he couldn't tell by her voice. "Before I realized the spell I was under and clawed my way out. He buried me alive, six feet beneath the earth."

Malcolm knew this part. It was one of the first things she'd explained to him; how she had escaped the grave that Casper had buried her in, but that didn't mean she was free. Casper and the others had turned her into all but an apparition, bound between worlds. It was the reason he had first decided to trust her. He'd just wanted to help. To undo a single fragment of the damage his father had left in his wake.

"I know what you've done," Malcolm said. "They're all dead. All the names I found for you. You said that you just needed their blood to be free. You said you would give them a choice to do the right thing."

"Malcolm," Mercy sighed. She sounded almost sorry. "I did give them a choice. And each time, they sided with him. Even after everything, even though they knew in their hearts what was right, I couldn't sever their loyalty to him."

"So you killed them."

"Yes."

He'd half expected denial, more manipulation maybe, so he wasn't prepared for the soft, earnest admission.

"When I first woke up here, he made me think that I was at home. I went through all the motions of my everyday life. Cooked, cleaned, called my friends. But then I noticed little oddities. Small things he'd missed. Cartons mislabeled. Buttons missing from electrics. Weather that never changed. Little details that you wouldn't notice unless you looked closely. Your father had never been one to get caught up on the particulars of things. He was there, you see, in the dream, so I never looked too closely. But eventually, the more I noticed, the more the wrongness of it all became unavoidable. When

I slept, I would get the taste of dirt in my mouth. I would find these little needles of wood lodged in my palms that I didn't remember getting. There would be dirt under my nails that I couldn't scrub away. It took me a while to pick at the seams of his spell and realize what he had done. To realize where I'd been the whole time. I hadn't been sleeping next to him at all. I was buried, six feet under the earth, locked away in the world between the living and the dead." She tilted her head. "In an odd way, I think it was a gesture of kindness on his behalf. The deceit. So that I wouldn't suffer."

Malcolm felt something tight coil behind his ribs. "He still locked you in a cage."

"And I clawed my way out," Mercy said. "Just as you climbed above the circumstances he left you in."

Malcolm inhaled, but his lungs felt like sacks of compost.

"It doesn't bring me joy to see what's happened to your mother," Mercy said. "We were friends once upon a time. It must be hard for you."

"Yeah," Malcolm said. "It is."

It happened gradually. At first it was just small things, names of distant family members, the day of the week. She would put things down and forget where they were. She would repeat herself a lot in conversation. Malcolm found it funny at first. *Mum*, he'd say as she was once again cussing out their supposedly unruly neighbor for not separating their recycling. *I know this already. You told me earlier, remember? We had a whole conversation.* And she would laugh and roll her eyes, and they wouldn't mention it again. But then things started to take a turn for the worse. She would go to the supermarket and get lost on the way home, and Malcolm would spend hours roaming the estate looking for her, until some sympathetic neighbor brought her home. She would forget to pay bills and Malcolm would spend school nights eating cold food in the dark.

And her magic. That was perhaps the worst part of it all. When she wasn't concentrating, it seemed to ooze from her like melting candle wax. She would have sudden bouts of frustration, and every glass object would shatter around her. Malcolm would shuffle them down to the ER to have the glass shards picked out of both of them. More than once, Malcolm found her in the middle of the night nearly drowning in a flooded bedroom, water streaming in from her dreams, only to wake up disoriented. *I was dreaming I was home,* she would say. And Malcolm would bring her warm clothes and try to remind her *You are home, mum.*

Then of course, there was the night of the fire.

"I know what it's like to have no one. To be abandoned by your own blood. To have to carve your own space into the world with nothing but your own hands. My father was never around. My sisters never accepted me. So I understand, is all. I know how that kind of loneliness can eat you from the inside out. How it will infect everything around you."

Malcolm had to blink away the tears that were burning at his eyes. "Why are you saying this?"

"She's getting worse, isn't she?" Mercy said. "Has been for a while. And she's only going to deteriorate. You've been clinging to the last scraps of her, but when that finally fades away, what will you have left?"

She wasn't wrong. The doctors had handed Malcolm a leaflet cheerfully titled "Dealing with Alzheimer's Disease: Preparing for the Worst," and sometimes at night, when Malcolm was feeling particularly self-flagellating, he'd spend hours going down wormholes of internet threads and YouTube channels of people describing the utter deterioration of their loved ones. He watched them with a numb sort of detachedness. Even though some of the symptoms he read about matched up with hers, he couldn't picture his mother losing her quick words and fiery competence. Yet with every passing day, she would get more and more confused, and Malcolm could feel himself losing more of her.

"What are you suggesting?" The question slipped from Malcolm involuntarily.

"Well," Mercy said gently. "It's just as you did before. You'll do me a favor. In return, I will fix your mother."

He thought of what Pam had said. How Mercy was nothing but hunger and magic; that her anger and greed had eaten through to her until there was nothing left. Yet that wasn't quite true. When Malcolm looked at her, he saw something else in her. Something that he saw in himself, too. Pain. Maybe you had to be broken to see the cracks of it reflected in someone else, but Malcolm knew it was there. And while he didn't trust Mercy as far as he could throw her, he knew he could trust that.

"You'll fix her," Malcolm said. "She'll be like—like she was before?"

"Just like she was before. When you wake up tomorrow, it will be done. You'll never have to worry about being alone again."

It was a trick, Malcolm knew that, and yet his mind spun with thoughts of his mother. He'd caught her the other day standing in the middle of the kitchen with a defrosted chicken in the sink. She'd just been staring at it when Malcolm found her, and he couldn't have said how long she'd been there. *Casper?* she'd said, when she'd turned and seen Malcolm there. Something in Malcolm had turned to ash at that. *No, Mum*, he'd said. *It's me, Malcolm.*

"What do you want me to do?" Malcolm asked.

"It's simple," Mercy said. "Set me free."

Malcolm exhaled, but he could still feel the soil in the back of his mouth. Something had taken root in him.

"We both know what it's like to be in his shadow, Malcolm. To have him underestimate you, abandon you. It has to be you, don't you see?"

"Okay," Malcolm said. He looked at her then. He knew he might regret it, but at that moment, all he felt was a gradual breath of hope. "We have a deal."

CHAPTER TWELVE

MALCOLM

The sun filtered in through a gap in the curtains, and for a brief second, Malcolm was able to tell himself that what had happened the day before had just been a dream. He lay there, not quite willing to jinx it. He was scared that this was another trick, that he'd open his eyes and end up back in the House of Spiders. But no, he was home.

He could hear his mother through the wall, rustling around in the kitchen. Unable to ignore the rumble of his stomach, he got out of bed, following the smell of food. Pam was right about what she said before; using a lot of magic did make you hungry. Drowsily, Malcolm stumbled to his feet, taking inventory of his various aches and bruises with every movement. His head throbbed, and his knuckles were covered in scrapes, plus his throat still felt like it was caked in mud.

He found his mother frying ackee and saltfish. That in itself was cause enough to falter. These days, his mother moved around their flat like a ghost. There had come to be a fragility to her that Malcolm hadn't yet gotten to grips with. When Malcolm wasn't there, she spent most of her time sleeping and watching old reruns of game shows. Today, however, she looked like his mother as he knew her. He found her gently humming to herself, hips swaying to and fro while the frying pan spit and spluttered. The TV in the living room was playing last night's *EastEnders*, and there was a battered copy of a dog-eared mystery novel left open on the coffee table.

"Mum?" Malcolm asked. "You're cooking?"

It had become a rule between them since that time with the chicken: Malcolm did the cooking now. They even kept a Post-it Note above the stove to remind her, though today it seemed to have been discarded. Nothing was on fire yet, and Malcolm didn't have the heart to stop her.

"Uh-huh," his mum replied. "You hungry?"

Right on cue, Malcolm's stomach gave a treacherous rumble. His mother shot him a knowing look, and he smiled. "A little."

"That's what I thought. This will be ready soon, so wash your hands. Where have you been? I didn't hear you come in last night."

"Oh, um." He wasn't used to having to explain his whereabouts these days. His mother continued to give him a long, placid look. She would wait all day for a reply if she had to. "Just staying at a friend's."

"You didn't text or leave me a message." She pointed a wooden spoon at him. "I checked, in case you had and it slipped me."

"Sorry," Malcolm said. "I forgot."

His mother raised an eyebrow. "I suppose I can't fault you that. Which friend?"

"Huh?"

"It's 'excuse me,' not 'huh.' I know I raised you to have manners. I said which friend?"

Malcolm paused where he was soaping his hands under the tepid water.

"Corey Johnson." A blatant lie. Corey Johnson had been Malcolm's only friend throughout school, mostly due to the two of them falling to the bottom of the social food chain and having no one else to turn to. They didn't have anything in common except for the fact that they both watched anime and played video games. Malcolm's mum had always liked Corey's mum, though, so Malcolm knew that she wouldn't mind if he stayed there. He hadn't spoken to Corey in years, but he was also certain that his mother didn't have Mrs. Johnson's phone number in order to double-check the fact.

"Uh-huh." If his mother didn't believe him, she granted him the small mercy of not calling him out on it. "Come cut this sweet pepper for me," she said, so Malcolm did.

He listened to her talk for a while, about mostly inconsequential things: her friend Cynthia's grandson had gotten his license, the bulbs she'd planted a few months back had finally started to blossom, how she wanted to go to the bank this weekend, and what did Malcolm want for dinner? Malcolm was quiet the whole time, a sharp, hopeful fondness in his chest, until she gently elbowed him in the ribs. Could it really be that easy, Malcolm thought, that he might be able to have this every day?

"You lost your words?" she asked. "Didn't realize I was practicing a monologue."

"Sorry," Malcolm said, dropping his chin. "Just thinking."

"About what?"

Malcolm shrugged a shoulder. "You seem better today."

"I feel better," she said, with a determined nod. She stuck the spoon in her mouth, wrinkled her nose, then added some pepper to the pan. "The doctors said there would be good days and bad days, didn't they? But today's different. I feel like—myself."

Abruptly, Malcolm put down the knife and wrapped his arms around her in a tight hug from behind. He buried his nose in her shoulder, the way he used to when he was a kid. She smelled sweetly familiar, like hair oils and cocoa butter and fresh detergent.

His mum laughed, but after a moment, she turned around to hug him back. "What's got into you?" She pulled away to frown at him, her face wrinkled with concern. "You in trouble? You're not behind with your schoolwork again?"

"No. It's nothing." He hugged her again, and this time his voice came muffled against the shoulder of her dressing gown. "I just love you, is all."

She patted his hand. "I love you too," she said. "You know that."

"Of course."

"And I know things haven't been easy for you lately—"

"They will get better," Malcolm said. He leant back to look at her seriously now. It was the two of them, in it together as they had always been. "I promise you. I have a feeling that from now on, everything will be okay."

"Baby," she sighed. "You can't will this away."

Malcolm raised an eyebrow. He'd been told he looked like her, when he did that. "We'll see."

Malcolm left the flat with his belly full and his heart a little lighter. All he had to do was keep his promise, and he and his mother could have endless mornings like this one. Open a door, that was all he had to do. Open one door and Malcolm could keep his mother.

He'd left her on the phone with some lady from church, laughing about something that had come up in a sermon the week before. He'd kissed her cheek, and the image of the memory kept playing in his mind as he took his backpack and jogged for the bus, eyes glassy from tears the entire way.

It didn't occur to him that he might have to construct something to tell the others until he reached Pam's. When he got there, the store hadn't opened yet, but Sunny was outside. She leant against the shop window, a scuffed Converse on the wall, one hand balancing a roll-up between her fingers, the other absentmindedly scrolling through her phone.

Malcolm saw her before she saw him, and he watched her look up and take him in. He'd found it hard to read her that first day, but today she seemed to be particularly inscrutable. Malcolm wondered if it was something she actively schooled her face into. After a moment, she stubbed the cigarette out on the wall and pulled herself up.

"Look who rose from the dead," she said, blowing a last tendril of smoke from the corner of her mouth. Something in her tone felt like he was being made fun of, but it was lacking the usual sting of malice that used to leave him flustered and shamed at school. If anything, she sounded impressed. "It's you, then?"

"Uh," Malcolm said. "Yeah?"

"Prove it." She didn't appear to be joking. She stared at him until Malcolm held out his hand, palm up. He sent a little pinprick of magic into his arm, just as he had the day before, until the scab reopened with fresh blood. When he looked up, something had loosened in Sunny's expression, though she didn't look fully at ease.

"So, you're all right, then," Sunny said, running a skeptical eye over him. "I mean, you seem to be in one piece."

"I guess."

"*I guess*," Sunny mimicked. "Something tells me you could literally be bleeding out from every artery in your body, and you'd still be like, '*I guess*.'"

"Well," Malcolm said. "Maybe not every artery."

Sunny's mouth twitched upward. Instead of answering, she looked over one shoulder to call inside, "Maxine, come out here."

Max's head popped from behind the door a second later.

"What?" she snapped, and then she saw Malcolm and her eyes widened comically behind her glasses. "Malcolm!"

Malcolm barely had time to register what was happening before she was in front of him, flinging her arms around him. Malcolm froze. Casual affection wasn't something that came naturally to him, and he had no idea what to do with his hands or his arms or how to stand. He didn't want to hurt her feelings, though, so he patted her a few times on the back and tried to pretend like it was something he did every day. "You're here! Eli, come, Malcolm's here, and he's not dead! Where have you been? Are you okay?" She pulled back to examine him. "You weren't body-swapped again, were you?"

"Um, no." Malcolm glanced over to Sunny, but she was just watching the entire exchange with a droll kind of amusement. "Wait, what was that about body-swapping?"

"Don't worry about it," Max said, and hugged him again.

Truthfully, he hadn't expected such a warm reception, and it left him feeling off-kilter. It was an odd conflict; his chest flushed with warmth and yet his stomach knotted with guilt. They'd accepted him so easily, and Malcolm knew that he didn't deserve it.

"I'm assuming we're out here yelling for a reason," Eli asked as he slunk into the doorway. He was wearing the same clothes as the day before, and he looked like he hadn't slept. Actually, as Malcolm took in each of their faces, he realized they all looked as though they could use some rest. Eli faltered when he saw Malcolm, and something passed over his face that Malcolm couldn't quite read. A second later, it was gone. "Oh. You're back."

Malcolm shuffled uncomfortably, which was hard to do with Max's arm still laced around him. "Hey."

Eli exchanged a wordless look with Sunny, and it wasn't until she nodded that he seemed to relax a fragment. "Where have you been?"

"I was stuck in the house," Malcolm said. "I couldn't get away."

"We waited for you," Max said. "But there was a whole thing—"

"Lagahoo," Eli interjected.

"—and then the doorway moved and none of the spells were working. We couldn't find you, so we thought maybe you were, you know—"

"Dead," Sunny finished.

"And then Eli's magic started acting crazy and blah blah blah, we ended up here."

"Oh." Something swooped in the depths of his gut. "You waited for me?"

"I promised we would," Eli replied, and it was the way he said it, without a single moment of hesitance, that brought Malcolm up short.

He wasn't quite brave enough to see what was on their faces, so instead, he looked down at his arm, where the line he'd just cut was starting to itch.

"Anyway, so yeah, we were kind of freaking out," Max continued. "But hey, the good news is we got the fang!"

Malcolm could feel his heart thudding mutinously behind his ribs, but he kept his expression carefully impassive. "Yeah?"

"Yep. Bad news is, we thought you were dead. Pam's AWOL, so we kinda didn't know what to do with it. We were up all night researching. But then we thought—well, Eli, show him what you found."

"Oh. Yeah, here."

He pulled a photograph from his back pocket. It was crumpled from having been shoved into the front pouch of his hoodie, but Malcolm recognized it instantly. He'd found it a while back in his mother's belongings. They'd been flicking through a box of memorabilia, a pastime that he'd resort to sometimes when she was stressed and not remembering things well.

It was a photo of a group of young people standing on the front step of a large Georgian house. There were ten of them in total, including his parents. Malcolm instantly recognized Casper in the back, a hand up to shield his eyes from the sun. He looked a little younger than the others, but there was something in the casual slump of his shoulders, the coy, knowing cock of his smile. He looked like a leader. Though it pained Malcolm to admit it, this young version of his father did look uncannily like Malcolm. His mother was on the other side of the group, smiling, wearing big gold hoops and double denim. But that wasn't what caught his eye. What made him pause was that there, behind them, was a woman he hadn't recognized at the time. *Who is that?* Malcolm had asked his mother, who had immediately frozen and put the photo away. *Don't ask me that,* she'd said. *That's a question for your father.* It was just a few days after that conversation that Mercy had appeared in his dreams.

When Malcolm looked up, the others were still waiting for his response.

"That's my dad," Malcolm admitted. Casper had been just twenty-one then, not much older than Malcolm was now. Casper had just taken his place as the youngest leader of the House of Spiders and had already begun cementing his legacy as the duppy king of North London. He looked young and at ease. He looked *happy.*

"Told you," Sunny said, pointing at Eli. "You owe me a fiver."

"They called it the House of Spiders," Eli said. "It was where they used to meet in secret. They were the ones that locked her away."

And it was true. As Malcolm dug more into his parents' history, he had uncovered the truth. The photo was proof of it all: there was his uncle Erwin, and so many other familiar faces from his childhood. Tiny, the six-foot-eight black-cabdriver who always brought his mum flowers whenever he came to the house. Martin, who smelled strongly of cigarettes and who was never on time. There were more he recognized, faces he'd seen before but hadn't necessarily been able to put names to until Mercy gave them to him. Romeo. Kev and Ronnie, the twins. Jem, the seer man. And of course, George. Malcolm recognized them all. It had been him, after all, who had tracked them down and handed their whereabouts to Mercy. Some had been more difficult to find than others. Some had taken great lengths to stay hidden. But all Malcolm had to do was say his name and doors would open for him. Shame warmed his cheeks, and he forced himself to look away from the photo.

"It was bothering me," Max said. "I've been looking through all the books. The spell your father used to lock her away, it didn't keep her alive. If all the stories are true, Mercy ate so much magic that she became reliant on it. Without magic, she should have wasted away by now."

"My dad thought someone had betrayed him," Malcolm said, keeping his voice perfectly even. "That someone was secretly keeping her alive."

"That's what we thought," Max said. "We did some Googling, but almost everyone we could find linked to the House of Spiders is dead. The others, it was like they didn't even exist. If someone is keeping her alive, we have no idea who it could be."

"So what do we do?" Malcolm asked.

"Well." Eli's eyes ran over him thoughtfully. "Actually, that's where we were thinking you came in."

The woman who answered the door was pretty and in her forties, with freshly pressed hair and a dressing gown wrapped tightly around her body. She took each of them in with a frown and folded her arms. In hindsight, Malcolm did suppose it was weird, four unfamiliar teenagers turning up at your front door in the middle of a weekday.

"Can I help you?" the lady asked.

She looked nothing like his mother. That was the first thing Malcolm noticed. She was small and shapely, where Malcolm's mother had always been tall and long-limbed. Her nails were perfectly manicured, and she wore two gleaming rings on her ring finger: a sparkling diamond, just the right side of flashy, and a sleek silver wedding band.

The others were taking Malcolm's lead, waiting for him to answer, yet when Malcolm opened his mouth to reply, he found himself unable to form a sentence.

The woman looked between them, confused. "Well?"

"Hi," Max said, when it became clear that Malcolm wasn't going to speak. She gently squeezed his elbow as she steered him behind her. "Are you Mrs. King?"

"Yes?"

"Sorry to bother you. We're looking for Casper. Is he around?"

The woman's frown only intensified. "There's no one by that name here."

"Andrew," Malcolm corrected Max, and he felt his cheeks warm as their gazes landed on him. "His name's Andrew. Casper's a . . . it's, uh. An old nickname."

Of course his father didn't go by Casper here. The only people who knew that name were the people who whispered about the duppy king, but it was becoming rapidly evident that this woman possessed zero knowledge of either the existence of magic or Casper's reputation in their world. Casper King was the boogie man that haunted their ends. Andrew King, however, was a respectable, hardworking father who worked in the city and drove an Audi.

"And what is it, exactly, that you want with my husband?" the woman asked.

It was Sunny who stepped forward with a prompt lie. "We're doing a school project," she said. She didn't so much as stutter. "Mr. King offered to give us career advice."

"Career advice," she repeated skeptically.

"Uh-huh. It was hard to come by someone with his expertise, so we're all very excited."

"And you're all . . . interested in finance." Malcolm caught her gaze lingering on the holes in his jeans and felt his face warm with shame.

"You bet," Sunny said. She was using the same voice that Malcolm would shift to, sometimes, when he was talking to social care workers or his welfare case manager.

"Sure," Eli agreed. "We just love those . . . numbers."

"Well, okay." Mrs. King looked deeply confused. "I suppose you can come in and wait. I'll get Andrew."

Malcolm had never been inside his father's house before, and somehow it was worse than he expected. The first thing that greeted them was a family portrait, the kind you took in front of a fireplace and then sent around in Christmas cards. There were pairs of shoes by the door, the kids' book bags. The place had been newly renovated, by the looks of things. It was clean and airy and bright. They followed Casper's wife inside, who disappeared into the house to look for her husband. Malcolm passed drawings the kids had done of their parents displayed next to wedding photos. There was no indication that Casper even had another son.

It had been a miscalculation to come inside. There was abstractly knowing that your father abandoned you to start a new family, and then there was walking into their big Muswell Hill house, past coats hung for four and snapshots from birthdays that Malcolm had never been invited to. He picked up a framed holiday photo of the four of them on a sandy beach. Wherever they'd been, it looked hot. Malcolm had never even been on a plane before.

Sunny whistled. "Shit, Grim, your dad's place is nice." She stopped by a random ugly, headless sculpture and squinted at it. "You think this is worth anything?"

"Don't even think about it," Max said, and swiftly steered her away.

In any other context, Malcolm might've laughed, but it hit him in that moment just how little he knew his father. His father's disappearance had left a huge, gaping hole in his life, and it had eclipsed everything for him. It changed the way he defined himself, his understanding of family, his ability to trust people. As he wandered around the house, it occurred to Malcolm for the first time that this was not a mutual feeling. Malcolm's absence had barely made a dent in Casper's life. There was no space for him here.

"Hey," Eli said, shaking him from his thoughts. "You okay?"

Sunny and Max had disappeared up ahead; they were poking their heads into each room, not even bothering to hide their curiosity.

Malcolm didn't know how to answer, not without revealing too much of himself, so he just shrugged.

"This must be weird," Eli said.

"Yeah." Truthfully, Malcolm was embarrassed by how much this was affecting him. This place *was* nice, with its high ceilings and hardwood floors and long, neatly kept garden. It was a corner house, too, which Malcolm thought was odd. His parents had always cautioned him against living in houses at the end of the street because they were easier to break into. He supposed they probably didn't have to worry about that in this area. They probably had CCTV and a neighborhood watch that shared recipes on their group chat.

"I have to say, when I pictured where the duppy king lived, it wasn't somewhere like this," Eli murmured.

"Yeah," Malcolm admitted. "Me neither."

"I was thinking more, like, Gothic manor. Or an ice castle. Maybe a cabin in the woods."

"Cabin in the woods is impractical," Malcolm replied automatically. "No Wi-Fi."

There was a beat; then, like a dam breaking, they were both laughing. It wasn't even particularly funny, but the buildup of the last few days had maybe made them slightly hysterical. Plus it felt good, Malcolm realized, to share the absurdity of the situation with someone else.

"I'm going to have a place like this one day," Eli said. His hands were stuffed in his pockets, and he was smiling crookedly, but Malcolm could tell he meant it. "Somewhere I don't have to worry about Pam cussing me out for sleeping past nine a.m."

"Yeah?"

"I mean, your dad did it. I don't see why we couldn't." *We.* The word wasn't lost on Malcolm. "You work with cars, right?"

"How do you know that?"

"Oh," Eli said. He seemed embarrassed by the question. "I don't know. You must have mentioned it."

"Right," Malcolm said, though he didn't remember that, since it wasn't something he ever tried to be open about. "Well, not anymore. My dad and I used to when I was a kid. I hated it. I think I just went along with it so I could spend time with him. He'd have all his friends hanging out in the garage, playing music, cracking jokes. It made me feel, I don't know, grown. Like I was part of something."

"He had you fixing cars as a kid?"

"Yeah," Malcolm said. "He'd buy them used, fix them up a little, double the price, and sell them as new. Pretty sure I was changing number plates before I could even ride a bike. I didn't realize until I was older that it was probably not exactly legal."

He didn't know why he'd admitted that—in fact, it had always been something he'd been ashamed of—but standing there, in his father's home, he felt an uncharacteristic and overwhelming urge to be seen.

Eli didn't laugh. Didn't comment on the depressing realities of his childhood either, just raised his eyebrows.

"So what do you actually wanna do?" Eli asked. "You know, if it's not scamming car buyers."

"I, uh, like to cook," Malcolm said. He didn't know why it felt like such a precarious thing, just offering up that tiny admission, but it did. "My mum taught me. I don't know, it's dumb. I always imagined we'd move somewhere far away. Maybe outside of London. Somewhere with a big kitchen."

He'd never said the words out loud before, and he felt a little like he'd just pried open his rib cage with a crowbar.

"It's not dumb," Eli said, and he said it with such certainty that Malcolm almost believed him.

"What about you?"

"Me . . ." Eli laughed. "I don't know. Max keeps hounding me about applying to college, but . . . I mean, I don't even remember what I wanted to do with my life before all of this."

"Sometimes you just have to focus on making it through the day," Malcolm said.

Eli gave him an odd look. "Right," he said.

Malcolm figured he'd been too presumptuous and that Eli was going to tell him to mind his business. Whatever he was about to say, however, was interrupted by the looming shadow of his father appearing in the doorway. He wasn't wearing the Andrew King facade. His rage was palpable, and this, at least, was familiar to Malcolm.

"Outside," Casper said. "Now."

The door had barely closed before he spun on Malcolm. They were roughly the same height, but under the force of his temper, Malcolm felt every centimeter of the difference.

"What on earth," Casper said venomously, "made you think you could come here?"

Malcolm felt a surge of anger at the core of his chest but found that he couldn't summon an answer.

"Well?" Casper demanded. "What is it? Did you have something to prove? Did you come here to provoke me?"

"No—no, of course not."

"I didn't teach you to mumble. You have something to tell me, I want to hear you say it with your whole chest."

"That's not why I'm here."

"No?" Casper said. "Then what is it?"

"We have Osebo's fang." He'd meant to say it himself, but a voice behind him cut in before he could stammer out another response. It was Sunny. Malcolm looked over his shoulder to see that the three of them had followed him outside and were now leaning in the doorway.

"Sorry to interrupt," Eli said, though he didn't sound very sorry. "But that is what you were looking for, wasn't it? The fang."

Casper's expression was one of genuine surprise before he carefully masked it. "You found it?"

Malcolm nodded. He was mortified that even after all these years, he was still so unable to defend himself, but the real shame came from the fact that the others had witnessed it.

"Where?" Casper asked.

"We stole it," Malcolm said, and then because this part felt important: "From a lagahoo."

Malcolm watched Casper's face closely as he registered that, and it was like he was experiencing all seven stages of grief in the span of three seconds. Then, to Malcolm's horror, he started to laugh.

"Well," Casper said, once he'd caught his breath. "Okay then. Nicely played."

He ran a hand over his face, looking exhausted, and the whites of his eyes were a little bloodshot, like perhaps he hadn't been sleeping well. Malcolm wondered if Mercy had made any trips to his dreams as she had to his, and if he was frightened by her too. It occurred to Malcolm that he probably was, and he felt a small pang of satisfaction.

"We have a plan to stop her," Malcolm said.

"And you think I don't have a plan of my own."

"I know you do," Malcolm sighed. With at least three backup plans, probably, all of which most likely guaranteed his survival at everyone's expense. "But we're not going to do it that way."

"No?" And there was that laugh again, like this was a game for him. "I suppose this must be the part where you tell me that you're not going to just hand over the fang either." His tone was light, amicable even, now that the others were present, but Malcolm knew him enough to be able to read the indignation behind his eyes. He was pissed, and Malcolm was going to pay for this. "I'm assuming that's what all the theatrics are about. You want something in return."

"No," Malcolm said. He swallowed and consciously kept his gaze level with his father's. "We're going to stop Mercy. But if you want the fang, then we're going to do it our way."

There was a slight twitch in Casper's eyebrow. "Your way?"

Malcolm turned to the others, and it was the certainty in their gazes that stopped his voice from wavering. "We're going to recreate your spell."

CHAPTER THIRTEEN

ELI

Eli looked mournfully down at his trainers, now destroyed after the past week's action. He and Sunny had left Max and Malcolm with Casper, and the two of them were perched at their usual spot by the bus stop. They were waiting for Legs. Of course, because Legs was Legs, he was late. Eli had been inwardly cussing up a stream of expletives for the entirety of the half an hour they'd been waiting, but logically he didn't really have anyone to blame but himself.

He'd been the one to volunteer himself for Legs duty. The truth was that being in Casper's presence unnerved him. Eli kept thinking of all the stories he'd heard about the duppy king: that his veins spilled black, that he could find you in your dreams, that he'd once caught a bullet in the palm of his hand, just like Queen Nanny in the Maroon Wars.

Now that Eli found himself waiting in the cold for thirty minutes, however, he started to regret the decision.

"This is a bad idea," Sunny grumbled.

"Well, yeah, obviously," Eli said. "But you were the one that wanted to call him."

"Not the Legs part." Sunny sighed. "Everything else."

Eli rubbed his palms together. It was beginning to get dark outside, and the chill was nibbling at his fingers. "You've made that clear. Repeatedly."

"Someone needs to," Sunny said. "I don't trust him."

"Who?"

"Casper." She tilted her head thoughtfully. "Malcolm . . . he's all right, I guess. A little on the fragile side, but probably harmless."

"Fragile?" Eli scoffed. "He's like six feet tall."

"That's not what I meant."

"I know," Eli sighed. "Look, I don't trust Casper either, but what are our other options?"

"We could make a run for it. I'm thinking Europe. You reckon we could bump the Eurostar? We could be in Amsterdam by tomorrow."

"And get dashed off in Ashford?" Eli snorted. "I'm good, actually."

Sunny gave an unladylike laugh, but Eli could tell that underneath the bravado, she was being serious. Eli could say the word and she'd have them tickets out of there within a heartbeat.

"Look," Eli said. "I know this is dangerous. If you don't want to go through with this, I get it. I'm not forcing you."

"Oh," Sunny said, and Eli immediately regretted it. "You're not forcing me to?"

"That's not what I meant," Eli protested, but it was too late.

"Well, since you're not forcing me to, I'll just head home, then. Might order in some Nando's. Catch up on the latest episode of *Love Island*. You know, since you're not forcing me to."

Eli looked up at the sky. "I hate when you get like this."

"The feeling's mutual. So. You gonna tell him?"

"Tell who what?"

"Don't act dumb." She leant forward to flick him on the forehead. "Your bredrin. He's gonna figure out you stole his magic."

"I saved his life."

"Semantics."

Eli shrugged. He'd been avoiding thinking about it too closely. He looked down at the lines of his palm so he wouldn't have to read whatever was in Sunny's expression.

"I think . . . it might be doing something to me."

"What?"

"The magic. I don't feel like myself."

Sunny leant back to look at him properly, and Eli shifted under the weight of her gaze. "What do you mean?"

"I don't know. When we were back at the House of Spiders, the lagahoo said something to me. It told me I was *of the earth*."

The humor had vanished from her expression. She'd gone very still, like she was braced for a fight. "What does that mean?"

"I don't know," Eli said. "But I should probably find out, right?"

Sunny opened her mouth to reply, but Eli never got to hear what she was about to say because it was then that Legs finally deigned to grace them with his presence.

The thing about Legs was that he had the perpetual energy of an early 2000s garage hype man. Everything about him was loud: his pastel pink locs, his tie-dye graphic tee, his Fila bucket hat and matching fluorescent joggers. Eli had run into him at Carnival once, and he'd been wearing a puffer jacket even though it was the hottest day of the year. There was a lot to be said about Legs, but the one thing you couldn't question was his dedication to the aesthetic.

As soon as Legs saw them, his expression brightened into

something comically insincere, and Eli found himself reliving their last interaction, when Legs had hustled them with some dodgy information that had resulted in Eli walking with a limp for a week after his broken bone healed wrong. Eli knew for a fact that Legs was badmind enough to pretend not to remember, and he'd bet Sunny a fiver beforehand that he wouldn't even bring it up.

"Sunny, what you saying? You're looking nice, yeah? New hair? I like it. Eli." He paused, grinning wickedly. "We good?"

"We're good," Sunny answered before the rebuttal had a chance to leave Eli's tongue. "Did you bring what we asked?"

"Yeah, yeah. Listen, let me tell you, though, I had to search high and low for some of this stuff." He pulled the backpack from his shoulder and started to unpack its contents onto the bus stop bench. "Had to go to Brummie. You know, with the gold teeth?"

"Short, with the locs?" Sunny asked.

"Nah, that's Dennis from Birmingham. Brummie's not an actual Brummie, he's a Scouser. Dunno why we call him that. Anyway, he came through, said he knew this guy from Elephant and Castle that can get you anything. And when I say anything, I mean *anything*. Swear down, Brummie says this brudda can even get you, like, human remains if you're into that kinda thing."

"We're not," Eli said at the exact same time that Sunny asked, "How much?"

"Anyways, when Brummie told me, I was like, *serious?* 'Cause you know he's full of shit most of the time. But hear him, yeah, said he sold a whole human skull just the other week. I was like, rah, 'cause you know there's duppy magic, and then there's *duppy* magic, but I guess his bredrin's been making serious bread off it. Just bought a flat in Tooting—two-bedroom, two bathroom, a proper driveway and everything."

Eli unfolded the piece of paper from his back pocket, a

checklist that Casper had given him of everything they'd need for the spell to work, and sorted through the plastic bag Legs had just handed them. Most of the ingredients were natural stuff they often came across for bush medicine and rootwork, an old kind of folk alchemy that Pam had taught them: pomegranate oils, witch sticks, jars of dried leaves. Things you couldn't exactly get at your local corner shop.

"You're really going to do it," Legs said after a moment. He was shifting from leg to leg, and if he was anyone else, Eli might have thought he was nervous, but that was just Legs's hyperactive baseline. "You're gonna recreate the spell they did all those years ago?"

"How do you know about that?" Eli frowned.

"I hear things, innit," Legs said, and was quiet for exactly three seconds before he began talking again. "You know the last people that did it are all dead. Hearts pulled out. Like, literally. Out their chests."

"Well," Sunny said. "Not all of them."

"So it *is* true what they're saying." Legs lowered his voice, like the bus stop wasn't completely empty aside from one tired-looking woman in headphones and a nurse's uniform who was forcibly ignoring them. "You lot are running with the duppy king now."

Eli raised his eyebrows at Sunny. That meant *this one's all you.* Sunny rolled her eyes in response. That meant *okay, fine, but we're committing to this.*

"Yeah," Sunny said. "I guess we are."

He looked genuinely impressed. "So, like. If I help you lot with this, really . . . I'm helping the duppy king."

"Sure," Sunny said. "You can think of it that way if you want."

"Cool, cool." Legs seemed mollified now that he had this information. "So, have you ever, like—"

He raised his eyebrows meaningfully. Eli and Sunny stared at him.

"You ever kill a man and bring him back, just to flex?"

"That . . ." Eli took a deep breath. "That would be murder."

"Would it, though?" Legs said. "Like, technically?"

"Okay," Sunny cut in. "Eli, was that everything on the list?"

"Yeah," Eli said begrudgingly. "That was everything."

"Course it is," Legs said, and just like that he was back to smiling. "I told you I'd come through."

"How much?" Sunny asked.

"So cynical, Sunshine." Legs grinned. "All right, all right. How about . . . for you, just owe me a favor."

"And there it is," Eli sighed. He turned to leave, fully ready to call it a day, only Sunny grabbed him by the elbow and pulled him back. She scowled at Legs, weighing their options, and after a moment, she relented.

"What kind of favor?" Sunny asked.

"A proportional one." Legs leant back across the grimy bus stop glass, arms crossed, all smiles. "I'm not gonna ask you to, like, murder someone for me. Though I guess shit like that wouldn't matter to you anymore, since you're running with the duppy king now."

"Wow," Sunny said flatly. "That's so reassuring. How could we not agree to your extremely vague and ominous terms?"

"A favor. Take it or leave it."

"Fine," Eli cut in. "A favor. And just one, so don't start getting gassed."

"A favor from the duppy king." Legs grinned. "Today is a good day."

"That's not—" Eli started to protest, but Sunny just put a hand on his arm and shook her head. This wasn't the hill to die on.

"You can have your favor," Sunny said, though she sounded like she wanted to laugh. "But keep the whole Casper thing quiet, yeah?"

"As a mouse," Legs said, and mimed zipping his mouth shut. Eli rolled his eyes. He had no doubt that this would spread across the entirety of North London before the sun even set.

They found Max, Malcolm, and Casper in a corner table at Pam's, bent over scrawlings of spells like medieval kings in a war room. Max had initially been thrilled when Eli had shown her the notes he'd found from the House of Spiders, but he could tell from her expression that any excitement she'd possessed had long since waned under Casper's tutelage. He was supposed to be teaching her how to recreate the spell he'd done all those years before, but instead, he and Malcolm seemed to be engaged in an intense, murmured conversation, while Max's head swiveled between them like a spectator at a tennis match.

"I'm telling you," Casper was saying. "Even channeling the magic from the fang, it won't be enough to hold her for long. In my day"—and at this, both Max and Malcolm gave a wholehearted roll of their eyes—"it took eight of the most powerful witches in the world giving everything they had to seal that door. *Eight.* Not four untrained, frankly *disorderly* teenagers—"

"Respectfully, Mr. King," Max interjected, "Malcolm has the same magic that you do. And Sunny and Eli and I were taught by Pam, just like you were."

"Pam? Teach me?" At this, Casper laughed. "Lord have mercy, is that what she's been telling you? The only thing that woman taught me is what *not* to do. Not to be so frightened of my own kin that I hide away. Not to turn my back on the people that need me. Not to spend decades, shit, probably centuries, if we're being honest, sitting on the fence because I'm too frightened to pick a damn side."

"You don't need to be disrespectful . . . ," Max started, but Casper's voice boomed over her.

"Oh, Auntie Pam has got you hooked, hasn't she, little girl? I feel sorry for you. You think you know that woman? You don't know anything about her. She's pulling you into war, and you don't even know you're blindfolded."

Eli realized he should probably intervene. He went to cross the room but stopped when a walking stick landed in front of him. He looked up to find Mr. Palmer, a regular who came by once a week to pick up red pea soup and dumplings.

"Hello, young man," Mr. Palmer said. Beside him, Sunny dipped and hurried across the room to hide behind the counter. Max immediately leapt to her feet and disappeared into the back. Eli didn't blame them. Mr. Palmer was a nice man, but he had a tendency to pry. If you got trapped in conversation with him, it was nearly impossible to escape.

"Hi, Mr. Palmer," Eli said. "Are you keeping well?"

"Not as well as you, I hear." Mr. Palmer sniffed. "My nephew Peter tells me that he heard you're following around the duppy king. I told him *not Elijah*. Not that good-mannered young man that works so hard to better our community. He would never lower himself to such devilry. But then I walk in here, and who do I see?"

They both turned to look where Malcolm was still being quietly lectured by his father.

Eli resisted a laugh. He knew Legs could run his mouth, but this was a record pace even for him. He snuck a glance over Mr. Palmer's shoulder at Sunny, who mouthed *devilry* and snickered.

"Yeah, well, you can tell Peter I haven't forgotten about the tenner he owes me. How about I get you something to drink, Mr. Palmer? On the house. You want a ginger beer?"

He used the excuse to duck behind the counter, where Max was placing trays of food she was carrying out from the back. He was met with a gust of heat as he entered the kitchen, and he pulled down the neck of his T-shirt to fan himself.

"Uh, thought you were keeping Casper at his place?" Eli asked, nodding toward the main floor. "Didn't Pam banish him from the diner? You know. For life?"

"I unpicked the spells barring him," Max said, and then, at Eli's raised eyebrows: "What? It's not like Pam's around. I can break rules too, you know. Besides, what else were we supposed to do with him?"

"Where is the old witch?" Sunny asked. She handed the bag of their findings to Max, who immediately tipped it upside down onto the counter to sort through it.

"Dunno. Haven't seen her. You know how she gets." To say that Pam was elusive was an understatement. She tended to disappear for days at a time without any warning and then reappear later with no explanation as to where she had been or what she'd been doing. *Wha*, she'd snapped at Eli the one time he'd made the mistake of asking where she'd been. *Are you mi probation office? Mi under house arrest?*

"How are things going here?" Eli asked.

"Slow," Max said. She sifted through the various ingredients, picking one up, sniffing, then humming in approval. "There's still so much Casper refuses to say. The main problem is that in order to cast the spell again, we'll need to unpick the existing one. Which hypothetically shouldn't be a problem, since it's already fraying at the edges."

"Okay," Eli said. "I'm sensing a *but* here."

"Like I said. It should be simple. *Hypothetically*." Max looked like she was about three seconds away from pulling out her hair. "Except for the fact that I have, like, a million questions for Casper, who apparently crafted this spell to exist like a minefield, so that if you pull even just *one* of the wrong threads, it will explode in your face. Getting any information from him is like getting blood from a stone. Plus, this magic . . . it's more than a little above our pay grade.

So, yes, *hypothetically*, it should be simple, and maybe it would be if Malcolm's dad wasn't such a raging—"

"Max."

"Right. Sorry." She shoved an unruly curl behind her ear. "I'm working on it, is all."

"He doesn't trust that we can do this," Eli said. He glanced through the kitchen doors to where Casper was still reclined in his seat, ceaselessly ranting about something else.

"He thinks his way is the only way to end it," Max said. His way being that they simply plunge Osebo's fang between Mercy's ribs and let it eat the magic from her inside out.

"Maybe he's right." Sunny shrugged. "You know we're only delaying the inevitable."

"No," Eli said. As far as they were aware, Mercy didn't even know that they had the fang at this point. If she found out, she would only be a bigger threat. Eli was exhausted. It felt like a curse, this endless cycle of trying to fix the mistakes of the generation before them for new problems to spring up each time. "We use it as a last resort only."

"Okay," Max said. "If you're certain."

Eli didn't quite have the heart to tell her that if there was one thing he craved, he grappled and yearned for, it was the single promise of certainty.

Malcolm was folded up on one of the squeaky plastic chairs, looking anywhere but in his father's direction. He looked like he needed rescuing. Eli hesitated, then ducked back through the kitchen doorway into the main diner.

"Malcolm, can we talk?" He felt Casper's gaze land on him, cool and calculating. "It'll be quick."

Malcolm glanced in Casper's direction, but then he nodded and followed Eli out to the hallway. They ended up sitting on the stairs leading to the upstairs flat, which was the only place in the cramped building with any semblance of privacy.

"What happened to your hands?" Eli asked once they were alone. There was bruising across the knuckles, swollen and tender-looking, like he'd gotten into a fight. The same sort of cuts and bruises that had been across Eli's own hands when he'd lost control of his magic and felt like he was suffocating. Eli's hands had since healed, and he hadn't known how to broach the subject. Not without revealing everything.

Malcolm shoved them into his pockets. "It's fine," he said.

"I can probably fix that for you, you know," Eli offered.

"No." The refusal was blunt, and from anyone else, Eli might've thought that he was angry. But Eli was beginning to learn Malcolm's silences. He had more to say, Eli knew; it just needed to be coaxed out of him. "I . . . knocked it. When I was trying to escape."

"Oh." Eli kept his face carefully neutral. "Are you okay?"

From one room over, they caught a burst of muffled laughter from Sunny and Max.

Malcolm picked at one of the scabs on his knuckle, and fresh blood welled.

"I will be," Malcolm said. "When this is all over."

As if thinking the same thing, they both looked through the door toward Casper, who was now slumped in his seat and flipping through a newspaper, reading glasses balancing on the end of his nose. From here, he just looked like a regular guy.

"Is he . . ." *That bad?* Eli almost said, before catching himself. "Like everyone says?"

"Honestly, I don't know. I haven't seen him since I was twelve. I think that's how he still sees me. As that little kid." Malcolm shook his head. "I do kind of get it, though. The urge to leave."

"That doesn't mean you're like him."

Malcolm gave a humorless laugh. "Yeah, everyone keeps saying that." He took a deep breath before speaking his next words. "He told me something while you were gone. He said that when they locked Mercy away, he claimed most of her magic for himself, but he also took a piece and hid it away. I think he knew that the magic he had would dry up one day, or he suspected one of the others would betray him, and he needed a backup plan."

Eli's head perked up at that. "So he hid it? Where?"

"He wouldn't tell me. He said he's the only person that knows, and that it's going to stay that way. He likes to play games."

"Maybe he's just trying to keep you safe."

Eli caught a look that seemed to be almost sympathetic before Malcolm shrugged it off. "Maybe" was all he said.

Truthfully, Malcolm wasn't the only one who was ready to be through with this. Eli had barely slept since it had started. The nosebleeds were getting worse, and he was frequently racked with headaches that lasted for hours on end. He wanted to sleep and rest and take a breather to figure things out. Only, Eli had no idea what his life would look like a week from now. They'd be compensated enough for the fang that they should be able to get through the next couple of months, but Eli knew how quickly things could dry up. Pam had mentioned something about a den of soucouyants in Lewisham that he and Sunny had been meaning to check out, so that was at least one paycheck he could count on. But still. Soon the summer would be over, and Max would go back to Sixth Form, Sunny would probably disappear doing god-knows-what with god-knows-who as she often tended to, and Eli . . . Eli would have nothing but an unfinished college application and more unanswered questions.

"Did you mean what you said back at your dad's house?" Eli asked.

"Huh?" Malcolm looked up from where he was pulling on the strings of his hoodie. He had coiled himself up so small that it was easy to forget he was over six feet tall.

"About leaving."

"Nah," Malcolm said, deadpan. "I'm gonna die never having left Edmonton."

Eli huffed a laugh, knocked their shoulders together. "I'm being serious."

Malcolm's brow was furrowed in that contemplative way of his. "It would be nice to start fresh, I guess. Someplace new. Somewhere where I don't have to carry all this—this stuff with me."

"You think it would be different?"

For so long, Eli had been frugal with his dreams. His focus hadn't extended past basic requirements: keeping his lungs breathing, his heart beating, his stomach full, the lights on for another month. Wanting anything past that seemed like a luxury.

Abruptly, Malcolm turned to Eli. "I have to tell you something," he said, only at the exact same time, Eli turned to Malcolm too.

"About that night you were attacked—"

"Oh," Malcolm said. They stared at each other, then both laughed, embarrassed. "Sorry. You go first."

"No, uh. It's nothing. What were you going to say?"

"I—" Malcolm started, but it was then that Sunny reappeared in the doorway.

"You lot need to get back in here," she said. "Max wants to run through something, and she's doing that thing where she's being really intense. Her and Casper are going at it again."

"Sure," Eli told Sunny. "We'll be one sec."

He waited until she'd gone back inside before turning back to Malcolm, who seemed to be studiously avoiding eye contact.

"What were you saying?"

"Nothing. Don't worry about it."

"Okay," Eli said. "Look, I know things are messed up at the moment, but it will be over soon. Five years from now, we'll be looking back on this laughing."

Malcolm gave him an odd look; that same, slanting half smile. "You sound so sure."

"I am," he said. "Tomorrow we'll end this for good."

He bumped their fists together.

"Yeah," Malcolm agreed. "Tomorrow."

CHAPTER FOURTEEN

MALCOLM

The thing was, Malcolm didn't have until tomorrow.

He waited until the others had fallen asleep. They'd set Malcolm up on the sofa in the spare room at the back of the diner. Max had draped a blanket over him, and he'd borrowed a pair of joggers and a sweater from Eli that came up a little small. Sunny had wheeled in an ancient-looking space heater, mumbling something about drafty old walls, and he'd been left staring up at the ceiling through the synthetic orange glow. The good thing about the kind of old English buildings the diner was set in was that you could hear every creak and groan. It took a long time for the house to settle. He heard Eli and Sunny bickering in the hallway over who got the best blankets, and then over who got to use the bathroom first, and then again over the blankets, before Max finally intervened and they all went to their respective rooms. Malcolm waited until the footsteps above him subsided and the lights in the hallway went out, until he was certain that the others had fallen asleep, before he pulled himself quickly to his feet and silently got dressed.

The fang was where they'd left it, with Sunny and Max. Offi-cially, watching over it was Sunny's job. They'd settled on leaving it with her after even more bickering. *Why'd I have to keep it?* Sunny had scowled. *You know I'm not historically good at being respon-sible.*

Because . . . Eli had replied, fumbling around the words. *You've got no magic.* Malcolm had waited to see how Sunny would react to that, but she'd said nothing. Just turned on her heel, face completely blank, and left. Eli had caught him watching them and sighed. *She doesn't like to talk about it,* he'd explained. *But Sunny's got no magic, so it's like . . . she's an unloaded gun. Less risk of a misfire.*

Now, Malcolm pushed the door open as quietly and carefully as possible. When the door made no creak, he crept inside. Max was staying in Sunny's room, since they figured it was better she didn't go home tonight. They were both buried deep under the cov-ers; through the darkness, Malcolm only caught a glimpse of Max's satin headscarf and Sunny's socked foot hanging out from the duvet. Sunny hadn't been lying earlier when she'd said it was cold. He felt a chill now, and fought back a shiver. He pushed it aside and got to work quickly, his heart beating rapidly inside his chest; he was hyperaware that any moment he could be discovered or they could wake up, and then he would have no feasible explanation to offer. He checked drawers and cupboards; at one point he fumbled over a pair of trainers left on the floor. There was a tense moment when a floorboard creaked beneath his foot, and Malcolm froze, certain that one of them would stir. Luckily, the moment passed. Max rolled over, and their breathing continued undisturbed.

He dropped to his knees and felt more than saw it: Sunny's small denim backpack was shoved haphazardly under her bed. He knew without looking that the fang was inside. It was like raising his hand to an open flame.

Above him, Sunny mumbled in her sleep and rolled over. Malcolm took a deep breath. Careful not to unfold the tea towel wrapped around it, he slid the fang out of the backpack and returned the bag to its position under the bed.

It wasn't until he'd closed the bedroom door behind him that he allowed himself to exhale. It would probably take them a while to notice the fang's absence in the morning, but by then, it would already be done.

He knew Max had closed up the front, and since Malcolm had never been good at untangling spells, he went for a window at the back. He could see that it was unlocked, but when he went to open it, it remained stubbornly shut, despite him pulling on it with considerable strength. Magic, then. After a moment, he sighed, wrapped a tea towel around his hand, and punched through the glass. It took two attempts, but eventually the window caved in, and Malcolm knocked away the shards to pull himself out.

He landed with a grunt and waded through the unkempt weeds at the side of the building to unlock his bike. He kept the fang stuffed in the front pouch of his hoodie, careful not to touch it, but mindful of its presence. It was dark as he made his way to the main road, and his focus was on not tripping over bin bags. He didn't notice Casper languidly leaning against the front.

"Fancy seeing you here," Casper said as Malcolm stepped out into the open.

"Oh." Malcolm tried desperately to school his face into something neutral. The streets were mostly empty at this time of night, all the shops having closed their shutters and turned off the lights. One taxi place was open across the road. Malcolm could just about make out a bored-looking employee slouched behind the counter. "I, uh, thought you'd gone home?"

"Decided to stick around." His father was smoking again.

Something about the act made him seem a lot younger. Malcolm wondered how long he'd been out there. There were a bunch of cigarette stubs by his feet, but Malcolm couldn't tell which ones were new. "Couldn't sleep. You want one?"

Casper didn't seem to be making fun of him. He briefly toyed with the idea of accepting, but then imagined himself going home with the scent of nicotine on his fingers, having to tell his mother that he'd smoked his dad's cigarettes.

"No," he said. "Thank you."

"Suit yourself." Casper leant back against the glass and turned to look at Malcolm from the corner of his eye. "Big day tomorrow."

"Yeah."

"Lot of pressure for someone like you."

Someone like you. Malcolm flipped the turn of phrase over in his mind a few times but still couldn't dissect where exactly the cut in it landed. Still, it stung.

"I guess."

"No one could fault you for wanting to leave."

Malcolm searched Casper's expression for any signs of irony, but he appeared to be sincere.

"I'm not running away," Malcolm said.

Casper only shrugged. "It would be the smart thing to do."

"It would be weak," Malcolm said.

"The two aren't mutually exclusive."

Malcolm kept his voice even and shoved his hands in his pockets. "Is that what you think of me? That I'll just run away?"

A police car sped past them, sirens blaring, briefly casting flashes of red and blue on them. Casper gave him a long, sideways look. "Malcolm, I don't think anything of you."

Malcolm didn't know what to say to that, so he let it settle somewhere in his chest.

Casper sighed heartily and stood up. "What I mean to say is that it's what I would do, if I was in your position."

"Right."

"You're my blood. Believe it or not, I'm trying to look out for you."

Malcolm almost laughed outright at that. "You're trying to look out for yourself."

"Well, like I said, the two aren't—"

"—mutually exclusive. I get it."

They both fell quiet. Casper took a drag of his cigarette and tilted his head back, like he was tracking stars that neither of them could see. "You're just like me, you know."

"Yeah?" Malcolm said. "How's that?"

"Selfish."

Somehow the way he said it didn't make it seem like an insult. It was just a fact, in the way he might've been commenting on Malcolm's hair or eye color. Still, something about it made Malcolm's blood boil. "Me and you," Casper continued. "We're always looking for something more. I don't think your mother ever really got that. But I do, and I know what you need."

"I don't need anything from you," Malcolm said.

"No?" Casper sounded genuinely sympathetic. "Look at yourself, Malcolm. She has you living in the same council flat she was in when I met her. Scrounging off benefits and hanging around with these youts? Your mother's rotting away, Malcolm. Soon your entire life will be spoon-feeding her mashed potatoes and reminding her of her own name. Be realistic, son. You're my blood. What are you without what I've given you?"

The truth was, Malcolm could count the things his father had given him on one hand, and yet he was right.

He was careful to keep his voice even. "Where is the rest of Mercy's magic, Dad?"

"Is that what you think?" Casper laughed, humorless. "That it's hers? That magic is *mine*. I earned it. I worked hard for it. The things I had to give up just to hold it in my hand—" He shook his head. "If you think I would ever give that up, then you don't know me at all."

"No," Malcolm said. "I know exactly who you are."

"Malcolm," Casper sighed, but Malcolm ignored him. He turned his back and swung his leg over the seat, and just like that, he rode into the night.

To an outsider, the council estate Malcolm lived on looked like any other regular block of flats: a lively, redbricked new build where kids did wheelies on the pavement and drew chalk hopscotches on the sidewalks. Malcolm had lived there long enough to know the magic of the place, though. He knew which walls had protective sigils carved into the brick, which flats housed shadows that were best not to be disturbed. He knew which balconies caught the best views of the moon and which windowpanes he could walk past and always find lined with herbs and greenery.

For Malcolm, though, it was just home.

It was the alleyway where he had learned to ride his bike up and down with his neighbors. The corner shop he stopped by every day after school to buy fizzy drinks. The NO BALL GAMES sign where he tore his jacket running from some kids at their rival school.

That night, Malcolm tried to let the place anchor him as he weaved through the familiar maze of buildings to get home. He felt unmoored by his father's words, and they looped through his head. *You're my blood*, he'd said. *What are you without what I've given you?* The truth was Malcolm had no idea.

The flat was still when he let himself in. Washing was strewn over the balcony, and there were a few unopened letters on the doorstep. Malcolm took a key from his back pocket and locked up behind him, leaving his shoes by the welcome mat and flipping on the lights.

His mother's bedroom door was closed, which he at first assumed meant that she must be sleeping. When he went into the kitchen to pour himself a glass of water, however, he found a handwritten note stuck to the fridge. *GONE OUT WITH BRENDA*, his mother had written. *BE BACK LATE. DINNER IN THE FRIDGE. LOVE YOU X.*

Malcolm felt a swell of affection. His mother's friend Brenda was known for hosting what the aunties called "a true Big People Shubz," the kind of old-school house parties that lasted way, way into the early hours of the morning. Malcolm stared at the note for a long time, something resolving in him. She'd been well enough to call up her friends. To put on her good dress and do her hair and go out and have a nice time.

What are you without what I've given you?

He supposed he was going to find out.

He started with the candles. The notebook he'd taken from his father showed them being set out into a circle. He took some extra-long matches from the kitchen and, careful not to get any wax on the carpet as he lit them, laid them alongside the ingredients they'd got from Legs but kept the fang covered. Even through the fabric, he could feel its magic rushing and pulling him in like a tide.

He turned the flat's lights off. Then he took out a bowl and found a bottle of rum from his mother's drink cabinet, and paused. The spell called for something with sentimental value, a gift to sacrifice. He looked around, and the oil landscape of St. Elizabeth that hung above the television, the one his father had gifted his mother, caught his attention. Fleetingly, he considered using it, imagining the thrill of satisfaction that would come at watching it shrivel and burn in flames, but then he envisioned his mother's face when she inevitably found out. Instead, Malcolm carefully lifted the painting off its hook and disposed of it in the next room over, where it couldn't taunt him.

He fingered the pendant he always wore around his neck, an heirloom from his father. But no—as appealing as it would be to watch that burn, it wasn't technically a gift. He'd taken it from his father's belongings. Plus, he liked to wear it as a reminder of everything he wasn't.

It wasn't until he was sitting down again, cross-legged on the floor, that he noticed he still had on the bracelet that Eli had gifted him back at the House of Spiders. It hadn't been a small gesture to Malcolm. *To keep you safe*, Eli had said. Without thinking too much about it, Malcolm placed it in the bowl with the ingredients and the written incantation, doused it with the alcohol, and dropped a lit match.

Once they had burned, he took the mirror from the hallway and placed it at the center of the circle. Malcolm took a deep breath and put his hand to the floor. He felt something distantly. It was almost like hearing a party from a few walls away. The vibration hummed at his fingertips.

From this angle, he should have only been able to see the ceiling of the flat in the reflection. Maybe an inch of the top of his own forehead. Instead, he was looking down at the unmistakable roots of a tree, sloping and twisted, just like he'd seen at the nine night. And there, underneath, was the hastily dug grave marked with a wooden cross where Mercy would have lain buried for all those years. A blink later, it was gone, replaced with the normal reflection of the light swinging above him.

Twenty years ago, his father would have sat in the same position, gazing into the same doorway. He, of course, wouldn't have been alone. There would have been seven others, sat in a circle around him. Malcolm wondered if they would have been joking around as they always seemed to be in photographs, or if the weight of what they were about to do was heavy enough that there had been a somber air to the proceedings. Regardless, it didn't matter; they were dead now. Casper's blood was the last key to opening the door. The same blood that ran through Malcolm's veins.

By now, as Casper had explained to them, the spell would be threadbare and tattered, like the fraying ends of a rope. In order to recreate the spell and seal Mercy away, Casper had said they would first need to unpick the original one. Malcolm was just cutting the final cord. The thing was, Malcolm had no intention of redoing the spell.

Before he could lose his nerve, he sent a shard of magic across his hand, sharp enough that the blood welled in his palm, and let it drip into the bowl. He reached out his hand, sticky and wet, and picked up the fang.

Malcolm screamed.

It was like holding a branding iron. All at once, he felt the magic soar through him, desperate to escape the fang's hunger. It shot white and electric behind the lids of his eyes. He almost let go, but he fought through it. He only had seconds.

What are you without what I've given you?

His father's voice looped over and over in his mind, but Malcolm pushed it away. He focused on breathing, on reciting the words of the spell, as his father would have all those years ago. Even though his voice wasn't loud, he knew she would hear. The spell didn't want to break. It lashed at him with razor-edged tendrils of magic, a failsafe undoubtedly put in place by his father, determined to make him crumble. He felt it all, like dozens of tiny needles, everything he was and wasn't. His rigid bones; his rotten, corrupted magic; he was his father, right down to his marrow.

And then, just when he had reached his limits, when he was seconds from thinking *I don't think I can do this,* he heard a voice, crystal clear in his ear. Her voice.

Yes, you can.

Trembling, Malcolm raised his arm, fang in hand, to plunge it into the glass and sever the last thread of the spell. It resisted him. He had to use all of his strength to push through it, until his arms ached with fatigue, the fang sizzling at his skin. He had to. For Mercy. For his future. For his mother.

"Malcolm?"

His eyes opened, but it wasn't the daughter of Death he found himself faced with. It was his friends. Magic crackled at Eli's fingers from where they'd forced open the door. As soon as he released the fang, it went flying from his grip and landed between them, rolling to and fro. There was Sunny, hands held out placatingly toward him, and Eli, calm and steady as always, a book under one arm. No Max. She must have been back at the diner, watching his father, who, of course, would have sold him out. He'd probably known what Malcolm was doing all along. Malcolm almost wanted to laugh. Of course Casper could not allow him even this one thing, Malcolm thought viciously. Of course, he would never allow Malcolm to possess an idea that wasn't dictated by Casper's own thoughts and feelings.

"Malcolm," Eli said, tentative. He edged forward, only stopping once he reached the ring of candles separating them. Neither of them reached for the fang. "Please don't do this."

Malcolm didn't move. He couldn't, even if he'd wanted to. The magic rushed out of him, and in its absence, he was left feeling limp and drained, gasping for breath. There were cuts and scratches up his arms from where the magic had torn at him.

"Stay back," he warned. He needed to reach the fang, but his body wasn't cooperating. He had to do this. He couldn't let them stop him.

"It was you," Sunny said. If she was surprised, he couldn't tell. Her voice was completely devoid of inflection. "You kept Mercy alive all this time. You fed her your magic."

Malcolm set his jaw. It was as if he had sold them out for thirty pieces of silver. "Yes."

"How long?"

"Two years." Malcolm couldn't look at them. "She came to me in my dreams after . . . after my mother. I thought it was just a night-mare at first, but then she offered to help."

"And the others?" Eli said. "Did you kill them?"

"No," Malcolm said. "Of course not. I just . . . found them. Tracked them down."

"And let Mercy send her monsters after them. Let her rip out their hearts and feed off the magic."

It was true, but he didn't know how to explain that Mercy was just doing what she had to. They hadn't seen where she'd been locked away. They hadn't felt the claustrophobic darkness, the soil dusting their lips and the earth under their nails.

"Malcolm," Eli sighed. "Whatever you're about to do—you can still stop this. We can figure this out together."

"I don't have a choice," Malcolm spat.

"I know it feels that way," Eli said. "But we can still go through with our original plan. We can recreate the spell and keep her from hurting anyone else. Nobody has to be hurt. Let us help you."

"Help me?" It came out brittle, a hollow laugh. "You stole my own magic from me and thought I was too stupid to notice."

Eli flinched as if he'd been hit. "No," he said. "That's not . . . I didn't mean for—"

"It doesn't matter," Malcolm said. He felt the magic stirring in the palms of his hands, low and steady like an old engine. "I have to do this."

"If you let her go, she won't stop at just hurting your father," Eli said. "You realize that, right? More people will get hurt."

"Don't you get it?" Malcolm frowned. "People will get hurt if I don't."

"Look, Grim," Sunny said. She took a cautious step forward. "I know what it's like to have so much anger inside your chest that you feel like it's eaten everything good inside you. I promise you I've done much worse, and I'm still here. We can fix this. Come on. Don't make me beg. You know that shit's undignified."

She smiled at him, this sad little half smile. Eli edged forward alongside her, and Malcolm knew. He just knew. If he let them get any closer, they would talk him out of it. He would hand over the fang and change his mind. They might even forgive him. They'd probably go back to Pam's and finish their original plan. But he also knew his mother wouldn't find another chance like this. She would only get worse. She would forget. He would be alone, and that felt . . . intolerable. Because now he knew. Now he knew what it was like to *not* be alone. He couldn't go back to how things were. He wouldn't.

"I'm sorry," Malcolm said. He raised his hand and sent his magic shooting toward them. It poured from his palms in a hot, blinding white light that he felt all the way down to the roots of his molars. Before he could lose his nerve, before either Sunny or Eli had a chance to register what was happening, he leapt forward, grabbed the fang, and plunged it straight into the mirror.

CHAPTER FIFTEEN

ELI

Eli closed his eyes. If he had been braver, he might have opened his eyes and seen the world warp under the force of Malcolm's magic. One second they were standing in the dim light of Malcolm's flat, illuminated only by the candlelight. The next, the fang hit the mirror and all the magic in the room sizzled and dispersed like water flung on a hot pan. Eli felt an ice-cold shiver shoot down his spine, and then all three of them went hurtling backward from the force of it.

Eli landed hard enough to bruise. He raised his head in time to see the shards of broken mirror tremble as something stirred below. And then he saw it.

A hand clasped the mirror's edge, groping its way out. Slowly, it pulled itself up, prying open the shards of the mirror with the pads of its fingers and unfurling from the space between the cracks like a spider. She unraveled from the darkness, coiling her way to the surface. One arm. Two arms. A head of long, dreadlocked hair. She wasn't just the stories that were whispered behind closed doors. She was here, in the flesh. There was a hole through her chest, gaping and black, where her magic had been. It almost looked like her rib cage had been pried open and she was hollow inside.

She stood, shakily at first, as if the gesture was unfamiliar to her after such a long time, and then raised her chin and set her shoulders back. There was a regality to her that Eli couldn't tear his eyes away from. A determination in the set of her jaw. People didn't hold themselves like that in Edmonton.

All at once she flung back her hair and laughed, arms stretched out wide enough to engulf the world.

Eli must have hit his head harder than he expected, because it took a moment for his vision to refocus and for his ears to stop ringing long enough to take in the words being exchanged.

"—and I did what you wanted," Malcolm was saying. "So it's over now."

"Not everything," she said. "Did you bring what I asked for?"

There was a long pause. Eli rubbed at the back of his head, trying to clear his vision. If he could just get his hand to stop shaking for a moment, he could pull himself up and stop this. Sunny was across the room. She was lying motionless. He needed to get to her.

"I—I tried to find the rest of your magic," Malcolm said. "But he's hidden it. I looked, really, I did, but I couldn't find it—"

"Hush," said the daughter of Death, and at once Malcolm fell silent. She reached down to touch the side of Malcolm's face, her eyes narrowed and hungry.

"You kept your word," she said softly. "Just as I did, so I don't want to have to hurt you."

"I don't know where the rest of your magic is," Malcolm said. "If I knew, I would tell you, I swear."

"You swear," Mercy said. She laughed. Ran her finger up and down Malcolm's jaw. "You know, your father swore a few things to me too. He swore we'd be together forever. He swore he'd leave his wife. He swore that we'd eat the world whole. Each and every one of them turned out to be a lie."

"I'm not him," Malcolm said, and Mercy sighed.

"I know." She sounded genuinely sympathetic. "But unfortunately, he's still in your veins. You're a walking embodiment of every promise to me he broke."

Malcolm opened his mouth to protest, but before he got the chance, Mercy reached forward. In one rapid motion, as if she were simply plucking an apple from a tree, she reached inside Malcolm's chest—the soft part, the space between his ribs, right where his soul rested in the center of his heart—and tore the magic raw from his body.

Malcolm stood still, startled. It was like that moment in old black-and-white Westerns when the cowboy gets shot; he froze midair, his body unable to register what had just happened. A blink later, the witch's hand slipped out of his chest, fist full and bloody, scorching a hole straight through Malcolm's chest.

If Eli thought the small piece of magic that he'd held was a sight to behold, the thing in its entirety was another matter. It was almost too bright to look at directly, a gleaming silver light that left dark spots in Eli's vision. It was undeniably beautiful. And the heat of it: Eli could feel its warmth from feet away. Mercy held the magic out, palm up, watching with faint curiosity as it twitched in resistance between her fingers, like a dying light bulb.

Malcolm held out a hand as if to touch it, a last drunken sway before gravity pulled him down, but his limbs were clumsy and uncoordinated. Mercy watched him stumble toward her in amusement. Eli wondered what it must have felt like to be Malcolm at that moment. To see the very core of yourself like that.

Malcolm's eyes flitted in Eli's direction, but they were hazy, unseeing.

When he fell to the ground, it was soundless.

The witch tossed his magic casually hand to hand, to and fro, like it was nothing but a piece of fruit. Then, with a smile, she raised it to her mouth and took a bite from it.

It couldn't have been pleasant. The splintering crack as her teeth made contact was enough to cause Eli to wince. He knew from experience what pain like Malcolm's could do to a soul; he still had faint scars on his palms from the first time he'd mishandled a fragment of magic. It fractured and splintered like shards of glass. Malcolm's pain would have been razor-sharp, and yet the witch devoured it all, piece by piece, even as the jagged corners snagged at her mouth and left her ragged and bleeding. She took one bite, then another, then another. Crunching and cracking, magic spilling over her lips and running down her chin like the juice from a grapefruit, until the whole thing was gone.

When she was done, she wiped the blood from her chin with the back of her arm. Her chest heaved from exertion. There were bloody smears across her cheeks. Her hands and wrists were stained white with magic. She licked her palms, ravenous for another taste.

There was a glow to her that there hadn't been before. The hole in her chest had healed slightly. Even that small amount of magic had loosened some of the lines around her eyes and lessened the gray in her skin.

Was Malcolm alive? Eli couldn't tell. If he was, he wouldn't be for long. Eli's mind raced. The three of them might've stood a minuscule chance minutes earlier, but that was before the witch had peeled the magic from Malcolm's bones. Sunny still lay a few feet away from him. The crown of her head was matted with blood, and she wasn't moving. He spotted the fang near her. It was his only chance at defending himself.

Slowly, painstakingly, he dragged himself across the floor

toward the fang. He had barely made it two steps, however, before a force like a hammer landed across his arm. There was a brittle crack, like a branch snapping in winter, and Eli let out a piercing yell before he registered what had happened. The ball of Mercy's foot had landed on his forearm.

He rolled over, squinting and disoriented, to find Mercy standing over him. She was shrouded in candlelight, and her long white dress danced in the breeze. Malcolm's magic dripped down to her elbows like melting ice cream.

"I didn't forget you," she said.

She crouched on the balls of her feet to get a better look at him. Eli was struggling to register anything past the blinding white-hot pain shooting from his elbow to his fingertips. It occurred to him that he might be about to die, and he spared a thought for Sunny. He hoped she was still unconscious. She shouldn't have to witness it.

Mercy reached down then and touched the side of Eli's face, just as she had with Malcolm. Warmth radiated from her fingers, and then he saw it. A hazy memory, edging into the back of his mind.

It was a simple scene: Eli walking through a flat. He was younger. Wearing a school uniform, though his tie was loose, his blazer unbuttoned. He had a backpack slung over one shoulder. He was late, and he'd forgotten to do his homework the night before. He was trying to think of an excuse that didn't get him detention, when a hand snagged his arm before he could reach the door. A woman: small, messy hair, tired eyes, skin a few shades darker than Eli's own. Her hands began knotting his tie for him with practiced ease. *Did you pick up your lunch money?* Yes. *And you left me change for the car park?* Yes. *Remember you're getting the bus home today because your sister has practice.* I know. *And make sure you don't forget your keys, because I won't be here to let you in.* Okay, okay, I know. *I love you.* He felt a rough kiss on his forehead.

The witch snatched her hand back with a hiss, as if she'd touched a flame. Her brow was furrowed slightly, a guardedness in her eyes.

"What was that?" Eli whispered. He could still feel the touch against his forehead. He ached for it. His mother, it had to be. He had a family. A sister. People who loved him. "What was—who was that? What did you do to me?"

"I didn't do anything," Mercy said with a hollow laugh. Eli didn't think he was imagining the genuine surprise in her voice. "What *are* you?"

"I'm—Eli," Eli said. It felt like the wrong answer somehow.

"Well," Mercy said, and she pulled herself back to her feet. "It seems like that's not all you are."

"What?" Eli asked, but she had already walked away, laughter following her like a shadow.

There was a long, high-pitched ringing in his ears.

Sunny was talking to him. He watched as her mouth moved and her arms gestured frantically, but Eli wasn't taking in anything she was saying. His palms were clammy, and he was struggling to catch his breath. His brain kept replaying the image in his mind. His home. His mother's face.

"Eli," Sunny said, and he could hear her now over the rapid thrum of his chest. "Eli, I've got the fang. We need to help Malcolm. Can you—"

"Right," he said. He couldn't focus. His arm hurt. His lungs hurt. Had she done something to his chest? Why couldn't he catch his breath? "Right," he repeated, like that would center him. "Okay, I'm just going to. Yeah."

"Concentrate," Sunny said, and suddenly, she was in front of him. A slow, steady heartbeat in a cacophony of noise. "We're helping Malcolm, then we're leaving. Simple, yeah?"

"Sure," Eli said, before Sunny's words caught up to him and he registered what she had said. "You want to help him?"

"You would prefer to leave him here?" She wasn't even being sarcastic for once. Eli knew that if he told her that, yes, he wanted to leave Malcolm behind, Sunny would turn on her heel and not look back.

"No," Eli admitted. "We can't leave him."

"All right, then." She nodded, and she held out a hand to help him scramble to his feet.

Malcolm lay motionless, head tilted to one side, eyes gray and unfocused. There was a huge black tear through him, just as there had been with George and the others. He looked dead, except for a slight rise and fall of his chest. Eli raised a hand, the one that wasn't hanging limply at his side, to try to heal him as he had before. But his magic wasn't listening to him. He was in too much pain.

"It's not working," he said.

"It's all right," Sunny said. "You tried. Let's not stress about it." She took a deep breath and suddenly looked very tired. "New plan: we get him back to his dad."

"To Casper?" Eli frowned. "He'd hate that."

They stared down at Malcolm's body. Truthfully, he didn't know if there was anything left in Malcolm to heal. The familiar hum of magic around him was gone. There was only cold.

"Well," Sunny said. She sounded just as weary as Eli felt. "You got a better plan?"

CHAPTER SIXTEEN

ELI

Eli leant over the sink, coughing and spluttering. His throat was raw, and the white porcelain was painted with flecks of blood. He'd been trying for almost an hour to remove the magic from himself, but it was stickier than he'd expected. He caught sight of his reflection in the mirror. His cheeks looked sallow, and there were dark bags under his eyes. He leant down to splash water against his face, and when he looked back up, he found that his reflection had company.

Pam was in the doorway, leaning heavily on her cane. She inspected the mess in the sink and then stepped forward and reached across the doorway to pass Eli a hand towel. He dabbed his face, spat a mouthful of bloody water into the sink, and turned off the tap. Only then did Pam break the silence.

"He's still sleeping," she said.

They'd barely exchanged two words since he and Sunny had arrived back at the diner with Malcolm, having somehow managed to manhandle his deadweight from in and out of a taxi. Pam hadn't even asked what happened. Instead, she'd calmly and methodically inspected Malcolm's injury, then helped to settle him on the thread-bare sofa in the back room, the same one he was supposed to have been sleeping on when he'd snuck out. It still held the blanket Max had left him, neatly folded off to one side, because of course Malcolm had nothing if not good manners.

"That's good," Eli said. "One of us should be, at least."

"I gave him a little something to keep him steady for now, but it won't last long. He'll need your help. You should be resting too," Pam said. "Your arm is broken."

"Yeah." It also appeared to be healing. That in itself was odd. Usually healing involved a conscious effort on Eli's behalf, but his arm seemed to be knitting itself together of its own accord. Some of the pain was subsiding, and he could feel the tips of his fingers begin to tingle.

"You won't be able to fix him until you fix yourself."

"I know that."

Pam crossed her arms, and there was a twitch in her eyebrow like he was two seconds from receiving a swift lick upside his head, but for once she let him be.

"It was like he said?" Pam asked. She meant Casper, who they'd left with a half-empty bottle of rum on the closed restaurant floor. "He went to her?"

Eli nodded. His brain kept replaying the moment Mercy's hand had slipped from Malcolm's chest. The blinding glow of his magic between her fingers. He closed his eyes, trying to wring the memory from his mind. When he opened them, Pam's gaze was still on him.

"You're not surprised," Eli realized.

"Hm," Pam said. "It's what I would have done, if I was young and lonely and desperate." Eli felt a low, simmering fury right in the base of his gut at that. Because no: Eli had been in that exact same situa-tion, yet he'd never turned his back on the people who had offered him kindness. Friendship wasn't supposed to be this delicate, precarious thing. It was simply finding people who made you feel less lonely and granting them the same favor. "You don't agree?"

"I don't know. Maybe Sunny was right about him."

"Is that what you think?"

Eli sighed and rubbed at his eyes. "No."

Pam gave him a speculative look and turned on her heel. "Come," she said instead, and before he could bother arguing, she'd hobbled out of the room.

As they made their way downstairs, they were greeted by the sound of an argument. Though as Eli took in the scene, he realized that *argument* probably wasn't the best choice of words. *Argument* generally implied two sides. Instead, Sunny and Max were going off on Casper in careful, hushed voices, while Malcolm slept in the next room, oblivious to the turmoil in his wake.

"You knew this would happen," Sunny was saying. "You knew Mercy would try to use your son, and you let him go through with it."

Casper tilted his head, neither confirming nor denying. "Malcolm made his own decisions," he said. "I'm sure we all hoped he'd make smarter ones."

"I just don't understand why," Max said. "What was the point of it all?"

"Seems obvious to me," Sunny said. "If Mercy killed Malcolm, she would have one less reason to kill Casper. Plus, Casper was probably scared that Malcolm would figure out where he'd hidden the rest of Mercy's magic and wanted him out of the way."

It was only then that Eli caught the first indication of irritation on Casper's face underneath the meticulous performance of indifference.

"Malcolm is my son," he said, voice like steel.

Sunny gave a scathingly bitter laugh. "Let's be honest," she said, and she was wearing that razor-edge smile that usually preceded Eli having to drag her away from a bar fight. "I don't think he's been your son for a while."

Something thunderous stormed Casper's face, and he pulled himself up to tower over her. Sunny went to step forward, and there was a moment when Eli actually thought they were about to tussle, so he moved to situate himself between them. The sound of Pam's cane hitting the tiles beneath their feet brought everyone up short.

"*Enough*," Pam said. Silence fell on the room. "Sunny, Maxine. You know what this man is. You know all he has done, and yet you act surprised by his cowardice. What have I always told you? You cyaan expect nothing from a pig but a grunt." Casper at least had the decency to look slightly indignant at that. He opened his mouth to defend himself, but Pam cut in with a glare. "And you. This is your mess we're all up to our knees in. The least you could do is spare us some humility." She sighed, hobbled over to Casper's half-empty bottle, and poured herself a drink. "Now, we don't have time for this. We are all on the same side here, and we must work quickly. Where is Mercy?"

That last question was directed toward Eli, who startled, shame warming his cheeks. "She got away."

She turned back to Casper, her face twisted into something sour. There was something heavy in the air between them, something Eli couldn't identify.

"You understand that means she'll be coming for you now," Pam said.

Casper shrugged. He seemed less like someone who was being hunted down by a murderous god and more like someone enduring a particularly tedious play. "It would appear so, yes."

"It means that you're not safe here."

"No."

"And none of us will be while she lives."

"I'm aware."

"Then what do you suggest?" Pam asked.

He glanced around at the others, then dug into the pocket of his coat. When he opened his fist, it was to reveal a large, thick golden coin. Eli wondered when it had come into Casper's possession; it had been in Malcolm's pocket when they'd carried him back to the diner, just a short while ago. Eli knew this for certain because he'd taken it upon himself to inspect all of Malcolm's belongings for anything dangerous. Then again, Casper was infamous for his lightning-quick hands. He could change his name and move away, but he was still a thief through and through.

"I think," said Casper, "that it's time to finally cash in that debt."

Pam went very still. It was odd; Eli didn't think he'd ever seen her surprised before. "Now?" she said flatly. "When we're so needed here?"

"Now," Casper insisted. He held out his hand, palm up, and after a moment of hesitation, Pam reached out and took the coin from him.

"Be sure," she said. "After you use this, there is nothing more, Casper. We are done."

"I'm sure," Casper said.

"Fine." She closed her fist, and when it reopened, the coin had dissolved in the palm of her hand like a sugar cube. She turned to where Eli, Max, and Sunny were watching their odd exchange in varying degrees of confusion. "I'm afraid it is up to you now—all of you—to stop her."

"What?" Max said. "What do you mean?"

Pam's attention was on the doorway leading to where Malcolm was still lying vacantly on the sofa, his chest rising and falling in gentle succession.

"You'll need him, too," Pam said. She patted Max gruffly on the cheek. It was the most open gesture of affection Eli had ever seen from her. "If anything happens to me, the diner falls to you. All the paperwork is in the back room. I trust you understand the importance of this place."

"Of course." Max blinked. She looked just as confused as Eli felt. "But—"

"Good," Pam said. "Look after each other."

She hobbled back toward Casper, and Eli realized belatedly that their entire conversation was sounding eerily like a goodbye.

"Wait," Eli started, but it was too late. He'd barely gotten a chance to form the words before Pam turned back to Casper and put one leathery hand to his shoulder. Even he looked surprised by the contact, and his eyes widened cartoonishly. Then, just like that, the world folded into white, and in the blink of an eye, the two of them disappeared into thin air.

"What," Sunny said, which just about surmised Eli's own feelings, "the fuck?"

The three of them stared down at where Malcolm slept, unmoving.

There was something bitter on the tip of Eli's tongue. Something sharp and difficult to swallow. Malcolm had betrayed them. Or maybe they'd betrayed Malcolm first. At this point, it was hard to discern where their friendship had clearly started to sour—if there was even a friendship at all.

Eli's arm was starting to feel better now. It was still a little stiff, but he had the feeling back in his fingers and he could move it without wincing.

"So," Eli said. "Pam said we'd need him."

Sunny rubbed her forehead. "Yeah. But then she also disappeared into thin air with our best chance at stopping Mercy, so maybe she's not the most trustworthy source of information."

"We can trust Pam," Max insisted, and then when they both turned to look at her with equally dubious expressions, she faltered. "What? We can. Can't we?"

"Does it matter?" Sunny gestured vaguely toward Malcolm's unconscious body. "What's he going to do, betray us twice?"

"I mean . . . yeah?" Eli said. "That's a valid concern."

"Okay, so we wake him up. Then what?" Max added. "We're just going to lock Mercy away, like Casper and the others did? What makes us any better than them?"

"You weren't there," Sunny said. "You didn't see what she did." The humor had faded from her expression, and her arms were crossed tightly across her body. "She ripped the magic clean out of Malcolm's chest like it was nothing."

"I saw something," Eli said. They both turned to look at him. "I felt it when she came out of the mirror. Something was broken . . . right at her core. Probably from when Casper first stole her magic. What if I could heal it? After everything that's happened to her, don't you think we should at least try to help her?"

"Eli—" Sunny started, but he cut her off.

"Max is right," Eli said. "If we recreate the spell, we're no better than those who came before us. Malcolm knew that. That's why he went behind our backs."

"He went behind our backs for his own gain," Sunny said blandly.

"He went behind our backs to help his *mother*," Eli protested, and then realized that he was defending him, which was not at all what he intended. He wasn't ready to move on from being mad about it yet.

"And if we can't help her?" Sunny asked. "If you're not able to heal whatever you saw that was broken?"

"Well," Eli said, "we'll cross that bridge when we get to it."

Max leant across and knocked their shoulders together. "I think it's a good plan."

"Uh-uh," Sunny said dryly. "Except for the question of what to do with Brutus over here."

Once again, their heads swiveled back to where Malcolm was deep in sleep.

"Yeah," Eli exhaled. "I don't know what to do about that one."

"Just wake him up already," Sunny said, waving her hand. "We're only delaying the inevitable."

She turned and walked out of the room, and Eli felt a stab of envy at her casual confidence in her decision. He caught Max's eye, and she gave him a small, knowing smile.

"If we're going to take on Death's daughter, it might be helpful to have the duppy prince on our side," she said. "But whatever you decide, I'm with you."

"Okay." Eli exhaled. "So no pressure, then."

She left the room, and then there was just Malcolm.

Even with the two of them gone, Eli still felt a tight knot of tension in his chest. Max was right, probably. *Pam* was right. He looked down at where Malcolm was sleeping. After a moment, he raised a hand to Malcolm's chest once more and willed the magic to listen to him. It didn't. Eli clenched and unclenched his fingers, but he'd left it too long; the magic had weaved itself into him too tightly. It was in his bones, lining his tendons and under his fingernails. He tried to shake it, but it was like wringing droplets from a dry dishcloth.

He found himself thinking back to that conversation with Malcolm. The small, embarrassed way he'd admitted that he wanted to cook like his mum, that he wanted to move away. He thought of how he'd first seen Malcolm under that silk cotton tree.

The anger dissipated and instead a new feeling bloomed from

him. *You're of the earth*, the lagahoo had said to him. It hadn't made sense before, but now he could feel it. His ties to this place, his home. He felt it in the ground beneath his feet. He felt it whisper against the slight hairs on his arms. He didn't force it this time. As he channeled it, the air in the room got thicker and warmer.

He opened his eyes, and it was there: the small piece of magic that he had taken from Malcolm that first day. Its light was a little dimmer than before, but it was there.

It seemed reluctant, and Eli thought, *It's okay*, said it loud and clear in his head so that it could hear him. He reached out and pushed the piece of magic back toward Malcolm's chest. There was no resistance this time; it was like moving his hand downstream in water. The magic swam back to Malcolm, and Eli felt it the moment it returned to him. It was like the snip of a thread between them.

Malcolm took a chest-deep breath. He was still asleep, but something had shifted; Eli could feel it. The balance of something broken healing.

He stood back to dust the last remnants of magic from his fingertips. In the absence of the magic, a chill had run through his body. He shivered, and when he coughed, his breath came out in puffs of ice, as if he'd been standing on a street corner in the middle of winter. The weight of the past few days started to feel heavy on his bones. Dealing with that much magic felt like lead in his bloodstream.

But it was done. Malcolm would wake, this much he was certain of. All that was left to do was wait.

That night, Eli slept like the dead.

When he woke, it was to something scratching at his window. He pulled open his blinds to find a small black cat perched on the edge of his windowsill, staring up at him with big, wide eyes. Eli scrambled backward. He'd never had much of an affinity for animals in general, but he'd always been particularly dubious around cats.

Eli shooed it and tapped at the window to scare it away, but the cat only looked at him blandly. It was a wild-looking little thing, an ugly tangle of matted black fur. It was, Eli imagined, the kind of cat that only existed in the city. Brittle-boned, rough, and covered in scratches. It looked like it wanted to fight him, and Eli had to admit the feeling was mutual.

"What?" Eli asked. "Are you lost? Go away."

The cat yowled and swiped a determined paw at the window.

"How did you even get up here?" Eli asked. "We're, like, ten feet up. There's no trees around here." He scowled, immediately suspicious. "Did you fly?"

The cat tilted its head slightly, a little too human to be feline, and Eli groaned.

"You've got to be joking," he muttered, but after a moment, he leant forward and pulled the window open. Immediately, he inhaled a metallic, coppery scent.

He was half expecting the lagahoo to change into another form, into something he could have a conversation with. It didn't. It just stayed there perched in the center of the room in cat form, craning its neck to blink slowly around the room.

Eli shoved his hands in his pockets and dropped back onto his mattress, bouncing a little as he sat. "So you were right, I guess," he mumbled. He didn't specify what, exactly, the lagahoo had been right about. About Mercy. About Casper. About Malcolm.

The cat didn't move, just watched him steadily, and Eli's temper flared.

"You're not gonna say anything?"

The cat gave an unhelpful meow, more of a yowl than anything, and Eli was about to complain again, but that was when he noticed. One of its paws hung limply in the air, and the side of its fur was matted with blood.

"Oh." Eli frowned. "That looks painful. Does it hurt?"

The lagahoo stared at him.

"Okay, that was a dumb question. What happened?" The cat meowed. "And you can't talk, great. This is perfect. I love today."

The cat continued to stare at him blankly, so Eli leant closer. "Can I look?"

He reached out a hand, but the cat gave a vehement hiss and bared its teeth. Eli snatched his hand back, raising his palms in a placating gesture. "Hey," he said. "I'm not going to hurt you. You came here, remember?"

When the lagahoo didn't hiss or try to bite him again, Eli took that as an invitation to squat down on his knees and look closer. He inched forward gradually, making sure to narrate his movements. "I'm gonna touch you now." He tried to keep his voice as calm as possible. "Just to see how bad it is. Please don't bite me."

This close, he could see the source of the problem: there was a tiny sliver of magic lodged in its paw, just around the size of a penny and as clear as a shard of glass.

"It's stopping you from changing," Eli realized. The lagahoo meowed, which Eli took as confirmation. This was way beyond his realm of expertise, but he found himself reliving the last time he'd seen the lagahoo, after they'd left the House of Spiders. He'd lost his temper. Eli had been feeling guilty about it ever since. "I can probably get it out for you, but you'll need to be still. I've never healed a lagahoo before."

He raised a hand, but there was nothing. No familiar buzz of magic. No hum in the air. After helping Malcolm, he was dried out. The lagahoo tilted its head, as if sensing Eli's exhaustion.

"Sorry," Eli said, feeling a little embarrassed. "Guess we're gonna have to do this the old-school way."

He found an empty shoe box under his bed and held it out until the lagahoo got the gist and hopped into it. He lifted it, careful not to rustle the cat too much, and placed it on his bed so that he and the cat were eye level. The lagahoo glared at him the entire time, and Eli didn't blame it.

"Maybe I should get Max. She'll know what to do." The cat let out a little meow; then, when it realized Eli couldn't understand, nipped at Eli's knuckle hard enough to make him yelp. "Ow—*all right*, jeez, no Max. Well, believe it or not, I don't exactly know how to fix a broken paw without magic."

The lagahoo stared at him.

"Don't give me that look. I'm telling you because I don't want to mess it up."

The lagahoo meowed.

"Okay, fine, but if you're stuck like this forever because it goes wrong, don't blame me."

That was how Eli ended up cross-legged on his bed with a half-empty Adidas shoe box full of rustling fur while a YouTube tutorial titled "How to Treat a Feral Cat!" played on his busted old laptop. The internet at Pam's was bad on a good day, so the video kept pausing to buffer, and every time it did, the lagahoo clawed at him as if he were personally responsible.

As a peace offering, he crept down to the kitchen to fill a saucer with water and sneak away some leftover chunks of oxtail. He waited until the lagahoo was distracted enough that he was certain he wouldn't get his eyes clawed out; then he reached forward and pulled the tweezers from the lines of its fur. The jagged piece of magic didn't come out easily—it snagged a little, and the cat let out an angry hiss—but Eli ignored it. The magic smelled rotten, and as soon as Eli removed it, it crumbled and floated away like ash. Eli turned back to the cat with a raised eyebrow. It seemed he wasn't the only one to encounter Death's daughter.

"You all right?" Eli asked, once it was done. Eli hadn't known it was possible for a cat to look sardonic, but this one did. "Yeah, yeah, I know. Sorry."

He wrapped the paw with gauze, the sticky kind like the guy used in the video—tight, but not tight enough that the lagahoo yelped and scratched him again. As a cat, the lagahoo wouldn't be able to walk very well for a while, which meant that it probably wouldn't be able to change into another form.

"I'm sorry about before," Eli said once he was done. The saucer that he'd put in front of the lagahoo was empty, and now that its paw was wrapped, it looked content. "I was scared."

The cat stared at him.

"Not that it's an excuse. You were scared too. I should have realized we were on the same side. Or that we can be, maybe."

The cat stepped forward and rubbed its head against Eli's hand until he stroked him.

"You can stay here until you're better, but this doesn't make us friends. Allies, maybe. You know, since you lied to us and almost cost us Malcolm's life. Not to mention, if we hadn't left Malcolm behind, he never would have—"

Betrayed us. That was what he'd been about to say. It sounded melodramatic, and yet the sting of it was still fresh. He scratched behind the lagahoo's ears, and it gave an approving purr.

"I don't even know what you look like," Eli said. "I mean, actually look like. When you're not being a cat or a bull or whatever. Do you carry a coffin around with you, like in the stories? Are you male? Female?" He caught himself and huffed a breath. "What am I even saying—you can turn into a fly, it doesn't matter."

He was quiet for a moment, and he picked up a piece of oxtail, which the lagahoo then proceeded to devour from the palm of his hand. "It would be nice if I knew your name, though."

He wondered if it even had a name, though maybe the concept of a name was meaningless when you could shift your skin and be anything or anybody within the blink of an eye. Eli supposed they weren't really that different in that regard. They were two completely blank slates, in their own way.

"Rah, you're really going at that oxtail," he said before the words registered, and then he grinned. "Hey, that's what I'm gonna call you. Ox."

The lagahoo—Ox—looked up at him briefly, then nudged him gently with its head, until Eli surrendered more pieces of meat.

"You're not cute," Eli said, which was true. The cat was ugly and mean-looking, not to mention that it smelled bad, but his words were mostly undermined when Eli reached out to ruffle the tufts of fur behind its ears. Ox didn't move, just purred contentedly and dug into its food.

"I've been thinking about what you said back at the House of Spiders," Eli said. "You said that Mercy took one of your kind captive and would use them for her bidding. It was you, right?"

Ox stopped chewing momentarily to send Eli a flat look.

"Oh," Eli realized. "Not you. But someone close to you."

Ox turned away, which Eli took as a yes.

"I'm sorry you had to go through that." He slumped back against his pillows and stared up at the ceiling. "Her magic isn't like anything I've ever seen before. I think if I can get through to her, we can stop her. The question is, how do we get close?"

Ox stopped eating and raised its head to cast what Eli could only interpret as a highly unamused look.

"What?"

Ox jumped off the bed and limped across the floor. Eli swung his head over the side of the mattress, and he found Ox dragging his backpack out from under his bed with its jaws.

His backpack, with the fang tucked into the side pocket.

The lagahoo had probably known it was there the whole time. Had probably sensed the magic in there from the second Eli had let it in. The fang was probably why the lagahoo was even here.

"Yeah, all right," Eli said. "Good point."

CHAPTER SEVENTEEN

MALCOLM

Once, when Malcolm was little, he had a chest infection. His mother had fed him endless supplies of chicken soup and cerasee tea, and he'd spent a week in bed feeling like a small hive of bees was trapped in his rib cage. It wasn't dissimilar to how he felt now, as he sat in the back room staring at the slightly peeling wallpaper opposite him. Pulling himself upright was a slow and humbling experience. Breathing hurt. Moving hurt. Even thinking too hard hurt.

His reflection in the mirror looked sickly and gray, and he had heavy bags under his eyes. He pulled up the bottom of his T-shirt and took in the damage. It wasn't as bad as he expected. There was a knot of welts at the place right over his heart. It was raised and itchy, but it was already beginning to scar around the edges. He poked at it and found that the skin around it was still tender and inflamed.

A knock on the door made him look up. It was Sunny, of all people, leaning against the doorframe, her arms crossed. Her braids were bundled on her head, and she wore a faded Aaliyah T-shirt, gray joggers, and slippers. She looked completely at home here in the chaos of the diner with its sloping old Victorian walls and sticky floors.

Malcolm immediately found himself reliving their last interaction. *I know what it's like to have so much anger inside your chest that you feel like it's eaten everything good inside you*, Sunny had said. He wondered if she still meant it when she'd said they could fix it.

"Hey," Malcolm said, pulling down his T-shirt quickly.

"You're up," Sunny said. Her hands were shoved in her pockets. "Not planning on sneaking off and betraying us again, are you? My stress levels can only take so much in one week."

Malcolm looked down to hide his flinch.

"That was meant to be a joke," she said. "Too soon?"

Malcolm huffed a laugh. "Maybe a little."

"Well, you'll build up an immunity to it if you're sticking around," Sunny said. "I'm assuming you are sticking around."

Malcolm stared at her. He couldn't tell if she was joking or not, but her face was completely straight, aside from the one eyebrow that was cocked upwards.

"I don't really, um . . ." He picked at one of the scabs on his knuckles that hadn't yet healed. "I don't have anywhere else to go."

Sunny waved a hand, dismissive. He wondered if it was intentional, the casual aura of calm she radiated. Before this, he'd probably found her to be the most intimidating of the three. She seemed unable to be anything other than herself, unapologetically, at any given time. For Malcolm—who was someone who had never taken so much as a single step without calculating the exact risk—it had been difficult to reckon with.

"I'll let you in on a little secret," Sunny said. "None of us have anywhere else to go. That's why we're here."

She crossed the room and planted herself on the sofa, resting her feet on the coffee table. Malcolm felt awkward standing across the room while Sunny was sitting down, too conscious of what each of his limbs were doing, so he moved himself to the other end of the sofa and forced himself to sit next to her.

"Look," Sunny said. "Casper told us about your mum. It's messed up, what you're dealing with. Shit, if I was in your position, I probably would have done the same thing."

"Yeah?" Malcolm asked.

Sunny shrugged. She pulled at a stray bit of thread on the sofa. "Sometimes you have to do messed-up things to protect the people you care about."

Malcolm couldn't tell if she was speaking from experience, and he didn't know how to ask her about it without causing her guard to rise back up, so he just stayed quiet.

"You said she found you in your dreams," Sunny said.

It wasn't quite a question, but it caught Malcolm off guard.

"Yeah. It was the only way she could talk to me."

"Hm." Sunny just nodded, grim and accepting. "Makes sense. Get to you while you're alone."

"She didn't force me to do anything I didn't want to." That part felt important. He'd done what he'd done. He wasn't going to shirk responsibility for it.

"I know," Sunny said. Though her tone was light, there was a tic in her jaw. "But she didn't need to. She knew your weakness. In this case, it was your mother, and she dangled a solution for it in front of you to make you do what she wanted. Textbook manipulation."

Malcolm remained quiet. It didn't feel right, hearing it simplified like that.

"You wanna know something?" Sunny said.

"Okay?"

"I'm good at math. Like really good. Got an A+ in my GCSEs and sat all my exams a year early. Max and Eli don't even know that about me. I try to keep it that way, because otherwise they'll try to rope me into doing all the accounting stuff for the diner, and I don't have the attention span. Anyway, my point is that I'm good at problem-solving, and when there's an inconsistency in data, I can't help but find it. In this case, the thing that was bugging me was when she first came to you. Two years ago, right—you were, what, Year Eleven?"

"Yeah," Malcolm said. "It was, uh. After my mother's accident."

"Makes sense." Sunny nodded. "You were vulnerable. Probably, like, traumatized. Social workers come around a lot?" Malcolm nodded numbly. "And I bet you had the school breathing down your neck too. You were probably having a generally shit time, which made you easy pickings."

"I don't know where you're going with this," Malcolm said.

"My point is that it was only a couple of years that you were bringing her magic to feed on, right? To keep her alive?"

"Right."

"So she'd turn up in your dreams, call you into the half world between the living and the dead because, of course, you're one of the only people that can easily get there. Told you she needed your magic to survive. Probably made you open up a vein for her."

There was no malice in her voice, but the truth of it still made the back of Malcolm's neck prickle with shame.

"But your father and the others, they locked her up almost twenty years ago," Sunny said. "So my question is, how was she surviving before you?" At Malcolm's startled expression, she gave him a small smile. It wasn't sympathetic, not entirely. It was understanding. "She should have starved. That's what Casper said. Unless, of course, there were others like you. People she went to before, who she offered the world to get what she wanted."

Malcolm wanted to deny it, but now that she had spelled it out to him, it was obvious.

"She played you," Sunny said, matter-of-fact. "And when she got what she wanted, she ripped the magic from your chest."

Malcolm didn't know what to say to that, so he looked down at the frayed ends of his hoodie strings.

"I'm not saying it to upset you," Sunny said. "I'm telling so you know it's okay. Because now we know her game. Now we can win."

Malcolm was so taken off guard by her casual use of the word *we* that he couldn't even stutter out a response.

Sunny pulled herself to her feet and stretched. "I just wanted you to hear that. In case you were thinking about, like, hurling yourself out a window or something dramatic. It's not necessary. We're on your side. Plus, it would probably only be more inconvenient because then we'd have to, like, clean up your brains or whatever. No one wants to do that."

"The fall is too short anyway," Malcolm replied, deadpan. "I'd probably just break my arm."

Sunny looked surprised for approximately three seconds, but then her face split into a giant smile and she erupted into laughter.

"I knew there was a sense of humor in there," she said. "See? You'll be all right." She reached the door but stopped and squinted at him. "You hungry? There's food out here if you want it." Malcolm opened his mouth to decline, but something in Sunny's face cut him off. "And before you say no, I was serious when I said we're cool. Try not to hide in here forever, yeah? Plus, we could do with an extra hand downstairs, because, seriously, Pam and Casper have disappeared, and we have no idea what we're doing. I'm, like, two ancient histories of magic away from smothering Max with a leather-bound."

Could it really be that easy? Malcolm wondered. Was he being let off the hook? Sunny seemed sincere in her kindness, but Malcolm had never been good at reading people. He feared this could be yet another subliminal test that he was failing. Then again, what he did know about Sunny was that she wasn't the type to stay quiet about something that bothered her. Malcolm didn't know what to do with it—this forgiveness she'd just handed him.

"Wait," he blurted, just before she could slip through the door. "Just—thank you, by the way. I didn't say that before."

"Don't thank me," Sunny said. "It was Eli that saved your life." She slipped him a quick, easy smile before disappearing, and the lightness in Malcolm's chest lasted way after she'd gone.

Malcolm did come out of hiding eventually, after an intense ten-minute pep talk with himself. He went downstairs to find Max in her usual corner, surrounded by books, while Sunny was behind the cash register, serving an actual, honest, in-the-flesh customer. It was rare to see anyone on the premises who wasn't some kind of acquaintance, staff member, or tenant. Even the rare few customers were all regulars known by name. Malcolm was beginning to think that Pam's was just a front.

"Sorry," Sunny was telling the customer, though she didn't, in fact, sound very sorry at all. She was twirling a braid around her finger and chewing bubble gum. "I told you already. We don't have that."

"How can you not have rice and peas?" The customer, a construction worker, judging by the reflective vest and the hard hat under one arm, was turning increasingly pink. "It's not even midday. You're a *Caribbean takeaway.*"

"I don't know what to tell you." Sunny shrugged. "We're out."

"This is ridiculous," the customer complained. "Let me talk to your manager."

Sunny waved a hand vaguely in Max's direction, who looked over the rim of her glasses to take the man in and then shrugged, equally nonchalant. "Sorry," Max said. "We're out."

"Look," Sunny cut in when it looked like the man was about to burst a blood vessel. "I'll tell you what. You're that desperate, take my card, head to the market up the road, and get some kidney beans. We'll whip it up quick for you, then you can come pick it up in a few hours. Done."

The customer stared at her blankly. "You're having a laugh."

"Okay, fine, go hungry, then! Rah," Sunny said, rolling her eyes as the man retreated in a rage, slamming the door behind him. "Some people have no manners."

Still a little tender, Malcolm settled down next to Max and picked up a book discarded on a large pile. It was a hardback children's picture book showing various stories of Anansi, the spider god. Malcolm flipped through it and landed, at random, on a story he knew well; the one where Anansi tried to steal from Death, but Death followed him home. In the drawing, Death was illustrated as a sour-faced old man, swathed in white light, and Anansi was a small black spider dangling from a tree.

You can't trick death, the cartoon man said, pointing a finger.

Not with that attitude! the spider replied.

"You all right, Malcolm?" Max asked. Her glasses were wonky, and she had ink smudged on one cheek.

"I was thinking I could, uh, help," Malcolm said. He snuck a glance at Sunny, who gave an infinitesimal nod of encouragement. "You know, try to find the rest of Mercy's magic."

"Of course," Max said. Her face had brightened like he'd said the exact right thing. "We're still trying to figure out where your dad hid it. As you can see, we're really scraping the bottom of the barrel here. You didn't . . . hear from him, did you?"

"No," Malcolm said. "Nothing." He wasn't surprised. His father had made it clear that he had no intention of giving anything up. Not even, it seemed, to save his own son's life. "No word from Pam, either?"

"Nope," Sunny said. "They've fully ghosted us."

"I'm sure they'll be back soon," Max said, and she sounded so cheerfully optimistic that Malcolm felt bad for her. He didn't have the heart to tell her that coming back wasn't necessarily his dad's specialty.

"Sure," Malcolm said. "Maybe."

They worked mostly in silence. Sunny clattered in the kitchen while Max and Malcolm pored over books. Max was an impossibly fast reader and would devour entire chapters while her hand moved simultaneously, taking notes with the veracity of an ancient scribe. Sunny would occasionally slide a book across the counter and make a few humming noises as she skimmed. There was something comfortable about it all—being here, with Max and Sunny, being useful.

Malcolm read through everything he could. There were stories of Mercy existing for centuries. He read about sailors barely surviving shipwrecks, catching glimpses of her floating above them in a white dress before they were dragged under by the storm. Stories of children walking past a silk cotton tree only to hear her whispering their names. Other times the stories made her out to be a savior, appearing at the beds of slavers and ripping their souls out with her bare hands. Once she made the journey across the waters to their small gray island, history lost all trace of her.

Malcolm was so absorbed in his reading that he didn't even register when Eli entered.

"The hell is that?" Sunny exploded, half leaping out of her chair at the sight of him.

Eli was cradling a cat in the crease of his arm like a baby, despite it being almost half his size. It was an ugly thing, scruffy and jet-black, with what looked like blood matted in its fur.

"It's not what you think," Eli said.

"That's a lagahoo," Max said. She was the only one of them to not have leant back in trepidation. She sniffed cautiously; then her face twisted into something surprised. "That's *the* lagahoo."

"Okay." Eli lifted the shoulder that wasn't currently being nestled by the surly-looking cat. "Then yeah, I guess it is what you think."

"*Eli.*"

"Relax, it just needed help. What was I gonna do, turn it away?"

"Uh," Sunny said. "Yeah?"

"It did leave us for dead," Max added.

"In its defense," Eli said, "we broke into its home. And be real: Who hasn't left us for dead these days?" Malcolm sank into his chair, his cheeks warming with shame, but Eli continued without noticing. "Look, it's hurt, so it can't change its form yet, but once it can, it's gonna help us."

"It told you that?" Max asked, dubious.

Eli looked at the cat. The cat gazed back placidly. "I mean," Eli said. "Like . . . in a manner of speaking."

"Give me strength," Sunny muttered.

"We're all on the same side here," Eli said. "We all want to stop Death's daughter." He swept an arm toward the stack of books Max had been unsuccessfully bent over the past few hours. "Unless you have any better ideas?"

Max sighed deeply. "You know if Pam sees that thing in here, we're all dead."

"Pam's gone, Max," Eli said. "In case you didn't notice, this is kind of our only option right now."

Sunny moved closer to scowl down at the lagahoo with obvious distrust. "So does that thing have a name, or what?"

"Maybe, I dunno," Eli said. "I've just been calling them Ox. Like oxtail, 'cause you should have seen the way it nyamed it up quick."

"You gave oxtail," Sunny said flatly. "To a cat."

"To a *lagahoo*," Eli corrected her.

He raised a hand, and the creature nuzzled into it, like it was a real house cat. The rest of them watched in horror.

"Eli," Max said. She sounded like she was trying really hard to contain her hysteria. "A lagahoo is not a pet. It could switch and be a panther and claw out your eyes within a matter of seconds. This is not something to cozy up to."

"I know that," Eli grumbled, though it was difficult to believe him with the lagahoo coiled on his lap and purring contentedly.

"Whatever," Sunny said. "Don't come crying to us when it scratches your eyes out."

She turned away, a clear dismissal, and on that note, Max turned back to her book. There was an awkward beat where Eli and Malcolm were just staring at each other. They hadn't exchanged any words yet. A million things flew through Malcolm's head but died on the tip of his tongue. Instead, he kept his gaze on the words in front of him, so he wouldn't have to read whatever was on Eli's face.

"I can go, if you want," Malcolm offered.

Eli was quiet for a long moment before answering. "Why would I want that?" he said, his voice completely devoid of any inflection whatsoever. Malcolm couldn't tell if he was being sincere or not, and he didn't get a chance to find out, either, because Eli swiftly turned his attention to Max. "So, what do we have?"

"Well," Max sighed. "Wherever Malcolm's dad hid the magic, he didn't intend for it to be found."

"He didn't say anything to you?" Eli asked, turning toward Malcolm. It sounded a little like a challenge. "Leave you any coded hints, or anything like that?"

"Oh, uh, no," Malcolm said, when it became clear he was serious. "No, that's not something he'd trust me with."

"So we haven't found out anything," Eli said.

"Well," Max said. "In all the old stories, she tends to gravitate to places filled with pain and a lot of bloodshed. She feeds off the grief. Things like wars, famines, massacres . . ."

"Funerals?" Malcolm suggested, and they all looked at him, the same idea blossoming in all their minds.

"We'd have to get to her first," Eli said. He was slumped in the chair and stroking his shape-shifter cat like a Bond villain. "Before she gets to the magic, we draw her out. Trap her somehow. Then I heal her."

"Heal her?" Malcolm repeated, surprised. "You want to help her?"

"I think," Eli said, "that she deserves at least a chance."

"That sounds great and everything," Sunny said, "except how do you expect us to do that? You saw what she did to us last time. I still have bruises from it. You're dried up. She took most of Malcolm's magic. We might've stood a chance before, but not now."

"It's a valid point." Max shrugged.

"Well," Malcolm said. "We do know what she wants more than anything in the world."

This time when their heads swiveled toward him, he didn't shrink under the weight of their gazes like he normally would. He kept his chin high. This was largely his doing, and the parts that weren't his doing were most certainly his father's. He wasn't going to hide from the responsibility of it anymore.

"Yeah," Eli said. "And what's that?"

Malcolm shrugged. To him, it seemed obvious. "To kill my father."

There was a moment of silence as they all digested that. "That may be true and all," Sunny said. "But your dad's not here. And neither is his magic."

Malcolm resisted a snort. His dad was never there. Malcolm was used to figuring things out without him.

"*We* know that," Malcolm said, and his eyes shifted to where the lagahoo was watching them, taking this all in. "But she doesn't."

CHAPTER EIGHTEEN

ELI

Camden Lock was rarely empty, even at this time of night. Usually, in the summer, it was flooded until way after sunset with tourists spread out on picnic blankets, eating Chinese food from silver containers and balancing pints from nearby pubs. There were always crowds coming in and out of the station, heading to the bars further up the high street. Eli didn't know if it was the unusual cold for this time of year keeping people away that night, or if it was just a general restlessness in the air. A knowledge of something coming. Either way, when he looked around, he found that they were mostly alone. Most of the shops and market stalls had closed, so it was only the few pubs still open that shined light on the streets. He and Sunny put the diminishing buzz of the high street behind them and followed the path along the canal, past a group of drunken students ambling outside a pub and an old man offering fortunes for a fiver.

They kept moving up the canal, until it all faded behind them. Tourists didn't generally venture this far up at night. This was where the market shifted from being a carefully curated tourist trap to something more solidly residential. On one side of the river, beyond a wall of trees, were long rows of identical Victorian terrace houses, painted white like something out of a postcard, and home to doctors and lawyers and politicians. The other side of the river, that was the side Eli knew well. Most of this side of London was a boneyard if you knew where to look. Concrete estates carved out of the rib cages of dead gods, and roads paved over the veins of giants. You could walk down the street and see red, black, and gold flags hung over balconies of redbrick estates, and uncles on road knew you by name. This was the side Eli walked along.

The canal cut down the middle of these two worlds. Eli could see the last few lights up ahead from boats on the water, but aside from that, it was dark enough that they had to watch their step along the cobbled pavement. The water was dim and murky beside them. The last thing they needed was to discover what was lurking under the surface.

They followed the canal through lines of flats, their surroundings silent apart from the gentle rush of water. None of the streetlights were on. Eli didn't think that was a coincidence.

"This is a bad idea," he said.

"Yeah," Sunny agreed, sounding largely unconcerned. "Probably."

Eventually, they reached a narrow overpass that led from one side of the canal to the other. In the summer, Eli would see kids up on the bridge, dropping things into the water to frighten unsuspecting tourists taking selfies on the waterbuses below. For people like them, the bridge was one of the only places they knew where the two opposing sides of the world collided, where one side of the river crossed to the other for things they couldn't find on the other. Eli and Sunny would see them sometimes, rich people from dull, magic-less worlds who heard the odd rumor of something unimaginable occurring on the other side of the river, crossing the bridge in the hunt for cheap thrills. Most would get sent away, since the secret of magic was something sacred to everyone who possessed it. The reality, of course, was that everyone had a price.

Legs was at his usual spot when they arrived. He was with a group of four other kids around Eli's age, whom he vaguely knew from around their area. Legs had a pit bull on a lead, but it looked as though it hadn't quite finished growing yet, because it barely reached his ankle. As conspicuous as ever, today's outfit was a lime-green ski jacket with matching luminous shorts. His locs had also changed from the pastel pink color they'd been just a few days ago and were now a royal blue.

"No shit," Legs said as soon as he saw them. "You're actually alive, then."

"Don't sound too happy about it," Eli said. He was already annoyed that they'd had to delay their plans for a whole day in order for Legs to squeeze them into his busy schedule because, quote, "he was dealing with big man tings." This did nothing to alleviate Eli's irritation.

"Nothing personal," Legs said. "Just that last I heard, Death's favorite daughter had ripped the ground open and was nyaming the magic of anyone involved in putting her there. So, like. You can see why I'm not trying to get involved."

Behind him, his crew were watching with interest. Eli remembered the first time Sunny had brought him to meet them. Eli had been nervous back then, unsure of himself, of who to trust, of his magic, and desperate to impress Pam and the others. He'd found Legs and his crew intimidating; the casual easiness and familiarity between them, their seemingly boundless knowledge of magic. Now he'd been around long enough to know most of them, at least by name: there was Shay, who just got four A+'s at A Level, and Nadia, who was a huge sneakerhead and worked at a hair salon in

Haringey. The tall one with light eyes was Light-Skin Rahim, not to be confused with Short Rahim, who was, like, five feet tall and loved Naruto. Then, of course, there was Legs.

Sunny leant around Legs to wave at them, and she received a couple of nods in return. "You mean you don't want to be any more involved than you already are," Sunny said. "Since you helped us before. I'd hate to let that involvement get out."

Legs huffed a sigh. "Be a bit more bait, yeah?" He ushered them further along the bridge, away from the prying eyes of his friends. "What's this about? I thought we were cool. You weren't happy with the product?"

"We're just looking for some protection," Sunny said.

"Protection," he echoed.

"She's going to come for us," Eli said. "We need to be ready."

Legs looked back at his friends, who were suddenly pretending not to watch.

"Funny, yeah." His voice had something of a hysterical edge to it. "Great joke."

"Legs," Sunny said, voice low.

Legs shook his head. It was unsettling to see him so nervous. This was the guy who, according to the stories, once put his hand in a sleeping dragon's mouth to steal the gold tooth out of its jaw. Who once used the flames of an actual soucouyant to light the candles on his birthday cake.

"Look," Legs said. "The way things are moving . . . we shouldn't even be talking about this out in the open."

"Spooky," Eli muttered.

"Very *Nineteen Eighty-Four*," Sunny agreed.

"I'm serious," Legs said. "You know how many people are in her pocket? People will sell out their own blood to get good in her books. They say she's even got shadows working for her. The way the stories are going, you say her name, the next day she'll come and snatch it out of your mouth. One word against her, I could be dead."

Eli and Sunny turned to each other. Eli shrugged, which meant *this one's all you.*

"Okay," Sunny said. "So don't say a word against her. Just tell us what you know."

Legs crossed and then uncrossed his arms, glanced back toward where his friends were still hovering nearby. "You didn't hear?"

Further along the bridge, a man approached from the west. He was white, middle-aged, wearing a messenger bag over a disheveled suit like he'd hopped off the tube straight from work. There was a nervous edge to his walk that told Eli that he wasn't from around here. Eli watched him approach Legs's friends. He pulled out some money, and Legs's friends started laughing. Eli didn't know what he was here for, but it was always the same kind of thing. A love spell, a voodoo doll, a hex bag. Something they saw in a film once, magic that had real roots and practices and spiritual repercussions that they would never truly understand. Most of the time, Legs would just sell them watered-down ginger beer and send them on their way. Whoever this guy was, he was a rookie. It wasn't enough to deal in bread and pennies here; they traded in secrets and sacrifices.

"Hear what?" Eli asked.

"They found another couple of bodies this morning, just like the others. Holes in their chest. Magic drained from their bones. They're saying she wants her magic back. Even though it seems like she's gonna pull the heart out of anyone she can find until she gets it, nobody knows where it is."

"Well," Sunny said, "that's not exactly true."

Legs looked between them, but Eli kept his face blank. This was the plan, and he'd taken the bait, just like Sunny had said he would.

"The only person that knows that is the duppy king, but everyone said he's missing."

Sunny shrugged, purposefully coy, and Legs's eyebrow shot up comedically.

"Wait—you know where he is? Shit, I should have known. Where's he hiding?"

"Come on," Sunny said. "You know I can't spill for nothing."

"The favor you owe me, then. We'll scrap it and call it even."

"A secret of this proportion?" Sunny laughed. "There's not enough favors in the world."

"Okay," Legs relented. "What do you want?"

"We need something to hide the scent of a lagahoo," Sunny said, and Legs flung his head back and cackled.

"Oh no," he said. "You lot are up to something. There's no way I'm getting involved. Nope. Nah. Absolutely not. Exclude me from this narrative."

"Come on," Sunny said. She pulled off her red beaded bracelet, and Eli almost objected. He'd become oddly attached to it. He didn't want Sunny to give it up. "Like this. I know you've got to have some-thing."

Legs squinted at the bracelet, but it wasn't an outright no. "When a lagahoo changes, it's like they're . . . they're making and unmaking themselves. Undoing the shit around them and breaking the magic in two. There's no way of erasing that kind of magic."

"Not erasing," Eli said. "Just . . . covering up. Temporarily."

Legs was quiet for a moment, thoughtful; then he turned and walked over to Light-Skin Rahim and whispered something in his ear. Rahim headed off the bridge and disappeared around a corner. When he returned a few minutes later, he pulled from his pocket what looked to be fishing wire.

Eli had seen something like it before. It was a kind of busted old magic. It appeared as a long, golden thread that faded into the air if you knew the right words to whisper. Back in the 1950s, when London had been filled with witch hunters determined to keep England "English," magic like this was common for people trying to assimilate, because it could be worn like jewelry and hid all traces of magic on the wearer. Now it was seen as toy magic, really—prank stuff, the kind you learned as a kid. It was, however, nearly unbreakable without the right words. Rahim handed it over and then jogged back to where the white man on the bridge was still nervously hovering around the others.

"Your lagahoo won't be able to change while it's wearing this," Legs said. "But that will hide the scent of its magic."

Legs handed it to Sunny, and it immediately coiled around her wrist like a hatchling snake. She hissed a little as it tightened around her skin, but after a moment, it snapped closed like a bracelet.

"Do you feel anything?" Legs asked. "You know, with your whole—" His eyes drifted to the scars along Sunny's fingers. "No offense."

"Do you want to find out?" Sunny said, smiling sweetly.

"All right, sunshine," Legs said. "Point proven. Now talk."

"Well," Eli said. He glanced sideways at Sunny, who nodded. "Word is that Mercy's magic is with the last one to betray her."

"George?" Legs said. "But he's dead. And the last night of his nine night is . . ." Legs counted on his fingers. "This weekend. Friday?" Eli and Sunny kept their expressions perfectly neutral. "That's where Casper King will be?"

"You can't tell anyone," Sunny cut in. "It's just a rumor. You said yourself what will happen if word gets out."

"I won't breathe a word," Legs said, miming a zip across his lips—the telltale sign that it was sure to be news across the whole of London before the sun had even set. "I promise."

Sunny waited until Legs was out of hearing distance before she raised her now-gold-encrusted arm with a grin. "What did I tell you?" she said. "Easy."

"Nicely done," Eli laughed, and he bumped his fist to hers. Above them, the moon was waning, a perfect C shape. If all went to plan, Legs would get the word spread. Then it was just the matter of it finding Mercy's ear.

Over the next few days, an odd sort of calm had fallen over the diner. It was the anticipation of what was to come. It hung over their necks like a hangman's axe. Even Max, who generally buzzed around Pam's like a hoverfly, seemed to have sobered.

The night before the nine night, Eli went upstairs to ditch his bag, but when he opened his bedroom door, he stopped short.

"The fang isn't in here," Eli said.

Malcolm's head snapped up from where he was poking around a particularly large cactus that Eli kept by his window. When he registered that it was Eli leaning against the doorway, he winced. "Oh, I wasn't—" he started, before taking in Eli's expression. Some of the tension slumped out of his posture. "You're messing with me."

Eli shrugged a shoulder. He had been, a little bit. "Why are you in my room?"

The guilt on Malcolm's face managed to evolve into embarrassment within the span of three seconds.

"I thought Ox might be hungry, so I brought up some leftover food," Malcolm said, and sure enough, he was holding a little saucer of brown chicken. "Max did buy cat food, but Ox wasn't feeling it. And, you know. Tomorrow's a big day. Figured we'd all need all the energy we can get."

Eli didn't get it. He thought he had Malcolm figured out. Malcolm had used them. He'd lied to them. He'd sold them out for his own gain. But then there were moments like this, when Eli found himself stumbling smack into a wall of unexpected kindness. He had no idea what to do with it.

"So how does it work?" Malcolm asked, and Eli realized that they had both been standing there staring at each other in silence.

"What?"

"The plants. You said it helps with your magic."

"Oh." Eli blinked. "I don't really know the mechanics of it. Max showed me this photo once, of how if you zoom in close to the rings on the stump of a tree, it looks exactly the same as a fingerprint. And if you look really close at a leaf, you'll see all the veins and capillaries and roots. It's all the same thing, really." He lifted the broad leaf of an elephant ear in a nearby pot. It was the wrong climate for it to exist here without magic, so Eli had to check on it regularly. He pressed his fingers to it, and under his touch, the crispy brown edges turned thick and green. It was the most he'd been able to use of his magic since he'd woken Malcolm.

Malcolm kept his voice low, like he thought if he spoke too loudly it would break the spell. "I've never seen magic like that before. Where do you think it comes from?"

"No idea," Eli said. "Probably nowhere good."

Outside, it had started to rain. Eli had opened the window so that Ox could come in and out, and now the sound of the steady pitter-patter against the windowpane filled the room.

"Tomorrow," Malcolm said. "When you go to the nine night, I want to be there."

Eli took his hand away from the leaf, and it went back to being limp and lifeless. "No." It came out blunter than he intended. "What I mean is . . . you should go home. Check on your mum, get some rest."

"My mum is fine," Malcolm said. "She's—good, actually. Better than ever. She doesn't need me."

"You're still hurt," Eli said. "You need time to heal."

Malcolm heaved a breath, but he wasn't wholly unsurprised. "You don't trust me."

Eli considered softening the blow, then decided against it. "Would you?" Eli asked. "If you were me?"

"I trust you," Malcolm said, like it was that simple.

Eli snorted. "I lied to you from the day we first met."

"Yeah, well, same. We'll call it even, then." He stepped forward. "You'll need me. My magic—"

"Is what got us into this mess in the first place."

"Then let me use it to get us out of it."

Eli stepped back, putting space between them. They were too alike. Eli hadn't seen it before, but he could now. They would both happily take a bullet for those who were important to them. Eli just didn't know if that extended to Malcolm yet.

"If you want to help, stay here with Max and figure out where your father hid the rest of Mercy's magic. We have the fang, which is powerful enough to kill a god. It will be enough."

Malcolm stuffed his hands in his pocket and looked anywhere but at Eli. "So that's it?"

"That's it," Eli said.

Malcolm turned to leave, but at the last minute, he stopped in the doorway.

"I've been trying to figure it out," he said. "What was taken from me that night in the alleyway when you took that piece of my magic. There's always a price, right? I've heard about it happening. This boy I knew from West, he got jumped. They bled the magic from him. He survived, but after that, he couldn't taste anymore. He said everything he ate tasted like ash. I keep wondering if there's some vital part of me that's gone, that I should be missing, but the only thing that's different about me is that this feeling . . . this, like, constant dread that has been following me around for as long as I remember. It's gone. I'm pretty sure—" He stopped then, huffed a laugh, feeling awkward. "I'm pretty sure it's 'cause it's the first time I've ever not been alone. If staying behind is how I get to help, then fine. I'll do it."

Eli didn't know what to say to that, so he just nodded, ignoring the twitchy, gnawing feeling in his gut.

"Good luck tomorrow," Malcolm said, and Eli couldn't tell whether Malcolm meant it, but he decided to take it at face value. After all, they would need it.

CHAPTER NINETEEN

ELI

Eli didn't need Malcolm's magic in order to see between the veil of the living and the dead this time. That was the magic of a nine night; the walls between life and death were at their thinnest. It was the only time the dead could cross over to the living, without worrying about being stuck there. It meant that the last night of the nine night was always the most raucous. They could hear the music from all the way up the street. It seemed that all of George's friends and family had made the journey to say their final goodbyes. As they made their way up to the front door, Eli could see them, the dead and alive alike, bodies two-stepping to familiar offbeats, rum already thumping through veins. They'd made the right decision, Eli thought, to come here. There was no way that Mercy would resist the pull of a place like this, where the grief was ripe enough that you could skin it, cut out its core, and boil it into something sweet.

He'd been carrying Ox in his arms as they walked, still in cat form, but as they got nearer, he crouched down and let Ox hop to the pavement. Ox had been uncharacteristically amiable since they'd left Malcolm and Max back at the diner and hadn't so much as hissed at him once. In truth, that only added to the general feeling of foreboding. More than once, Eli considered asking if Ox was okay, before thinking better of it. He expected he might get an eye clawed out in response.

"You ready?" Eli asked instead as he stepped back.

The cat peered back at him, head tilted into something unimpressed.

"All right then," Eli said. "Like we discussed."

All at once, Ox wasn't Ox. Ox was Casper, and the likeness was truly uncanny; the same looming height and perpetually disgruntled expression, the same gray-speckled beard, the same sweeping black peacoat. It was only the slight scent of burning in the air that was any indication that Ox was Ox, and not the duppy king of North London. Eli had known abstractly what to expect—he had seen Ox in others' faces—but he hadn't anticipated the coiling nerves that tangled in his stomach when being faced again with Casper.

"That doesn't get any less impressive," Sunny said.

She handed Ox the instrument Legs had given them, and as soon as it was around Ox's wrist, the faint scent of burning magic disappeared.

"She's not wrong," Eli said. It was strange to think that just a few hours ago, Ox had been curled up on the end of Eli's bed eating leftover ribs.

"It doesn't normally take that long," Ox grumbled, sounding a little put out.

Eli snorted. "We'll try not to hold it against you."

"What do you reckon?" Sunny said, and elbowed Eli. "You think she'll buy him as Casper?"

Ox's expression was carefully placid, which, on Casper's face, reminded him of Malcolm, now that he was able to properly assess it up close. The artful, carefully concealed ambivalence that they both seemed to wear like armor. The absurdity of the situation only hit Eli at that moment. It was a skill, he realized, to warp yourself into someone else's being. To not just wear their face, but to inhabit the weariness in their shoulders, the weight of their ego in the cock of their hip. With the instrument Legs had given them wrapped around Ox's wrist, nobody would be able to tell otherwise.

"Yeah," Eli said. "She'll buy it."

"You realize that if this goes wrong, she'll likely kill us all," Ox said.

This was true, though it was only then that a thought occured to Eli. "Hey," Eli said. "If we're going to die, we should probably know your name."

Ox waved a hand, airy and dismissive. It was the same vaguely imperious attitude they'd possessed as a cat; Eli was beginning to learn that this, perhaps, was just Ox. "My kind shed our names with our first skin."

"Cool," Eli said, and Ox gave him an odd look, like his answer was unexpected. "What? It is. Sounds like it could be kind of lonely, though."

"Perhaps," Ox said. "Sometimes."

"Well, is there something you'd like us to call you?" Eli asked. "Or not call you, maybe?"

Ox smiled. The gesture might even have been considered fond if they hadn't been wearing Casper's face. "Ox is fine."

"Okay," Eli said. "Ox it is."

The three of them headed to the house and knocked on the door.

"What's that?" Sunny asked, gesturing to the small plastic container Eli had wrangled from his backpack.

"What?" He looked down. "Oh. I brought fritters."

"Why do you have fritters?"

"Max made me." Eli shrugged. He risked a glance at Ox, whose face was carefully blank, as if they were trying extremely hard to not be pulled into the conversation. "She said it's bad manners to turn up empty-handed."

It was what Pam had drilled into them. Undoubtedly, if she were around, she would say the same thing. Eli almost laughed at the thought of her cussing them. *Yuh mean fi tell me*, she would say, *you turn up wid yuh two long hand?* He spared a thought for Malcolm and Max, who they'd left flicking through more dusty spell books.

Of course, Pam wasn't around to tell them what to do anymore. He wondered where she'd taken Casper, and then cast the thought out of his mind. That wasn't his concern. It was just up to them now.

As the door swung open, any humor he'd been feeling sobered. The house was rammed. They had to sidestep their way through the narrow hall, waving at various partygoers they recognized from last time and politely nodding at the ones they didn't. Guests were leaning on the walls and hanging off the stairs. They got more than a handful of speculative looks, but it wasn't Eli they were looking at. It was Ox—or more accurately, Casper. Eyes followed them everywhere, and it was the same expression on all their faces. A mixture of reluctant awe and fear. "The duppy king has returned," he heard one person say.

"We're being watched," Sunny murmured, voice low.

"Good," Eli said. "That's what we want."

There was a different feeling tonight. Everything felt heightened, as if dialed up a notch. The music was louder, the lights were dimmer, there were more people shoulder to shoulder. Even the air felt thicker.

They found little Tia in the back room of the house, where all the coats and bags had been stacked. She was lying on her stomach on the floor and playing on a game console, but she looked up when they entered. Eli pulled out the Capri Sun he'd brought along especially for her, and she caught it midair, grinning.

"You're back!" She seemed to be missing a tooth from the last time they'd seen her. "And you remembered! You've come to help Uncle George?"

"He's still here?" Eli asked.

"Kinda," Tia said, and scrunched up her nose. "He's different."

"Different how?" Sunny asked.

On cue, the light bulb above them began to flicker, casting them in sallow gray light. The music from the next room stuttered and jumped, slowed and distorted. Eli heard a series of grumbles from the crowds. He felt a gust of cold run over his body. Seconds later, it was over. The music resumed; the party went on.

"Different like that," Tia said. "I don't think he can help it."

"Huh," Ox said dryly. "You neglected to mention we would be intruding on an angry ghost."

"In our defense, he wasn't angry when we met him." Eli turned to Sunny, who looked thoroughly unenthused by the whole deal. "We should go up there."

Sunny was cussing him out under her breath before he'd even finished. "Why did I know you were going to suggest that?"

"Are you here with the men?" Tia interrupted. Her attention was mostly on her game, so the question was asked innocuously. Eli's heart still lurched.

"What men?" Eli asked.

"Uncle George called them black-heart men. They're in suits, and they've got blue paint on their hands. They look like they're made of clay. He said not to pay them any attention, that nobody does, and all sorts of funny things can happen on the last night of a nine night. But I think they're looking for him. Uncle George, that is. He's hiding."

"Tia." He bent down to Tia's height so that they were eye level. She tore her eyes away from her Nintendo just as the screen whirled with the unmistakable flash of a *GAME OVER* message. "It's really important that you stay in here, okay? If you need a grown-up, find your granddad. You don't trust those men."

"Are you coming back?"

"Course," Eli said. "Just stay here, enjoy your Capri Sun, stay out of trouble, yeah?"

Tia nodded dutifully, and Eli felt the first prickle of fear run down his spine.

"Okay," he said to the others. "Let's go."

They had just started to weave their way back through the people when Eli caught something in the corner of his eye. Mercy. Right there, in the mix of swaying bodies. She looked the most alive they'd seen her. Her hair was flung over one shoulder, and her skin was slick with sweat. She was surrounded, of course, by men and women alike. Eli recognized the look in the eyes of the people around her. The willingness to hand over their souls there and then. She was feeding off it all. The love, the bond of blood and family, the music, the grief, the magic.

The sound system warped and jolted again, and the lights flickered off. By the time they came back on, she was gone. The crowd around her continued to dance, unperturbed. There were ghosts of magic in her wake. Swirling and black like smoke, the only sign that Eli wasn't losing his mind.

Eli opened his mouth to alert the others, but something wrenched his arm. He turned and immediately found himself looking up at cool white eyes. Under the grip, his arm prickled and blackened as if frostbitten. The creature was nearly identical to the one that had attacked them at Pam's, painted emerald-blue over cracked, porcelain skin. Black tailored suit under a long windbreaker. He smiled and Eli spotted one golden canine, a last remnant of his decaying humanity.

"Fancy seeing you here, little witch," the creature said with a Cheshire cat grin. "She's waiting for you, and she's so, so hungry. Have you come to return what is hers?"

Eli tried to pry his arm away, but its grip was inhumanly strong. "We've come to end this."

The creature laughed. With his spare hand, Eli rustled in his pocket for the fang, but by the time he pulled it out, the creature had gone.

Sunny knocked into him from behind, and Eli took a deep breath.

"What just happened?" Sunny asked.

"Well." Eli resolutely did not allow his voice to tremble. "She's here."

CHAPTER TWENTY

MALCOLM

Malcolm poked at the wound that was starting to scab over on his chest. He wondered how deep it went, if his rib cage was charred from the magic. He was sitting by the front window at Pam's, watching the comings and goings outside. Some kids across the road were taking turns practicing ollies on a battered skateboard that was too big for them, but their dedication was impressive. Every time they fell over or skittered across the ground, they would immediately get up, laughing and jostling one another.

"Stop it," Max said. "You'll only make it worse."

"Sorry." Malcolm dropped his hands, feeling abashed, but the itchy feeling under his skin didn't go away.

Max raised an eyebrow behind her book. "You're a much better patient than Eli or Sunny. They never listen to anything I tell them."

"You patch them up a lot?"

"More than I'd like," Max said.

"You're good at it," Malcolm said. And it was true. Max had

steady hands, an even temper, and what seemed to be a nearly infinite supply of kindness.

"Thanks," Max said, with a shrug of one shoulder. "My mum's a nurse, so most of it came from her. Plus, I'm the oldest of seven siblings. That's a lot of scraped knees to tend to."

"Seven." Malcolm blinked. "Wow."

He thought about the silence of his childhood and tried to imagine it filled with the laughter and chatter of six other children, instead of quiet Friday nights in the kitchen with his mother. "Must have been fun, though, growing up like that?"

"Fun is one way to describe it," Max said. She counted on her fingers. "It's loud. Like, all the time. You have to share everything. The good snacks are always gone before you get to them. The internet is slow, people are constantly in your business, oh, and good luck ever trying to decide on a film. On the other hand, there's always someone to hang out with. So you're right. You're never bored."

"Sounds nice." Malcolm smiled. He'd always known that he was lonely, that he probably had been for as long as he could remember. He'd known it in an abstract sort of way, in the way of someone who'd always eaten lunch alone and been forced to entertain themselves. He'd never really experienced *not* being lonely, and now that he'd been around Eli and Sunny and Max with their loud overlapping voices and echoing laughter, it only reinforced how starved he was for that sort of friendship.

Max hummed. "Sometimes you do need your own space, though. A place of your own. That's why I'm here so much."

"Seems like Pam lets this place be that for a lot of people."

"Yeah," Max said. "I guess it is. You wouldn't believe some of the riffraff she's taken in over the years."

Malcolm turned back to his book but couldn't take in any of the words. Outside, one of the kids successfully flipped the board and the others erupted into voluminous cheers, gassing her like she was Tony Hawk or something. Malcolm looked up to find Max watching him, her expression twisted into wry amusement.

"Maybe you should stretch your legs. Have a wander around," Max said.

"You think?"

"Go on." Max nodded. "It'll be good for you."

The walls were lined with photographs and paintings. Max had been telling the truth; it seemed everyone and their mother had inhabited Pam's through the years. There were signed photos of local celebrities. Handwritten letters to Pam, thanking her for housing them. Culinary awards for the best neighborhood patties. Photos of block parties.

He stopped at the oil painting in the back room—the clifftop scene in Jamaica—framed with dark mahogany wood. He'd noticed it earlier, because it was so like the one they had back at his flat.

It was a piece of home, his mum would always say, though truthfully, everything was a piece of home to her, from the Buju Banton greatest hits CD she kept in the glove compartment of her car to the Dunn's River All Purpose Seasoning that permanently inhabited their shelf. The painting, though, his mother had kept for all those years, even after his father left. Even after all his other things were packed away into black bags and flat-pack boxes and taken to the charity shop, the painting had remained on their wall, a reminder of home.

"Where's this painting from?" Malcolm asked.

"Huh?" Max was barely listening, her hand still moving when she was scribbling notes. "Oh, that painting's older than me. Pretty sure it's been here since they opened."

When he was younger, Malcolm thought the painting was so lifelike that he used to squint his eyes and tilt his head, pretending he was looking through a window. Like he could reach through and skim his fingers along the water. Only every time he'd try, his mother would knock her hand hard against the top of his knuckles. *You look with your eyes, not your hands*, she'd say. The landscape was nearly exactly the same as the one that hung in Malcolm's flat, only it was painted from a slightly different angle. Here the sky was rich and clear and blue and empty. Whereas the one at home . . .

"I'll be back," Malcolm blurted, already heading for the door.

"Wait . . . what?" Max frowned through her glasses. "Where are you going?"

"Home. There's, uh, something I need to do."

"You're leaving?" He heard the implicit *again* in her voice and stopped short.

"Yeah. I mean, no. It's not like before, I swear." Max just continued to stare at him, and Malcolm felt his cheeks start to warm. He was aware of how this looked. Like he was going behind their backs, again. "You can come with me."

"Malcolm—"

"I just need to check something." He looked down at his hands so that he wouldn't have to see the little wrinkle between Max's brows. "It's important."

"I don't think it's safe to leave right now," Max said. "Plus, the others—"

"This could help them," Malcolm said. He didn't know how to explain any of it without making himself sound ridiculous. "Please. I need you to trust me."

After a long and agonizing moment, she put down her book. "Okay," she said. "Let's go."

His mother opened the door in a worn dressing gown, a pile of laundry under one arm. Their ancient cordless phone was nestled between her ear and shoulder. She was midconversation, but when she saw Malcolm, her eyebrows rose dramatically. Malcolm knew that look. "It's okay, Brenda," she continued into the phone, though her glare was fixed on Malcolm. "He's just walking through the door now. Yes, it seems he finally remembers where he lives and has deigned to grace us with his presence. We can call off the search party."

"I did text?" Malcolm offered meekly, once she'd hung up the phone and stood in his line of sight, arms crossed. His mother's lips puckered, but then she noticed Max's presence behind Malcolm and he watched her pack her anger away to deal with later.

"Hi, Mrs. King," Max said politely. "I'm Max. It's nice to finally meet you. I've heard so many great things about you."

"Uh-huh," Malcolm's mother said, eyeballing Max. She wasn't used to Malcolm bringing home any friends, least of all any who were as wholeheartedly earnest as Max. "Ms. King, actually. Malcolm didn't say to expect guests."

"Sorry, Mum," Malcolm said, and kissed her on the cheek before shouldering his way past her. He left Max in the hallway politely exchanging small talk with his mother, which she was apparently an expert at.

He paused as he crossed into the living room. Malcolm was used to the flat being a mess lately. They had a carer but most of the time, Malcolm was the only one doing the washing and cleaning, which often meant that bundles of clothes were piled on the back of the sofa when the washing machine was full, and that the sink seemed to be eternally stacked with dishes he hadn't had time to clean. As Malcolm walked into the flat now, however, it was like the home he'd known in his childhood. The carpet had been hoovered, the surfaces dusted. All the dishes were washed and put away. He had a mother again. The realization almost floored him, and he was so consumed with terror that Mercy might not keep her word, and this might not last, that Malcolm almost forgot why he'd returned.

The painting wasn't in its usual place, and his heart sank in horror before he realized that he'd taken it down during the spell. He hurried to the kitchen and then skidded to a stop when he realized that it wasn't where he'd left it either.

He poked his head around the corner to find his mother slyly interrogating Max about her career ambitions. He could tell by his mother's increasingly impressed expression that Max's answers were the right ones.

"Mum, where's the painting?"

"What?"

"The Lovers' Leap painting you got from Dad."

"Oh." His mother gave him an odd look. "Well, I was cleaning and I saw you'd taken it down, so I assumed you'd finally tired of it. I thought we could put something else there instead, so I started going through our photo albums to find something. You know, Max, Malcolm really was the sweetest baby. He had these huge cheeks, just like a cherub. Do you want to see a photo of him at Legoland?"

"Oh." Max beamed. "I'd love to."

"That was the day he tripped and knocked out his front teeth, you see."

Malcolm tilted his head and tried desperately to bite back his impatience. "The painting, Mum. Please."

His mother put her hands on her hips and frowned. "I thought you hated that painting. You said you couldn't bear to look at it."

"I don't. I mean, I do. I just— This is important."

She gave him a flat look, like she would have cussed him out if it'd hadn't been for the fact that they had company. "I put it in the cupboard," she said. "Your old school is having a fete next week, and they need donations, so I thought they could take it. It's a nice painting, and one of a kind. Your father had it painted specially for me."

His mother hadn't been exaggerating. There were boxes of photos everywhere, half-open albums strewn about in stacks. Malcolm paused. Had she been going back through them now that she remembered, or was she starting to forget again? He glanced back into the living room to where his mother was giving Max a detailed breakdown of the time that Malcolm had projectile vomited after going on the teacup rides. So, not forgotten everything, then.

He found it underneath an old VHS recording of what appeared to be Malcolm's Year 4 school production of *Joseph and the Amazing Technicolor Dreamcoat*. The painting was just as Malcolm remembered, only the view was from a slightly different angle from the one that hung in Pam's diner.

They were nearly identical. The only other difference was that in Pam's painting, the sky was clear and blue, the way it never was in England. In this version, the sun shone brightly, a small, glowing speck in the center of the canvas. There was something odd about it, though. When he picked up the painting, it left white spots in his eyes, like he was looking directly at light. He moved his hand toward it, and miraculously, he felt warmth radiating on his skin. But it was more than that. It was the smell—like sand and salt water and fresh sea air. Tentatively, he let his skin brush the surface of the canvas, just like he'd always wanted to as a child but never had the nerve to. At first nothing happened. When he traced his fingers across the painted clifftops, all he felt was the thick, oily canvas. He lifted his fingers and brushed where the painting was warmest, right over the sun, and there, the slightest hum of electricity—

He exhaled, just a little, and his hand slipped through the painting until his fingers brushed the little ball of light. He had to tug at it, like plucking a grape from a vine, and it was hot enough to burn.

Then he pulled back his hand, and with it, the sun from the painting. It was no bigger than a penny, glowing between his thumb and forefinger, but he could feel the steady pulse of it, aching to be used.

"Malcolm, did you find what you were— Oh shit." Max stood in the doorway, her eyes wide behind her glasses. The whole room was illuminated by the light in Malcolm's hand. It hurt Malcolm's eyes to look at it directly. "Is that what I think it is?"

"I think I found where my dad hid the last of Mercy's magic," Malcolm said.

"No."

"Yep," Malcolm said, and he couldn't help it. He started laughing. Then Max was laughing too. The two of them bent over in the dancing, glimmering light, cackling hysterically.

In the next room, his mother clattered around, half muttering to herself as she hefted boxes.

"So, what now?" Max asked.

Malcolm stared down at the magic. He could rid himself of it. He could hand it over to Mercy and let her destroy everything. He could give it to his father and watch him do the same. Or he could stop living in the footprints of giants and do something to help his friends.

"I started this," Malcolm said. "It's only right that I finish it."

"Wait." Max grabbed his wrist. She looked frghtened. That was what cemented his resolve. He was sick of being someone who everyone was afraid of. Someone who was constantly being pulled by other people's strings. He could do this, he realized. He could use his magic to be something other than his father's son. "Are you sure? It will be dangerous."

"I'm sure," Malcolm said.

Max stepped back but nodded, accepting. "Well, all right then," she said. "Bottoms up, I guess."

Malcolm smiled. Before he could talk himself out of it, he lifted the magic to his mouth and swallowed it whole.

It felt like every nerve ending was on fire. The void that he hadn't realized was inside him suddenly started to fill. It wasn't like before; there was still a gaping hole in him, but he felt more like himself again, whoever that was. It was different from the magic he knew. There was a clearness to it that he hadn't felt before. He understood, in an instant, why Mercy had found it so addictive. He felt hungry. He wanted more.

He pushed the feeling aside and looked back at Max, who was watching him nervously.

"You good?" she asked.

"Yeah," Malcolm said, and for once he meant it. "I'm good."

CHAPTER TWENTY-ONE

ELI

Eli pushed through the crowd, despite every fiber of his being rebelling against the action.

"I've lost her," he hissed.

The air was thick and dewy with magic, like a summertime storm. It was seeping into the guests. Their eyes had turned glassy and vacant under the weight of the magic. A boy around Eli's age was leaning on a wall nearby. Eli waved a hand in front of his face, but it didn't seem to register: Nothing. No reply. It was like they were all entranced.

Shit, shit, shit.

The crowd seemed to be getting denser with every passing minute. Eli turned and bumped into someone, only to flinch. Their eyes were completely white. Eli gasped and leant back, knocking into another body, just as eerily unmoving. He couldn't tell the living from the dead.

"What has she done to them?" Sunny called over the music.

"She's feeding on them," Ox said. "On their grief and their magic. We should hurry—she'll be getting stronger every second."

This wasn't their world anymore; it was hers. Or at least, the world between theirs and hers, the living and the dead. Here the magic was as tangible as the sweat thickening on Eli's brow. It was intoxicating. He could feel himself succumbing to it. To the music, the warmth. It would be easier, he thought, to give in to it. To stop fighting. To let himself drift into the fog.

"Eli," he heard Sunny snap from behind him. "Keep moving."

Right. The fact that Sunny didn't possess any magic for Mercy to corrupt was a small blessing. She would have to act as their North Star. Eli and Ox wouldn't be so lucky. Even with Sunny there steadying them, it was difficult for Eli to keep his thoughts straight. He recognized the heat from the first night of the nine night. It seemed to have only intensified since then, leaving his skin sticky and moist. The music droned on and on.

He couldn't shake the feeling that he was being watched. If he listened, he could hear whispers easing from the shadows.

He caught sight from behind of another tall figure with long locs, swaying rhythmically. *Mercy.* Eli elbowed his way to her and grabbed her by the shoulder to spin her around, but when he turned her, it was just another partygoer, lost in the magic.

He felt a trickle of something from his nose. He brought his finger to his nostril, and it came away dark and inky. It was his magic. All around, he saw the same thing oozing from the others: magic dripping from their noses, their ears, their eyes.

They had to get out of here. He shoved his way through the crowd and up the stairs, Sunny and Ox hot on his heels. This time, when he entered George's bedroom, it was empty. He didn't have Malcolm's magic to see the dead anymore, but it was the last night of the nine night; George should have been visible to all of them.

"George," Eli called to the space at large. He felt panic start to rise in his gut. What if the door had already closed forever for

George and he wouldn't be able to pass along? What if George was already gone? "Please tell me you're here."

There was no reply. Eli felt wet around his ear and raised his hand to find it dripping with magic. Fighting the pull of Mercy's magic was making him weary. A glance at the others, and he knew they were feeling the same.

"Eli," Sunny muttered behind him. "It's the ninth night. Maybe we're too late."

"We're not too late," Eli said, jaw set. "We can't be."

"There's definitely something here," Ox said speculatively. "I can smell it."

The light bulb above them began to flicker, and they looked up. By the time Eli glanced down, George was standing right in front of them, shuddering and pale. He had faded even more since last time. Cold came off him in waves, and Eli knew he was struggling to stay tied here. They were witnessing his second death. Soon he would be nothing; trapped and invisible inside his home, while his friends and family went on beneath him.

"You came back," George said.

"Yes," Eli said. "I told you I would."

"Holy shit," Sunny exclaimed. They all turned to look at her, and she raised her eyebrows. "Sorry, it's just—I can see him this time."

George was not paying her any attention, though. His eyes were on Ox, who of course was wearing the face of one of his oldest friends. "Casper." George exhaled. "I should have known that you would be the last one standing."

Eli looked between George and Ox and realized that this per-haps had been a miscalculation on their part. They hadn't stopped to consider what George's feelings might be toward Ox wearing Casper's face.

"Erwin's dead because of you," George said, voice low and full of warning. "Tiny, Martin, Kev, and Romeo—all of the House of Spiders, everyone that followed you. Gone, because of your greed."

Around them, the lights flashed on and off. The weight of George's anger was palpable and sickly. The floorboards began to rattle. Eli felt the hair along his arms rise. They needed to calm him before he lost control, but they couldn't risk telling him the truth, not when Mercy could be anywhere listening.

"George," Eli interrupted. "We don't have much time. We need you to open the door to the other side for us. Like you did last time, so that we can fix this."

George's eyes were still on Ox. "You don't need me," he said. "The walls between the worlds are crumbling. Soon anybody, dead or alive, will be able to come and go as they please."

Eli opened his mouth, ready to plead again, but Ox placed a hand on his shoulder and stepped forward. "I won't let her hurt anyone else," they said.

This was Ox talking, and not Casper; George must have heard the sincerity in Ox's voice because after a moment, the room stilled. George turned away and poured himself a drink. His hands were shaking ever so slightly, but he no longer looked angry, just tired. "You'll make it right," he said.

Ox nodded. "You have my word."

George took a long swig, then crossed the room to where the mirror hung on the wall. He reached out, and just like before, the mirror turned inky and wet under his touch, like a flat pool of water.

"Your word is worthless to me. Pay me back by not dying," George said, and just like that, he faded and disappeared.

Impossibly, the silk cotton tree had grown since last time. It had all but overtaken the entirety of upstairs, blocking out each window and any daylight that tried to creep through. The result was that the room was in near-complete darkness. It wasn't until Sunny pulled out her lighter and flicked it that they were able to make out their surroundings. The tree just kept going up and up and up, until Eli was sure that if Ox were to change into something with wings, they probably could have followed its trunk up through a cavity in the ceiling, and right up to the clouds. Standing there, so within touching distance, Eli felt that same call from before, like a drumbeat right at the center of his chest. A need to go toward it. He pushed the feeling aside.

When he exhaled, his breath came out as ice. It was jarring compared to how warm it had been on the other side of the mirror, as well as how hot it had been here last time. Mercy must have fed off so much magic here that now it was barren.

"Is this where you were before?" Sunny whispered. She moved her lighter around, aiming for some break in the shadows, but there was none.

"Yep, this is the place."

"It's creepy."

"If it's any consolation, it's definitely creepier than it was last time."

"Yeah, I don't think that's as comforting as you intended it to be," Sunny muttered.

In the darkness, they unpacked their bags and laid out the ingredients in a circle. Eli laid the small compact mirror on the floor. He didn't want to do this, but they needed some way to hold Mercy in one place while they spoke to her.

"We're not alone," Ox said, looking around the darkness with mild curiosity.

Eli paused from pouring some of the ingredients into a container he'd brought. He shifted his weight and could feel the crunch of something underneath his trainers. He held out Sunny's lighter and could just about make out the dustings of forest foliage from oceans over, which covered George's nicely laminated floors. There were no sounds of the city around them, no distant passing traffic. Ox was right, though. It was more than that. It was the smell.

"Lij?" Sunny whispered. "You good?"

"Wait," Eli said, and waved a hand. "Don't move."

The first things he saw were the eyes.

Eli thought maybe his own vision was playing tricks on him. Like when you squinted too hard and saw balls of light in your periphery. This wasn't a trick. Two yellow eyes blinked down at him, unmoving. In the darkness, there was a wet, dripping sound, and the creak of something being dragged across the floorboards. From the shadows came a low, chest-deep growl, and Eli felt the vibrations of it through his bones. Whatever it was, it had teeth.

He barely had time to register what was happening, and just about enough time to form the thought *Oh shit*, when the beast came hurtling out of the shadows and toward them with the force of a train. Malcolm had warned him that La Diablesse would be back, and it bought him the second he needed to shove Sunny to one side, ignoring her yelp of protest as she hit the floor. In the scurry, Eli dropped the fang and heard it roll away, just out of his reach. He felt a searing pain rip through his shin and looked down to see the bottom half of his leg engulfed by the jaws of the monster.

He kicked it in the face, hard enough that it let out a high-pitched yelp, but the jaws around him only tightened.

"Sunny!"

"Yeah," Sunny said, wiping smeared blood from her chin from where she'd hit the ground. "On it."

She leapt onto the creature's back, wrapping her arms around its neck in a chokehold. It screamed and writhed beneath her, trying to force her off, but her legs were clamped tightly around it. With his free foot, Eli struck it again, but its grip was relentless, grinding into the bone, causing excruciating pain with every jolt of movement.

"Hold on!" Sunny yelled, but Eli could barely concentrate on anything except not passing out from the pain. Behind him, Eli saw that the silk cotton tree had begun to unravel and open up like a doorway. He realized in an instant what was going to happen if he didn't get his leg free: the monster was going to drag him into the depths of that trunk, along with all the rest of the lost souls, and he would be nothing but another duppy story told by aunties to their badmind kids.

He felt the scrape of the floor against his fingernails as the creature hefted him toward it. One tug. Two tugs.

"Sunny!"

The skin on his calf tore underneath the monster's jaw.

"I know!"

Just a few more feet and they would have reached the tree. Eli took a deep breath and braced himself for the impact, only it never came.

Suddenly, he was blockaded by a wall of Ox. Ox was no longer Casper; they were a wolf. The instrument they'd taken from Legs was disposed of on the floor, sizzling. Ox stood over eight feet tall, gray and on hind legs, and Eli realized instantly: this was Ox's true form. Ox roared and brought their claws across the monster's face, causing it to shriek. Black oozed from the wound, and Eli saw what was underneath it. There was nothing but shriveled bone, eaten away by magic.

It was enough of a distraction. Eli lurched forward, freeing his leg from the monster's grip, and crawled the few feet it took to reach the fang. He seized it, and even though he was careful to hold it through the sleeve of his hoodie, he still felt a blistering sizzle of pain seep through to his palm.

"Enough," Eli said. He wielded the fang right over the creature's head. It immediately went limp. As soon as its grip loosened, Ox jumped, turned into something with wings, flapped into a spiral, and shot off into the air. The creature tried half-heartedly to grab Ox, but Ox was too quick and it only landed a handful of feathers. Three beats of their wings and Ox was gone, streaming through the shadows. They landed behind Eli, once again on two legs, this time wearing Casper's face.

Sunny was still slumped on top of the monster, her weight holding it down. She was covered in black blood, smeared across her face and hair. Eli pulled himself up and limped forward, the fang in his hand. His leg was ruined, that much was clear; it hurt so much it almost gave out on him. His hand, when he held out the fang, trembled.

"I know you're here," Eli called into the darkness. "Come out. We just want to speak to you."

All it would take was one gesture, and he could splinter its skull. It wouldn't be difficult. Even though he was careful not to touch the fang, holding it through the sleeve of his hoodie, he could feel its hunger seeping through, willing him to let it feed. Eli resisted.

The creature grunted and rustled beneath Sunny, but she held it tight.

"Lij . . . ," Sunny murmured, but Eli waved a hand.

"Just a minute," Eli hissed. "She's here. I can feel it."

The shadows bent, the darkness split in two, and then Mercy stood before them.

She looked different. The glow around her was stronger. The last time Eli had seen her, the hole over her chest had been black and vacuous. It was smaller now, healed over a little with the return of some of her magic, but it was still there, gaping and empty. Her eyes were jet-black from the pupils to where the whites should be. It gave an erratic edge to her and made Eli feel even more uneasy, not knowing exactly where she was looking.

"The lagahoo was a nice touch," she said. "You actually managed to trick me. I thought the duppy king had returned. I should have known he would never be that brave."

"Call her off," Eli warned, gesturing toward the creature. "We don't want to hurt her."

"And yet you're holding the weapon of a god over her head," Mercy said.

Slowly, Eli lowered his hand. Mercy smiled and stepped forward. She placed her hands on either side of the creature's face in a soft, almost placating gesture. For a second, Eli thought that they were going to be able to discuss things calmly. Then, in one quick movement, she ripped the creature's head clean from its shoulders. It broke off and crumbled, disintegrating into dust before it even hit the floor. Sunny scrambled to her feet, and it was the three of them, Eli, Sunny, and Ox, staring her down.

"She thought I didn't know that she had been scheming behind my back," Mercy said. "The reality of the situation is that I kept her alive. If it weren't for me, she would have died, powerless and hungry, centuries ago. I saved her."

"Like Casper saved you," Eli said.

The dry, mocking smile Mercy had been wearing disappeared. She dusted off her hands with a sigh and moved to where the contents of Eli's backpack were littering the floor. She picked something up, sniffed it. "You know, when your friend Malcolm and I struck a deal, he spoke to me. Told me things he'd learned about you all. The little tinker girl with her collectables, and the angry girl scarred down to the bone. Oh, and you, of course. The silver-tongued thief with an affinity for all things green. He told me all about you. He told me you can pull the magic from a soul. That you can heal. I must admit, that's very impressive. It's been a long time since I've seen one of you."

She reached down to touch the side of Eli's face, just as she had with Malcolm. There was blood on her fingers. Eli felt it, warm and wet, against his cheek.

"I can help you," Eli said. "I know that Casper hurt you. That he left a hole in your magic. Let me heal it."

"Heal it?" Mercy laughed. Her gaze roamed over the three of them before landing on Eli, speculative. "You know, we're not so different, you and I."

Eli felt a spike of irritation wedge its way between his ribs, but he ignored it. She leisurely started to circle the room, almost waltzing. "How so?"

"You don't know?" Mercy asked. Eli blinked, and she was beside him, lowering her head to whisper in his ear. "You've got the magic of the old gods in you. Part of you has been locked away. You've been deceived by those closest to you. I think we're more similar than you'd like to admit."

"What are you talking about?" Eli asked.

"Oh," Mercy laughed. "Oh dear. You didn't know. Well, in that case, maybe I can help *you*."

She traced a nail across his cheek. He felt the warmth radiating from her fingers, and then he saw it. The same hazy memory he'd had before, edging into the back of his mind.

It was the same scene: Eli was walking through a flat. He was younger. Wearing a school uniform, though his tie was loose, blazer unbuttoned. He had a backpack slung over one shoulder. He was late, and he'd forgotten to do his homework the night before. He was trying to think of an excuse that didn't get him detention, when a hand snagged his arm before he could reach the door. A woman: small, messy hair, tired eyes, skin a few shades darker than Eli's own.

Her hands began knotting his tie for him with practiced ease. *Did you pick up your lunch money?* Yes. *And you left me change for the car park?* Yes. *Remember you're getting the bus home today because your sister has practice.* I know. *And make sure you don't forget your keys, because I won't be here to let you in.* Okay, okay, I know. *I love you.* He felt a rough kiss against his forehead. This was all familiar to him. He had seen it before. But then he turned and saw his sister waiting for him in the doorway. She was wearing his hand-me-down blazer, and her hair was freshly braided. Her head was tilted scornfully at an angle, like she was tired of having to deal with him even though he was older. *Hurry up, Lij!* she snapped, the way she always did. Eli grumbled to himself. She was always so impatient. . . .

The witch moved her hand away, and just like that, it was gone. Eli couldn't breathe around the memory. Because all at once, it made sense. He knew that face. Knew it better than anyone else in the world. Knew the sullen clench of her jaw, the tiny scar she had above her raised eyebrow. And *Lij*. There was only one person who called him that.

"Sunny?" he asked, feeling strangely distant. He'd lowered the fang at some point, and now it was hanging limply at his side. "You . . . you know who I am?"

His voice sounded weird, even to his own ears. It was like hearing a stranger speak.

Sunny didn't deny it. She looked straight at Eli and said, "I can explain."

But she didn't need to. Eli knew her well enough to read the guilt in her expression. The realization curdled in his gut like spoiled milk. He almost wanted to vomit it out. He wanted to wring the sensation from inside him.

"It was you," he said. "You're the one in my head. In my memory. You've . . . you've known who I am all along."

Sunny, to her credit, didn't lie. Her jaw was set firmly, like she was bracing herself to be hit. "Yes," she said.

"You're my sister," Eli said.

"Yes."

"Were you ever going to tell me?"

There was a beat, but then Sunny took a breath. "No," she answered.

The ground began to shake. It was his doing.

He looked at his friend, at his sister, but all he could see were the hundreds of lies she must have told him throughout the course of knowing her. Every time she'd found him after a nightmare and said nothing. Every time she'd followed him around, feigning innocence as he'd searched for answers.

Eli finally understood it. The sting of betrayal that Mercy must have felt the moment she opened her eyes and realized she was six feet under the ground. That she'd been put there by those closest to her. All he could feel was rage. It lit up his veins like wildfire and he could feel it stirring, sour, in the base of his belly. He was distantly aware of the magic around them tightening and turning acidic, of the glass in the windows surrounding them beginning to rattle and the heat in the room intensifying. Healing was making, stitching things back together. Eli was ready to pull the world apart by its seams.

"Eli," Sunny said, low and careful. She put her hands up in a placating gesture and took a step toward him. "If you could just calm down, we can talk about this—"

"Talk about what?" Eli spat. "How you lied to me?"

The silk cotton tree started to uncoil its branches, summoned by the hum of Eli's magic. He felt it shoot through the air involuntarily, and every glass surface in the room immediately shattered and burst inward. Sunny went flying across the room and hit the wall.

He heard Ox call his name but ignored it. He was tired of constantly having to keep this feeling shackled. He let the white-hot anger he'd held pent up in his chest for so long slip out. He watched it curl out of his veins and into darkness, and that seemed simpler somehow. He could make sense of that.

Behind him, he could hear Mercy's voice, barely louder than a whisper.

Go on, she said. *Let it out.*

Eli exhaled, and the world around him twisted and bent and unmade.

CHAPTER TWENTY-TWO

MALCOLM

By the time Malcolm and Max arrived, death was already thick in the air. Malcolm might not have recognized the scent of it, had he not spent hours trying to scrub it out from underneath his fingernails just the day before.

They made their way up to the house, only to be met with complete stillness. The party was full of people, but the guests stood vacant and dazed, completely unmoving. Some seemed to have frozen midsentence, others with their arms outstretched, struck while dancing, a drink in their hand. It was as if he and Max had walked into a museum. Magic dripped from the guests, thick and waxy, like a molten candle. Even the music was affected, playing slow and warped, as if they were all underwater.

"What happened here?" Max whispered.

Malcolm could feel his own magic—Mercy's magic—singing in his veins. He was hungry for it, but he pushed the feeling down.

"Nothing good," Malcolm said. "We should move quickly."

They made their way through the hall, cautious to not knock

into any of the partygoers. They had to duck under a few arms, ease sideways through the middle of halted conversations. One guest was holding her glass askew, and red wine trickled down the side of it and down her sleeve. This was the only time Max disturbed any of them; she wordlessly steadied the lady's wrist, a small, kind gesture, and wiped away some of the liquid with the back of her sleeve.

They paused when they saw a little girl, her hair in two pigtails, peeking around the corner of a coat cupboard, completely frozen.

"Oh," Max said. She could barely look at her. "I know her. Her name's Tia. She helped us last time."

"It's not too late," Malcolm said. "We can still help them."

"Yeah . . . I know," Max said, though she was still staring at the little girl in horror and continued to until Malcolm pulled her away.

Malcolm was concentrating on not tripping over any feet, when movement up ahead made him stop in his tracks. It was Mercy's creatures, wading through the crowd. They were flocking like vultures, filling their pockets, sniffing out magic they could steal from the partygoers. There were at least four of them, which immediately caused Malcolm's heart to sink. One of them, he might have been able to take. The magic in him was itching to come out, to stretch its legs and fight. But *four*?

"This way," Max whispered to Malcolm. She grabbed his sleeve and hauled him into the next room before they could be seen.

"What are we going to do about them?" Malcolm asked, once they were out of sight.

"I guess we hope that when we take out Mercy, they'll go with her."

Malcolm didn't feel confident in that, but he decided against saying anything. "We need to get upstairs," he said, instead.

That was where the magic was bleeding in from. A small rain forest seemed to have flooded in from up there, thick and unyielding. It was the silk cotton tree. Its roots had burst through the ceiling and coiled around the staircase, and the higher they got, the more cloy-ingly warm and thick the air became. Even the walls, when Malcolm put his hand to them, were damp with condensation. Someone was crumbling the barrier between worlds. Between life and death.

"Okay," Max said. She poked her head around the corner, then gestured for him to follow. "Quickly."

As they made their way up the stairs, Malcolm heard the house groan and creak around them. The roof could come down at any moment. It was suffocatingly hot, enough that Malcolm took off his hoodie and tied it around his waist.

"Over here!"

He caught sight of a familiar figure stumbling down the stairs, hunched over and wheezing. Sunny. She had in her arms a feral-looking cat that Malcolm instantly recognized as Ox. Max was at their side in a heartbeat.

"Hey," Max said. "You're all right. You're okay. Where's Eli?

Sunny's hairline was matted with blood. She'd clearly taken a hard knock to the head, because her eyes were glazed and unfo-cused. "He's still . . ." She gestured, but the words wouldn't come out. "I couldn't."

"It's okay," Max said. "He's back there?"

Sunny nodded.

"We'll get him."

Max turned back to Malcolm, and the conflict was clear on her face. "They need help," she said. "But Eli—"

"It's okay," Malcolm said. "I'll get him. You get them somewhere safe."

"Are you sure?" Max asked. "This magic is intense, Malcolm."

"It'll be all right," Malcolm told her. "Death works different on me, remember?"

Max nodded in acceptance. Her arms were full with Ox, so she couldn't hug him, but she did squeeze his arm once and gave him a quick smile. "Be safe," she said.

Malcolm took a deep breath and turned back to the staircase.

The higher he went, the thicker the magic was. It was heavy and palpable, to the point that even raising his arms required effort. "Eli?" he called. He stuck his head into each room, but there was nothing. More of the same, frozen people. Two ladies leaning against the landing. Someone midshout over the banister. A couple sneaking off to the spare room, with their arms looped around each other's necks. No sign of Eli.

He made his way across the landing, stumbling over vines and roots that had engulfed the floorboards. He reached the door at the end and had to shoulder it open, the wood splintering against his weight.

He burst in to find Eli on his hands and knees in the middle of the floor, gasping for breath. Magic soared around him, inky and black, as high as the ceiling. Eli didn't notice Malcolm. His eyes were as white as milk. Magic spewed from his veins like vines, bleeding into the roots of the silk cotton tree. He was feeding it.

Seeing him like that, Malcolm was taken back to the night with his mother. He'd found her in the ruins of their flat in almost the same way, looking down at her own hands, confused and violently trembling. *What have you done?* Malcolm had asked. His mother had only shaken her head. *I didn't mean to,* she'd whimpered. She'd said the words over and over again, like a mantra. *I didn't mean to. I just wanted them to feel what I felt. I didn't mean to. You have to help.* Malcolm closed his eyes at the memory. He'd failed her that day. She'd been acting off all morning, but Malcolm had been sick of looking after her. He'd just wanted a day, one day to breathe. He'd taken his bike and ridden around the block, knowing that she was upset. Knowing that she shouldn't be alone. She had just lost control for a moment, but her magic had destroyed their home, had nearly taken down their block, had almost brought down the building on half of their neighbors. It was Malcolm's fault that it had happened. She was his responsibility and he had failed her. He wasn't going to fail Eli, too.

He took a step toward Eli, but the magic spiraled around the room like a hurricane. Eli seemed to be in conversation with it all, the wind and the earth and the magic. The silk cotton tree was perfectly framed behind him, enveloping the whole room.

Malcolm found himself wishing his father were there. That he'd appear out of thin air and rescue them all, the same way he'd disappeared. If he did, Malcolm might forgive him. He would forget all the missed birthdays, the no Christmas cards, the ignored phone calls. Of course, Casper didn't appear, just as he hadn't appeared all those times before, and Malcolm had no choice but to accept it. No one was going to save them but themselves.

"Eli," Malcolm tried again, but it was lost over the roar of magic. "Elijah!"

Eli looked up then, but it was like he was seeing straight through him.

Malcolm went to move closer, but he had barely taken a step before a force as strong as a freight train suddenly came hurtling at him, sending him slamming straight into the wall. He opened his eyes to find himself staring up at Mercy. Her hand held the fang against his neck. It hummed at his jugular, hungry and eager. It had already tasted his magic when he'd first opened the door to let Mercy out, and now it wanted more.

"There you are, little duppy prince," she whispered. She was taller than him, tall enough that the tips of his trainers grazed the floor as he scrambled. He clawed at her hands, but she was inhumanly strong. "I was wondering when you'd arrive."

The sound of her voice brought back that moment when she'd reached her hand inside his chest and ripped out his magic. Her hand traced the same place now, as if she was remembering too. It didn't hurt anymore—Eli had made sure of that—but the skin was soft and raised. He swallowed back the panic and tried to wrench her grip from his neck.

His instinct was to fight, but then he'd thought of what Eli had said to him. *You want to help her?* Malcolm had said. *I think,* Eli had said, like it was simple, *that she deserves at least a chance.*

"Wait," Malcolm panted. "I know you're angry. I'm angry too. I know how it feels to be cast aside—to be forgotten. But you don't have to do this. You don't have to let it control you."

"Control me?" Mercy laughed. Her fingernails dug into his neck hard enough to draw blood. "Is there any part of this that doesn't look like I'm in control?"

"You're not," Malcolm said. He stopped struggling, kept himself still under the weight of her gaze. "Not as long as this is about him."

Mercy leant back ever so slightly, and the grip around Malcolm's neck slackened. He almost thought he'd got through to her, but then she leant in, voice low.

"You know, I thought it was your father that you were most like, but I was wrong." He felt the warmth of her breath against him. "You're just like your mother. Always sticking your nose where it doesn't belong."

Mercy saw his confusion and laughed.

"Oh, you sweet boy, you haven't figured it out?" She leant forward and spoke barely louder than a whisper. "She pretended it was just concern when she told me to stay away from him, but I saw it. The jealousy. She knew he was going to leave you both for me, and she couldn't take it."

Malcolm felt as though he'd slipped out of his own body. As

though he was watching their conversation from a third-person perspective. He watched Mercy's mouth move, but for some reason the words were not registering. He tried to concentrate on things that would ground him: The trickle of blood at his jawline. The ragged coils of her hair.

"What did you do?" he asked, numb.

"I made it so that even if he went back to her, there'd be nothing left. I planted it in her, a tiny piece of rotten magic, like a sickly little disease, and watched it eat her mind from the inside out. And your father, he wanted my magic too much to care. He watched me do it. He let her mind slip away. All magic requires sacrifice, after all. She was his."

Malcolm felt a slow, icy rage run through his gut.

"But you said you would fix her," Malcolm said. "That you would give her back to me. And she seemed better. We were . . . we were doing okay."

Even as Malcolm said the words out loud, the reality of it dawned on him. Of course Mercy had granted him that temporary reprieve; she'd needed him to trust her. She didn't need him anymore.

Malcolm had been afraid last time. When she'd reached inside him, it had felt like being buried alive again. He'd felt like he was suffocating, like he might not ever breathe again. He remembered seeing Sunny and Eli behind him, and he'd felt a sharp and all-consuming terror at the realities of miscalculation. In hindsight, he realized that there was probably a part of him that had wanted to die that day. That had half expected it. He was only able to reconcile that feeling now, in the absence of it. He wasn't afraid anymore.

He grabbed the hand that was holding the fang, and his mind raced through a carousel of images. Standing in the kitchen the night after his father left, while the radio crooned with lover's rock. His father, head cocked. *Malcolm, I don't think anything of you.* Of

Eli and Sunny and Max laughing in the dingy corner of Pam's. Eli's voice, so sure of itself. *I think that she deserves at least a chance.* He thought of his mother, of finding her wandering the streets, lost and disoriented. All the times he'd sat up with her at night during her frantic episodes. There had been so many moments Malcolm had raged at the injustice of it. When he'd wished that there was someone he could blame, something palpable he could put his hands around and make feel just a semblance of the suffering he and his mother endured. Now here she was, staring down at him with a smirk on her face.

He watched the magic—Mercy's own magic—bleed from his fingers and seep into her skin like acid, slow and syrupy. She jerked backward, but Malcolm grabbed her other hand and held her against him. It stung, a razor-edged chill in his veins, but for once he didn't fight it. They'd said it was only the fang that could eat her magic, but that wasn't true. The magic of a god could kill a god, and her magic was in Malcolm's veins. She wasn't the only one who could control death anymore.

"You stupid boy," she hissed. "What did you do?"

"I'm not going back to how things were," Malcolm said. "Tell me how to fix my mother for good."

Mercy laughed outright at that. "There is no fixing her."

Malcolm didn't need to hear any more. Mercy stumbled away, releasing him, but it was too late. Where Malcolm's fingers had brushed her, her skin started to blister and swell. She began to wilt under his touch. The darkness started as just a small patch, but then he watched it spread along her veins. It happened within the span of just a few moments. Her body went stiff and unmoving as rigor mortis hit her muscles. Gradually, she began to dissolve: first her locs, then her eyelashes one by one, then her eyebrows. She shrieked and brought her hands to her face, but it was too late. Her skin was already turning gray and blotchy and swollen, decomposing more and more with every second. Her hand, when she raised it, had rotted down to its tendons. Her fingernails shriveled and fell off one by one. She screamed viciously, a sound that Malcolm was sure would haunt him for the rest of his life. She raised a hand to undo the magic, but it was already too late. Death had taken hold of her.

"I should have killed you," Mercy said. Even as she spoke the words, parts of her broke off and flaked away.

"Yeah," Malcolm said. "You should have."

He stepped back and watched her crumble to her knees, deteriorating with every second. Her skin corroded away to reveal tendon and tissue and muscle and finally bone, and there was a foul smell that soured the air like rotten meat.

"He'll come for you next," she said.

"Who?" Malcolm asked, but in his heart, he already knew. Casper. That was what this had always been about. That had always been what it was going to come to.

Malcolm didn't wait to hear anything else. He grabbed the fang from her hand, ignoring the flare of blinding pain that coursed under his fingers, and plunged it hard into the soft part between her ribs. Mercy screamed as it ripped through her, devouring the last remnants of her magic. She stumbled backward, toward the trunk of the tree. She looked small, Malcolm thought. Small and lonely. Malcolm watched it dawn on her, a brief, shared moment of understanding. She had been alone for so many years, cast out by her family, locked away by the person she loved. At least, Malcolm thought, he could give her one thing. At least she would not die alone.

On cue, the silk cotton tree's branches unraveled and opened, as if it had been waiting for her. He heard the whispers from inside, calling her name, centuries of ghosts waiting to feed. *Mercy,* the voices said. *Your sisters are waiting.* The roots rose and latched themselves around her shins and wrists. She tried to peel them off, but the fang continued to eat away at her, devouring the last of her skin and bones. One of the roots wrapped around her thigh. She threw out a hand to clasp Malcolm, an act of desperation, but he leapt out of the way. The last image Malcolm saw of her was one of wide-eyed surprise, hand outstretched to him as she clawed at the ground. She let out an earsplitting shriek, fighting the entire way, but the silk cotton tree didn't relinquish its grasp. One tug, two, *three*, and she was dragged into the sunken folds of its trunk. The bark sealed over her in a satisfying swoop, and it was like she'd never been there.

Malcolm exhaled and let himself fall against the wall, his heart thrumming manically inside his chest. He looked down at his hands, which were trembling. He was still holding the fang, and it had left burn marks across his palm. He dropped it, the pain finally registering against his nerves, and it clattered to the ground.

Malcolm saw movement in the periphery of his vision, and he turned his head to see that several of Mercy's creatures, ghostly and fractured, stood to attention. They were each watching the space where Mercy had just been in. They looked lost.

Malcolm should have torn through them. He should have ripped them apart and turned them to ash. But he could still feel the lingering pull of something between each of them. It was Mercy's magic; it was the same thing keeping them alive, as it was him.

"Go," Malcolm said. He saw one or two of them hesitate, but he stood his ground. "Please."

One of them turned to bow, low and deferential, then, one by one, they left.

The relief was short-lived. The building around them groaned;

the house was going to come down any minute if Eli continued.

With Mercy gone, Malcolm launched himself to the middle of the room, where Eli was still curled on the floor, in an odd trance-like state.

"Eli," he tried gently. "It's over now. We've got to go."

He reached out to touch Eli's shoulder, but a wall of magic sent him hurtling backward.

He sat up, gasping for breath. They wouldn't be able to take much more.

His gaze went back to the fang, just a few feet away. Reluctantly, Malcolm used the sleeve of his hoodie to pick it up. He stared down at Eli. He didn't want to do it. He couldn't do it.

"Eli!" he shouted, but there was nothing. Eli was slipping away. His own magic would consume him if this went on any longer.

Malcolm walked across the room. A floorboard gave beneath his feet, and he almost fell, but he kept moving. He stood in front of the silk cotton tree, which was still lined with white buds. He looked at it and took a deep breath. It was odd; he felt an affinity with it. But he knew it wouldn't stop.

"Sorry," he whispered, and plunged the fang as deep as he could into the bark.

The effect was immediate. Blackness oozed from its core and trailed across the floor.

Eli's eyes opened, and he let out a piercing yell, as if he were the one who had been bludgeoned. He bent over, wrenching and coughing, hacking black leaves from his mouth. Eventually, the milky-white haze cleared from his eyes and he was Eli again. He looked the same as the first time Malcolm had seen him. Scared and coiled tight, like he was ready for a fight. It took a moment for Eli's eyes to adjust, but when they did, the magic ceased as if it had been doused by water. He could hear the building creak as bits of debris fell, but there was now complete calmness. In the distance, the music downstairs restarted.

"What happened?" Eli asked, blinking rapidly. His eyes, quietly curious, fell to the fang, which was hanging limply at Malcolm's side.

"It's all right," Malcolm said. "It's over now." He shoved the fang in his pocket and held out a hand for Eli to take. "We need to get out of here, though."

Eli nodded. He looked around, skittish and seemingly surprised by his surroundings. He took the hand that Malcolm offered, and together the two of them limped out of the room.

As they stumbled down the stairs, the partygoers started to come back to life. There were lots of murmurs of confusion, people not sure what was going on. Malcolm pushed their way through the crowd and outside, politely avoiding concerned guests, to where Max was waiting across the street with a slightly frazzled Ox, who still hadn't changed from cat form. As soon as she saw them, she set Ox down and rushed forward to envelop them both in a crushing hug.

"Sunny's gone, isn't she?" Eli asked. It came out muffled against Max's shoulder.

Max pulled back with a frown. "I lost her in the crowd," she said. "I figured she'd gone after you—she's not with you?"

Eli laughed, but he seemed entirely unsurprised. He looked like there were a thousand things that he was about to say, but instead, he shook his head.

"No," Eli said. "She's not with us."

Across the street, the little girl they'd seen earlier was waving her arms. Tia, Max had called her. Malcolm followed her gaze and then realized she was pointing upstairs to the window of George's bedroom. He was there, looking down at them, taking it all in, the faces of his family and friends. He must have felt their attention, because he raised a hand in their direction. Malcolm caught the tail end of a grin. He looked younger at that moment. Like the man Malcolm remembered from the family functions.

"What are you looking at?" Max asked.

"It's George," Malcolm said. His outline was faint and gray behind the reflection of the window.

"I don't see him anymore," Eli said softly. His eyes were on the shadows, as if he expected something to step out of them.

George nodded, a small goodbye, and Malcolm lifted a hand in response. He turned and walked farther into the house, and Malcolm knew. Mercy was gone now, so there was nothing holding him here anymore; George would finally be able to cross over. Not only George, but the others, too. Everyone who had suffered at her hands.

Max knocked her shoulder against him, pulling him back to the land of the living. "Come on," she said. "Let's go home."

CHAPTER TWENTY-THREE

ELI

Eli stared at the web page he'd pulled up on his computer, willing his nerves to still. It didn't work. His brain kept tormenting him with what-ifs.

You have submitted your application to North London Sixth Form College.

Oh well, Eli thought. *Too late now.*

"Hey, whatcha doing?" Max asked, coming in from the kitchen.

"Nothing," Eli said, slamming his laptop shut and sliding it across the counter until it was out of reach.

Max raised an eyebrow and exchanged a look with Malcolm, who was perched on the stool by the counter. It was Sunny's spot, really. She would usually sit there and stretch her legs across the aisle, but of course Sunny wasn't here—hadn't been since the nine night, which was three weeks ago now—and it had been such a painstaking experience to try to make Malcolm feel like he wasn't taking up space that there was no way either of them was going to point that out to him.

"Sure," Max said. "Because that's not suspicious behavior at all."

Eli groaned and covered his face with his hands. "*Ischubmitted-myplication*," he grumbled, garbled and half muffled, into his sweater.

"Wanna run that by us again?" Max asked. She sent a sweeping hand in Malcolm's direction. "Unless you speak caveman?"

"Nah." Malcolm smiled. His hair had grown out a little in the last couple of weeks, and it made him look a lot younger. "Sorry."

"In that case, maybe try speaking with your whole mouth," Max said.

Eli lifted his head to glare at her.

"I said I submitted my application," he repeated, with all the enthusiasm of someone prying off his own fingernails. "To college. And with about, uh . . ." He glanced at the time. "Ten minutes until deadline. Hope they don't penalize you for that."

As soon as the words were out, Max's face broke out into a huge, blinding smile and she immediately started jumping up and down and screaming. "You did?" She flung her arms around him. "Eli, that's amazing! I'm so proud of you! Did you hear that, Malcolm? He's going to college!"

"Yeah." Malcolm had a small, quietly fond smile on his face. "Congratulations."

"Thanks," Eli said, rubbing his cheek where he was sure Max had left a makeup smear. "I mean, it's not like I've been accepted yet."

"You will be," Max insisted, and she said it with such fervent sincerity that Eli almost found himself believing her. "This is a huge step. I'm really proud of you."

Eli buried his head in his hands, embarrassed, but he couldn't quite resist smiling either.

"Oh, now we can finally be study buddies," Max continued. "I can share all my study techniques with you. Do you have Post-it

Notes? I'll get you Post-it Notes. Oh, and you'll need new pens. And a notepad."

"What kinda noise this?" Pam asked, hobbling into the diner. She paused to stare in their direction, and Max immediately started pretending to wipe down tables.

"Eli's thinking of going to college," Malcolm said, because he was a traitor and hadn't yet learned not to spill every earthly secret to Pam just because she asked.

"Is that right?" Pam said, raising an eyebrow.

Eli tried to not squirm under the weight of her gaze. "It's just one application," he said.

"Hmm," Pam said. "Well, it's about time you did something with that brain of yours other than to hover around here and make trouble."

After they'd gotten back to the diner from the nine night, Pam, of course, had been there waiting for them. She'd taken one look at them, bruised and beaten, and turned on her heel. That had been that. No *thank you*, no *good job*, no *sorry for abandoning you in your time of most dire need*. Certainly no explanation for where the hell she'd gone. Eli hadn't been surprised. There had been no sign of Casper either, of course, but Malcolm had barely flinched at that revelation. He'd simply shrugged, hands shoved deep in his pockets, eyes looking anywhere but at them. *I'm sure he'll come back when he needs something*, Malcolm had said. Eli had felt a slow rage start to simmer in the base of his belly at that, but when he'd felt the familiar sizzle of magic in his veins, he'd forced himself to bite back the poison on his tongue. His magic had been slippery since that night of the nine night. It would flare in sudden bouts with his temper, and each time, it took a controlled effort to reel it back in. Something had awakened in him, and he wasn't sure how to put it back to sleep.

He'd handed the fang over to Pam with raised eyebrows. "We'll be splitting the money three ways this time," he'd told her, but then he'd heard a little yowl come from below and looked down to find Ox glaring up at him. "Okay," he'd added, with a roll of his eyes. "Make that four." Pam had laughed, a vacuous echoing sound, but she'd done exactly that.

Since then, Malcolm and Ox had just sort of kept coming back. Malcolm would come after his shifts at work, when he wasn't with his mum. Ox tended to come and go as they pleased. More often than not, it would be in the form of four legs, but sometimes they'd wear an unfamiliar face. The others would only know who it was because of Ox's tendency to barge in unannounced and go straight for the oxtail. Eli found he didn't mind much. The combined presence of the two of them helped cover up the fact that there was one person noticeably missing.

He hadn't told the others that he'd seen Sunny. He'd received an ominous anonymous text in the middle of the night a couple of weeks earlier, and he'd followed the Google Maps pin he'd been dropped to Camden Lock.

He'd found Sunny sitting under the bridge, chain-smoking like a middle-aged divorcée in a black-and-white film noir.

"How's your leg?" she said in greeting, like no time had passed.

"Still attached."

Sunny had given him a long, tired look, before Eli finally caved. "I'm fine," he'd said, and the corner of Sunny's mouth had lifted into an almost-smile.

"Liar," she said.

"Takes one to know one, I guess."

They sat in silence for a long time, with just the sounds of the city surrounding them.

"I'm so fucking angry," Eli finally said.

Sunny exhaled a breath of smoke. "I know."

"I'm gonna be for a while."

"Sounds reasonable," Sunny agreed.

Eli inhaled deeply. He'd always hated the smell of cigarettes, but he was surprised to find that he missed the familiarity of it. "Are you coming home?"

He was staring ahead as he spoke, so he felt more than saw Sunny's sideways look at him. She hesitated. Eli didn't think he'd ever seen her hesitate before.

"You want me to?"

Eli felt a surge of irritation spike through him. He hated this. He was used to them finishing each other's sentences, exchanging wordless glances, and knowing exactly what the other meant from just a quirk of their eyebrow. Now, Eli didn't have a clue what was running through Sunny's head.

"Are you going to tell me the truth?" Eli countered.

Sunny huffed a laugh. "Touché," she said.

Eli sighed, but this, at least, was familiar. He looked down, picked at a stray thread on his jeans so that he wouldn't have to see the rejection write itself across her face.

It was Sunny who broke the silence this time. "I can't tell you what you want to hear," she said. "And I don't expect you to forgive that. But I'm not gonna change my mind about this. I promised I wouldn't."

"Promised?" Eli frowned. "Promised who?"

Sunny, of course, didn't answer.

Eli felt a fierce prickle of frustration in his stomach.

"I'm going to keep searching," he said. "With or without your help. Are you gonna try and stop me?"

"Yes," Sunny said. "However I can."

Eli laughed. It echoed against the walls of the bridge. "Of course now's the one time you decide to tell the truth."

For the first time in a long time, Sunny didn't laugh off her sincerity. When she looked him in the eye, her face was oddly sober.

"I need you to trust me," Sunny said.

Trust me. Eli thought of everything they'd been through together. How Sunny had saved his life over and over. How she had lied to him the entire time. Despite everything, they were family, though truthfully, Eli didn't know how much that was worth.

"I don't," Eli said.

Sunny had nodded once, accepting, and that had been that. She stubbed her cigarette out against the pavement and pulled herself to her feet. "See you around, Lij," she'd said. If he didn't know her so well, he would've missed the hurt in her voice. He'd stood there for a long time, watching as she retreated into the darkness.

He thought of that now as Pam drummed her fingers against the solid wood of her cane.

"So," Pam said. "Did you tell them yet?"

"Tell us what?" Eli asked.

"We've got another job for you," Max said. "If you're up to it."

Ox jumped onto Eli's lap, and he immediately began scratching behind their ears. Eli turned to Malcolm, who had his chin perched on the heel of his arm resting on the counter. He raised his eyebrows, and Malcolm raised his in return. Eli thought they were maybe getting a little better at this whole understanding-each-other thing.

Eli leant back in his chair and crossed his arms. "What you saying?"

Malcolm huffed, and his face was so serious that Eli was expecting a polite but stuttered decline. Instead, he gave a slow, sly look out the side of his eye.

"Well," he replied. "How much?"

Eli laughed, because it was all he could do.

ACKNOWLEDGMENTS

I'm infinitely grateful to the team that made this book possible: Naomi Colthurst, who was the first person to help me start this journey back when it was just five hundred words and a pitch; my agent, Izzy Gahan, for her endless patience; the incredibly generous Tamara Kawar, Roxane Edouard, Isobel Leach, and Josh Benn; and of course, my editors India Chambers and Kristie Choi, who have elevated this story further than I ever imagined possible. I'm also thankful to Penguin Random House's WriteNow program for all the continued support and mentorship.

So much of this story is about the chaos of family, blood or not, so thank you to my mum and dad for being absolutely nothing like the terrible parental figures in this story. To my brothers, Adem and Joseph, thanks for being my first readers even though I basically had to hold you at gunpoint to do so. Han, most of this book was conceived in rambling voice notes to you, so I'm forever indebted to you. Em, thanks for always being my biggest cheerleader. Thank you to all of the Holnesses, Cadogans, Rileys, Rentons, and Sidkis. Nana, I know you always wanted a journalist in the family—hopefully this is a close second.